Praise for *Hawker and the King's Jewel*

... with verve and pace. Hawker is a

Bernard Cornwell

'A highly enjoyable ride through a story rich in detail. Bale takes the reader from the terror of battle where a crown is lost and won to the sparkling jewel that is Venice, teeming with intrigue and treachery. Loyalty tested, love for a woman reclaimed, a quest beckons to reclaim the English crown. Great storytelling'

David Gilman, author of *Master of War*

'An absolute gem of a novel. I was taken aback by Bale's skill and talent. Meticulously researched, with a totally authentic medieval feel, the novel fizzes with action, romance and intrigue. A gripping yarn'

Angus Donald

Ethan Bale was a defence journalist in both Washington and London before he turned to writing historical novels, non-fiction and short stories. Despite covering modern military technology for much of his professional career, he was always passionate about times past, particularly the Renaissance and early modern Europe. Indeed for many years he donned full medieval armour to participate in fighting tournaments in the US and UK. These days, he is usually found wielding a pen and not a sword.

www.ethanbale.com @EthanBaleAuthor

Hawker
and the
King's Jewel

ETHAN BALE

CANELO

First published in the United Kingdom in 2022 by

Canelo
Unit 9, 5th Floor
Cargo Works, 1–2 Hatfields
London, SE1 9PG
United Kingdom

A CIP catalogue record for this book is available from the British Library.

Print ISBN 978 1 80032 968 3
Ebook ISBN 978 1 80032 967 6

Look for more great books at www.canelo.co

Printed and bound in Great Britain by Clays Ltd, Elcograf S.p.A.

I

MIX
Paper from
responsible sources
FSC® C018072
www.fsc.org

For Emil and Felix

Prologue

A northern wind carried the mournful, rhythmic moaning of the last surviving lion in the royal menagerie across the night air and through the mullioned windows of the Wakefield keep.

Inside, climbing the stone steps up to the royal apartments, Sir John Hawker halted. The forlorn beast had stopped its complaints for a second before letting out a defiant roar. Then silence. Hawker turned and raised his tin lantern to check that no one was following, then continued up. His long woollen cloak partially obscured the glint of a polished breastplate.

When he reached the top of the stairs, he saw a starry firmament in front of him – a dark blue curtain of halfmoons, stars and white heraldic roses – a tapestry that covered the oak door to shut out the draught. He swallowed, trying to soothe his parched throat. It did nothing. His mouth was just as dry. For what he had been told to do had shaken him to the marrow and, even now, poised at the threshold, he did not know if he could muster the mettle to see through what needed to be done. Hawker swallowed again, pulled the tapestry aside and entered the chamber.

A huge fireplace cast its fading light across the circular, high-ceilinged room. There was no longer a roaring flame, but the coal embers burned a deep cherry red in the grate, affording just enough illumination for him to see the bed near the hearth. It was a large four-poster, painted red and green, its wine-coloured curtains pulled back and tied off despite the damp cold of the place. Hawker raised his lantern to look upon the sleeping occupants.

Two young boys held each other in slumber, and Hawker could see a mountain of pillows arranged about them like some gentle castle wall, a child's attempt to keep night terrors at bay.

The older of the two awoke with a start, hearing the jangle of Hawker's harness and boot buckles. He saw a haggard-looking soldier before him: grey hog-bristle stubble of a beard, deep crow's feet around piercing eyes, and a beak-like nose. His eyes then went to the long, silver-hilted dagger slung from the soldier's waist. The boy shook his companion, his younger brother. This boy, too, pulled back upon awakening when he saw the intruder at the foot of the bed. His brother put a protective arm around him and stared at the soldier.

'I know you,' he said after a few seconds, his soft voice steady. 'You are my lord Buckingham's retainer.'

Hawker nodded. He lowered the lantern. 'You must ready yourselves. Now.' His voice was rough, strained by his frayed nerves.

The younger boy, no more than eight or nine, started to cry silently, a slow stream of tears running down his cheeks.

'Hush, Richard,' said the elder. 'Don't worry.' He pulled back the covers and climbed out, pulling Richard after him. The elder dressed hurriedly in his hose and doublet, and then began to help his brother. He started to cough from the exertion, phlegm-filled and deep.

'Quiet that,' said the knight, knowing the nursemaid slumbered on the floor below. 'And hurry yourselves,' he added, this time more sympathy in his voice.

They complied. The elder boy retrieved their heavy cloaks lying atop a wooden chest and swung one around his brother's shoulders. The knight stepped forward and Richard shrank back against his brother. Hawker tried to smile and reassure, but this somehow came out as a twisted grimace. He lowered his chin. 'We must go. And go quietly.'

The older boy opened the chest and pulled out a prayer missal bound in leather and secured with golden clasps.

2

Hawker reached forward and slowly took it from the boy's hand, laying it down upon the lid. "You won't be needing that, my lord."

He led them out, listening intently, down the wide winding steps of the keep, the way he had entered. They had reached the flagstones of the entry hall and the great archway that led out to the yard when the elder brother began a fit of coughing again. The knight pulled him back gently by the shoulder.

'I beg you, for the love of Christ! You must stop that,' he hissed in a whisper.

Richard began to cry again, and this time the sobbing was audible. It echoed around them.

The older boy restrained his coughing fit and turned to look at his captor.

'Where are you taking us?'

Hawker regarded the boy. He had once been a king, the other, a prince. He couldn't think of words to give either of them much hope. The griping pain seizing his belly tightened further. 'You will see. Fear not.' His smile was as insincere as a street beggar's. Hawker then drew out his dagger, its accompanying rasp barely muffled by his cloak.

'Let's go.'

Part I

THE WHITE BOAR

1

Two years later...

Eavesdropping might be a sin, but eavesdropping upon a king is treason. The priest lay face down, cheek stinging as it pressed the gritty garret floorboards of the White Boar Inn. Although it looked like he was prostrate in prayer, in truth he was doing no such thing. He tilted his head ever so slightly and looked down. Down through the narrow, thumb-wide gap that he had enlarged earlier, scrape by surreptitious scrape, with his eating knife. His right eye searched what he could see of the room below. The sound of conversation floated up to him as if he were in the very chamber, but he could not *see*.

Frustrated, he moved his right hand to pick up a small piece of mirror glass, but in so doing, his silver crucifix dragged along the floorboards. The scoring noise made him freeze, his heart nearly stopping.

They were still talking below. No alarm. Priest or not, if he was discovered it would mean a blade rammed down his throat or driven into his belly. *At least I shall go to my death without sin. It's no sin to spy on a usurper*, he thought.

He edged the mirror over the crack. Angling it downwards, he tilted it until it framed the object of his search. The priest allowed himself a thin smile. *He* was indeed there, talking with another. He pressed his hairy ear to the crack. Snippets rose up from below: whose troops were arriving, whose were late... all of it a monotonous drone.

Leicester was stuffed to the brim with soldiery and, on the morrow, Richard Plantagenet's army would venture out on the road south, searching for the enemy that was hunting him. The priest had spent the day ministering to the troops of York, at least those that would listen to him, hearing the confessions of a few pious ones as the hour of battle drew nearer. The hour, no doubt, of their wretched deaths. And for the whole of the afternoon he had hidden himself in the garret, waiting and hoping that he might gather something useful. Something secret.

The priest knew that young Henry Tudor was fast approaching with what he hoped was a vast force. A force that would see King Richard and his cronies cleansed from England's ravaged land. One last fight to end the bloody quarrel and heal the kingdom. The two great houses, Lancaster and York, grappling each other for the right to rule, had surely earned the Lord's wrath. God willing, the impending battle would be an end to Richard and just punishment for his having murdered two innocent children, the true and rightful heirs to the throne. If he could learn anything to help make that happen — and convey it to Henry's men — then it would be worth risking his life.

The king's voice suddenly broke through the priest's musings, and the other figure's monotonous babble.

'John Hawker? Fetch him to me at once.'

The priest's brow furrowed. The name bore no meaning to him, but it had caught the king's interest quickly enough. The sound of shuffling boots, the tinging of a soldier's glaive and a thump of its haft, and then a shrill call down the stairs for John Hawker. Just a few moments later, boots pounded the staircase. The priest's buttocks clenched as he prayed for them to stop at the floor below and not continue up to his. The door below groaned open and he heard the king speak again, a gentle voice that was surely as sweet and beguiling as Lucifer's.

'You may leave Sir John with us.'

The priest raised his head up off the floor and, neck aching, angled the glass again with a slight twist of his wrist. He saw a man bow his head and bend his knee before Richard – a head of black hair streaked with grey, round-cropped and oiled in the fashion of his boyhood years. Watching like an owl perched in the rafters, the priest viewed the knight from the top down. Sadly, it revealed little. A proud nose like the beak of a kite, a reddish sort of velvet brigantine and pointed brown boots. Not much more. The voice, when the man spoke, a raspy sort of growl, told him this was no young blade sworn to serve the cause of York. Whoever John Hawker might be, he was an old campaigner. The priest had seen many of his sort over the years, stone-cold killers whose loyalty usually balanced on the promise of coin and favour.

'Sire, you summoned me?'

When Richard Plantagenet replied, the priest, who possessed an ear well tuned to the confessions of frightened men, heard worry in the king's voice, well disguised though it was.

'There is this matter of an old gift from abroad. One you won't have forgotten, since you're the one who brought it here. I have need of your service again.'

Heart thumping, sweat prickling his armpits, the priest knew that God was about to reward his patience and daring. Jaded cleric though he was, he was quite unprepared for the bounty of secrets that soon floated to his ears. Sweet fruit indeed for the table of Henry Tudor.

—

Beneath the priest's spy-hole, the king faced his retainer, a man he'd known since his youth. 'The Venetian trinket must go back,' he said, slightly peevish. '*Your* trinket. This stone. This *Tear of Byzantium* – or whatever it was my brother called it. I need to buy allies. The return of the jewel will sweeten things to that end.'

Sir John Hawker and the King of England had an understanding, of sorts. The king told Hawker what to do, and Hawker – without fail – did what he was bid, no matter the deed. A knight of modest means but still hale for all his forty and nine years on God's good earth, John Hawker suddenly felt a little older as he looked into the face of his king. Hawker had not seen him in many months and the pallid and haunted face that met his gaze took him aback.

Worry had eaten away at King Richard's youth. Ceaseless worry – worry over rebellion and intrigue. The king who stood before him could have been his own age. He remembered the youth he had fought alongside at Tewkesbury years gone by: cheeks flushed red with the delight of battle, eyes a livid grey that pierced enemy and friend alike and were possessed of a quick intelligence, a cunning for the judgement of men high or low. There was now a gauntness in those cheeks, a weariness in the eyes, crow's feet spreading towards the temples and a brow as furrowed as a villein's furlong. What remained were a strong jaw and those thin, miserly lips – a trait of his family.

Hawker knew the king had suffered loss. His young son was dead and buried. The month of March just past, gale-blown and deathly damp, took with it his queen. He was alone now. That was probably the only thing Hawker had in common with the king: a dead wife and child. His own had died on her birthing bed, bled-out blue. The babe survived three months in the care of a wet nurse – until he too succumbed to a fever. It had changed Hawker's view of the world, hardening his heart to cover the emptiness. Now, some fourteen years later, he still carried the guilt for ignoring his infant son for those brief months. A deep dull pain that sat like a lump in his belly whenever the memory came upon him.

The king's eyes bored into him. 'As you're the one who delivered the gift to my family, it's you who should return it to the doge. Gain his goodwill before I send a delegation there in the spring. You will do this for me when the current business is finished.'

'If that is your will, sire, it shall be done.' It was a light reply for what was not a light matter. This single 'Tear' of Byzantium, a gem of great worth, he had borne back from Venice for the last king, Richard's brother, Edward. A gift from the great Doge of Venice. Hawker had never seen so large a ruby or indeed one so strangely crafted, set in a golden armature. It was his experience that princes, like children, were captivated by shiny things. They ought to be more careful about accepting gifts from strangers. He had just been the courier. Now, ten years later, he was to be the courier again.

Richard turned, left shoulder drooping, and moved off to his bedside, crushing underfoot the fresh rushes and lavender that the innkeeper had strewn before his arrival. The sweet, pungent scent drifted up to Hawker, a far better one than the smells outside: camp mud, sweaty arming doublets and mildewed linen.

The king picked up his red velvet cap, which was lying on the coverlet. Hawker watched as he prised off a jewel, tossed the cap down, and returned, hand outstretched. 'Here, take it. Edward used to amuse me with the tales of this little thing. I never believed much of it. But he never told me why he was given it.'

Hawker bowed and took the jewel. 'The Venetians never told me. I assumed it was an act of goodwill… friendship. I was only the courier, sire.' But Hawker knew a bit more than that. It was a crimson treasure crafted ages ago in Constantinople, now crushed under the Turk. The stone was as he remembered it: a large, blood-red oval with a surface as uneven as a crumpled bedsheet. By the looks of it, it had never seen the skilled hands of a gem-smith. It looked almost alive, a glistening crimson slug held fast in a cage of yellow gold.

The king gave a thin, wan smile that didn't linger. 'But we both know the tales around this thing. Foolish, don't you think?'

Hawker kept his gaze downwards and fumbled with the flap of his belt pouch. He tucked the jewel down inside, anxious to have it out of his sight. 'Sire, I was told only, long ago, that it must never be sold – only returned to the giver.' Hawker didn't think it was wise at that point to confirm the king's suspicion about the warning that went along with the jewel.

The king retrieved his wine goblet and took a sip. 'Well, perhaps giving it back will buy me a new trading concession. I had thought to keep it – for luck – until I finished with Henry and his shit-stirring uncle, as well as his hag of a mother.' His fingers played absently around the rim. 'You will see that the stone returns to the hands of the doge.'

Hawker bowed, remembering the cryptic instructions of the doge's councillor ten years earlier. It had struck him as strange even then, the Venetian's vehemence in stressing that the Tear must be returned if ever the king tired of possessing it. Hawker looked up again and into Richard's eyes. 'It shall be done, my lord... after you defeat the rebels.'

The king nodded. 'Tell me, you still have your Flemish soldiers in service with you?'

'I do, fifteen lances, five crossbowmen. All of them skilled at polearm and sword, blooded against the French and the Swiss, too.' No great number for any captain he knew. He hoped Richard wouldn't press the issue.

The king stuck out his lower lip for a moment. 'Ah, well, I had expected more. But no matter, however few, they're still likely to settle some scores in the next day or two. The Welsh bastard has a fair few French mercenaries, I'm told.' He took another sip of his wine but made no move to offer Hawker any. 'And what about you? Still fitting into your harness? I've not forgotten the bruises you gave me when I was a boy at Middleham.'

'That was a long time ago, sire,' the knight replied, already wondering where this conversation was leading. 'And you were quick to learn. I'm sure you would knock my head off in a tournament now.'

Richard fixed him with a curious look, almost puzzlement. 'My brother picked you to train me from a dozen of his knights. I was never quite sure why, you come from no great family. But I think I understand. It's your loyalty, John Hawker. Whether it be to the House of York or to the Doge of Venice. Loyalty that's constant against any storm.' He raised a finger. 'Like a hound! Yes, I'd say like a hound. Loyal to a fault.'

Hawker didn't relish being called a dog, but took the point. 'Your brother saw some worth in me even if my family possessed little, sire. He took me in as a man-at-arms and I proved myself.

He saw fit to reward me with chain and spurs after Towton when he secured the crown. I'm forever grateful for that.'

Richard folded his arms across his chest. 'Now then, when my brother gave you your arms, what motto did you settle upon?'

'Steadfast.'

'*There* you have it. You see my point. That's why I want you in *my* formation, John Hawker. My personal formation. You and your men.'

For some reason he wasn't quite sure of, Hawker was being extended the royal favour on the eve of battle. He sensed a royal snare waiting for his ankle. 'I am grateful, sire.'

Hawker was a henchman, a king's knave, and he knew it. More useful as a jack-of-shadows when the Plantagenets needed something done by stealth. He knew what other members of the court thought of him: he was some greying *condottiere*, a mercenary whom most believed had spent far too much time in the Italian republics. Too much time imbibing their dubious ways to be believed or respected in England any more.

'There's something else I must ask of you,' said Richard. 'Do you know of Sir Giles Ellingham? The lad knighted on the road yesterday?'

Hawker shook his head. 'Our paths had not crossed, sire, until I saw you and the holy men give him his spurs. Should I know him?'

Richard waggled a forefinger playfully – or threateningly. 'You *will* know him. He's eighteen years, as strong and brave a lad as you will ever meet. He'll do well – with a guiding hand. Yours.'

Hawker could feel the royal snare pulling tight at his ankle. 'I will give him instruction, sire. If that is your wish.'

A change came over the king, a sudden earnestness that bore a whiff of offence. 'You will give him *protection*. Do you understand me?' He shifted his stance and looked away a moment. Then his voice softened some. 'He is my son.'

Now Hawker could see what was on the cards. The silence seemed to last an age. Before Hawker could think of a reply, the king continued. 'His mother was a miller's daughter from the village. My brother had her brought to a priory for her lying-in. When she was safely delivered, the boy was taken and given over to Sir Thomas Ellingham and his lady. Raised as their own.'

'Indeed, sire,' replied Hawker, realising just how young Richard had been to sire the lad. 'Your boyhood was a fulsome one.'

'Aye, though not half as fulsome as my brother's.' The king looked away again, past Hawker, into the middle distance. 'I was lucky that Ellingham's wife was so fat that one could never tell whether she was with child or not. Thus the ruse worked the better. No one knows of his parentage – except Sir Thomas and his wife, and they are sworn to the secret. Not even the lad knows.'

'I understand, sire. And Sir Giles's true mother? What of her?'

The king's attention snapped back to Hawker, a look of mild irritation on his face. 'She was told the child was given to a good family. Nothing more. I know not whether she still lives.' He paused a moment. 'Giles is not to know the truth. Leastways, not yet. He's seen a skirmish or two in the last year and is well spoken of, which is why I gave him his spurs. He already fights like a lion with the long sword, if a little foolhardily. Rushes in with the power of youth but not with cunning. He's young, but I was commanding soldiers at seventeen. He'll be new to open battle and I want him with you tomorrow on the march.'

That presented more than a few problems, thought Hawker. For one, by what right would he take charge of the king's bastard? 'It will raise curiosity, sire. I mean… with no apparent reason for my… custody. He is now a knight of the realm in his own right.'

'I realise that. I will issue an order for a rear-guard within my formation – you, Sir Giles and a third knight to command.'

'And who is this third man to command, sire?'

'Roger Beconsall.'

Hawker felt his jaw tense. Beconsall was a brash knight, built like a siege tower and with a head as empty as a beggar's pantry. But if one needed an ox in armour, he was it. 'Beconsall? To command?'

The king looked mildly amused. 'Jealous, Sir John? You'll have your hands full with your new charge, and Sir Roger is capable enough. You might wish to know him better.'

'I don't question your wisdom, sire,' said Hawker, bowing his head.

'If any should ask of your audience here this day,' said Richard, 'it's by reason of this rear guard that I appoint you to. Watch the lad's back. Keep him safe.'

Hawker bowed low, the weight of his new responsibility sinking in. 'I will watch him as if he were my own.'

The king reached over and laid a hand on Hawker's forearm, nearly causing him to draw back in surprise. 'My dreams these last days have been filled with disquieting visions. I don't know why I am plagued – I've confessed my sins and prayed to God. He's already punished me enough, don't you think? Taking my queen... my son.'

Hawker had never seen Richard so distracted, so disturbed, so weak. He attempted a gentle, consoling smile. 'Such dreams are not uncommon before battle. I've had them myself, many a time. They steel us for the fight.'

The king looked Hawker in the eye. 'I hear them whispering. *Murderer.* I was sworn to protect my brother's boys, to uphold my promise to God.'

'Sire?'

'It was Lord Buckingham's treachery. All of it. Though he wouldn't admit it before he died. And the hands of Henry Tudor and his wretched mother are red with the blood of innocents. It was *she* – that witch – who set Buckingham to the task. Destroy my brother's children and then come against me.'

His hand squeezed the knight's arm, whether seeking agreement or absolution, Hawker could not tell. '*You* were there at the Tower, weren't you, Sir John? While I was in the north. But you didn't follow that traitor. You were loyal to me.' The king suddenly remembered himself and drew his arm away as if he had touched fire, turning. Hawker watched as the veneer of authority peeled away like a scab off a wound.

Hawker fought back the queasiness that was beginning to roll in his belly. 'My lord, the day will be yours.' He could not stop his voice quavering slightly. In his head, images from two years ago rushed past his mind's eye. Things he had seen and done, things he had told no one, things that even this king did not know. About the Tower. And John Hawker had not kept his head on his shoulders this long by being foolish enough to offer advice – or confession – to a king.

Richard struggled to smile. He extended his hand and the knight saw something gleaming on the king's palm. A ring of gold. 'Here, take it,' he said. 'A token of my thanks for your good service.'

Hawker took it and bowed deeply again while his brain tried to make sense of everything he had just heard. Whether he had turned a blind eye to the princes in the Tower or not, Richard's dynasty was a family of fallen angels, mighty and powerful yet as flawed as any mortal. The Plantagenet compass did not always point north.

'You may go now, Sir John. God keep you.'

Their eyes met briefly – an awkward, embarrassed moment – and then Hawker backed away, bowing, and reached for the door latch. Outside, he walked a few steps along the corridor that overlooked the hall below. He brought the ring closer to his eyes. Upon the fiery yellow gold was a charging boar in filigreed silver, great tusks curling on themselves while at its other end prominent bollocks and an erect member proved its virility. The king's personal sigil. He placed it on his little finger, but the thoughts that ran through his mind dulled any pleasure in the gift that now adorned his hand.

Jacob de Grood, Hawker's chief man-at-arms for many years, was waiting for him across the muddy square near the stone cross of the market, his thick, scarred hands crossed and tucked up into his armpits. He watched Hawker approach, trying to decide whether things had gone well or not. Difficult to tell, since Hawker wore a sour grimace on the best of days. It didn't really bother de Grood one way or the other, though. Hawker would see it through, duty done. De Grood had decided a long time ago that he was better off with the taciturn knight as a master than someone he didn't know from Adam, and he had known Hawker for a very long time indeed.

They had fought side by side in the Italian republics, Austria and France, surviving what seemed a hundred battles and skirmishes. Sometimes stabbed, bruised and broken, but always alive on the other side of it all. Thinking about it as he had these past weeks, de Grood felt he had survived beyond the odds. And far, far better than his success at either cards or dice. They'd been in harness together so long that in battle he and Hawker could almost think as one. He wasn't exactly a friend, though. De Grood probably hadn't had a real friend since he was a boy in Flanders, running with his gang through the narrow streets of the market and stealing bread loaves off the baker's stall. His relationship was servant to master but with a master who probably needed him the more. He was content.

He gave a nod as Hawker reached him. 'How did it go, my lord?'

Hawker wasn't sure if de Grood was actually worried or just appeared to be. The Fleming always looked deeply pensive, as if he was carrying the weight of a sin-laden soul, his right cheek hollowed and sucked in between his teeth. But that look was chiefly because, some time ago, he had taken a thrust of a halberd spike to his face that had knocked out every tooth in his upper jaw and broken his cheekbone, so Hawker could never quite tell what was on his mind.

Hawker gave a snort and shook his head. 'I'll need a strong ale first. And when I tell you what I've been told you'll need one too.'

De Grood's brow creased as he swept off his rust-stained arming cap and ran his hand over his long, greasy blond hair. 'He isn't going to arrest you, is he?'

'No. Hardly that. The good news is that you get to see Venice again. The bad news is we have to fight a battle before we can go there.'

De Grood smiled, a little relieved for the both of them. 'Well, your bad news isn't news, my lord. But the good news is welcome enough.' His eyes moved to survey the square, riven by deep wheel ruts from the legion of carts bearing provisions for the army, now massing near the south gate in preparation for tomorrow morning's march. They bore tents, armour, weapons and barrels of salted pork, bread loaves and cheeses, all piled high. Wagons creaked along, their drovers cursing at their mules, dray-nags and anyone foolish enough to get in their way. 'I've heard cursing in at least four different tongues,' he said. 'I think half the world has come over for your king's little battle.'

Hawker nodded. 'And I hope it will be the last.' He clapped de Grood on the shoulder, jangling his studded leather brigantine. 'God willing, we shall both see Venice again when this business is done. Now, let's get back to the Bull, I'm parched and we'd better herd the men in for the night. And I must tell you the rest of the tale.' He set off briskly, making way around a gaggle of holy-charm vendors and locals selling pies and pickled eels to hungry soldiers. The king's army had invested the town, inside and out, and though daylight was fast disappearing, Leicester was not yet abed, not when the chance to make a few pennies was in the offing.

'The *rest*?' yelled de Grood, hurrying after.

Hawker stopped and turned back to him. 'We are in the king's personal guard!'

'Sweet Jesus!' muttered the Fleming, rubbing at his scalp with renewed vigour.

—

When they reached the Bull, its high archway looming over them like some cavernous maw, a gaggle of mud-flecked children ran towards them, begging coin. Hawker's eyes were caught by a girl, no more than eight, who was holding out something in her hand. Her undyed kirtle was blackened with road filth but her linen coif was clean, tied about her head, mouse-brown hair spilling out. She extended her hand upwards. Leaning in, he saw it held a corn dolly fashioned of straw, prettily plaited and tied with a bit of red thread. And she was offering it to him. De Grood moved to shove the child aside, but Hawker stayed his arm.

'Nay, give her a penny.'

De Grood's brow creased. 'My lord?'

'I said, give her a penny.'

He undid the latch on his purse, irked at his master's strange kindness to urchins. 'Most generous. Would have thought a farthing would do.'

Hawker reached out and took the corn dolly from her. She gave him no response, not a word, her dark brown eyes wide and unblinking.

De Grood stepped forward and thrust a small silver coin into her palm. 'Now, off with you!' he barked. She turned without a word. He waved his arms to shoo off the rest of the children, sending them scuttling to either side, shouting and laughing while they made their way down the narrow street, the overhanging eaves of the reed-thatched houses muffling the high-pitched screeching.

The knight gently tucked the corn dolly between his belt and his robe. Hawker had a feeling that the child had not expected payment. It had seemed to him when he plucked it from her hand that she was bestowing it upon him as a gift. 'Find Will and Jack. And get the keeper to draw us a pot of ale.'

The Bull was always dimly lit. Horn windows at the front allowed only an amber-tinged glow through, even in the strongest light of day. Now, with the sun low on the horizon, tallow-lit lanterns were the only illumination in the hall. The square hole in the centre of the massive oak-beamed roof permitted a cone of weak light onto the flagstone hearth. This was barely aided by the light of a log fire that sputtered and smoked upwards.

Hawker's men-at-arms, at least those who had not wandered off, were spread around the hall or up in the communal bedchamber, its long railing overlooking the hall below. They swore and laughed, a mixture of English and Flemish – a few French words here and there – as they threw down their cards on an upturned washtub, their rush-seated stools gathered round close. Others, stooped low and huddled together, arses peering out of slipping hose and braes, bounced dice against an upended side table. A Flemish sergeant named Jan Bec, a short stocky fellow with a squashed nose whom Hawker had known nearly as long as Jacob, arm-wrestled with one of the English. His filthy mop of straw-like hair practically stood on end as he strained to throw over his opponent, all the while trying not to laugh. At length, he sputtered loudly, cheeks blowing, losing the bout in an explosion of mirth. He shoved his opponent in the chest and sat back. 'Bastard!' he said, still grinning. 'You farted just to make me lose concentration. Make me laugh. The wager's off!'

Hawker's eyes slowly adjusted to the gloom. 'God keep you all, for I've just seen our king. He asked after each of you – by name!' There was a ripple of laughter from the men and the knight grinned back at them. Half of them were new recruits to his worn banner but the rest had served at his side from Venice to Burgundy, fighting French, German and Swiss mercenaries. Hawker had their measure, well and truly. They were blooded and loyal. He waved them off to signal they should resume their games. It would be different in the morning once the march westwards towards Wales resumed.

Hawker sat on the bench at the empty end of the table and did not wait long before de Grood reappeared, followed by his two servant lads, one with a large pitcher in hand, the other bearing two clay vessels. Will and Jack were Lincolnshire boys, both fourteen, whose fathers had begged the old knight to take them into service. They had already proved their worth in the year he'd known them: mending clothes, polishing plate armour, finding fodder, driving the wagon when needed, bearing messages; a thousand tasks always undertaken with eager energy.

Will was the shorter of the two, black-haired and cautious. Jack was tall for his age, a curly mop of dull brown hair on his head that he perpetually seemed to be flicking back from his prominent ears. His upper lip had burgeoned with fine blond down of late to match his increasing awkwardness at becoming a man. And the two were dedicated to Hawker as if he was their own grandsire. Not once had Hawker raised a hand to them, nor would he let any of the men strike them. They trusted him and, in his own way, he trusted them. That, now, would come to the test.

Jack handled the pitcher and poured while Will angled the clay mugs. Hawker could smell the bitter ale, freshly made, as it foamed into the vessels. The boys stood back a step from the trestle, shifting awkwardly, and Hawker beckoned them to sit. The two exchanged a quick glance and clambered onto the bench opposite. One of the soldiers across the hall called for de Grood to join them and the Fleming hefted his mug and crossed the hearth, kicking a log back into place that had rolled beyond the flags. That left the knight alone with his charges, and he levelled his gaze at them, hands cupping the brown glazed mug.

'Well, my lads, you know what happens in the next days?'

Jack spoke up first. 'Aye, there'll be a fight. A big one.' Will nodded his agreement. 'And you will fight for the king.'

Hawker leaned forward. 'Yes, there'll be a battle. A battle where all must play their parts.'

'Will the king win?' asked Jack.

'That's for God to decide. But we will fight with the king and do what must be done. Now, I've told you that on that day you both must stay with the baggage and wait until it's over, haven't I?'

Will scowled. 'You told us you would train us to fight with a knife and then a sword so we could defend the camp.'

'I let you try your hand with the crossbow, didn't I? Much better for someone of your years. With practice, you'll get better – and faster.'

'But you promised to teach us how to fight. Fight with *steel*.'

'Aye, I remember that promise. But the time hasn't yet come for it. I need you both for something else. Something secret.'

Jack's eyes grew larger, his hands gripping the trestle. 'Something important?' he whispered. 'Are we messengers again?'

'It's a secret that must be shared by you equally – like brothers. Brothers that trust each other. Even to the death.'

They looked at one another.

'First, you must swear by our holy Lady, and to our Lord in Heaven above, that you'll help each other and never betray each other's trust. Or my trust.' He pointed a crooked index finger at them. 'Go on, take his hand. Swear it.'

They awkwardly grasped right hands. 'I swear to God, like Sir John says,' said Jack. Will's voice was even softer. 'I swear to God, likewise, never to betray you nor Sir John. Or may the Lord send me to hellfire.'

'Good lads. Now I must entrust you with something. Something to keep safe and which you must not tell a soul about. Something your life will depend on. You can hand it over to each other – if need be – because you shall share its burden.'

The two had now become wary, even frightened by Hawker's words, Jack fidgeting on the bench. 'It's only a small trinket, but nonetheless a king's ransom. And it will be in your safekeeping until the battle is won and I ask for it back from you.' Hawker reached into his belt pouch and pulled out the gemstone. Casting a glance to ensure none of his men were watching the conversation, he moved his right hand across the trestle, fist clenched. 'Who will bear the treasure first?'

'He can take it first,' said Will, his voice barely a whisper.

'Very well.' Hawker opened his palm, exposing the dull blood-red jewel in its golden armature. Jack reached across and plucked it as if it were a scorpion poised to strike. Hawker grasped his wrist. 'Look at me, boy. Wrap it fast in a scrap of linen. Keep it safe on you.' Hawker looked over to Will. 'And if he be killed, then you must take up the treasure. Do you understand?'

The boys both nodded, terrified at the secret they now were part of, for better or worse. Jack drew his hand back, cradling his new, dreadful charge in his lap.

'And if I should die, you are to go home – as fast as you can fly. Do not stay with the men. And tell no one of the gem. Throw it away in the deepest pond you can find. It's not worth your soul to sell it to anyone. Do you understand me?'

The boys nodded, earnest, if a little confused and frightened by it all.

Hawker leaned back, raised his mug and drank. 'There. You're sworn to it. Now, off to bed with you! We're up with the dawn and you two have to ready the wagon. Good lads.'

He watched them scurry away. It would be another year before they were of fighting age, but this was a charge that only required them to keep silent – or run if they must. He knew they wanted to learn the art of war, Jack being the keener of the two, but Hawker had resolved he would never send them into battle until they were trained enough to defend themselves properly. He would see that they were ready as they grew from boys to men. Hawker turned and watched de Grood laughing with a few of the other Flemings in the corner. He called him over to the trestle table.

'Scaring the boys again, my lord?' The Fleming threw a leg over the bench and placed his mug down on the table before plopping his backside down. 'Looks as if you gave them some telling-off.' His eyes followed Will and Jack as they made their way along the railing upstairs.

De Grood always spoke English with Hawker and Hawker had always been impressed by the Fleming's gift of tongues, whether French, Tuscan or English. He had been a godsend to Hawker over the years. He trusted de Grood, a trust forged over the years and several wars. He was also the closest thing Hawker had to a friend. Once, the Fleming had, on hands and knees, dragged Hawker out from under a thicket of clattering Swiss long-spears, and Hawker in turn a year later had fought like a demon with a poleaxe over a wounded de Grood until he'd driven back the Austrians around him.

'No,' said Hawker, 'I just told them to stay in the baggage once battle is joined.'

'Did you? I'd look a damn sight more happy if I'd just been told I could bugger off to the camp and not have to face a hail of arrows.' He wrapped his hands around his cup, his ruined cheek twitching slightly. 'But you're right. They're better off out of it. I've got a feeling it will be a difficult business, this fight.'

Hawker nodded. He felt the same.

A serving girl brought over a trencher with cheese and bread and de Grood stuck his knife in, liberating a wedge of the white stuff.

'You could be right,' Hawker said. 'Don't know why but it feels wrong. Still, our numbers are good. Just depends on what some of the northern lords will do with their armies.'

De Grood nodded. 'The Stanleys. It's all the talk here. Whether they'll come to the standard or not.' He picked off a large lump of mould from his bread and flicked it across to the fire. 'Rumours are like mouldy bread,' he waxed, 'you can cut away the green and yet it's back before you can finish the loaf.'

'No, I expect the northern armies will come. Might already be waiting for us towards the Marches. Question is, whose side will they take?'

De Grood's heavy-lidded grey eyes met Hawker's. 'So, then. What did the king tell you?'

'He had other business with me. A message for Venice. Asked for me to deliver it in person.'

'So you say, my lord. And why does he want you in his personal formation? Does he know he can count the number of your men on his own two hands?'

Hawker shrugged. 'He remembers me from the days when I trained him in arms. And I did tell him our numbers. He wasn't best pleased, but neither did he make much of it.'

The knight could see de Grood's eyes move to the ring on his forefinger, the gold and silver boar glinting in the candlelight. 'Sentimental *and* generous, it would seem,' said de Grood softly. He raised the cup and took a deep swig of beer. 'So, we make it through this scrap, kill the Welsh pretender, and then we're off to Venice. Would have thought the king could have told the Venetian ambassador or given him the message, instead of you.'

'The king doesn't trust the ambassador with his personal business. He trusts me.' Hawker paused. 'And I trust you, Jacob de Grood.'

De Grood raised his mug. 'And I'll serve you well until they hack me down.' He looked over to the others. 'As will these lads. This house will give them a soft bed tonight, bugs and all, for a few days at least. Maybe their last one.' He scowled. 'Don't much like sleeping rough on the ground. A little too close to where I'll end up one day – six feet lower.'

Hawker grunted at that thought and reached for a hunk of the greyish bread. For once, he was starting to share de Grood's mood, his mind opened to Lucifer's dark mutterings of doom. The jewel was back in his hands. That wasn't necessarily good. It could attract attention. The king was wounded inside, eaten up by doubt, and beset by enemies seen and unseen. That wasn't good either. 'We've braved these seas before, you and I. Many times. We'll do it again. Perhaps an extra Ave Maria or two tomorrow wouldn't go amiss.'

De Grood smiled broadly, revealing the few teeth he had left. 'I'll begin my prayers tonight.'

Hawker pulled out the corn dolly from under his belt. The Fleming shook his head in bewilderment. 'Whatever for, Sir John?'

He turned it over in his hands. 'I don't know. Perhaps for luck. The child seemed to will it upon me – with some purpose.'

'She saw you for an easy mark, a grandfather with a full purse. But you fooled her, you did. You made *me* pay for it.'

Hawker placed it in his purse and changed the subject, irritated as to why he had taken the foolish bit of straw in the first place since he was not usually given over to such mawkish sentiments. 'The king said we fight alongside Roger Beconsall's men and this newly belted knight, Giles Ellingham.'

De Grood shrugged. 'Beconsall fights like a lion but he has the brains of an addled flea. Stout heart though. The other I don't know, but I hope he has a strong arm.'

Hawker nodded his agreement. 'And after, if there is an after, it is Venice.'

The Fleming's eyes took on a mischievous gleam. 'Do you think she'll still be there? You stole more than kisses from her. And what you stole you didn't give back when you left.'

Hawker's face looked set in stone. 'You forget yourself.'

'You'll see her. If we make it there.' His finger wagged. 'I know you better than you think.'

'Then you know I have struck men for saying far less.'

Jacob shrugged and leaned back on the bench. 'I don't know why you didn't take her away with us when we left. She would have come freely, I know it.'

De Grood probably enjoyed more privilege than most retainers with their knights. But there were limits. Hawker pulled his shoulders up, baited by the words. Jacob raised his palms. 'Forgive me, my lord. For what my miserable thoughts are worth, I thought her a good woman.'

'You damned well know why I didn't bring her out.'

De Grood gave a small nod. He himself had never felt the need for the entanglements of women. Being shackled to Hawker, even by his own oath, was enough to keep him busy. When he felt the need for the arms of a woman, he would seek out one from the gaggle of camp followers or visit a brothel if one was close by. That was a contract with a beginning and an end.

A crash of crockery and a woman's scream turned their attention. The serving girl came flying out of the pantry followed closely by one of his men. One of his new recruits from Stamford who had been with him only a fortnight. He was red-faced and sweating but stopped up short once he saw Hawker and de Grood rise from the table. Hawker noticed straight away that the girl was clutching at her kirtle, torn at the shoulder revealing her chemise, also ripped. She sobbed and spluttered, looking to Hawker and shaking her head.

In the time it took him to leap over the bench, Hawker had the man by the scruff of his doublet before he could even start protesting. By now the others had also stood up, silently watching what was unfolding. Hawker propelled the man, an archer, across the hall and towards the door.

'My lord!' he squeaked as a wooden bead popped off his collar. 'She was playing me, sir! Begging she was! I swear it on my honour!'

De Grood was at Hawker's heels when the knight kicked open the door to the courtyard, pulling the archer along. A gaggle of laughing soldiers followed, clambering over each other to get a look.

'You choose to behave like a pig then you may dine like one as well!' Hawker put his boot toe into the back of the archer's left knee, collapsing him, and shoved his head into a bucket of kitchen slops that was set alongside the wall. He held it there a goodly while, as the man wriggled like an eel, blubbering into the stinking mess. Hawker then stepped back and shook the slops' spatter from his hands. The archer sat on his backside and wiped his face with his arm. 'Damned fool,' muttered Hawker. He then turned to the others. 'No one is to insult my host, his house or servants. Understood?'

They all nodded.

The innkeeper was out so he gave a coin to the shaking girl and told her she would be safe. She curtsied, wracked by sobbing hiccoughs, and went back to her chores. De Grood shrugged.

'At least he didn't kill the wench. That would have been hard to square with the tavern master.'

'It still won't be squared if she's his daughter,' said Hawker.

—

That night, sleep came reluctantly while he lay in a sagging bedstead in the eaves of the Bull. Jacob's foolish prattling had brought *her* into his mind again, dredging up the past of four years ago. She was there for a fleeting moment in his head – a swirl of her gown and a tress falling over a bare shoulder – and then she was gone again. A woman who had rekindled embers in his heart that he had thought were long dead after the death of his young wife.

When he had left Venice, he had begged her to come back with him. And she had refused because she could not bring herself to do it: to leave her husband. He was no kidnapper though. He returned without her, and tried to forget. King Richard's problems had soon become his own and that had kept thoughts of her and Venice far away. Now, his past came flooding back.

He had survived the butchery at Barnet and at Tewkesbury, those monstrous battles that had secured the throne of England for the White Rose of York. Yet something inside him had died just the same. The wars had made him a skilled knight bachelor, if not a wealthy one, but so too had they hardened his heart into a brittle lump of stone. He had prayed and prayed for his sins, for killing those who had expected mercy.

The summer of Tewkesbury, he took a wife to salve his conscience, but even this joy had been plucked from him by a vengeful god. England had become a place of ghosts for him. At the end of that terrible winter in 1472, King Edward, comfortable in his victory and magnanimous to one who had served so faithfully, had released him from service that he might find his fortune elsewhere.

Through sheer doggedness he managed to gain himself a contract with the Venetians – a mercenary's *contratto* – giving him the right to raise a company of light horsemen and men-at-arms. Venice was the jewel of the Mediterranean Sea and a power to be reckoned with, a city wealthy beyond imagination. He threw together a ragged band, most culled from the denizens of the inland Terra Ferma provinces that Venice ruled: poor village militia who wanted more money, men who saw war as their chance to make a life. He added mercenary veterans from northern lands as well as the Balkans, whose contracts with other captains had ended before their lust for gold and glory had. Within two years he gained a reputation as a cunning raider and a captain of men.

Hawker rolled over and fluffed up his reeking pillow, unwanted memories pushing to the fore from the recesses of his mind. Regrets for poor decisions he'd made – the eastern disasters with the Hungarians into Ottoman-conquered lands, the siege of Scutari – things he had seen that shivered even him. It had been the tipping point in his life when fortune leaked away like so much grain from a ripped sack; the end of his *contratto* with the city after his last campaign. And then, the journey back to England, a decision he had never expected to make.

Leaving his house in the care of Venetian retainers and half his remaining gold in the hands of his banker, he had returned home. But part of him had hoped he might one day go back to Venice – and her.

He finally drifted off to sleep. Anxious dreams followed. About the king, the jewel, all the secrets that had poured forth that day. It was a light, tortured sleep only half surrendered to. But that, strangely, is what saved his life.

He snapped awake as soon as the stinking hand clamped down over his mouth. Hawker's right arm flew up, blocking his attacker's as he was pushed down into the thin straw mattress. Straining to hold the lethal blade hovering above his throat, Hawker could smell the oiled steel in the man's hand. He twisted towards his assailant, a stifled cry on his lips, struggling to force back the blade tip that quivered just inches above him. His left hand scrabbled for his constant bed companion – a Florentine stiletto.

They grappled, and though it was nearly pitch black, Hawker knew it was the archer who was trying to kill him because the man's bicep was as big as his thigh – a bowman's arm – driving the dagger even lower until Hawker felt the point grazing his cheek. But Hawker had managed to reach his stiletto. Grasping it and twisting his body again, he sank the blade into the archer's ribs to the hilt, taking the lung.

The man screamed and rolled off the bed. Hawker staggered up, seized him by his hair, and dragged him out of the chamber, down a few steps, and into the common room where the others slumbered. A candle still burned there and the commotion had already roused de Grood. He was up, sword in hand, and the others tumbled out of their beds.

Hawker licked the blood that was trickling down into his mouth from his nose and cheek. 'Have a look at who would murder me!' The knight brought the stiletto across the side of the archer's head. The man was spitting blood and it bubbled and sprayed pink as he fought for every breath. He was crying but unable to plead. Hawker recognised his own red leather purse strapped at the archer's waist.

'My lord, I beg you!' De Grood moved slowly towards Hawker, seeing the blood pooling. Jan, too, had risen, his pot belly spilling over his stained braes. De Grood raised both hands, palms spread, his eyes first on the bowman, whom he recognised, and then on his master. He knew Hawker well enough to know what was coming next.

'Sir John, don't do it. Spare him. We can fetch the watch.'

Hawker seemed not to hear him, he was almost looking past de Grood and into a wider world. And when Hawker spoke, his voice was pinched and quavering with fury. 'All of you! See what his cowardice has gained him.'

Hawker shoved the thin, square blade into the man's ear to the hilt – all seven inches of it – and the archer went rigid, legs kicking once. Hawker let go and the archer fell forward, stone dead. No one said a word. Sir John Hawker now had one less bowman to offer King Richard. It was only when he saw Will and Jack, their faces ashen, that his conscience returned, the rage of the moment subsiding like a summer thunderhead. For a moment, he was ashamed. But only for a moment. This was the life they were all in, for better or worse.

He took a few steps back, the stiletto twitching in his hand. 'Get this dog down into the stable yard. We'll get rid of him in the morning before we leave.' He gave them all a slow look, his eyes still flashing with the wildness of an animal. Betrayed, in the dead of night.

3

'No, Will, no. You got the straps crossed. Here, let me!'

Hawker glanced down as the lads worked to buckle on his greaves. Jack stood up and fetched the set of cuisses from the ground and handed them to the knight. Hawker buckled the clattering pieces about his waist while Jack worked quickly to fasten one on each leg, fingers dexterously threading straps through brass buckles.

Hawker cinched the wide leather belt across his stomach as tight as he could bear. Other knights had squires. He did not. He had never been in England long enough in the last ten years even to run a household, never mind find squires to school in the ways of sword and court. There was little need in his life for that kind of hierarchy: page, squire, knight, lord. He had de Grood and he had his soldiers. He also now had his liberty again since his previous liege, Lord Buckingham, the king's good friend, had turned traitor and was hanging in pieces at the Southwark end of London Bridge.

'There's a good lad, Will,' Hawker said, staring out over the sea of tents. 'Fetch me my breastplate and back.'

The Yorkist army was spread out on both sides of the road, across the flat golden fields of harvested corn and green pastures of disinterested sheep, the squat tower of the church at Sutton Cheney village just in view. The sounds of priests droning the Mass came to his ears – an abbreviated version, no doubt, bells a-ringing as soldiers took their last opportunity to cleanse their souls before battle. He had already seen the procession, a shining crucifix bobbing along in front, voices of chaplains, chantry priests and the odd adventurous monk all raised in chorus. The king and his commanders had taken Mass inside the church while the rest of the army was ministered to by the roving clerics.

It was mid-morning, the dew burned full away in the warming sun. The raucousness of the camp had now given way to quieter conversations. A near silence had descended as final preparations were made. He could already see lines of soldiers making their way down Fenn Lane, marching west.

Will stood back after fastening Hawker's breastplate, while Jack finished attaching the armour for his arms. 'Can you sit on the stool, Sir John, so we can lace the points?'

'Aye, you're proper squires — the two of you. No lord has better.' They worked fast, pulling and adjusting, tying and tucking. Hawker reached down from the camp stool and retrieved the little corn dolly. He managed to tuck it down into the gap between breastplate and gorget. Will and Jack looked at each other and smiled. 'For luck,' he explained, returning their grins. 'Now, when we're gone, you both stay here and watch our things. Don't trust anyone, you hear? And if you see men coming into the camp wearing the green and white, you run. Understand?'

A booming voice carried across the field and Hawker turned to see a huge figure on horseback, surrounded by a number of men-at-arms, one trailing a pennon upon a pole. The group approached at a walk until they were practically among the tents, their mounts tense and twitching. 'Well, well, I see you've taken your tongue out of the doge's arse long enough to fight for your rightful king!' It was Roger Beconsall. Mounted upon his great courser he looked even bigger than he was, a Goliath among his Philistines. Hawker had not seen him in over a year, but he looked much the same and sounded just as insufferable.

Hawker hefted his sallet helm and pulled open the visor. 'And your tongue still remains in your head to pester us all!' De Grood came to his side, and leaned on his spear while watching Beconsall, mumbling curses in Flemish.

Jan, too, wandered over, a cold stare of his piggy eyes directed at the new arrival. The Fleming, like de Grood, remembered the braggart knight from a year gone by and the memory of his mouth had not faded. 'Who said you can't put armour on an ass!' he said, the guttural Flemish carrying more than a hint of disgust. De Grood nodded.

Beconsall grinned. 'Come on, old man. Time to move those bones and mount up! You and your men are with me this day.' He leaned forward in his saddle. 'Where's the rest of your army, Sir John? Looks like you're a bit lean on lances for this fight.'

Hawker gave him a cold smile. 'Given that one of my men count for three of yours, seems I've got enough for the day ahead. More than enough.'

Beconsall let out a belly laugh and pulled his reins to turn away. Jan trotted out behind him as the big knight left, waving his hand in front of his crotch and waggling his buttocks as if pissing on him.

De Grood shook his head and smiled at his shorter compatriot's antics, then turned to Hawker. 'Jan is right. The man is a prick among pricks.'

Hawker nodded. 'He is just that. And as most men are led by their pricks it's our lot to be led by that prick, whether we like it or not.' He buckled on his sword belt as Will led over his horse, the sun glinting off its polished *chanfron* and cruppers. He took the reins and Will guided his boot toe into the stirrup as he gripped the pommel and sprang up and into the high-backed war saddle with a jangle of harness.

Jack returned bearing a war hammer and looped its leather thong over the hook near the saddlebow. He placed his hand on the bridle and looked up at Hawker, his bronzed and freckled face set determined in spite of worry. Hawker would have been proud to have him as a son, a joy that had been robbed from him more than a decade ago.

'We'll do what you've told us, Sir John. Come what may. God go with you.'

'All will be well, lad.' And he said it as much for himself as for Jack.

As they rode westwards over the crest, the landscape opened up before them. They emerged from the wooded hilltops and followed Fenn Lane down into a wide valley, the Redemore. De Grood rode by Hawker's side, bearing his pennon on a spear shaft and, behind him, four of Hawker's other men were also in the saddle. Jan Bec brought up the rear, leading the remainder who went on foot, their hauberks, helms and chainmail clanking and rattling as they kept pace. Ahead, Sir Roger Beconsall and his forty retainers made their way, part of the vast host that was spilling out from the east over the lane and Ambion Hill on their right, the little town of Bosworth half a league further north over a ridge.

Already, Yorkist lines were forming below on the field just south of the road: the Duke of Norfolk's vanguard three ranks deep and winding like some giant serpent as it covered a front a thousand yards long. Silk banners and standards of knights and nobles were twitching lazily in the near-still air.

Hawker was never sure how many fought for Richard Plantagenet that day, some said seven thousand, but they covered the plain like a roiling grey wave, captains coaxing soldiers into battle lines, bowmen up front. He could see more of the Yorkist host marching down from the north onto the plain. The lack of gleaming armour told him they were militia: too dull-witted or slow to avoid the round-up by the commissioners and sheriffs, or maybe just too keen to die wearing only a studded leather jerkin, an old helm, and armed with nothing but a farmer's pitchfork. Poor fools.

De Grood trotted up close to Hawker's side. 'Looks like the enemy have cut off the road west. But why in God's name did Richard deploy lower down? We could have made them come up here to us, instead. Kept the high ground.'

Hawker reined in and looked down into the valley, his eyes squinting. The Lancastrians had arrayed themselves at an angle, two hundred yards from where the Yorkists were pouring out to match their lines, three deep. Their left flank was anchored by a huge mass of soldiers – probably French or Swiss – their spears raised ten feet high. The great banners were a riot of colour, reds and greens billowing in the brisk breeze. 'What do you make of their lines, Jacob?'

'Looks like marshy ground on their right flank; I can spy reeds and tall grass there. A lot of mounted men in the rear. Ground rises up a wooded slope behind their line. Steep. Could be a village at the top. A few serpentine guns on the far left.'

Hawker nodded in admiration of the enemy. 'They are well situated, I give them that. The only good thing I can see is that we probably outnumber them.'

De Grood stroked the nape of his mount, skittish with the din around them and the scent of sweat and horseflesh carrying across the hill. 'And they have the sun at their backs. Richard will have a devil's ride to outflank them either end. They've played well.'

And Hawker knew then and there that they had been outfoxed before the first arrow had been loosed. Cavalry would not get around either end without sinking into marsh on the left or riding into cannon and long-spears on the right. It would be a foot soldier's work this day to break them head on, vanguard for vanguard. 'Order the bowmen and halberdiers down to the front. The rest of us will join the king and the second formation.'

He and his six Flemish men-at-arms followed Beconsall's little army down onto the plain to join several hundred of the king's retainers and chosen men. The king's white boar banner rose high above a knot of finely armoured horsemen, their caparisoned mounts fit for a holy-day procession. The flag of St George dipped and waved, manhandled by an over-exuberant bearer, and the mass of riders curled onto itself, horses prancing and stamping, sensing the impending battle that filled their ears and nostrils. Hawker caught a glimpse of the king, some fifty yards ahead, speaking with his captains and confidently holding his tall white destrier in check while it whinnied.

If Hawker was not destined to fight in the vanguard then it was time to do what he had been bidden: find Sir Giles Ellingham, and then make sure he did not get himself killed. He caught up to Beconsall even as the formation began to take proper shape, spilling into ranks.

Hawker called out. 'Who are the other belted men among us?'

Sir Roger pivoted around and pointed into the sea of armoured horsemen. 'There, next to the white pennon with the gyrfalcon and red lozenge, that is Sir James de Lacey. And there, behind you, sits Sir Giles Ellingham, who just won his spurs this week. Not even time for a seamstress to stich him a banneret! He has but three men with him.'

Hawker spied him, close behind where they stood. Ellingham was sitting up straight in his saddle, visor raised while he conversed with a man-at-arms mounted next to him. He was a boy in a man's armour. His eyes were wide with anticipation and he was pale as death itself. A nervous, half-hearted smile appeared on his lips, the soldier next to him probably cracking a jest.

Hawker, with Jacob following, trotted over to where Sir Giles was waiting. It was growing warm now and myriad tiny flies buzzed about the horses, diving in little black clouds. He approached Sir Giles and halted, bowing and extending a hand in greeting. 'Sir Giles, we share the honour of the king's rear guard. I give you greetings and wish you well on your white belt and spurs. I am Sir John Hawker.'

Ellingham's pale grey eyes, near frosty white, focused on the knight and a scowl contorted his features. 'I do not know you, sir. It seems you have the better of me. But a good day give you our Lord.'

'I see you have just your sword with which to fight.'

The youth's voice dripped with disdain. 'And what of it?'

'I offer the advice of one who has seen heavy battle. A sword is hard work against plate armour. Better to swing an axe or hammer at your foe. Crush them if you can't cut them!'

Ellingham's face flushed, and he let out a high-pitched laugh. 'It's rather bold to offer advice on battle. You think I'm still some squire? What makes you think I need or even want your counsel?'

Hawker gave him a flourish with his gauntleted hand. 'I did not mean to offend. Forgive the directness of an old warrior.'

Ellingham turned towards his man-at-arms, smiling. 'Maybe too old a warrior?'

Hawker knew fear on a man when he saw it. He returned the smile. 'No doubt, Sir Giles, as I've seen a fair few years in harness. And battle. And I'm still here. God be with you this day!' Hawker nodded, smiled again, and turned his mount back towards where Beconsall sat, roaring at some bit of wit from one of his men.

De Grood lifted his sallet up on his forehead and looked at his master. 'I would ask you why you bothered, but that is not my place.'

'It was because of a favour... to his father. It was a poor choice of words on my part, I'll give you that. But we must keep watch if the boy charges in. I'll be praying that Henry Tudor catches an arrow first.' Hawker shook his head, embarrassed by the exchange that Jacob had witnessed. 'I suppose I spoke a little like a high-handed prig... an arsehole.'

'Even an arsehole has its purpose, my lord.'

Hawker looked down and shook his head again, grinning. While they waited the breeze picked up, snapping the standards. A blast of trumpets sounded from the Yorkist side and moments later the dull thud and crack of a cannon reverberated from behind.

White, acrid smoke drifted over their heads, guns thumping in quick succession before falling silent. Once the lines of men engaged, jabbing and hacking at close quarters, the guns would not be able to fire any more. Trumpet blasts reverberated and Hawker saw a black cloud of shafts fly up as one, then arc their way towards Henry Tudor's lines. Almost instantly, the enemy loosed their own volley, a few well-pulled arrows whisking past where he stood.

This went on for several minutes, volley after volley, then the iron rain began to thin out, finally ceasing altogether. Hawker manoeuvred his mount, threading his way to get a better view of what was happening. He could see the vanguard rippling

– movement – and he caught glimpses of polearms rising and falling. The lines had clashed and archers had now dropped their yew bows and drawn swords and bucklers, wading into the melee. Hawker started chewing on the inside of his cheek and stood up in his stirrups to gain a better view. Beconsall and others were doing the same.

Behind, further up the gentle slope, rank upon rank of shire militias in the Yorkist cause stood or crouched, led by the Duke of Northumberland and his household troops. Two hundred yards ahead, the line of battle stretched across a front of at least a thousand yards. The ringing crash of steel Hawker knew well, but from where he sat it was a distant sound.

Nearly an hour passed, and Hawker was no wiser as to who was winning. They had not broken the Lancastrians despite their numbers, and the heavy horsemen up around the king were picking their noses while they waited. The trumpets sounded again and this time he heard battle cries as the armies fell upon each other anew. 'The Devil take this!' shouted Hawker. 'Ride!'

He and his men pounded fast around the mass of cavalry towards the right flank. As they cut clear across the width of the army, Northumberland's rear guard, all three thousand of them, stood rooted as fence posts. Hawker could not understand why they had not been ordered to advance down towards the road.

He reined in, still well behind the front battle lines, and what he saw stole his breath away. The Swiss and French were turning the Yorkist flank with their tight block of spearmen, their long shafts and sharp barbs pushing the Yorkist host onto itself until it could barely move for the press. And beyond the Tudor spearmen Hawker could see their gun crews loading. The enemy now had a clear line of sight to Richard's quailing rear guard. The bolt from a Swiss crossbow whipped past Hawker's horse. He turned and rode back to Beconsall's men. Small groups of Yorkist militia began peeling off and leaving the field, heading back north. A slow melting of the rear guard had now begun. The king's fortunes were on a precipice.

Hawker dug in his spurs, his Flemings in tow, and rode back across the way he had come. When he reached the king's formation, all was in uproar. Groups of riders milled about, unsure of what to do, all waiting for a signal. All eyes were on the king and his captains, who were in a tight cluster on the left wing, watching what was unfolding. Hawker saw Ellingham and his soldiers trot past towards the king's foremost host and he shouted to de Grood for them to fall in behind too.

Closer to the front now, the old knight had a better view. The wily Earl of Oxford had re-formed his Welsh and English rebels into six tight wedges of men. This had opened gaps and through these Hawker could spy the enemy's cavalry, clustered tightly. The red dragon banner flapped into view – this was Henry Tudor's position.

Hawker could see the king, his fluted armour polished to a mirror's finish, gold circlet around his sallet helm, waving his arm in defiance at whatever counsel he was being given. Hawker did not need to hear what was being said. There were only two courses of action for the king to take: flee the field, or charge in. And Sir John Hawker knew Richard Plantagenet.

The king, war lance tucked under his arm, had kicked his spurs in before the trumpeters could even manage to blare their horns. And then the great mass of armoured men and horse followed behind him. They cantered forward in a vast wedge, the king and his standard bearer at the apex and some two hundred mounted men thundering just behind. A dozen halberdiers of the royal household, armoured head to toe, did their best to keep up, loping and clanking as they covered the open, spongy ground into the Lancastrian formations.

Beconsall kept yelling at the top of his lungs for the rear guard to fall into line, that is, the remaining two hundred or so horsemen that were struck near-dumb with the suddenness of it all. Some men-at-arms and knights were thrashing their reins from side to side, trying to decide whether they should ride in or hold their advance. But Hawker, old campaigner that he was, knew that no further orders would be coming down the line. Ellingham was forty yards ahead with his men. As soon as Hawker saw him draw his sword he whistled for de Grood and Jan and then slammed down his visor and unhooked the war hammer from his saddlebow.

Sir Giles Ellingham shot forward after his father and king. Hawker followed close behind with Beconsall's bellowed curses just drifting to his ears. Ellingham was an impulsive youth, but he was right about one thing at least: better to go in with numbers than commit piecemeal. Hawker and his men-at-arms pounded in, the heaving mass of foot soldiers in front of him becoming more distinct to his eyes with every second that passed.

Ellingham began to outdistance his men. Hawker kicked his horse to keep up and soon had moved to join the king's charge itself. His horse almost tripped on a grassy hummock, recovered, and pelted forward again. The king passed through a gap in the seething Lancastrian knot of glaives and spears, riding hell for leather to reach Henry Tudor. Hawker had one eye on Ellingham's horse while he saw the king – still at a canter – send his lance into the chest of Tudor's standard bearer, propelling him backwards out of the saddle. The dragon banner fluttered to the churned-up ground and some witless but brave fool of a foot soldier dashed in and scrambled to raise it up again.

Richard's knights slammed into Henry Tudor's mounted guard and Hawker slowed to a trot as the mass of men and horses collided in a metallic crash, yells and neighs filling the air. He didn't have to glance behind him. Hawker knew de Grood was at his back. He looked ahead, past the maelstrom, up onto the wooded hill slope. He could spy masses of soldiers gathered at the crest under long-tailed battle standards. It had to be the lords Stanley and their little army. And they were hanging back, waiting. Waiting to see who was gaining the upper hand.

Ellingham was hacking away lustily at a Lancastrian, doing his best to unhorse the man. But he was on his own and no one had his back. Hawker had no further time to follow his progress. A horseman came trotting up and engaged him. He caught the blow with the hammer, golden sparks dancing off its iron head, then turned in towards the Lancastrian as he moved past and around. He swung back. Hawker's blow hit the back of the man's helm, staggering him like a thumped cow in a butcher's yard. The rider went limp and the momentum of his mount carried him on and out of Hawker's immediate concern. There were others to contend with.

He had a second of warning before another Lancastrian's hand-axe glanced off his shoulder from an ill-judged blow meant for his head, while some other knight on his left tried to handle his maddened, stamping horse to come up alongside so that he could lay in, too.

Hawker pulled tight on his reins, jabbed the spike of his war hammer straight into the axe-man's visor and then rapidly brought it up and around his horse's neck to strike the other attacker. But there was no need: de Grood's spear took the man in the chest and unhorsed him, leaving him dangling, one foot twisted in a stirrup. Only in the fight for a few moments and now Hawker could hear himself wheezing inside his helm, sweat pouring down his face and stinging his eyes. He blinked hard, clearing them. Ellingham was in trouble.

He was ten yards ahead, horse whirling while he traded sword blows with another horseman. But a foot soldier with a polearm was bearing down on him from his flank. Hawker kicked in his spurs. He was almost there when he saw the soldier jag the hook of his bill around Ellingham's shoulder, yanking him back in the saddle. Ellingham's sword flew from his grasp. He tried to rebalance, his horse side-stepping. Hawker rode in on the left and the foot soldier saw him too late. The man made a futile block with his haft and Hawker brought the hammer down on his helm, collapsing it like tin, his skull with it. De Grood took the right, engaging the knight who broke off from Ellingham as de Grood aimed a thrust. The spear took the Lancastrian in his throat – a rapid, shallow thrust – sending a spray of bright blood spilling over his polished armour.

Hawker knocked up his visor and reined in alongside Ellingham. 'Here!' he shouted, 'Draw my sword!' Ellingham snatched at Hawker's hilt with his gauntlet, shaking like a snared rabbit. 'Draw it, damn you!' More foot soldiers were running towards them.

Ellingham tugged the sword out of its scabbard and Hawker immediately pulled his horse hard to the left as another enemy arrived, thrusting a glaive up at him. No time for finesse, he turned even tighter, forcing the soldier up against his horse's rump while he beat his opponent with a few well-aimed downward blows until the man slumped. It was a mad jumble of horses and soldiers, but Hawker could see they were pushing back Henry Tudor's guard. Both horse and foot were falling back and joining the knot of their vanguard, still engaged with the Yorkist host. Richard's headstrong charge had turned their flank and the white boar banner waved above all. The king, his battle axe drawn now, was hacking away at every side, cutting his way closer to Henry. But the pretender had fallen back, enclosed and buried deep among his long-spears, and heartened cries rang out among the Lancastrians.

Hawker had lost sight of his own retainers except for de Grood. The Fleming came up alongside, breathless, his muffled voice barely audible.

'The king is almost upon Henry! If he can kill him the day will be ours!'

But Hawker could see that the chance was vanishing fast. The Welsh coward was already backing into the hedgehog of his French spearmen, who opened up to protect the bastard's hide.

And that was the moment, the moment when they were hit from behind by a wall of steel.

Lord Stanley, his brutish brother, William, and all their men poured down the hillside, shouting murder, their knights and men-at-arms riding into Richard's army at full tilt. Hundreds of them fresh to the fight, pushing the Yorkist host between them and the Lancastrian melee. Someone near Hawker gave a strangled, anguished shout, 'Traitors!' and rode straight into them. It should have come as no surprise to any of them. Stanley was

Henry Tudor's stepfather. Maybe the king thought his enemy's ties of family were as weak as his own. It was a fatal miscalculation.

Ellingham was fighting off three foot soldiers, his horse prancing and kicking. A mounted man bore down on the youth and Hawker put spurs in to intercept him, de Grood at his flank. The man was so intent on taking Ellingham down he didn't see Hawker until the knight had practically ridden into him. He turned but it was too late, Hawker rained down three furious blows, hammering him into his saddle. De Grood scattered the foot soldiers, who ran off after easier prey.

'He was mine!' screamed Ellingham, flicking his reins and yanking his horse's head in his anger.

'Plenty more left to fight!' Hawker shouted back. Ellingham had no time to argue it further. Another mounted opponent was nearly upon him and the youth raised his blade to meet the attack. Hawker looked past him, twenty yards ahead. He saw Richard's standard flutter wildly, then fall to the ground.

The golden circlet on the king's helm flashed in the sun, drawing Hawker's gaze onto him. The king was surrounded by his enemies, horse and foot both. Richard wheeled and fought along with his bodyguards, a pile of armoured corpses scattered around him. The king's axe rose and fell, cleaving his attackers on both sides. Hawker kicked in his spurs to ride to the king's defence, but within a few yards a group of French spearmen intercepted him and forced him to turn his flank. As he tried to ride around, he saw Richard's mount stumble, go down on one foreleg, and then tumble over. The king was unhorsed. Hawker lost sight of him as he fell, a mass of struggling, roaring men enveloping him.

In the midst of the roiling melee, Hawker saw the glint of Richard's helm, the gold crown still upon it. The king was on his feet, axe in hand, raging at those who came at him. Hawker crushed some young, screaming Welshman who had reached his own saddle, clutching at him to unhorse him. When Hawker turned back to the melee, within the mass of men he glimpsed glaives and halberds raining down on the White Boar. A storm of steel. A moment later, he could not see the golden crown any more. Time froze, and Hawker felt as if his heart had been ripped from his chest for the king did not rise again. A horse pushed past from behind Hawker, knocking his own mount and stirring him to raise his war hammer to strike back. But it was Ellingham.

The youth carried on and rode down one foot soldier and took a mighty swing with Hawker's borrowed blade at a second. Behind Hawker, more of the Stanleys' men, now traitors to the Yorkist cause, were arriving. The old knight swore loudly, spurred forward and caught Ellingham up. Half mad, the young man swung at Hawker, just missing.

De Grood came up on his left and reached for the youth's bridle. 'My lord!'

'The king is down!' Ellingham yelled.

'The king is dead!' Hawker barked back at him while snatching at his forearm. 'We must fly!'

Ellingham, his eyes wide, looked as if he had lost his mind. Snarling, he shook off Hawker's grasp, but de Grood held tight to his reins. 'This serves no purpose!' Hawker shouted. 'The field is lost! It's done!'

Ellingham tried to kick his mount and wheel around, but Hawker seized the bridle and kicked his own horse forward, seeing a gap in the throng of men. Hawker pulled him along and de Grood followed after them.

They cleared the lines. Many men were running, some still fighting. The three of them moved at a rapid trot, north by northeast, outdistancing the Yorkist survivors who were heading in the same direction as fast as their feet could carry them. Ellingham reached up and managed to lift his visor. He spat out a heavy stream of snot that caught on his breastplate. 'My men! I won't leave them!'

'They'll have run if they have any brains!' said Hawker. 'We make for the camp and salvage what we can.' Hawker had lost his men-at-arms, too, disappeared into the maelstrom of steel and blood. But his Flemings were battle-smart, and he knew if they escaped they would head back to regroup at the camp.

Ellingham shot Hawker a look of enraged frustration, but said nothing and they kept riding. The lad was developing a good sense of self-preservation.

Hawker had experienced it only once before in his life: shouting, fearful soldiers grabbing what they could; drovers and servants carrying bundles of silverware, jewels, prayer books, clothing – anything they could sell once they got away. He swung out of the saddle and, stiff and aching, hobbled to the tents, practically a cripple. It did not look as if they had been ransacked yet, but the wagon was gone with his cart man. And Will and Jack were nowhere to be seen. He prayed that they had done as he ordered, fleeing when they'd seen what happened.

'The king is dead.' It was Ellingham, sitting in his saddle still, his sallet helm clutched in his hands. His voice was leaden, all fight gone out of him.

Hawker looked up. If the lad only knew that he had lost more than his king. 'Sir Giles, come with us. At least until the blood lust calms and we see who is declared traitor and who is not. Better for us to seek some safety in numbers.' Hawker remembered well what had happened after Tewkesbury years before, when the killing went on well after the last dead on the field had been stripped of their armour. Soon old scores would be settled once again. A small group of horsemen rode up towards them and Hawker reached for his sword, thinking it was the enemy. Seeing Roger Beconsall instead, he still wasn't sure.

Beconsall was bellowing, face bright red and dripping sweat. 'They've done it now! They killed him! Brought down by a pack of curs.' He waved an arm towards his few remaining retainers, all looking as grim as the rest. 'This is all I've got left. They'll be on us before you can finish a piss. Get out now, Sir John. I'm going back north.'

'We're going east. To Stamford. I'll wait things out there. Lie low.'

'I'm not going to Stamford,' said Ellingham quietly.

'You goddamned well are,' said Hawker. 'We need every blade we can muster to keep our heads attached.' He got no reply, only a sullen glare.

'Stamford?' said Beconsall. 'That is where you hail? Your house?'

Hawker nodded and remounted, his thoughts again moving to the boys and if they had gotten away safely with the jewel. De Grood picked up a scabbarded sword and a hand-axe, which was all that he could scavenge, and fastened them to his horse's cruppers.

Beconsall leaned forward. 'Then let's make company together. As you say, we're safer in numbers. Come along, Sir Giles! The old warhorse speaks some truth.'

Hawker heard cries behind Beconsall. A single horseman was riding full tilt for them. It was Jan. He had lost his helm, his face and shoulder were spattered with someone's greyish brains, his breastplate smeared with dried blood the colour of rust. He had wisely thrown off his Yorkist tabard. Reining in fast, the words tumbled from him, breathless. 'Couldn't find the others! But the enemy is upon us!'

A small band of horsemen bearing the colours of the Yorkist turncoat Lord Stanley hove into view below them, near the road that opened onto the plain of battle. Beconsall shouted to his men and kicked in his spurs and everyone else followed, shooting past the deserted tents and making their way up to the road again, eastwards, towards Leicester.

They rode hard for a while on the Leicester road, looking back from time to time for fear of the hordes of Lancastrians – and their sudden allies. There were none. Hawker slowed his mount to a trot and Ellingham pulled up alongside him, his lank blond hair plastered wet with sweat on his bare head. 'I still have your sword. You must have it back.' He sounded calm, as if he was returning a borrowed prayer book. Hawker knew the youth had never tasted the suddenness of defeat, the smothering sense of unreality that rolled in on one like a fog. He was tasting it now.

'Keep it, Sir Giles. You may yet have a need for it.'

4

'Tell me again,' whispered Gaston Dieudonné, the Sieur de Lian-court. He stroked the cheek of the youth whose head lay in the crook of his arm. Their bodies, glistening with sweat in the guttering candlelight, were still entwined. An acrid, metallic smell filled the tent, courtesy of Dieudonné's armour, haphazardly piled on the Flemish carpet next to the field bed they lay upon. Gaston Dieudonné had offered his sword in service to Henry Tudor in the hopes that it might bring him something more material than the lies that he had long worn like a coat of mail. For though at times he believed it himself, Dieudonné was not the Sieur de Liancourt, nor the Count de Montbard, nor the Baron Aubusson as he had styled himself over the years. In truth, he could barely call himself a squire. And that was only by dint of the generosity of a real nobleman.

The youth, a varlet of Jasper Tudor brought over from Brittany with the rest of the earl's entourage, gently shifted himself and pulled a sheet across his buttocks and thighs. 'It's just tattle. From a raving priest. Must I?'

Dieudonné smiled. 'Amuse me, again. And then I might amuse you... again.'

The youth's voice sank even lower. 'It was given in confidence to my lord... I was wrong to tell you.'

'But you did tell me. And I wish you to tell me more.'

The youth looked into the face of his lover. The eyes that now bored into his, he had not really noticed before. They shone with an intensity that he found strange. Such a handsome man and, though only a few years his elder, one who seemed to have the assuredness of one much older. 'I don't remember more of what the priest said. They whispered afterwards.'

The youth felt Dieudonné's hand reach under his thigh and then curl around his balls, cradling them. He smiled. 'You would convince me through pleasure?'

The nobleman returned his grin. 'That rarely works, I find.' The Breton stifled a cry as Dieudonné's hand gripped him tightly, sending a spasm of pain up to his belly. '*Dit moi, mon amour.* Else I shall crush your little olives.'

The youth felt the grip loosen a bit and he exhaled. '*Putain!*' He rolled over, one leg off the bed. Dieudonné was quick, his arm up and hand around the youth's neck, pulling him back down. His hand circled the youth's windpipe, pushing his head down into the feather pillow.

Tears came to the young man's eyes, the seriousness of his position now becoming apparent. 'The priest... he eavesdropped on King Richard before the battle. The king gave some knight a great jewel. Precious beyond measure.' The Breton felt the grip on his throat loosen but still he was held firm.

The bed creaked as Dieudonné leaned on his left elbow and pressed his body onto the youth's. 'Go on, my dove. I like this story.' Dieudonné's hand slid from the youth's throat and brushed down his chest like some amorous serpent before settling over his now shrivelled manhood. 'Tell me more of this spying priest.'

'He said he had lain above the king's chamber in the White Boar Inn. Listening through the floorboards.'

Dieudonné snorted and shifted his weight. The youth could feel the man's pistle hard against his thigh. 'The same place where Henry Tudor slumbers tonight? A lucky innkeeper. What of this jewel you speak of?'

'The knight was told to take the jewel away. The priest said it had been a gift from Venice... but... Richard no longer wanted it.'

'A king who gives away treasure?' Dieudonné's voice dropped a shade lower. 'Who was this knight?'

'I think the priest said his name was Hawk. Something like that. An old soldier who had once trained the king.'

'And where is this knight taking the stone?'

The Breton stuttered, the French words tumbling from his tongue. 'Something about him having to take it back to Venice.'

Dieudonné stroked the youth's loins. 'And that was all? He sent the knight away?'

The Breton nodded. 'That was all. I swear it.' He did not even have time to draw another breath before the hand was on his throat again, crushing his windpipe.

'I know when a man conceals! It could be written upon your forehead!' The words hissed out of Dieudonné as he pinned the youth down. 'What else was spoken? What else did Richard say?'

The lad struggled to plead. 'They would hang me if I said anything more. I beg you, let me go.'

'Hang you? I could strangle you here and now. Or perhaps turn you back to your master and say you are a sodomite who found his way into my tent. You know what they would do to you then, my boy?'

The youth tried to pull the noble's hand from his throat but the grip was iron. The words were strained. 'I would tell them you're the sodomite who thrust *me*!'

Dieudonné inclined his head and looked down at him. 'And just who do you think they would believe?' He felt the youth go limp under his weight.

'He told the Tudors of a secret.'

'Now then, that is more like it, my dove.'

A tear rolled down the youth's flushed face. 'They will kill me, my lord,' he whispered. 'If they find out, they will kill me.'

'We will keep our secrets between us, won't we?' Dieudonné wiped the tear away from the terrified youth's cheek. 'Confess them to me.'

'The priest told my master that Richard's bastard son was upon the field this day. That Richard charged this Hawk to look after him... that the son did not know who he truly was.'

The nobleman gave a little nod of encouragement. 'And his name? Who is he?'

'Giles… Giles Ellingham.'

'That is a secret indeed. What other morsels did your little ears receive?'

The youth reached up and gently placed a hand on Dieudonné's forearm. He had surrendered himself fully now. 'Most terrible intelligence. I… I can hardly repeat it.' The Breton's right leg started shaking.

'We're not slipping backwards, are we?'

The youth shook his head. 'King Richard told this knight that he did not kill the boy princes as people say. He said that it was the new king's mother who had guided Lord Buckingham to do the deed. That is a dreadful thing.'

'Dreadful, yes. But others have said the same. God knows they had reason enough to kill the princes. The only difference is that today it is treason to say so. Yesterday… it wasn't. So… how did your master, Jasper, and young Henry react to that?'

'Henry struck the priest across the face.'

Dieudonné sniggered. 'So much for good intentions.'

'You must pay me for what I have told you.' The youth pushed himself up a bit on his elbows. 'I've done what you have asked.'

Dieudonné frowned. 'Let us not be too hasty. Was Ellingham killed on the field yesterday or did he fly? What became of this Hawk fellow?'

'I heard that my lord had demanded of the herald if any such men had been counted dead or captured. They had not.'

'So, a royal bastard on the run with a jewel fit for a king, but that a king doesn't want. What did the earl do when the priest delivered this morsel?'

'He sent out a party of men to find them.'

'The Tudors waste no time. Richard's body is still warm on a tumbrel in the market square and they're after the next one.' His mind spun rapidly at the possibilities on offer. What if he found the jewel and the bastard first? Surely, great reward would follow.

The Breton spoke up, quietly, but his voice carried new resolve. 'Pay me, my lord. None shall hear of what we have done here, I swear it. Your secret is safe. But what I've told you, *mon Dieu*… it will get me killed.'

Dieudonné smiled and traced his right forefinger around the youth's nipple. 'Yes, my dove… it will.'

Instantly, the youth's body tensed to spring, but Dieudonné's right hand splayed and pushed him back down, pinning him. The pillow quickly stifled the cries and Dieudonné bore down with all his weight, the body underneath him arching and bucking. 'Hush, my dove,' whispered the Frenchman, again and again, until finally the young Breton lay still.

5

Sir John Hawker, nearly dizzy with fatigue, leaned back in his creaking saddle and surveyed the manor that lay beyond. Just a league east of Stamford, he had inherited it from his father, a wealthy merchant known for his tenacity in the wool market as much as for his sourness. It was a sturdy if somewhat dark abode, a grange built of grey stone, four-square and gabled, a pretty chapel tacked on beyond the great hall, barn and stalls on the other side. He knew his house was without a heart and he also knew that the fault for this lay entirely with him. Having no wife or children to fill it, the manor was a melancholy place, miserly in its welcome to both stranger and friend.

He looked over to Ellingham and Beconsall, flanking him either side. They, too, were studying his estate and probably already wondering why it had the look of a place forsaken.

Hawker's sister, Catherine, herself widowed for five years, lived there. And by dint that no one else was around to take charge, she had become the mistress of the place. She was years younger than him, but he believed she would remain a widow the rest of her days. Far too much of the bitterness in her soul had now leached out to discolour her temperament, enough to discourage but the bravest of suitors. She was aided in her role by a broken-down bailiff who had worked for their father, more often than not sunk into drink.

As Hawker entered the great hall, still in armour, stinking and sweaty, his sister was there to greet him with a curtsey and a pained expression on her thin, long face.

'Brother, God has delivered you. I am thankful.'

'He has. But not everyone. Not nearly enough of us.' He was quiet for a moment. 'Christ, I'm parched for an ale.'

She waved to the scullery girl near the door to the kitchen who nodded and disappeared. 'What news, then?' she asked. 'Seeing your condition, I almost dare not ask.'

She knew the answer already. He was downcast, unwashed and dishevelled, looking more like a robber than a knight of the realm. 'The king is fallen, sister. We're undone. Undone in less than half a day. It is over.'

Her mouth fell open, then shut, and she wrapped her arms around herself and strode to the tall leaded-glass windows at the end of the hall. 'You bring back all these soldiers with you? What are we to do?' She was tall and slender, once considered pretty, but life's travails had given her a pinched look and a taciturn demeanour to match his own.

De Grood waved, grinning at her through the grimy glass. She glared back. Ellingham and Beconsall were stripping their armour off in the courtyard while the small band of retainers milled about, poking their noses into doors across the way – no doubt looking for something to eat.

Hawker wiped a rivulet of sweat from his face. 'What are we to do? Why, food and beer for a start.'

Catherine turned on her brother, eyes narrowing. 'Food and beer? You'd better start thinking about allegiances. Thank God you're a knight of little consequence. You can pledge loyalty to the new king when the time comes. Where is Henry Tudor now?'

Hawker shook his head. 'No doubt celebrating in Leicester. My lady, I am fresh out of battle and fresh out of ideas. Filling my belly might help assist the latter. Where are the lads? I sent them back ahead of me.'

Her look changed instantly, eyes widening. 'What? You've managed to lose those poor boys? They've not shown their faces here. It was madness to take them with you in the first place. I pray they're still alive.'

The words struck him hard. He trusted them both. Still did. But what if they had been waylaid on the road and taken or

54

killed? Turning them into couriers with the jewel might have been foolhardy after all. Too much responsibility for them, and too dangerous. He tried to dismiss the possibility from his mind. 'They will turn up… I know they will. Where is Piers?'

'You've lost those boys, haven't you?' Hawker saw that she was clenching her fists at her side. 'Brother, your soul is heavy enough as it stands. And yet you burden it with more sin.'

'I've taught them well. They're cunning. They'll return here.' He had to believe it. 'Where is Piers now?'

His sister flung her hand about like she was swatting at a moth. 'Where? Probably with a jug in the barn. You think things have changed that much in two weeks?'

'I need the horses taken care of. We won't be staying long.'

'So now you're off again? With that rabble out there? And what about me? Do you expect me to deal with it all, negotiate with the reeve and the tithing men next fortnight? You are down to two bondsmen to work what's left of the land. Half of it is fallow already.'

Hawker shrugged. 'Don't worry. We shall see it through.'

'We?'

'I've given you my keys to the chest. You have coin and you have had my permission to use it.' He was tired, that was true, but he had other things to worry about. Will and Jack to begin with. Then, what to do with Ellingham. The scullery maid handed him a vessel and he put it to his lips, relishing the cool ale as it ran down his throat.

His sister grew uncharacteristically quiet for a moment and then her expression changed to one of distrust. 'Will they be coming for us, John? Tell me.'

Hawker lowered the cup and looked at her. 'To what purpose? Look around you. What do we have?'

'So why must you leave again? How can the war go on without the king? He has no heirs. There is no one to lead York now. You're a fool if you carry on fighting.'

He was about to tell her where he had to journey but then thought better of it. 'I have unfinished business. A promise made to my liege lord. A duty.'

She closed the distance between them and ripped the cup from his hands. 'Duty to a dead king? You'd better start thinking about the new one. The *living* one.'

Hawker grumbled a curse, seized back his cup and went outside. If he had wanted a scold he would have married one. Didn't matter that she was right this time. She had a way of picking at his conscience like a child picks at a scab – a bit at a time. Sir Roger, with young Ellingham in tow, had returned from the well in the yard, dripping wet but refreshed.

'A pretty place you have here, Sir John, though I confess I don't see a firm hand on the tiller. Who is the woman that's raining curses on us with her eyes?'

'My sister, Catherine.'

Beconsall smiled. 'Sister? Ah, worse than a wife, in my experience. Can she bring us some food and drink? Your hospitality is sorely lacking.'

Hawker looked at him hard. 'As are your manners. You'll receive the best my house can offer. And then you and your men can be on your way.'

Beconsall chuckled to himself. 'And, Sir Giles, what is your pleasure? Do you wish to stay in this place of abundance?'

Ellingham threw Hawker a look that still carried distrust. 'I'll accept Sir John's hospitality and a bed for the night. But I intend to return to Middleham now that we've made it here unscathed. We must all think about our futures, decide what is best.'

Hawker had witnessed most of the youth's haughtiness evaporate during the course of their escape east. Now Ellingham sounded almost dejected, and to Hawker's ear, not just because he had lost a battle. Hawker doubted he had very much to return to in Middleham, secret adopted parents or not.

'You may stay as long as you wish, Sir Giles,' said Hawker. 'To think upon things.' He called to the maidservant to fetch two cambric shirts of his for the knights while the washerwoman dealt with sponging down their arming doublets. That would have to do.

–

Just past vespers, they all gathered in the great hall, high and low, Catherine peeved that they had little to serve the two gentlemen other than some rabbit stew and a smoked ham. Even enough boiled parsnips to fill a handcart sadly did not compensate. But so hungry were they that none complained. Beconsall's men and Hawker's ate on a trestle at the end of the flag-stoned hall while the knights and the mistress of the house sat at the table.

Beconsall was deep into his retelling of the battle and Richard's fall, while Catherine, in a green dress, her hair coifed and veiled, listened in horror. The cook and the scullery girl must have scoured the pantry clean, for by the end of the meal they were reduced to nothing but cheese and bread. Luckily enough, there was wine for them – brought up to table by old Piers despite his best efforts to drink the cellar dry in Hawker's absence – and some sweet ale for the rest.

By the time the candles were lit, the wine raised the colour in Beconsall's face to apple red, his emotion stoked higher in the telling of it all. Ellingham had become even more morose with each cup he drained. He said little, glowering from time to time as Sir Roger embellished what had happened. Piers wandered in again and crept up behind Hawker's chair.

'A word, Sir John. Two men up on the ridge behind the grange. Watching the house. I seen 'em in the twilight, but when I move towards 'em they run off. Vagabonds most like.'

Hawker leaned back and told him to tell de Grood to post a watch. His sister, taking her eyes from Ellingham for once, asked Beconsall his intentions now that he was without a king, and Hawker quickly turned his attention back to the table.

'Intentions, dear lady?' said Beconsall, smiling at her. 'Why, we must gather our strength, go back north and prepare to fight off the Stanleys when they return home. That Welsh bastard will be depending on them, now that he has stolen the crown. He and his nit-ridden relatives will soon be filling their pockets.'

Catherine was sceptical. 'But who is left to challenge them? Who will claim the crown? Richard has no issue and the princes are declared bastards.'

'If they're still even alive,' said Beconsall, nodding.

'There is the Earl of Lincoln,' Hawker added, uninvited, 'if he managed to escape the battle. He is of the blood. Warwick also.'

Beconsall snorted. 'Boys.'

'Then we must bide our time. Until they become men.'

Catherine sat up and puffed out her chest. Hawker could see the lesson coming. 'You both talk like fools. The die is cast. Make peace and look to your lands before you end up dead. How well did either of you two fare under Richard or his brother? It will be no different under this Henry Tudor for they're all cut of the same cloth. Don't you agree, Sir Giles?'

The youth had been staring into his cup for some time. He looked up suddenly with a face so full of dark apprehension that Catherine instantly softened as she looked upon him, reacting to his distress. 'I know you must be of heavy heart now,' she said, trying to soothe. 'But surely, wisdom and preservation must prevail.'

'I'm going home, my lady,' he said softly.

Beconsall smacked his palm hard on the table. 'As am I! Gather up those that I can. Before the wolves come!' He was sweating in the heat and from the wine, shining beads standing proud on his sloping ursine forehead.

The mood had turned grim and Catherine, disconcerted by the conversation and the threat that hung over them, excused herself to go to her chamber. Hawker could not bring himself even to toy with the idea of swearing fealty to the Tudors. He might have to do so though if it meant saving his house and lands and protecting Catherine. But it would stick in his throat like a trout bone. He would wait and see what the next few days would bring. His immediate problems remained, however. What to do about Ellingham? And how to find the boys before someone else did. He thought about asking Ellingham to assist him in searching for them after he got rid of Beconsall and his men. No doubt they would move on in the morning, like locusts.

They continued to drink, mostly in silence, until Hawker summoned Piers to show the men-at-arms where they would sleep in the barn. His sister had already had the servants prepare two rooms for the knights. At length, he arose and bowed. 'I will show you to your chambers, my lords. We should all take what rest we may.'

Beconsall nodded and regained his feet, wobbling a bit. Hawker turned to Ellingham. 'You are resolved to make for Middleham in the morning, then?'

'I believe that is for the best. By your leave.'

'I will see you properly provisioned – and armed. You may keep the sword I gave you. The enemy will be going there too. To seize Richard's holdings.'

The youth shrugged. 'That goes without saying. But I am not he. I'm no one now. No one of any consequence.'

–

Hawker slept badly. He was up with the dawn and walked down to the weed-choked pond, where he watched a carp gasping below the green scum. The ageing knight had some sympathy for the creature even as he cursed Piers' laziness. Money had been tight these past few years: the fish pond was stagnant, the barn and stables sagged precariously, the servants had run off, and the apple orchard was filled with unpicked and rotting fruit. The whole of the estate had the look of decrepitude, an unloved place. Hawker felt that if the house had no heart it was because his own was elsewhere, along with the remainder of his wealth.

Of the furtive intruders that Piers had spotted the night before there had been no sign. Not a single chicken missing. He thought about Sir Giles. Perhaps it was right for him to return to his home, to his false parents, to his illusions. For his own part, Hawker had fulfilled what Richard had demanded: to look after his son in the coming battle. And he'd done more than that. He'd pulled the lad out of Death's grasp, by God. He had followed the king's orders in full. Now, maybe now, he could live out his life on his own terms, in service to whatever king he chose.

Before that, though, he still had to find Will and Jack. And the jewel. The damned jewel. Venice was a long way to go to fulfil a sworn oath, he realised that. And it was a sworn oath to a man now dead. His sister had spoken plain sense to him about the folly of allegiance. In her mind, allegiance was dictated by expedience, and she was probably right.

But that was not who he was. Why not return the gemstone? If he could kill two birds with one stone by giving the trinket to the doge and then gaining a command and gold in return, why not make the journey? Such reasoning did not lessen his honour in fulfilling his word. What life remained for him here? Even if he handed over the Tear of Byzantium to Henry Tudor on a satin cushion tomorrow, they would still more than likely take his head too. Surely they knew of his past work in the shadows against the Lancastrian cause? And then the vision of the Venetian woman sprang into his mind again, pushing in as she did, unbidden, whenever he was distracted. Would he find her as he had left her if he managed to reach Venice? Would she even hold any affection for him still after what had passed between them? The carp seemed to be looking up at him. It belched a gullet-full of stagnant water and then dived down into the mud.

—

Beconsall's eight men were up and making ready to depart not long after Hawker returned to the grange. He had to admit they were an orderly lot, some discipline at least, and he felt sorrow that he had lost nearly all his own band, for none had made their way back to Stamford yet. Beconsall was among his men, cheering them up as they saddled their mounts.

'There you go, my lads!' he said, spurring them. 'Make it all fast! We're not yet ready to take holy orders at the friary. Young Roland, you must put a smile on your ugly face! We burnish ourselves and ride on! Ready for the next fight.' The burly knight was dressed in his arming doublet and leg armour, leaving the rest until it was time to mount. His men were already armoured, lashing bedrolls to cruppers and checking girth straps and bridles.

He turned to Hawker. 'I must thank you, Sir John, for your hospitality in such hard times. You won't begrudge me for my jests of yesterday, will you?'

Hawker managed to smile. He was still distracted, second-guessing his own decisions for the coming days yet trying not to show such weak indecision to his men. Or to his equals. 'You are a comrade in arms. We've fought together. I would not refuse you shelter or food.'

He gave Hawker a quick bow of his head in respect. 'Aye, and I do thank you. I wish we might have become better comrades before these last few terrible days came upon us.'

'Our paths may well cross again, Sir Roger. It is in God's hands.'

Ellingham joined them from the house. He too was dressed and armoured and Hawker assumed one of the house servants must have helped him, for he was without a single retainer now. Hawker had gifted him one of his arming swords from Milan. He nodded to Hawker as Piers led out his horse from the stable. 'Your good sister was kind enough to help me dress for the ride. She insisted on it. Did you teach her to fit a battle harness?'

Hawker shook his head. 'No. But if you're in need of a squire you may take her with you.'

Beconsall gave a belly laugh and Ellingham began to blush.

A cry sounded from the gates. A man crossed the little foot-bridge and ditch into the courtyard and came towards them, arms waving wildly. Hawker recognised him straight away, one of his two farmers, his face nearly purple with exertion.

'Sir John!' he said, swallowing great gulps of air as he fought for breath, 'a party of men are coming up the road… from Stamford way.'

'Where are they now?'

'By my God... they are on your doorstep as I speak, Sir John.'

Hawker swore. 'And you could not have told me earlier?'

'Aye, had you lent me an ass or a mule when I asked a month ago!'

Beconsall and Ellingham exchanged looks, probably thinking the worst. Hawker called for Piers to fetch his sword – there was no time for armour. Beconsall's prodigious brow began to furrow deeply. 'Were you expecting visitors?'

Hawker snatched sword and belt from Piers and hurriedly buckled it across his waist. 'Could be the reeve to welcome me back. Or perhaps not.'

Beconsall moved to his horse and mounted, signalling his men to do the same. Ellingham looked confused. 'Would you have us stay and see who it is that challenges?'

'A goodly offer, Sir Giles, but the choice is not yours or mine. They're here.' Hawker could hear the neighs of several horses beyond the wall and a moment later two soldiers rode in, followed by three men dressed in velvets and brocades, swords at their hips, and a rear guard of some nine more soldiers. They entered the courtyard, the three gentlemen nudging their mounts towards him while their guard fanned out behind. It was not the fat local reeve and his men.

One of the party spoke up. 'Which of you is Sir John Hawker?'

Hawker took a step forward. 'And who is it that addresses me?'

'I am a sheriff of Leicestershire. And these men are sent from the king.'

'Then you're in the wrong county, friend. This is Lincolnshire.'

The sheriff screwed up his eyes at Hawker and then looked over to Beconsall and his riders. 'These are your men?'

'No, they are not. They're... friends.'

The sheriff nodded. 'Friends. And is one of them Sir Giles Ellingham?'

The young knight stepped forward to join Hawker. 'I am he. What is your business?'

The sheriff opened his mouth to reply but was cut off by one of the other gentlemen who, it seemed, could not decide whether he was off to battle or to court. He wore a rusted breastplate over his fine doublet and a cap of wine-coloured velvet with a pheasant cockade. 'We have warrants for the both of you under orders from the Lord High Constable and Jasper Tudor, Earl of Pembroke. The king's uncle. And we are to search your house.' He signalled to two of his men who quickly dismounted.

The sheriff shifted in his saddle. 'I will need your sword, Sir John. You too, Sir Giles. We will join the court at Leicester.'

Hawker's eyes drifted over to Beconsall. He had the unflinching, staring glare of a mastiff, eyes locked onto Jasper Tudor's two henchmen. He sat in his saddle, frozen, and the sheriff turned his attention to him. 'You there! I would ask you and your men to dismount. I will need your names.'

Beconsall didn't move.

Hawker heard a rasping sound next to him. Ellingham was loosening the sword from its scabbard even as he undid the belt buckle. It was a gesture that had not gone unnoticed. One of the gentlemen moved his hand to his hilt and began loosening his blade. Beconsall was coiled, a moment away from launching himself forward.

Hawker slowly raised both hands. 'You are duty bound to show your warrants if you are who you say.'

'God's nails!' spat out the sheriff. 'I would have us reach Leicester by day's end. *This* day's end.'

'Enough of this!' The man in the red velvet cap drew his sword and brandished it at Hawker. 'Take off your weapons!'

A loud *clack* echoed across the courtyard. Hawker saw the man's head jerk in a spray of blood. A crossbow bolt had taken him below his right eye. His sword flew from his grasp as both hands went to his face. He slumped out of the saddle and crashed into the mud. His well-dressed comrade drew and came at Hawker to run him down. Beconsall let out a cry of rage and ploughed into the man, his men spurring forward to join him, weapons flying out of their scabbards.

63

Hawker held his sword in both hands, planted his feet, deflected the first blow of a man-at-arms as he rode past, and reversed the blade to make a cut at his back. He saw the sheriff yank his reins hard and ride out, not waiting for the outcome, great clods of earth flying up as he made for the stone gate. Ellingham gripped his sword and let out a cry, running at the nearest Tudor man. Raining blow after blow, he beat the man into the mud, killing him three times over.

Beconsall ripped the other gentleman out of his saddle and onto the ground. Throwing himself off his horse, he hit the ground on both feet and rushed the fallen man, stabbing a dozen times, one hand clenching the hilt, the other halfway down the blade. He was as a wild beast, frenzied. Again and again his sword plunged until he hit the man's heart, a gush of gore bursting upwards and spattering him. The knight leapt up and searched for the next opponent.

Hawker raised his sword to defend against a blow from one of the mounted Lancastrian henchmen. His sword rang as he caught the man's blade. Before the man could strike again, he had yanked him out of the saddle and brought him down into the courtyard mud. Hawker raised his sword to strike but was knocked over by the wheeling mount of another horseman. Then de Grood was there, pulling that man from the saddle and spitting him before he could get up. Hawker staggered to his feet, chasing the man he had brought down who was still sliding in the mud, trying to right himself again. One of Beconsall's men was there though, blocking escape. A sword arced and the Lancastrian sprawled, nearly decapitated.

More than half the Lancastrians were down and just two of Beconsall's men. With little in it for the sheriff's men, the last five had spurred their horses for the gate, following their master in flight. Hawker hefted his blade and shouted to De Grood, 'The house!' De Grood and Jan Bec ran inside to find the pair of sheriff's men who had gone inside.

Hawker heard Catherine's wailing and bolted inside. He found her at the centre of the hall before the hacked body of a soldier, her hands covering her face.

Jan stood there too, looking awkward, his sword dripping onto the rush-strewn floor. He saw Hawker and shrugged. 'Sir John, made a mess of him... in front of the lady. I am sorry.'

Hawker waved Jan away and moved to embrace Catherine, but she pushed him back and darted up the stairs to the solar. He started to run after her, but stopped. A hundred things rushed through his mind. That Henry Tudor wanted him this soon after the battle was a surprise. That Henry Tudor was hunting Sir Giles Ellingham was a much bigger one. It meant to him one thing: that others somehow knew of the youth's bastardy. The remaining Plantagenets were now being swept up like yesterday's broken crockery. When the sheriff's men had tried searching the house this told him even more. They knew he had something in his possession. Something precious. King Richard's orders to him had been compromised, and probably on the very day he gave them.

Hawker went outside again and looked over to Ellingham. The youth's feet were rooted, his mouth agape as he surveyed the carnage in the courtyard, his sword hand shaking. Beconsall was breathing heavily, ranting about Welsh scum and traitors. Facing the incensed giant, Hawker's grip tightened on his sword. 'Well, Christ's nails! That's torn it! This has cooked us well and good!' He gestured to the bodies that sprawled around them. 'This is fine work, you bloody fool! Two gutted Tudor noblemen smeared across my courtyard and half a dozen of their men.' Hawker turned away, fist clenched, then swung around again to Beconsall. 'Do you realise you've made us all outlaws now!'

Beconsall shook his head and swore in a low voice. 'You ungrateful wretch! Do you long to be separated from your head? *Ask* yourself why they came for you! And for Sir Giles. By God, they *named* you both. So what have you done?'

Hawker knew the answer but even he was surprised at the speed with which the enemy had tracked him down. And Sir

Giles. The question was: how did they know? But he was not about to confide any of that now. 'I was finding a way to get us out of it when hell broke loose! And now, sweet Jesus – even better – we've let some of them get away to tell the tale. Which one of your simpletons shot that crossbow?'

'My men? Damn you, it was one of yours! Over there!'

Walking uncertainly towards them across the yard, a spent crossbow cradled in his arms, was the boy, Jack. The look upon his face was one of disbelief. Disbelief that he had now slain his first man.

6

Piers and the farmer, reluctant gravediggers both, dragged the corpses out of the courtyard and down towards one of the lower fields, aided by Beconsall's grumbling men. Meanwhile, Hawker sat in the hall with Jack, his head in his hands. He would have to fly again. And staying in England was probably not an option. The reach of the Tudors would stretch further with each passing day. It would have to be Flanders. And what would he do for Ellingham, who was now in grave danger? What *could* he do now?

Hawker rubbed his hand over his mouth. 'What happened to Will?'

Jack was covered in road filth, shoes caked in mud. 'I took him home, sir. After we watched the grange from the hill. We saw all the soldiers down here and didn't know if it was safe.' He looked out into the courtyard through the window. 'Didn't know they were your men.' He paused a moment. 'Will… Will said he had had enough of being a soldier.'

Hawker let out a weak laugh and tousled the lad's hair. 'So have I, I think. So have I.' Jack had settled himself after making his unexpected appearance in the courtyard but Hawker knew it would be a while before the boy could make sense of killing his first man. If he ever would. 'What about you?' he asked him softly.

The boy didn't reply straight away, looking at his shoes instead. 'I'm your servant. I have tried to serve you well. I thought the horsemen were going to kill you, so I shot. Did I ruin it all?'

Hawker sighed. 'We do what we feel we must. To survive. If you hadn't started it then Sir Roger would have an instant later.' He clapped the boy on the shoulder. 'You defended me.'

67

Jack managed a small smile. 'But I would like to be your squire… if you let me.'

Hawker felt a twinge in his calcified heart. 'Well then, you shall be, Jack Perry. You shall.'

He said this although he knew that Jack probably had not an inkling of what he was getting into. Hawker's own sense of morality told him he should tell Jack to go back to his father and mother then and there. But he knew that wasn't right for this boy. They didn't want him. Which is how Hawker ended up with Jack in the first place, the lad given over to him without remorse or regret or any conditions. Jack had been cast off like yesterday's slops in a pail.

Worse now though, Jack's killing of a king's man meant that the boy was no longer safe. Not just in Stamford, but anywhere in the kingdom. Jack would be lucky if he even got a trial. There were enough witnesses – the sheriff for one – to testify for the coroner. Others could be bought or persuaded, if need be. As for himself, being Richard's agent and shepherding his jewel and bastard son, there would no doubt be a writ of attainder. They'd execute him, give his estate to the Crown, and dispossess his sister. Hawker looked up to the wall over the high table, the cream-coloured plaster painted with the anchor and hawk's head from his armorial crest. It had been there fifteen years and would no doubt be whitewashed over soon.

Jack's quiet but firm voice brought him round again.

'I have it with me, Sir John. Like you asked. Will wouldn't touch it, so I was the one who had to carry it.'

The words drew him up sharply. How could he have almost forgotten? 'Good lad. You hold on to it a bit longer. Just in case, eh?'

'I've got your satchel too. Hid it in the barn. I knew when I saw all the soldiers running back to camp that we'd lost. Didn't have much time so couldn't get much. The cart man told us to climb up with him, but I never liked him. His eyes were lying to me. So I took a mule and got Will up on the front holding the satchel and I climbed up behind him and we got to the road.'

Hawker rubbed Jack's shoulder, a feeling of almost fatherly pride welling up. 'You did well, Jack. Very well.'

'Did they kill the king?'

Hawker looked down at the rushes. 'Yes, they did. But he fought them all the way. The White Boar brought down by dogs.'

'So... we're going away now?'

Hawker smiled again despite his fatigue. The boy was quick-witted indeed. 'Yes, this day, I think. And I need you to go and get my armour and pack me a bedroll with knife, bowl and spoon. Roll up a doublet or two, an extra shirt, and my hose and braes. Understood?'

He nodded, face brightening underneath the grime. 'Where are we going, Sir John?'

The knight put a finger aside his nose and winked. 'We make for Bishop's Lynn.'

'A ship?'

'Aye, my lad, a ship. If we can find one that'll take us.'

–

'Bishop's Lynn!' Ellingham shook his head. 'You mean to leave England? That may well be your fate, but I'll not leave.' He gestured in defiance, striking the air with his hand. 'Why *should* I leave?' The three outlaw knights stood in the courtyard, surrounded by patches of dark, blood-soaked earth.

Beconsall's voice was muted for a change. 'Because, my friend, you've murdered the king's men.'

'No, no, no. It was not like that. I *defended* myself. You broke the peace!'

'Well,' replied Beconsall, 'in truth it was a lad of fourteen, but do you think that will make it any better for you. Or for me?'

Hawker tried to sound reasonable. 'Giles, they called you out, by name. They want you as well as me.'

Ellingham's jaw dropped and he looked at Hawker and then to Sir Roger. 'And why me? Surely they're not after every belted knight who fought for Richard?'

'I cannot tell you why,' replied Hawker. Half a lie.

Ellingham fixed him hard. 'I don't even know you. You latched on to me before the battle. You found me later. What is your game, Hawker?' He turned to Beconsall. 'And you're fleeing abroad too, Sir Roger? With him? What about your men?'

Beconsall shrugged. 'They'll follow me to hell if necessary. I could ride north, but Sir John is right this time, I think. It will be far too risky to stay on these shores. At least for a while. But I, for one, plan on coming back.'

'Well where in God's holy name do you intend to go?'

'We can make for Bruges or Antwerp first,' said Hawker. 'Then see what happens. I doubt we will be the only soldiers of York turning up there.'

Sir Roger began nodding sagely. It was becoming apparent to Hawker that the man was as contrary as a leaf in the breeze. Too ready to agree to any plan. Too ready to follow him. And Hawker could not help but ponder why it was that Beconsall had made the decision to attack the sheriff's party when he could have just stood by and let them take him and Ellingham away. He glanced over to de Grood who was standing off to one side, listening to the exchange. The Fleming was staring hard at Beconsall while he stroked his scarred cheek. Hawker knew that de Grood trusted Beconsall about as far as he could throw him. He also knew that to make it out of England they would need the strength of numbers to beat back any pursuit.

'Aye,' Beconsall said. 'I could be convinced to go to the Burgundian lands. For a time. We would find allies there.'

'What?' protested Ellingham. 'We have *nothing*. The clothes on our backs, some half-rusted harness. I don't even have my own sword any more.'

'Think well upon it,' Hawker said. 'They will be back, you can be sure, and with more men. We have to leave this day. Sooner the better.' Hawker could tell that Ellingham wasn't convinced. He kept looking from him to Beconsall, jaw clenched tight. 'Together we stand a better chance on the road, Sir Giles. But it is your choice.' That was the truth of it as Hawker saw it. He'd done half his duty to his dead king. It was time to return to Venice, play the courier, and then find a new master to serve. But that plan he was keeping to himself for the moment.

Ellingham looked over to Beconsall, then down at the ground. 'Very well, Sir John,' he said, 'I will give way to you… your experience.' He didn't sound convinced, though.

Hawker nodded in approval. 'Good. Ready your mounts. And pray we can outpace Jasper Tudor's men.'

–

Catherine was upstairs in the solar, mid-morning sun streaming across the lavender-strewn planks. She watched Ellingham load his horse down in the courtyard, the fingers of her hand playing upon the stone windowsill. Her face, puffy and reddened from crying, accentuated her fading charms.

'If only you had come back victorious with that handsome young knight. Made a match for me, brother. It would be a different ending now, would it not?'

'I wish you would not stay.' Hawker had earlier offered to bring her to Bruges, but she had refused, lashing out at him with unrestrained anger. She had told him she could never leave. The grange was all she had and she would fight for it if need be.

Her voice became petulant. 'Of course I will stay. I will disown you and your actions. Swear allegiance to the new king and throw myself on his court's mercy. Perhaps they will let me live out my days here. Because you've left me no choice, have you, brother?' She turned to face him fully. 'Just why *did* they come for you? You're no real nobleman. What is it that you did? On the field. What did Sir Giles do? What could you have *ever* done that was so bad?'

'Old scores had to be settled,' he replied, the lie rolling off his tongue. 'The mean vengeance of lesser men. Revenge… for the Tewkesbury battle.' Hawker moved to the corner of the room and the iron strongbox. He opened it. Inside there were three sacks of coins, deeds, his award of arms, a few keepsakes. He folded the vellum adorned with King Edward's seal and shoved it into a deep pocket sewn inside his doublet. He then lifted out the three bags of gold, the last of his wealth in England, placing them on the foot of the bed. He pointed to the greasy green leather, 'I'm leaving you one... the largest. Take some coin, pay off the servants who wish to leave, and bury the rest of the gold. This day. Do you understand? Somewhere you will not forget. Soldiers will tear the grange apart when they return.'

She didn't even glance at the gold sacks. 'And you know what it is they will be searching for, don't you?'

He didn't answer her.

She glared, like a serpent ready to strike. 'I know that you do. You are vile, brother. And that we should part in this way is a great sin. A sin that falls upon you alone.'

'I am sorry, Catherine. More than you could know. Sorry for many sins. Against you.'

There was silence between them for a minute. Then, her anger suddenly melted, her eyes beginning to brim with tears. 'I will embrace you all the same. Come to me.' He hugged her but still felt the coldness of disappointment inside her.

'God keep you, sister. I will send word back. In time.'

She looked into his face and Hawker saw something like hopelessness appear on hers. 'I was a good wife. But the Lord took my husband from me just the same. I will never know why. And I had no choice but to seek refuge with you. I must have sinned – somehow, I must have – to have reaped such bitterness. None of us are blameless, brother.'

And that is when Hawker felt the tears come to his own eyes for the first time in an age. 'When they come, tell them what they want to know. Where I've gone. I will never hold that as a betrayal of me. You do what must be done. To save yourself.' He pulled away from her embrace, but Catherine held on to him.

'You have lost what mattered most to you, as have I. She was a good woman, your wife. She loved you and bore you a son. And

God took them. But you cannot keep running from grief. You must find your life again. Even if I could not.'

Hawker hugged her tightly and buried his face in her hair. 'Catherine, will you not come with me? We can find safety in Flanders. I will find you a new home.'

'No,' she mumbled. 'That is not meant to be. In your heart you know that too. I will find my own way. Here. You must go where fortune led you before.'

He pulled away, his throat thick, and then hefted the two sacks of gold. His house, his family, his very name, all were lost now. He gripped her arm, more gently than he had touched anyone in years. 'Fare thee well!'

—

It was fifty miles to Lynn. They rode steadily but not too hard, this for the simple fact that they could not get fresh horses. Even so, they were in the saddle until the sun was dipping behind them into a blood-red sky. A few merchant trains they passed by, these eyeing them with apprehension, probably taking them for a band of masterless rogues. They slept rough that night, well off the road in a stand of tall trees, which sat like an island on a sea of high grassland.

—

The party was strung out along the road, some in single file, others two by two. Jack rode last in line but for stocky little Jan, who brought up the rear. The gentle rocking of his horse's gait had lulled Jack into reverie. The images of the day before – the battle in the courtyard – kept repeating in his mind's eye. The moment he pulled the trigger on the rusted crossbow was as fresh as if it had just happened. He relived the moment of his decision, hand clenching tighter about the crossbow stock and his forefinger moving to the iron latch, slowing squeezing until finally the decision was made by his hand and not his heart.

But as he rode that day, his conscience had reconciled. He had saved his master by his actions. And if he was to be a squire to a knight then killing would be a part of that office. He reckoned that having now done that, another's blood on his hands, the remainder of his role as squire would be the easier. But he was asking himself other questions. He had never seen Sir John in defeat. Until now.

They had slowed to a walk for a few minutes to give the horses a rest before resuming the canter. Jan's horse stumbled in a rut and bumped into Jack's flank. Jan recovered and moved up alongside him. Jack thought he looked to be deep in his own thoughts, eyes straight ahead, body hunched low in the saddle. Jack glanced over again at the Fleming.

'Master Jan, how many years have you served Sir John?'

The man stuck out his lower lip as he raised himself up again. 'Eh? Well, lost count, boy. Enough to know I probably used up my credit with God's bank.'

'And you followed Sir John into all his battles?'

Jack saw the Fleming give a nod, but it might have been just the motion of the horse beneath him. He looked up ahead where he could see Hawker and Jacob riding parallel and in some animated discussion. Jack adjusted his reins and looked over again to Jan. 'Was he a great captain? Did he ever lose a fight?'

Jan grinned and shook his head. 'You're a shit-stirrer, aren't you? We fought many battles. We won many.' His head dipped. 'We lost a few, too.'

Jack looked down at his pommel for a moment. He was itching to know more but worried he might provoke, or worse, have his loyalty questioned. But he had had his own questions for some time. 'Master Jan, why does he have so little to show for it all? Was there no treasure? No fortune for you all?'

Jan exhaled and leaned over his saddle towards the lad. 'I tell you something, boy. Some things more important than coin. Sir John might not have treasure but he always pay his men. And when trouble came to us he never lose heart. Never let us see his pain. He is captain of men.'

That satisfied the youth for a while and he leaned back into his saddle as his mount clopped along beneath him. A few more minutes passed and then he heard a loud whistle from de Grood to signal that they were quickening the pace again. They rode on until the sun was sinking low at their backs, finding a copse that would afford cover a short distance from the road.

Jack had managed to kindle a small fire and so had Beconsall's men on the far side of the cluster of trees. Hawker stood off at the edge, facing the way they had come. Behind him, he could hear Sir Roger's men grumbling still, mainly about where they were heading. He began to worry that Beconsall's hold on his remaining men might be less than the grip of iron the knight claimed. Hawker watched the strange glow of the sun's last rays disappearing into a purple sky.

'Second thoughts, Sir John?' It was Ellingham, who had come up behind him.

Hawker looked at him and smiled. 'Hard to have second thoughts when there is but one path ahead.'

'I'm not sure why I am following you, even if you say it is the only choice,' said Ellingham. 'Or maybe, it was you who was following me.'

'You do not have to come with us, Sir Giles. It's your choice. But as far as I can see, it would be the wisest given the new harsh wind that is blowing our way. I have contacts in Flanders. Good ones. We will be safe there. Then decide what is next.'

Ellingham drew his cloak about his shoulders, given to him by Hawker's sister. 'You know nothing about me. I know nothing about you. And here we both stand, our necks on the block and I don't even know the reason why.'

A bellow and laugh from Beconsall brought them both around.

'You call that a fire!' Beconsall shouted at two of his retainers. 'I could fart a bigger fire than that!' The two men scrambled to add more sticks.

Ellingham turned back to Hawker. 'You understand my caution?'

'I do. I didn't seek out his company either. But the die is cast. How could your father protect you now if you returned to Middleham?'

Ellingham tilted his head slightly. 'My father? What do you know of my father?'

Hawker caught himself. 'I only assume your father is Sir Thomas. He is well known in the court. But even he will have to make a decision now whether to stay harnessed to York or else go on bended knee to the Tudors.'

'Why do they want you? And me? Those men had warrants for both of us. That was *before* we ended up killing them.'

The problem hung over Hawker as thick and heavy as coal smoke: when to tell the youth who his father really was. To tell him that he would be hunted so long as he stayed in England. He bowed his head for a second then looked up again. 'I know there are old scores to be settled. I am on that list. I will tell you the story when and if we make it off these shores.'

Ellingham gave Hawker a hard look. He didn't like half-truths and he suspected he was being served up one now.

Hawker saw the youth's dubious expression, the narrowed eyes that carried more than the fatigue of the day's hard ride eastwards. 'I cannot say what it is that's irked Jasper Tudor to be calling for your presence. But I for one would not answer that summons.'

Ellingham found that contained little in the way of assurance. 'So you run to Flanders. Have you seen campaigns in other kingdoms? Something tells me that your past is guiding your hand now.'

Hawker harrumphed and glanced towards his boots. 'The Italian kingdoms. The Swiss Confederation. Austria. Yes, I've made friends. And enemies. And now, it is time to lick my wounds and find aid where I can. In that you are welcome to join me.'

'You don't even know me.'

'I've seen a young knight who fights well. Thinks fast. Maybe a man who would seek his fortune if he were shown the open door.'

Ellingham's smile was as thin as a blade of grass. 'My father would probably tell me the same thing. He made me as his own squire and then sent me to the castle to train under Richard's men-at-arms. I suppose that is how the king came to find me. I helped to chase rebels down last summer in York. That was where I was blooded. But I don't know why that warranted the king knighting me on the road three days ago. Others were more deserving.'

Hawker smiled a little and placed a hand on Ellingham's shoulder. 'He must have seen what I've seen. A man of knightly bearing only in need of spurs.'

Ellingham edged away slightly, and Hawker withdrew his hand.

–

The next day, damp and shivering, they roused themselves to make the final leg to Lynn. A party of eleven armed and haggard men accompanied by a servant boy was bound to raise suspicions, the more so that they bore no colours or banners.

'I trust you know this place,' said Ellingham, riding alongside Hawker. 'I've never been here. Whose help do we seek?'

'Any we can find,' mumbled Hawker. 'We cannot afford to be particular any more.'

Sellers and tradesmen were just setting up for the day as they rode through the narrow streets heading down to the quay at the Purfleet. Without exception, all slowed their barrows and carts as the ragged group rode past, their eyes fixing the soldiers with a mix of distrust and disdain. Hawker avoided their gaze and questioning stares. They would get answers soon enough, though hopefully not before he had arranged passage with a ship's master. 'There are two inns down at the quay,' he told Ellingham. 'We should sell the horses and keep inside until I can make arrangements.'

Ellingham pursed his lips, doubtful of their chances. 'As if we haven't already been seen for who we are?'

Hawker nodded. 'I know that. All the more reason to stay out of sight.'

When they reached the wharves he saw three cogs and a caravel moored alongside.

'Well, which one is yours?' said Beconsall drily. The brash knight had kept his own counsel all morning, uncharacteristically subdued.

Hawker narrowed his eyes at the jibe. 'I'll speak with the masters. Get your men over to that tavern and stable yard. Sell your beasts as soon as you can and don't argue the point, we'll get new mounts in Burgundy.' It was a gamble, he knew. None of these vessels might be bound for Burgundian lands. Within a day, or two at most, there would be an armed party coming through the gates of Lynn. If Jasper Tudor had given the order to arrest them, there weren't many ports that couldn't be reached inside a day or two. It was either east or west, and the west – either Gloucester or Bristol – would have only been gained through the very teeth of the enemy who had come that way already. That left the east, and Lynn was the biggest port. If they could reach it in a day from Stamford, so could Henry Tudor's men.

Beconsall leaned forward in the saddle and crossed his wrists over the pommel. 'You're telling me to sell my horse and those of my men? And what if we can't find a ship going our way in the next day? You propose we fight it out here?' He sniggered and gestured towards Jacob and Jan. 'With your little army?'

Hawker remained expressionless, but his hands slowly took up the slack on his reins.

'Or maybe surrender?' added Beconsall.

'You're free to go as you please,' said Hawker, 'if you think you've got a better chance. They didn't have a warrant with your name on it.'

Beconsall leaned back and suddenly let out a deep belly laugh. His men, who had grown tense listening to the exchange, still showed no sign of approval.

'Aye. They didn't at that. But they might just as well now that I've put a blade into more than one of them. Have it your way,

Sir John, we'll sell our mounts.' He kicked his horse and started guiding it towards the stable yard. 'But you better get us that ship!' he barked back at Hawker, snapping his reins. 'I, for one, won't be swimming to Flanders.'

Ellingham reined in alongside Hawker while he watched Beconsall enter the yard, the bear of a knight bellowing at his men the whole of the time. 'How well do you know him?'

Hawker turned. 'Know him? Not well enough. Our paths crossed in the north once when I served King Edward. He's a braggart, to be sure, but good in a fight. And that might yet happen.'

'He's like a stray dog. He's only with you because he sniffs something to his advantage. You didn't exactly have to twist his arm to get him this far.'

'Everyone seeks advantage. But his won't come at my expense. I won't let it.' Hawker knew the youth burned to know why they were running. Those demands would get louder before much longer. And Ellingham was right to question Beconsall's eagerness to follow him: it was suspicious.

Hawker ordered de Grood to get them a room at the Tun tavern a few houses down, and to enquire about selling their horses. Jack followed close behind. Hawker laid a gentle hand on Jack's shoulder as the boy passed by. 'Take the bedrolls and sacks up to the chamber and don't take your eyes off them.'

Ellingham dismounted and handed his reins to de Grood, a look of misgiving on his face as he turned to look at Hawker. 'You are certain this is the best course for us to take? It still smacks of blind desperation to me.'

Hawker dismounted too, Jan stepping forward to take his mount. 'My advice to Sir Roger stands. If you have a better plan, you are welcome to pursue it.'

'A better plan? I don't think that this is a plan at all, Sir John. Perhaps *that* is the reason for my disquiet.' But both he and Hawker knew that he had come too far now, into a strange shire with nowhere to turn for help once Hawker had sailed.

'Faith, Sir Giles, faith. I'm going to the quayside now. You can come with me if you like.'

Hawker spied a sound-looking cog and, without hailing for permission, walked up the gangplank to come face to face with a squat, balding mariner standing on deck directing his crew as they hefted bales of wool and passed them down into the ship's hold. That meant he would be sailing soon. The master paused his labours at the sight of the two men approaching.

'What business have you on my ship?' he demanded as Hawker crossed the railing and strode towards him.

'Good business, for you. We seek passage.'

His grin showed blackened stumps. 'But I'm not seeking passengers.'

Hawker returned him a look of stone, voice quietly insistent. 'You may change your mind when you hear me out.' The man looked over to Ellingham, taking his measure, and then gave a slow nod to Hawker.

'Very well, but whatever you propose should have the colour of gold about it.' The mariner grabbed at a mast stay and beckoned them to follow him to his tiny cabin at the stern on the main deck, cramped and stifling but smelling of cloves and sweet cinnamon. 'Right then,' he said, reaching his map table and putting his hands on his hips, 'what do you offer?'

'We are soldiers... returning home to our employer. We require passage to Flanders. Antwerp or Bruges would do us, Master...'

'Cribbins. Master Peter Cribbins.' He folded his arms. 'So you be soldiers then. No surprise that. Half the Southside has guessed you and your comrades are on the wrong side of the law. Did you murder someone?'

Hawker's voice was flat. 'Would it matter?'

Cribbins smiled. 'Maybe not. But I'm bound for Castile – not Flanders. I shall be sailing round Plymouth way. Down and out and hugging the shoreline. Not to Antwerp, friend.'

Hawker smiled in return. 'Change your route and I will pay you handsomely. Not much of an alteration in course for you if you are bound for Castile.'

'So you're a mariner as well as a soldier, are you? I'll not be sailing clear across the German Sea just to save your skins. You'd better find another ship, friend.'

Hawker loosened a small pouch of gold at his belt and put it on the map table. 'Just drop us on the coast and then be on your way. No need to go upriver at Bruges or Antwerp. No customs men.'

His eyes went to the gold and he grinned at Hawker again. 'And saying I'm inclined to alter my course. Just what would you be willing to pay as fare?'

'I'll give you ten livres. More coin than you would see after ten voyages.'

'Seeing as you're in a hurry and I have the only ship ready to sail – first light if the winds be right – then I'd say you ought to pay any price. Any price I set.'

The knight moved one hand to the hilt of his sword while he spread open the top of the money pouch with the other. 'My business isn't commerce. I think you know that well enough. And I'm beginning to grow impatient standing here and listening to you flap your fat lips. So, I'll be generous and say *fifteen* livres. Accept that or you'll be swimming at the bottom of this river.'

Cribbins glanced out to see where his crewmen were standing, just for his own safety, then looked to Hawker again. 'You're a man of worth by the look of you. Maybe a knight. Maybe not. I reckon I might gain more by turning you over.'

'You might,' Hawker replied. 'But you would not live long enough to collect it.'

The master chewed on his prominent lower lip a moment before giving Hawker another grin of bravado. 'Very well, my lord. Fifteen livres it shall be. And my silence.' Cribbins stuck out his tar-stained hand and they shook on the bargain.

'I will give you five now, ten once we make the sea.'

'I sail at first light. Tide is in full flood then. And I won't be coming a-looking for you either.'

7

Ellingham and Hawker shed their rusting harness and Hawker tasked Jack with finding some sacks to stow it. Not that they looked much better afterwards, what with sweat-stained arming doublets several shades of yellow and brown, torn hose and muddy leather boots. Hawker sat in the hall of the inn sipping ale, fingers playing upon his dagger hilt. More than an hour went by. Sir Roger had not arrived as expected and Hawker told Jacob and Jan to go find out where he and the others were.

The Flemings were back quickly enough. They stumbled into the Tun, each supporting a half-conscious Beconsall, blood pouring down his face and a swollen purple bruise on his forehead the size of a goose egg.

'Here now!' shouted the landlord. 'Get him out of my house ere he dies and I have to fetch the magistrate.'

Hawker leapt up, warning off the man with a menacing finger, and saw to the knight as his men laid him down on the straw-covered flagstones. Beconsall started to retch and they rolled him over onto his side. Jan fetched a cup of ale and raised him up to take a sip. 'They must have thumped him good, Sir John. With a sword pommel.'

De Grood rolled his eyes. 'How would you know, you calf-brain?'

Jan protested. '*Nay, nay*, Jacob! I know what a pommel bruise looks like. I've given enough of them!'

Hawker rapped Beconsall's cheek to rouse him. 'Who did this to you?'

Beconsall blinked, then focused while he smacked his lips, the ale dribbling out. 'My men… decided… they don't much like boats. Or ships. Or me. Bastards have run off. All of them.'

Hawker ran a hand through his hair. 'Sweet Jesus, oath-breakers all. God rot them.'

'Fools as well,' said Beconsall, trying to rise up. 'They could have sold me to Henry Tudor for a goodly sum.'

Ellingham reached into his purse and took out a few coins. 'For your trouble,' he said, thrusting them at the innkeeper. 'And your discretion.'

He palmed the coins and nodded to Ellingham. 'You lot *are* the trouble. And you'll pay handsomely to stay under this roof but one night. Then you're out. Get your man upstairs and off my floor.'

In their bedchamber, Jack fetched some water in a bucket and cleaned up Beconsall while the Flemings watched in silence.

Jacob sucked his teeth and exchanged glances with his comrade. 'It's one thing being on the run,' he whispered in Flemish, 'but it's another being on the run and desperate. We're moving down that path, I think. Just five of us – not counting the boy.'

Jan shrugged. 'So what is there to do? At least we're going back home.'

Sir Roger, roused, batted Jack away and stood up, tottering like a drunkard. 'So when do we take a ship? Or do you propose barricading us in this hole and waiting until they knock the door down?'

Hawker re-entered from the landing, having just heard Beconsall's outburst. 'I've got us a ship, damn you. But you had better do what I say if you wish to live to see another Sunday.'

Beconsall shot Hawker a look of naked spite and then winced in pain after touching his bump. 'You think yourself a righteous bastard, don't you? You think you're the only one to have had Richard's favour? Sir John Hawker, the king's spy. Well, my lord, spies get watched too. Do you take me for a fool? I know where you're bound. I've always known. Leastwise, where you *should* be bound.' He smiled, savouring his secret knowledge. 'Venice.'

Hawker didn't answer.

'So, then. Where is it, Sir John? Where is the Tear? A heavy thing for one's purse, no?'

There was a long pause before Hawker gave reply. 'It is safe.'

'Aye, and the king bid me to see that it gets to where it should be. That *you* get where *you* should be.'

Hawker nodded at him. So he knew that secret as well. His voice dropped low. 'We both knew Richard's ways, how his mind worked. Always spinning webs to his advantage. So, what do you mean to do now, Sir Roger?' Out of the corner of his eye he saw de Grood tense, ready to spring if Beconsall made a move against him. Opposite, he saw poor Jan, frowning and completely bewildered by the exchange.

Beconsall pulled his disordered and blood-spattered doublet back down over his hips. 'I mean to keep my oath to my king, be he dead or alive. And I mean to stay alive to see that you keep yours. You are to deliver that jewel back to the doge and he bade me see it done!'

Ellingham swore. 'Am I the only one who doesn't know what is going on?'

'I not know,' said Jan quietly in his twisted English.

'What is this Tear he speaks of?' demanded Ellingham, rounding on Hawker.

'It is a jewel, called the Tear of Byzantium. A gift that the king asked me to return to the giver.'

Beconsall snorted. 'Aye, a gift that gets passed from king to king like a whore. You don't know the half of it, boy.'

'I would have told you in time, Giles,' said Hawker. 'You are free to go your own way or you may accompany me to the Venetian lands.'

'*Us*,' added Beconsall.

'You lied to me,' said Ellingham, his eyes flashing. 'You never had any intention of staying in England. You were always fixed on this course. You just needed an extra blade to back you up.'

Hawker nodded towards him. 'That is fair enough, I'll give you that, Giles. But we still have a common cause. And we're as good as dead if we stay here.'

Ellingham kicked a chamber pot across the floor and walked to the other side of the cramped room, a frustrated and trapped animal. He turned and looked at Hawker again and shook his head, smiling grimly. 'You're a cunning, wasted old mercenary, Sir John. That's what you are. And now I'm a mercenary too.'

Hawker looked at both the other knights in turn. 'If we stand by each other we stand a better chance of staying alive.'

Beconsall nodded. 'Well, now you know what my orders are, my duty. I am not riding away.'

Ellingham chuckled grimly. 'Nobody's riding away. We sold the horses.'

—

They still had hours to kill before taking ship. Not trusting Cribbins, Hawker had made a few secret visits to the cog to make sure there was no early departure being hatched. Walking back into the Tun, he stopped dead for a moment when he saw Sir Giles near the hearth. His hand wrapped around a leather tankard, the youth was deep in conversation with another. A stranger. That Ellingham could be so cow-headed as to strike up merry talk with someone whose intentions – for good or ill – he didn't yet know, was more than vexing and he prayed that he was not too late to intervene.

'Will you introduce me to your companion?' said Hawker. The man was young, but not as young as Ellingham, tall, curling brown hair to his shoulders, a dark complexion with hard cheekbones and a thin nose. He was dressed in a velvet doublet of the darkest blood-red, black hose and tall, close-fitting boots. A long dagger hung from his waist, a gentleman's blade, finely wrought.

Ellingham extended his hand towards the man. 'This is Gaston Dieudonné, the Sieur de... Orchamps? In the Burgundian lands.'

Dieudonné gave a courtly bow.

'He is seeking passage back home,' Ellingham continued. Sir John gave a shallow bow in return and Ellingham leaned in close to his ear, speaking in English. 'He says he is of the White Rose, like us. Commanded a company of crossbowmen but managed to escape.'

Hawker sized up the man. Margaret of Burgundy and the Habsburg archduke *were* allies of York. It was no secret she had sent troops to aid her brother Richard in fighting Henry Tudor. He had seen her bowmen and gunners at the battle with his own eyes. But was this man one of them?

'You are on your own, sir? No companions?' asked Hawker, addressing the young blade in French.

'I have lost all, my lord. As have you, it seems. My company was – to a man – killed, captured or run off.'

'A bitter harvest for us all. Where is your home?' To Hawker's ear, he sounded like a Frenchman, the lilt and accent was of the north. But French was the tongue of the Burgundian lands too, at least what was left of them.

'I come from Besançon. But my family were from lands west, near Dijon. Until the King of France stole that place too. I thought perhaps Bruges would be the best destination from here before I make my journey home. Have you had any luck in finding a ship?'

'Perhaps. These things take time.'

Gaston Dieudonné nodded. 'If you travel to Flanders I would be grateful to join your company. I can pay my way.'

'Besançon,' said Hawker thoughtfully. 'A very great city I have seen but once. Did you ever serve with Captain Derouche who leads the guard? I would have thought that the Habsburg prince might have sent him here to fight for Richard. I confess if Derouche was there upon the field this terrible week I did not spy him.'

'Ah, my lord, then you have not heard. Derouche died of fever more than one year ago. He is still mourned throughout the city.'

Hawker felt his suspicions ease a little. It was the right answer. Any other time he would have questioned how one man could survive when every other under his command was lost but, alas, he was nearly in the same situation as this Burgundian. What right had he to question the man's fate? He appeared to be of good bearing, forthright and, like all of them in that room, on the wrong side of victory. 'Word had not travelled to me of his death.'

'And whom do you serve, my lord? Sir Giles would not tell me your name. He said that would have to come from you.'

'John Hawker. A *condottiere* to the republics of the south. Therefore, I serve many masters. It was fortune that brought me back to England, or should I say, misfortune.'

'So, would you have another join your band? Bad business in the last months in Bruges. Local rebellions against the archduke, brigands now on every road. Another sword might make some difference, no?'

Hawker felt he was in no position to refuse when they had just lost five blades by way of Sir Roger's fleeing rogues. And Dieudonné was speaking truth about Bruges and Ghent. Thievery and murder were like daily bread now that the Habsburgs had crushed dissent. If you raise an army and don't put it to work, it will soon find work on its own.

'I suppose you may join us… for as long as our paths remain the same.'

There was confidence about the man, Hawker thought. A quickness of mind, a boldness of speech without *braggadocio*. And he saw that it might be better to have someone like that with him rather than against him. He listened as Dieudonné and Sir Giles each recounted their battle at Leicestershire. The two quickly found a common bond and after a short time and another cup of wine they moved to speaking French. By Vespers they seemed fast friends and Hawker began to take heart that they might just escape the claws of Tudor henchmen and make good their escape from a broken kingdom.

After a while, Sir Giles went upstairs to the chamber to look in on Beconsall and Hawker's three men. They would not all be able to sleep that night and Hawker took it upon himself to take the first watch. As the hour passed, Hawker watched the merchants and fishermen drift out of the Tun. Dieudonné had seated himself against a far wall, sipping his Rhenish while he eyed the heavy oak door. A waterfront inn is never a quiet place even late of an evening but the Tun had now grown quiet and empty. But it was not *that* late, he thought. The landlord bustled near his casks with vessels and wooden trenchers but avoided Hawker's eye. Hawker moved to sit on the bench next to the French imposter. 'It stinks of treachery,' he said to him in French. 'No more trade in this place. Where are they all?'

'I believe you may be right, Sir John.' His hand slid to his hilt and he edged his dagger out from the scabbard by a few inches.

Hawker pushed his cup of wine away and waited, torn between rousing the others and letting them rest before the early move to the waiting cog. He did not have to wait long. The door groaned on its iron hinges and five men walked in. Two wore chains of office over their robes while the three behind were clearly servants, swords at their hips. Hawker tensed to rise but Dieudonné calmly laid a hand on his forearm. In the torchlight beyond the door Hawker could glimpse the outlines of several more men. The sands of his glass, it seemed, had run out.

The officers stood square in front of them, one as tall and thin as a bishop's crook and the other a thick-set man whose pudgy face had not seen a barber's razor in a week or more. 'We are here to serve a writ of arrest on one John Hawker of Stamford, knight,' said the taller of the two. 'And his companion, Sir Giles Ellingham. And anyone else who is in their service.' Their escort had now fanned out behind them, moving cautiously between the tables.

'*C'est pas moi*,' Hawker growled, keeping his seat and reaching for his cup. It was a desperate move, he knew, but anything was better than getting into another murderous brawl when they were but hours from making an escape.

The man smirked. 'I come under authority of the king and the high sheriff of Norfolk. You may speak as much French as you like but you *are* John Hawker, and you are coming with us. I will give you the courtesy of reading the warrant, if you so desire. If you don't care for the authority of our new king I also have a writ from the magistrates in Leicester. They say you murdered a man there, at an inn. The Bull.'

This under-sheriff was only looking at Hawker. Not at Gaston Dieudonné. That as much as told Hawker that this officer knew who Dieudonné was, and it was he who had probably betrayed them. Making conversation for hours to keep them lulled. Hawker decided that if he was going to be taken he might as well slip his dagger into the Burgundian before the others wrestled him down.

Dieudonné edged away and slowly stood up. 'I don't know this man,' he said in his heavily accented English. 'We sharing some wine.' The remainder of the arresting party, another three armed men, were now in the inn and with a signal from the unshaven one, they began mounting the staircase.

Without warning, Dieudonné flipped the trestle table up and into the officials, clay mugs and jugs smashing. It staggered them just long enough for the Frenchman to leap forward like a leopard, dagger drawn in one smooth tug. He made for a man to his left, one of their retainers, who had just managed to draw his sword. A straight thrust to the henchman's throat dropped him, choking and gasping. As Hawker drew his own blade he saw Dieudonné grab the tall under-sheriff by the front of his robes and before the man could even make a plea he had thrust his dagger into his throat to the hilt, quickly withdrawing it with a savage twist. A spray of blood arced wide, spattering Hawker. Hawker lunged towards the other servant who had pulled back his sword arm to deliver a crushing blow to his head. Both of them tumbled to the floor, tussling and swearing, and Hawker found himself fighting for his life.

At the sound of the commotion inside, three more sheriff's men rushed in from outside to join the fight. A bellow sounded on the stairs and echoed through the room. It was followed by a tremendous crash of bodies as Beconsall threw himself head first into the fray. Hawker's attacker was getting the better of him. He was much younger and stronger and had managed to straddle the knight. Somehow Hawker was managing to hold off the man's arms as the retainer strove to throttle or behead him with his levelled sword, the blade getting ever closer to his throat. Hawker glimpsed a flash of movement behind his opponent and then a pitcher shattered over the man's head, tumbling him over. It was Jack, wide-eyed and beetroot red. In the confusion, Hawker pulled himself away to the side, searching for a weapon that had been dropped. Beconsall roared and chopped one of the retainers to the floor with a heavy blow, breaking the man's collarbone and carrying on into the top of the ribcage. Hawker, tottering to his feet, saw Jacob and Jan facing off against the others, exchanging awkward blows over up-ended benches and trestles.

Then, an arm circled his neck and in the next moment his head was jerked back by the remaining under-sheriff, a dagger poised to strike. The man's heavy silver chain dangled cold against Hawker's cheek, rancid breath filling his nostrils as he twisted and struggled to block his attacker's wrist. But the blow never fell. Hawker heard him cry out sharply, an exclamation that turned to a strangled gurgle. The officer dropped to the floor, released gently by Gaston Dieudonné. One of the remaining retainers snatched a jug with his off hand and threw it at de Grood, gaining enough time to make his escape out the door along with his comrade. Hawker steadied himself against a wall, wobbling for a moment. He counted that all were sound. Ellingham, eyes bulging with the shock of the raid, stepped back and promptly slipped in a rivulet of blood. He caught his balance and swore.

'Shit!' he said. 'We're not just outlaws. We're murderers now too.' He gestured with his sword towards the bodies in front of him. 'Christ's blood! Sheriffs of Norfolk. There's no coming back from this. Not now.'

'Fair fight though,' said Beconsall, glancing about him and nodding sagely.

Dieudonné gave a shrug of the shoulders and pushed out his lower lip.

'No,' Hawker said, 'there is no turning back now. But we still live. Which we wouldn't have for long if we'd surrendered ourselves.'

Giles swore again under his breath. 'Should we not leave – *now?* We cannot wait for first light.'

De Grood looked at Hawker and nodded.

Hawker sighed. They'd never get the master of the cog to push off in the darkness and with the tide slack, not without a blade to his throat. But, then again, they were getting good at that sort of thing. 'Jack, get our things down here. Leave my armour except the breastplate and back. Understood?'

'Yes, Sir John.' He was up the staircase, bounding two steps at a time.

'Jacob, you and Jan do the same. Take only what is necessary. We'll buy what else we need on the other shore.'

'Is *that* your plan, then?' Beconsall retrieved a mug from the other side of the room, squeezed one eye shut as he peered into it, and swigged it back. 'A boat ride in the middle of the night?' He shook his head in disgust and tossed the mug to the floor. 'Well, hell, I suppose there is nothing for it. Seems I've already lost most of what I own so I'm hostage to fortune. *Your* fortune, Hawker.'

Dieudonné whistled softly, moved to the barrels at the tap rack and pulled up the landlord who was cowering between them. He held him aloft by his thick black head of hair. 'What about this one?' he asked, in English.

Then the Frenchman answered his own question. Before the landlord could beg, Dieudonné had slid his dagger across the man's throat, opening it wide. The landlord died without a sound, slumping down to the slickened tiles. 'No tales. Is that what you English say?'

Ellingham started forward. 'Murderer!'

'*Ta gueule,*' spat Dieudonné, raising his dagger towards Ellingham. 'Who you think betray us here? Probably for a fat reward from these fellows. One he won't be getting now.'

'I would have preferred hearing it from his lips and not yours! You had no right!'

'I don't need no right.' He wiped off his dagger blade on the heap beneath his feet and sheathed it. He switched over to French. 'But you are correct, Sir Giles, in saying we should leave this place now. Sir John, we had best board before the magistrates arrive with more men.'

Hawker fixed the Frenchman with a glaring eye. The execution had been rash, and the landlord might have told them more if he had been given the chance. He spoke in slow, measured French. 'The next time you decide to kill a prisoner you ask me first. It was *you* who asked to join *us*. Not the other way around.'

Dieudonné smiled and inclined his head. '*Bien sûr*, Sir John. *Bien sûr.*'

Beconsall's brows knitted together, his mouth pouting. He pointed a bloodstained hand towards Dieudonné. 'And just who the hell is this?'

Master Cribbins held his lantern out towards Hawker across the gangplank as the tubby cog gently bobbed in its berth. '*You* again? You're too early, you damned fool!'

Hawker, sword drawn, barged past him and the others followed.

'Get off my ship, you brigands!'

Hawker raised his blade and the sword tip just tickled the master's chin. 'You're getting under way. Now. Otherwise I'm sure I can get one of your men to get this tub off the mooring. Without you aboard.'

'You're a damned pirate,' Cribbins muttered. Without taking his gaze from Hawker he pushed the blade slowly away from his face. 'And we'll be lucky if we don't run aground.' He barked orders to get under way. His sailors, stone-faced, said nothing and got to making the ship ready. Keel scraping horribly, the cog just managed to get out of the dock and downriver against the incoming tide. The company stood, gathered around the mainmast while the sailors leapt about the vessel, hauling lines and canvas and wrestling with the great tiller.

Thank God, thought Hawker. The ebb tide had stopped flowing and was now slack, if not beginning to run in again. The crew poled them out past the caravel and the other cogs, raising more than a few voices and curses at their foolhardiness. They were soon out into the wide, lazy Ouse, a silvery sheen of moonlight lying like gossamer over the water. Cribbins sang out that they must have the Virgin looking after their souls, for the sky had shed its clouds not more than an hour past and he had just enough light to navigate by. They went below, stowed their satchels where they could.

'Do we need to keep a watch?' asked de Grood. 'These men might attack us and take all your gold.'

Hawker's chin dropped as he weighed the risk. 'I doubt they would take the chance to overwhelm all of us. But maybe you're right. You and Jan take your rest now... while you may. I'll stand the first watch.'

The Fleming looked worried. 'Fear not,' said Hawker. 'You need your rest.'

'Why didn't you tell me? About the jewel.'

Hawker paused, taken off guard. 'Aye, well, because the fewer who know about the thing the better.'

'We have fought together for near upon ten years. You could not trust me?'

'Trust was not in question. I was protecting you.'

De Grood's brow creased. 'Protecting me, Sir John? Who else knew?'

'No one,' Hawker lied. 'It is my burden. And was mine alone until that great fool over there blurted the secret to you all.' Beconsall, who a minute earlier had been cursing the cramped lower deck, had already collapsed, face down and snoring, upon a pile of wool bales.

De Grood said nothing but gave a small nod of acceptance, if not belief.

'And remember,' said Hawker, 'you and Jan are to tell no one else of it. Including the Burgundian.'

De Grood nodded. 'As you wish.'

'Go take your rest. It's well deserved,' said Hawker, placing a hand briefly on his shoulder. He then went above to the main deck, his lungs drinking in the sea air, and wobbled to the sterncastle. It was here that Ellingham shortly joined him in the orange glow of a single lantern that was fixed there. His strong Plantagenet features shone starkly, cast partly in shadow from where he stood. For the first time, to Hawker's eyes, the youth appeared drawn and far older than his years.

Ellingham stared out ahead at the widening waters, the faint rim of orange on the horizon announcing the day. 'Will they pursue us?'

Hawker shook his head. 'Who would be so foolish? And for what gain? The magistrates of Lynn? Their authority ends at the water's edge. We've made our escape. We're safe now.' Hawker clapped Ellingham on the shoulder. 'Rest easy.' He turned and made his way unsteadily towards the forecastle as the ship rose and fell.

He was a little surprised to find Jack huddled there, backed away near a barrel.

Jack had said barely a word since the attack in the Tun. The lad had seen cruelty in the last months, to be sure, but there was a grimness all its own to the sudden brutality of a tavern fight at drawn daggers, and to murder.

'What are you doing up here, lad? You need your rest down below.'

Jack stood up and gave a nod. 'I'm sorry, Sir John. I started to feel unwell.'

Hawker smiled. 'Your first voyage. Aye, well, it's to be expected. It will pass.'

Jack nodded again and hugged himself. 'I keep seeing it all, Sir John. That man I shot. I cannot *stop* seeing it when I shut my eyes.'

Hawker stepped in and put a fatherly arm about the boy's shoulders. 'What is seen cannot be unseen. I will not lie and tell you otherwise. But you're of strong stuff, my lad, I know that. And what you did, you did to save us from attack.'

Jack looked up at him, his pale face tight with pain. 'Did I? It set everything alight. And now, now we're running.' He shook his head in disbelief. 'An hour ago I *brained* a man. And then he was stabbed dead. They were all dead. The innkeeper…'

Hawker pursed his lips, not really knowing how to reassure the boy about something as base as the business of killing. 'This is the life I have made,' he said quietly. 'And it is the life you have entered, too. It is no sin to kill a man who is trying to kill you. Are you my squire?'

Jack stood up straight. 'I am sworn to you, Sir John.'

'Then you have done your duty to me already. You saved me. For that I am grateful. And for my part, I will always stand by you.'

Jack managed a smile.

'Get below now. Once you lie down it will be like you are rocking in a cradle. Think upon something good to banish your dark thoughts.'

Hawker watched him go below down the narrow steps. He sighed a little and then noticed that Master Cribbins was glaring at him across the deck.

Whether or not the bald mariner had heard the exchange, he didn't know. But he was already feeling ashamed for what he hadn't told the boy. That killing grew the easier with each battle and that the true sin was when it no longer burdened your conscience.

8

Ellingham stared out at the flat, desolate shoreline while they pulled further and further away from everything he had known. And everything he had lost. Ellingham felt as if he were trapped in a swirling whirlpool, thrashing frantically but unable to swim out. Even if the others saw him as outwardly confident, inside he was scared. Scared to death. Fortune, blind fortune, now held the reins. He was on a voyage into the unknown with comrades who had been forced upon him. Men whose motives were as dark and churning as the waters underneath him. His life now in the hands of an old and broken knight still under the sway of a dead king.

He had stood there, clinging to a line and watching the shore for what must have been hours, the sun now fully risen.

'Changed your mind already?'

It was Hawker, chewing from a half-loaf of dark bread. He proffered some to Ellingham.

'I'm not hungry.'

Hawker shrugged. 'You will be. Once you settle in.'

There was an awkward silence between them, one Ellingham had no particular desire to end. Hawker leaned on the railing close by and broke off another chunk.

'I am sorry it's come to this, Giles. Fate hasn't been kind of late. To either of us.' He chewed the bread for a minute. 'Tell me of Middleham. How you ended up in Richard's army. Your family.'

Ellingham slowly turned to face him. 'And why the interrogation? I'm finding your curiosity a little suspicious. I have since the beginning.'

Hawker shrugged again. 'We're comrades now. Outlaws. Maybe we should get to know one another better. Build trust, no? Besides, we've a few days' sailing ahead and not much to do otherwise.'

Ellingham let out a cynical snort. 'Again, your idea. Not mine.'

'Well, humour me. I'll repay the favour before we reach land and tell you my own sad adventures.'

Ellingham dropped his chin a little. 'Very well. So, what do you want to know?'

'How you became a man-at-arms. A squire to a great lord and then a knight at such a tender age.' Hawker grinned broadly, his big teeth showing in full.

'I was squired to my own father, Sir Thomas. He had never paid much attention to me growing up. Nor did my mother. But once I was fourteen he thought I should train under arms, serve the king. I always thought it was strange because, since I had no siblings, I would have thought they might have paid me more heed as a boy. But they never really did.'

Hawker nodded. 'Did they beat you?'

'That was also strange. It was the opposite, as if I was some delicate object, a precious book they kept on the shelf, never to be held or opened. They were always distant and aloof. The only joy I felt was running wild with the servants' children and playing games. Sir Thomas paid to have me schooled at Middleham. Learned my Latin, grammar. Read scripture and spoke French.'

'And then... training at arms and the court?'

Ellingham nodded, looking across the stern and out to the water. 'Aye. My father sent me to the castle when I was just fifteen. A bit late, it was said. But I took to it, I did. We had a master-at-arms who patrolled the pell yard like some vengeful ogre with his oak staff. But I avoided getting my skull cracked more than the other lads did.'

Hawker laughed a little, nodding.

'I remember the king came once and observed us sparring. I could see one of his retainers pointing me out. My heart swelled.

It spurred me to train even more, get even better. I started to get noticed by the men-at-arms under the chatelaine at Middleham. Fighting with long sword, tilting at the quintain. Then one day – I think just after I had turned seventeen – my father came to the castle with his retinue. He made me his squire on the spot. Presented me with my own armour.'

'It was a fine suit of plate. I'm sorry you've had to leave most of it behind.'

It was Ellingham's turn to shrug. 'That's war, isn't it? Better to lose it than end up dead inside it.' He remembered Hawker and Jacob pulling his mount by its harness, out of the bloodbath where he probably would have died. 'I was proud then. But I saw little difference in my father. Except he was older and fatter than before. So I was squire to a knight who was too fat to fit into armour and too old to fight. I fell in with his men-at-arms though. They took me under their wing.'

'So that is how you ended up fighting in the north. Against Lord Buckingham.'

Ellingham nodded. 'I fought from Yorkshire to the Marches and into Wales. We skirmished a lot, riding backwards and forwards across the countryside in pouring rain and wind. Christ have mercy, but I loved it.'

'And the killing too?'

Ellingham returned a scowl. Not at Hawker, but rather at his own thoughts on battle. 'When I killed my first opponent I felt no remorse. Just a sense of rightful justice for one who had dared raise a hand against his king. I remember seeing him sprawled out, head split open wide like a cracked walnut. I didn't feel anything the next day either. Or the day after that. Does that make me a monster?'

'I've known many who enjoy killing. And many others who tolerate it because it is a part of what they must do. If you think you're a monster you need to exchange your sword for a crucifix. The sooner the better.'

'Last winter I spent riding to garrisons throughout the north. Keeping order for Richard. I saw many things up there. Did many things.' He paused, began again, then stopped.

'We've all done things,' said Hawker.

'A week ago I was knighted on the road to Leicester by my king. He raised me up and I was so proud. Arrogant even. And then everything was swept away in an instant by the hand of God. Now I'm penniless, and an outlaw for good measure.'

A sudden gust made the square-set sail snap hard and the cog rocked with the blast of wind. Two of the sailors scrambled to secure lines and take up slack. Ellingham steadied himself on a stay and mumbled an oath. Hawker broke off another chunk of bread and started chewing thoughtfully. 'I'm not one for counsel. You'd be better off with a priest for that. But for what it's worth I would tell you that self-pity won't get you far in our profession, lad. I've tried it and it always leaves you worse off than the day before.' He pushed himself off the railing and reached out for a stay before setting back towards the forecastle. 'Come forward and break your fast, Sir Giles. You'll feel the better for it!'

As Hawker made his way, Ellingham realised too late that he had revealed a sack-load about himself to the old knight without receiving so much as a grain in return. It made him angry with himself and he fell back into dark thoughts.

Someone called to him from across the deck. It was the shorter of the Flemings, Jan Bec. The man spewed a prodigious quantity of ale and half-digested bread over the railing before wiping the back of his hand across his mouth, head lolling. Ellingham moved towards him to offer help and Jan retched once again even as he reached him. 'But you've sailed at sea before. To get to England.'

Jan rolled his head up. '*Ja*, of course! Many time. Can you not tell? Jan Bec born for the sea!'

Ellingham smiled, forgetting his own miseries in the moment. He didn't know the clownish little soldier yet, but he liked him because he reminded him of the men he knew in Middleham. Men who, when not splitting skulls, were usually joking and laughing and sinking pots of ale. 'I have never been on a ship before now,' said Ellingham, trying to console. 'Perhaps I don't have enough sense to be sick.'

Jan snorted at that, the snot running down his nose. He smiled despite his nausea. 'Don't brag, my lord! We say in Vlaams, don't put on boot that is too big for you.'

Ellingham gritted his teeth and looked out over the rippling waves. There was truth in that. Today he felt like his boots were much too large for him.

9

The second day at sea, Jack busied himself polishing Hawker's breastplate, now blossomed with rust, encouraged further by the spraying sea. Beconsall – showing a bit of sympathy for once – gave him his hand-axe to clean as well, just to keep the lad busy. Jack sat cross-legged up in the forecastle, rubbing with his leather rag and a mixture of pig grease and sand that Cribbins had found for him.

Hawker made his way forward, the ship gently bobbing on a sea that was near glass. He managed to find an upturned bucket and sat next to the boy. 'Careful or you'll end up polishing that blade into a toothpick,' he said, smiling. Jack managed a smile in return but kept on rubbing. 'Flanders will agree with you, my lad. Good stews and roasts to be had cheaply. We're all due a good meal after this week.'

Jack looked at him, wearing the face of a man many years older. 'Is my soul damned, Sir John?'

Hawker rested a hand on the railing and watched the distant shoreline. 'We are none of us damned, my lad. Not with the salvation of Christ at hand. You know your catechism.'

'I know what you told me. But I'm still thinking about what I did. And it's still murder, isn't it?'

Hawker's brow furrowed a little. 'You saved us all, my lad.' The words almost caught in his throat for he knew how any magistrate would see it. 'He would have killed me. You stopped him. That is the truth of it.' Hawker had long known that God's world was an evil place and His design was such to test mankind at every turn. And Jack already knew life was cruel; that was no new thing for him. But his own role in this grim pageant was now becoming clearer. And it was like a bit of gristle between the teeth, not easily shifted.

'He would have killed me and taken you away to hang,' Hawker said. 'I told you it is no sin to defend oneself.' Jack gave a half-hearted nod. 'Fear not,' added Hawker, thinking fast. 'I'll take you to Mass in Bruges, to the cathedral. We can cleanse both our souls then. What do you say to that?'

Jack lifted his head, hair like a hedgehog's quills and matted with salt spray. 'I'd be grateful, Sir John, to see a cathedral!'

By late afternoon they had the wind with them again. Other vessels had been sighted during the day: caravels and cogs desperate to fill their sails, long, bluff-bowed herring boats hauling their nets. When the sun dropped low on the horizon, the master decided to drop anchor for the night within sight of shore. And with the fall of night again they ate their salt pork below deck and savoured the luxury of almost-fresh bread, but they ate mainly in silence while the hull bounced and rocked beneath them.

The isolation of the sea turns a man's thoughts inwards and Hawker was no different from any other. Sitting in the cramped fug of the cog's hold, he worried how he could keep his little band of felons together long enough to get to Venice. And what to do about Ellingham? He felt responsible for the youth, now more than ever, having convinced him to throw in his lot with them.

Even if his luck held out, what would the doge and his advisors offer him? He had sold out his mercenary command nearly four years earlier – no mark of dependability, that. But then his heart had been sick over his defeats in the eastern provinces. The loss of so many men under him. And, increasingly, he had grown homesick for England. The thought ate away at him until he could not wait any longer. But the biggest mistake he had made was in leaving his lover behind. It was a regret that bore heavily on him, regret and a suspicion that her love for him maybe had not been strong enough to break the bonds that held her in Venice.

Now, even if he reached Venice again, he would be begging the Council for another chance. This time, sadly, with but a handful of men-at-arms to offer. Not much of a bargaining position, it would seem, particularly in such a dangerous maze as the Serene Republic. He had one bag of gold, a sword and the clothes on his back. Maybe a sack of gold still in the bank of the Medicis. His little *palazzo* too, if it had not fallen down or sunk into the canal. But he also had something else with which to bargain: a Tear of Byzantium.

Jacob sidled alongside Hawker at the little four-legged trestle, careful not to bump his head on a crossbeam while he dabbed at his lumps of soggy pork with his bread crust. 'Just when I was getting my sea legs, now this swell rises up again. Will probably be a waste of my time putting this slop into my stomach.'

He gestured over to Dieudonné, who was further forward than they, near the foot of the thick mainmast, reclining on a bed of bales with hands folded calmly over his belly. He was half propped up on a bale that leaned against one of the ship's oaken knees, his gentle expression regarding them with little interest. 'Jan thinks he saw him in the battle. Says he fought without a helm. But, hear this, he says he was well back *inside* the Lancastrian line. Swinging like a madman.'

Hawker leaned in towards de Grood. 'You mean he had cut his way in – and survived? That seems a fantasy, though he is fast on his feet. I will give him that.'

De Grood shrugged and his voice went low. 'Jan's not sure just *whose* side he was on when we fought. He swears he was wearing Tudor colours. But it was all a blur. Glimpsed in an instant, he said.'

Hawker shook his head. 'Unlikely, given he saved my life in the tavern.'

'Aye, true enough. But Jan *asked* the Burgundian. Put it to him in French. Dieudonné laughed and told him to get buggered. Tell him, Jan.'

Jan, who had recovered from his bout of seasickness, scrunched up his face and tilted his head, swallowing a mouthful. 'Not really sure now,' he said in Flemish. 'It was from a distance, but it *looked* like him. But I was more worried at the time about being knocked from my saddle by a spearman. I'm probably wrong...'

Hawker stared hard at Jan who, once noticing, let his bread drop into his bowl, jaw slack. 'You would have to be sure,' he said softly, in Flemish. 'For that is a heavy accusation.'

'Why it's like I said, Sir John. It was all very quick.' He threw a glance over to Dieudonné. 'And I don't want to believe it anyway. He seems a good blade to have around, given our situation. Not a bad fellow really.' He chucked his chin towards Ellingham, who was already asleep on wool bales a few feet away. 'Like that lad. If he stays with us. He has a stout heart.'

Hawker gave a nod of reassurance to the little Fleming and again glanced over to Dieudonné. 'I wouldn't want to believe it either, Jan Bec. We all see things in the madness of the fight. Rest easy and get some sleep if you can.'

As the night grew deep, the cog was whipped about such that the bow anchor dragged and the master ordered a second anchor from the stern. The winds whined shrilly, the ship creaking and groaning, and Hawker had to wrap a noisome blanket about his head to try and stop the din. But he slept, mercifully, less worried about the raging elements than about Tudor henchmen.

He awoke suddenly, damp and sodden in his clothes, to find de Grood shaking him by the shoulder. 'Sir John, wake, my lord.'

'What is wrong?'

'It's Jan. He's gone.'

Hawker was on his feet in an instant. His waking comrades looked at each other before Beconsall said, 'He must be here somewhere. Further forward. Maybe scrounging for food or something to thieve.'

Dieudonné stuck out his lower lip. 'I saw him rise and head out on deck at some point. Probably had the shits and went forward to the bow.' Poor Jack was standing wide-eyed, just beginning to realise what might have happened to the Fleming.

Hawker swore and stormed up the stairs to the sterncastle and found Cribbins. The master shook his head forlornly but ordered his crew to search the vessel anyway. They searched from stem to stern, the band of soldiers frantic in their haste to turn over bales and barrels while the crew followed Cribbins' orders with a little less urgency. Search as they might, the Fleming was nowhere on board. Jacob swore under his breath and began another pass amongst the cargo in the forlorn hope his friend slumbered somewhere dark, curled up tight and drunk on stolen wine.

'He's here, I tell you! The little shit has fallen into the bilge down here somewhere.' Jacob began trying to shift a loose plank to get to where the ballast stones lay – barely enough room for rats to hide, never mind a man. Hawker placed a hand on his shoulder as the Fleming strained.

'Jacob, he's gone. He's gone.'

The Fleming stood up and roughly wiped his sleeve across his eyes. 'No, Sir John. He wouldn't have jumped or fallen. He's been to sea before.' He made to stoop again to tear at the planks, but Hawker hauled him up, gently, with a meaty hand under his arm.

'Jacob, it is over. We have lost him.'

Jacob turned to Beconsall, who shook his head slowly, and then to Ellingham. Ellingham found he could not hold the Fleming's agonised gaze. He looked down instead.

Jacob shook his head over and over until the tears came forth again. 'The stupid sot. Stupid damned little sot.' He lapsed into a string of muttered Flemish curses.

Hawker felt his own eyes begin to sting with tears as he guided Jacob back to the ladder leading up through the hatch. Little Jan had, like Jacob, been more friend than man-at-arms, more brother than retainer. A decade of risks, battles, feasts and death cheated a hundred times. Now he had ended ignobly in a churning grey sea. Better the Fleming should have died swinging his sword at Bosworth field than by this cruel misfortune.

'Bad luck, that,' said Cribbins, when the truth finally settled over them like a cold fog, crew and passengers standing together on the deck. 'Happens a fair amount of the time when the sea gets rough. You stick your bum out over the side and try and pinch your turd. But then, aye, well, you hit a trough and next thing you're arse over tits and in the drink. I've lost more than one man that way over the years, more's the pity.'

It was now full light, the sky hazy and the sun a weak ball of dirty yellow in the east. A gust whipped across the deck. Cribbins clapped his hands together and gave a shrill whistle. 'Right, lads! Weigh anchor and raise canvas. We run for Flanders!'

Part II

THE WIDOW OF BURGUNDY

10

Gaston Dieudonné felt remorse about the little Fleming. And in as far as he could feel such things, it was sincere. But, when the opportunity had shown itself, he knew he might not get another. He'd followed the man out onto the main deck, saw that the night watch was busy dicing on the quarterdeck, and moved up to where Jan had balanced himself over the gunwale of the bow, one hand on a stay. A good-natured smile then – viper-like – a quick thrust with dagger to the throat, a shove, and the Fleming was gone.

There had just been one sudden look of surprise, clutching at his punctured neck, eyes wide, and then he tumbled over backwards. Not a sound before he slipped under the ship, borne away by the swirling Norfolk undertow. Unfortunate, yes, but he could not afford to have that man's memory spark a light and unmask him to Hawker. Hawker was a crafty, battle-hardened old fox and not one to underestimate. He had come up against others like him in the past. They had a keen sense of smell for deceit as well as for profit. A help, really, that the little Fleming had voiced his doubts to Hawker. And good fortune that he had overheard the conversation. His English was poor, but his Flemish was better.

Back in Lynn, it had been his intention all along to lull them into trust and then have them taken by the sheriffs. He would have gained reward from Jasper Tudor for his daring and cunning. Maybe preferential favours. He was the one who had informed on the Yorkists at the inn, keeping them occupied. That was true. By design and ingrained caution, he had not given his name at the time, so the sheriff's men did not know who he truly was. But as the evening wore on, he had found himself ensnared by the young Plantagenet, a man who was unaware of his birthright and equally unaware of his own well of natural charm. As handsome a knight as he had ever glimpsed. And there was something else that attracted him to Ellingham: the lad had a darkly cynical, hardened shell that hinted at further secrets, perhaps worth wheedling out...

And so, Dieudonné had pondered what might be the better path to his own fortune: capturing this bastard of King Richard and taking the jewel to the Tudors, or spinning out the adventure a bit longer to see where it would all go. His mission was, after all, a self-appointed one. He did not truly know if Jasper Tudor would grant him favour for his actions. There was the nagging worry – not insignificant – that his deed might throw up more questions than answers. Such as, how did he know of Ellingham's siring? Or of the Tear of Byzantium? He should not have known about these things in the first place.

He had never trusted anyone his entire life, only his instincts. Such a life creed afforded one wisdom because it meant he was never disappointed by the actions of men. He had chosen the cloak of a Burgundian lord to hide himself in. Ironic, since it was the Burgundians who had burned his family out in Nevers, raped his mother and killed his father. Ruined them all. A salutary first lesson in life, for which he owed the Burgundians thanks. Thanks for giving him this one hard truth of the world. Yet Gaston Dieudonné knew his own nature. He was a fickle creature, perhaps even fey, and it had never bothered him. He followed his instincts, whether they took him to a man or a woman, for fortune was blind to sex or station.

His service as a mere man-at-arms, a poor squire to a broken-down French nobleman, had yielded him meagre reward. But it had given him the chance in Paris to meet Jasper Tudor and his cap-in-hand nephew, Henry. They needed men and ships for their cause and he had been daring enough to sign on. Jumping over to the scheming, by-blow Tudors had already been more profitable, and now with the crown of England in their hands money would not likely be a problem for them ever again.

Gaston Dieudonné watched as Hawker and his comrades crossed themselves and said a prayer for the drowned Fleming. He even joined in with his own reedy voice, evoking Saint Nicholas and the Virgin to speed the poor man's soul to heaven. A laughable wish. As if any soldier ever born was headed there and not to the other place. And it hurt his wind-chafed face to hold back from smiling.

If Hawker was playing a longer game to aid the Yorkist cause, Dieudonné might learn more by joining them. The stakes would be higher, to be sure, but so might the prize. Besides, he knew himself to be a curious man and this strange jewel, this blood ruby, seemed to be more than just an ornament of idle wealth. There was a story with it, a story he knew nothing about but one that tempted him. Kings didn't throw away gems, they hoarded them, lusted after them. Hawker might, in time, reveal what lay behind this jewel. Bruges, he realised, made perfect sense, if that was Hawker's first destination. Yorkist ties were strong there and with Richard dead it would become a lodestone for the disaffected. He might learn rich intelligence now that he had proved himself of value to the knight. There was no rush to decide whether to go to Venice with them. And if he did, it would be a small matter to find out who were the Tudor spies in Venice and then feed them what he chose to. He could drift down this dangerous, enticing stream and find what he might. For there was always his original plan lying safely tucked away in his mind: a dagger into Hawker, the jewel into his own pocket, Giles Ellingham in chains – or his pickled head in a cask – and a ship back to England.

11

Master Peter Cribbins kept his word. After a long day's voyage across the open sea, the vessel began a meandering course within sight of the coast until they found the mouth of the river Zwin. Shortly after Cribbins left them on the shore, they managed to find a river barge willing to take them up to Bruges – but for an exorbitant price that made Hawker grit his teeth as he counted out the coin.

Once they were inside Bruges' hulking walls they found the place in a foul temper, as Dieudonné had warned. German soldiers of the Archduke Maximilian, the Holy Roman Emperor, had spread across the town like a plague, putting the local burghers off their business as well as their food. Nearby Ghent had suffered far worse though. Those townsfolk who had rebelled against the archduke had been hanged.

As the little company dragged their meagre belongings across the cobbles, a gaggle of anxious merchants heard Hawker speaking to his comrades and the boldest of these burghers asked about the battle for the English crown. Terrible rumours had already reached Bruges and they were eager for more news.

Hawker gave it to them, leaving them as poleaxed as if King Richard had been their own close relation. They set to shaking their heads, groaning out dark predictions and saying it was grievous news indeed. For even a fool would know that this meant ill tidings for Flanders. The Tudors were allies of France and no friends of the Habsburg-ruled cities. Hawker knew that these merchants would be feeling sick at the very thought of what would likely happen to trade now. All that English wool going somewhere else.

'Tight-fisted bastards,' mumbled Beconsall. He then stuck out a wagging finger, speaking loud enough for them to hear even if their English wasn't fluent enough for them to understand. 'I don't give a fig for their fine words! Where was their money when Richard needed it? A company of Switzer spearmen or two might have made the difference if they'd had thought to send any. I hope their bollocks rot off. They don't deserve 'em!'

The company did not linger. It was enough to clothe and feed themselves, procure reliable palfreys that could cover distance, and then make their way east across Flanders. Yet, already, the gold was disappearing faster than Hawker had hoped, despite the Burgundian paying his own way and outfitting himself anew. Having reached Bruges, the young blade seemed curiously vague about what he proposed to do with himself. He had yet to bid them farewell, content to treat himself as part of the company, and he stuck to them like a Norfolk lamprey.

Young Jack, having never even glimpsed London town, was agog at Bruges with its soaring towers and steeples, its merchant palaces and guildhalls layered in gold. He rode next to Hawker as they left, proud to be seated on a horse of his own like the rest. Indeed, they could have passed to an inattentive bystander for merchants themselves, dressed in velvets and cloaks and only their tall strapped boots and swords giving them away as men of more martial experience.

'Such a great city and we've seen nothing,' Jack lamented as they passed under the massive grey twin towers that led them out the east gate. 'And we didn't even go into the cathedral.'

'Fear not,' said Hawker, 'Mechelen is nearly as grand. We shall spend a bit more time there, I think.'

Dieudonné pricked up his ears. 'I had been thinking myself of that place. You would seek new employment there, Sir John?'

'I have a few friends there. And they'll afford me the time to gather my thoughts. And to perhaps find out a few things.'

Dieudonné smiled broadly and touched a gloved finger lightly to his temple. '*Tout a fait, mon sieur!* Let us hope we find a paymaster.'

'We?'

He gave Hawker another of his sheepish looks, like an ill-behaved child who knows what he has done. 'If you seek to put together a company, I am for you, Sir John. But, that is your choice, naturally.'

De Grood shot Hawker a cautious look and Hawker returned an almost imperceptible nod. Dieudonné had proved himself thus far, but a week is little time to judge a man. Trust was a precious substance, especially now. It was not to be given lightly. Ellingham was mostly silent as they rode across the flat, lush countryside, his eyes off into the middle distance ahead. Hawker wondered what thoughts swirled through the youth's mind and he knew he could not put off the inevitable truth much longer.

The weather held fair for them, the season still balmy, September clinging to summer and the leaves not yet turning brown. They bypassed conflict-torn Ghent and stopped in a small village a few miles east, where they found an inn to water the horses and take refreshment. Dismounting, they led their horses forward towards a stone well that lay in the grounds. Bringing up the rear, Beconsall caught Hawker's arm. He looked intently at the older man.

'Why do you suppose young Giles was named in the writ against *you*? I've been trying to puzzle that one out. What could he have done? Seems to me you might know the answer.'

The unshaven Beconsall looked even more ursine than a week ago, Hawker thought. He hoped the man's nature had not grown wilder to match his appearance. And he had to think very carefully about what to reveal and when. 'Do you remember Tewkesbury?' Hawker said casually as he looped the reins around a hitching post.

Beconsall nodded. 'Do you think me completely witless?'

'Well, revenge, like meat, is sweeter when it has had time to season. When we had won the field, we dragged the Lancastrian lords out of sanctuary to put them to the sword that day. Direct orders of King Edward and carried out by his brother's men, me included. That was a sin the House of Lancaster will never forgive.

Is it any surprise they have come after nobles and belted knights of the White Boar?'

Beconsall's heavy brow furrowed a bit. 'Pursue *every* Yorkist knight that fought for Richard? Every a one? I might not have the brains of a magister but a man with as thin a claim to the crown as Henry Tudor ought to be winning over knights and nobles, not executing them.'

'I wasn't about to stay there long enough to ask them how they composed their list. I only know why they came for me. And you know why, too.'

Beconsall nodded, his eyes almost narrowed to arrow slits. 'Yes, the jewel, no doubt. They probably had many spies in Leicester. That makes sense, even to a buffle-head like me. But why the youngster? Who is he?'

Hawker gave the reins of his tethered horse a yank, testing them. 'I know as much as you. He is vanquished, like the rest of us. Now let us get these mounts watered and fed before I die of hunger myself.'

—

After they ate, Hawker sent Jack up to their chamber and de Grood along with him, just to keep an eye on the lad. The inn was full of merchants on their way to Mechelen and Brussels as well as a few soldiers, card sharps and sturdy beggars who had just enough coin for the landlord to tolerate their presence. Hawker knew that it was not a place to lose one's head in drink, particularly after what had befallen them in Lynn. He watched the Burgundian sitting as contented as a cat, drinking wine and watching the guests about the crowded room.

When Dieudonné arose to refill his wine jug from the barrel tap, Hawker leaned over to Beconsall. 'We need to keep an eye on the Burgundian. He's a quick swordsman but as dangerous as a smouldering hand cannon and I don't want him picking a fight here. We need to keep him out of trouble.'

Beconsall lowered his ursine head. 'I'll sit my arse next to his and keep him occupied if need be. I for one have tired of tavern brawling on this voyage.'

Ellingham, who seemed to have been lost in his thoughts, pushed away his goblet, still half full. 'I would have a word with you, Sir John. Outside.' Hawker gave him a brief, puzzled look, then nodded and rose.

They went out to the stable yard, the sky full of buzzing insects enlivened by the approach of darkness. 'We made good distance today,' Hawker said, stroking the neck of his horse. 'And on the morrow – with God's grace – we shall reach Mechelen by midday.'

Ellingham took a few steps to close the distance between them. 'It is time, Sir John, to talk of the jewel.'

Hawker was silent for a moment. 'Yes… you deserve to know about that. But… not here.' Hawker led him out to the front of the ramshackle inn, jetties sagging with age and moss, and crossed the road, finding a grassy bank that led down towards a ditch smelling of mud and full of reeds. Hawker hunched down, knees cracking, and took a seat, his back to the single old willow growing there. He then gestured for Ellingham to join him. 'This is a tale that must be guarded well from the ears of others,' he said quietly.

The youth sat down cautiously next to Hawker, hands on his knees, belt and dagger jangling as he settled. 'Aye, well, you've guarded it long enough from me. Out with it. Why did the king give you this thing?'

Hawker craned his neck skywards through the leafy canopy over them. 'Where to begin? Some say it was part of a Byzantine cross of gold, a holy relic that was spirited out even as the Turks took Constantinople. A few years before you were born, I should think.' Hawker threw him a sly smile, but Ellingham's frozen stare remained unchanged. 'The story I was told – in Venice – is that this crucifix was cut up, the rubies of each arm sent far and wide – as gifts to princes in the west. I was the bearer of one of these. Gifted by the Doge of Venice to King Edward. And it was upon his death that it came into Richard's hands.'

'If it was a gift then why did Richard order you to take it back to Venice?'

'That is best explained by telling you about the other Tears of Byzantium. It is said that they ended up with the Duke of Burgundy, the King of France, the King of England, the Emperor of the Germans and the Doge of Venice. My instructions from the doge's advisors were clear: the jewel was not ever to be sold or gifted out of the household of the recipient. If ever the gem was no longer wanted, then it was to be returned to the giver. No exceptions.'

Ellingham shook his head. 'That is most strange. Is it because these stones are sacred?'

Hawker smiled to himself, staring into the reeds. 'No, it is because they are cursed. Or so the story goes. The Duke of Burgundy had conquered all before him but he ended up hacked down by the Swiss when his horse stumbled crossing a stream. His entire house was snuffed out by that thrust of a single halberd. The King of France, the Great Spider, had defeated even his most cunning enemies but he ended up suffering agonising fits – from which he died. Our own King Edward was fit one day and dead the next. Richard falls in battle hours after giving me the stone to take away. What happened to the doge's Tear I do not know but his brother, the previous ruler, is dead now too.'

Ellingham cracked an awkward grin. 'So what are you saying? That means they're cursed? Men fight. Men sicken. Men die. One does not need a curse to explain such things.'

'I'm only telling you the story. I've heard that the Tears bring fortune in life, until, suddenly, that fortune gives way to calamity. The trick, they say, is knowing when to give them back – not too early and most certainly not too late. King Richard was most eager to be rid of that jewel, I can tell you, hand on heart.'

Ellingham followed Hawker's gaze down into the ditch. 'I believe a gemstone might act against poison and ward off illness – that is a fact well known and attested. But can a gem hold a curse down through the years, festering like a blood debt? Deliver bounty and then – without warning – strip fortune and life away? Is this not God's will alone?'

Hawker gave a shrug. 'I myself do not believe in curses. I have my favourite saints, that is true. I'm not ashamed if a paternoster or Ave Maria tumbles from my lips when a fight looks to be lost, I give you that. But, you see, when enough men believe something to be true it often becomes so. I believe the Tears are like some great game of hazard – without the dice. Charles of Burgundy didn't give his back. Cut down by the Swiss crossing a stream and now his bloodline is no more. The King of France? Healthy as an ox and then suddenly sickens and dies. The story goes that the Emperor of the Germans took one look at it and sent it back to the doge. He lives still. Luck?'

Ellingham turned and looked at Hawker again, those steel-grey eyes suddenly reminding the older knight of the late king. 'Foolishness. I believe that it is only God who determines our fate. Richard is dead. So what do you owe him? Why don't you just keep the jewel and sell it? Like any other man would. You expect me to believe you'd journey a thousand miles merely to return this trinket?'

'I don't expect you to believe anything. But I'm going to Venice just the same. To return what was given. I am sworn to it. Sir Roger is sworn to it.'

Ellingham let out a short harsh laugh. 'I'll wager he'll try and take it from you before you make it to the Alps.'

'You're too young to be so cynical about honour. Or motive.'

'Really? You know my upbringing well enough?'

Hawker stood up and brushed the soil from his hose. 'Honour and profit are not incompatible. You might remember that. I fully expect reward from the doge for bringing the jewel back – as well as service in the Venetian army. As a matter of fact, it's precious all I have to barter with.'

Ellingham didn't answer. He stood up, likewise brushed off his hose, and turned to head back to the inn. He took a few steps and halted. 'And this boy... your so-called squire. What honour or profit is there in dragging him along with us, taking him away from a father and mother's love? And now, now you've taught him to kill for you.'

Hawker felt his ears burn, face flushing with anger. He closed the distance between them until they stood toe to toe. '*I* might as well be his father for all the love that boy has seen. I would not send him back to be beaten again, like I was. And I will teach him skill at arms. And honour – in service to a worthy man. You would do well to think twice, Giles, before speaking.'

Ellingham didn't flinch. 'And I still think you're telling me half-truths. If you want me to follow you, I deserve better than that.'

Hawker shut his eyes a moment. 'You are right. The jewel is only half the story. We were pursued for it after we rode to Stamford. That is true. But there's another reason.' He pursed his lips a second.

Ellingham folded his arms across his chest. 'Come on, then. Let's hear it.'

'You are the son of King Richard. His bastard.'

A smile slowly took form on the young man's face. 'Are you that desperate to keep me in this company of fools? You spin me a madman's tale that I'm the son of the king! I asked for truth and you play me with more games.'

Hawker stood motionless, eyes locked onto Ellingham's. 'I sought you before the battle began. I gave you a sword. I begged you to ride out with us when the king fell. That was for a reason. Your father bade me watch over you. His last orders to me were the jewel... and you.'

Ellingham shook his head slowly. 'Where is your proof for this... *miracle*?'

'I swear by the blood of the Virgin. But search out your heart. Why else would Richard have knighted a boy who had barely been a squire? Do you carry the features of either Sir Thomas or his wife? Look in a mirror glass. You are a Plantagenet. Your true mother was a miller's daughter in Middleham. Your father's first bed-mate.'

Ellingham sprang and gripped Hawker by his doublet, their noses nearly touching. But Hawker didn't move, his arms hanging loosely at his sides, his face as stone. 'You lie! As you have since I joined this godforsaken pilgrimage.' Already Ellingham's mind was throwing out images from his past that gave truth to Hawker's words. The coldness of the Ellinghams, their overbearing concern that still somehow lacked the basic milk of kindness or love. He had been a valuable object, needing protection, nothing more. They had been his guardians, his watchers.

His hands relaxed and he released Hawker.

'See, not so hard to believe, is it?' said Hawker quietly.

Ellingham was stunned, almost light-headed. 'What else can you tell me?'

'I do not know if your birth mother still lives. The king told me she was in a nunnery when she gave birth. I am sorry. Sorry that I must deliver this hard truth. I assume Sir Thomas was well compensated to be your surrogate father, your keeper. I know nothing more.'

Ellingham swallowed hard. 'So that is why they tried to arrest us? Me.'

Hawker nodded once. 'That... and the jewel. Even though you are a bastard, if your presence became known you might serve as a rallying point to relight the Yorkist cause. Men like the Tudors and the Stanleys will stop at nothing to purge every male Plantagenet they can find. Henry Tudor is a usurper. He can afford to do no less if he wants to keep the throne.'

'Would they come this far?'

Hawker could see in the youth's eyes the weight of the dilemma crushing down on him. 'They have spies everywhere and men willing to do their work for them. I have no doubt they will dog us as we ride south. You must not tell a soul of your true bloodline. Do you understand? Not Sir Roger. Not the Burgundian. No one. Because you can trust no one.'

Ellingham absently moved his hand to his dagger hilt, his brow furrowing. 'My father didn't expect you to nursemaid me for the rest of my life. So why do you help me?'

'I don't know why. Maybe because it is the right thing to do. The Lord Himself knows I stand to profit nothing from it. But I might be able to offer you a chance at a new life. A chance to find fortune where others will not know you except for the skill of your sword arm and the cleverness of your tongue. And – for what it is worth – I will pledge myself to you as your protector. Until you wish otherwise.'

Hawker watched as the youth pressed his lips together, thinking. The leanness of that mouth was that of King Richard. 'It seems I am at your mercy, Sir John. For I have no other way to turn. Not now.'

Hawker gave him a weak smile. 'Venice beckons. But you will need a new name. Ellingham is now known by our enemies.'

Giles looked down at his boots, his hand tightening on his hilt. 'If I am now an outlaw then I shall be Robin. Robin Hoode.'

Hawker's right eyebrow arched. 'I doubt the Venetians will have heard the song. But perhaps Sir Robin will do. Robin Middleham.'

12

The next day, they were treated to a few long stares by the guards when they rode beneath the great white stone towers of Mechelen's west gate. A light, drizzling rain drifted down on them, slicking the stones of the road underneath. Avoiding eye contact with a burly sergeant, Hawker thought it was good fortune that commerce never truly ceased, even in uncertain times. There were dozens of merchants with pack animals and wagons streaming in along with him. The knights barely stood out from the rest of the heaving crowd. Once into the town square, Hawker raised a hand, halting the little company. 'Well, which way, Jacob?'

De Grood gave a grunt of indecision though he knew the way well. 'Not certain my father will let me over his threshold, never mind that I'm bringing along a company of English knights. He wanted a weaver for a son. He got a mercenary instead.'

'He'd be a fool to refuse my money,' said Hawker. 'Show us the way.'

Beconsall looked at Hawker, mouth agape. 'You mean to say we are staying with this fellow's sire and dam! Are we already so poor we can't plump for a mean hostelry in this rabbit warren? Are we to share a bed with his other relations, too?'

Dieudonné whistled at Ellingham who still seemed lost in reverie. 'You coming, English?' he called out. 'I'm hungry.'

Ellingham gave a nod and prodded his mount forward.

The house of Bertrand de Grood was near the end of a street so narrow and tightly built that the sunlight had work just to find the cobbles. Yet it was the largest and sturdiest house on the street, rising up three storeys high. They halted, and Jacob dismounted and entered the doorway. The rest of the party remained in the saddle, waiting, the horses snorting their annoyance, jostling and nosing one another. At last, Jacob emerged, and with him, a grey-hair who must be his father.

'My son has returned,' the man said to Hawker in Flemish so thick it seemed stuck in his throat. 'He says he is in service to you, a knight of the English king. He also says you would all lodge here for the night.'

Hawker nodded. 'That is true – and I'll pay handsomely for your hospitality.'

'I did not expect to see my son again when he left me. Considering I chased him halfway to the city gates with a piece of the loom I broke over his ignorant head, I'm surprised to see him returned to me alive.'

'Then I am glad I've been the means to reconcile father and son. That is how things should be in a world so full of sorrow and heartache.'

Bertrand de Grood glowered. 'That is yet to be decided.'

'I would not impose, but I have need of your good counsel.'

'My counsel will cost you nothing. My hospitality plenty more though. Get your horses round the back. Jacob will show you the way.'

The ground floor was Bertrand de Grood's workshop. Five large looms filled the room and five men sat hunchbacked on stools over each, deft hands playing the clacking spindles of brightly coloured thread through the warps, building their tapestries by candlelight. As they passed through towards the staircase, Jack stopped in his tracks, enthralled by the enterprise and by the magical scenes that were taking shape upon the racks, one thread at a time. 'Look, Sir John, here is a battle! Horsemen and soldiers and a forest of trees behind them.'

Jacob guided him away, firmly gripping his shoulder. 'See, you little nose-picker? Now you know what I could have been doing these last four years. Stuck upon a stool with arse ache and sore fingers.'

Upstairs were the living quarters, sparse and clean with a large table covered by a madder-dyed rug far simpler than the woollen pieces in the workshop below. Bertrand went to his larder and came back with a few pewter mugs and a clay jug. He put them on the table and motioned for Jacob to play the tavern keep by pouring out for the rest. Before he filled the second cup, the father had said something and Jacob had spat out a reply and the next moment they were hurling abuse at each other so fast Hawker could not keep up.

'Sounds as if this is one son whose return is not particularly welcome,' said Beconsall, reaching for a cup of beer. 'Do we have to stay here, Hawker? For the love of Christ.'

Dieudonné grabbed a mug and walked to the open leaded window and surveyed the street. He called for Ellingham to join him and the two were soon both chuckling at some altercation going on below. Bertrand's fist slammed down on the table after Jacob said something else that rankled the old man. 'Let them fight it out,' Hawker said to Beconsall. 'Better they purge the poison now. I have questions for the weaver.'

'What? Are you in the market for a tapestry or something?' He snorted and took a swig.

'He might know when the next merchant convoy sets out from here bound for the Italian kingdoms. Or at least know someone who knows. The weaver's guild here is powerful. They'll have goodly intelligence. You can depend on it.'

Beconsall tilted his head back where he sat and studied the ceiling beams. 'Aye, well this is your expedition, Hawker. Do as you must.'

There was a definitive burst of oaths from the father and then he turned to Hawker and jabbed his finger. 'Ten silver groats!' he said, then stormed down the stairs.

Jacob shook his head. 'I am sorry, Sir John, but it was not a good idea to return here. He hasn't forgiven me for leaving him. For leaving the trade.'

Hawker sighed and motioned for Jacob to take a drink. 'Well, at least he relented enough to speak to you. It will pass.'

'His entire shop is working on a commission for the Duchess Dowager of Burgundy, Margaret. Five great panels and every one of them is late. I think he is worried she will ask for her money back. He has only a few months left to finish them. He is vexed beyond reason.'

'We're all vexed,' grumbled Beconsall, reaching again for the pitcher. 'So let us find a meal somewhere.'

'Sir Roger is right.' It was Dieudonné who had turned from his observations. 'Sir Giles and I go to the square and find something to eat.'

Hawker was not convinced that was wise but could not begrudge them a full belly after a day's long ride. 'Very well, but don't let your tongues wag. And be back here after the bells strike vespers.'

Dieudonné bowed his head. '*Bien sur*, Sir John!'

Beconsall stood and straightened his voluminous velvet robe. 'I'll keep an eye on these two.' He turned back and winked at Hawker. 'And they can keep an eye on me.'

Hawker saw Jack begin to follow them down the stairs. 'Where do you think you're going?' The boy halted, turned slowly, and gave Hawker an embarrassed look, his pale face blotching.

'Begging your pardon, sir.'

'A squire does not move without his lord's permission. You'd do well to remember that.'

Jacob, quiet after his tempestuous reunion with his father, pulled out a bench from the table and sat down while Jack did the same. Hawker looked at his little retinue. 'We've come this far but there is further to go. We must find a group of southward-bound merchants to join. We can offer them protection and they will afford the same for us.'

'You are very cautious compared to the last journey from here south,' said Jacob.

'Because everything has changed. You know what I carry. So does the House of Tudor. They had spies everywhere before they usurped the throne and now they'll have even more. The exchequer is a near-bottomless pot of gold for the Welsh bastard. And I have a price on my head.'

'So, strength in numbers then?' Jacob sounded unconvinced.

'Something like that. We get to Venice. I return the jewel. The doge, grateful, offers me a commission with his army. Maybe even a commission with the Council of Ten.'

'And what about the others, my lord? Something tells me they're not listening to the same song. And the Burgundian is too slippery for me to even think of turning my back on him.'

Hawker reached for his ale pot. 'They are the wildcards in our deck, Jacob. But we need them to get to Venice. After that... well, it is up to them.'

Jacob merely grunted in reply. There was silence between them for a few moments and then he spoke again. 'I have been thinking of Jan Bec. It pains me still. And I miss the little bugger. It was not right that he should meet his end... not that way.'

'My heart grieves for him too, old friend. But we both know the lot of a soldier's life. We can never know when our time will come.'

Jacob absently rubbed his hand along the trestle table. 'But he had been to sea *before*. Been seasick *before*. And many times. I cannot believe he slipped and fell overboard. Too simple.'

'You think he was murdered, then? Why would one of those sea-rats have wanted to do that and risk losing their ship and their lives if we found out? Sometimes the simplest reason is the most obvious.'

Jacob nodded slowly. 'Aye. But it still does not sit right with me. It never will.'

–

Two hours later, Hawker was growing restless, his mind wrestling with his motives for the journey and whether indeed this was the wisest course of action. Jacob's doubts played on his mind, too. Early evening had descended and still the comrades had not returned. He could, of course, still sell the jewel to a goldsmith who would pay handsomely. The man would never know what it truly was. For him it would only be a large, blood-red ruby as deep as the night. Valuable yes, ready to be turned into some nobleman's hat brooch. But Hawker had given his word to his king and he would keep it, even if that king was now food for crows. And more than that, Venice held something else. Her. God willing, she would still be there if he made it back. With forgiveness in her heart.

At length, he stood up and stretched, joints cracking. 'I am going out for a walk. The others should have returned by now.'

Jacob jumped up. 'I'll go. I know the town.'

Hawker raised his hand. 'No, I want you to stay. Keep an eye on Jack. I need the air. To think.'

Jacob smiled. 'Then, Sir John, we should all go. Better to keep an eye on each other that way.'

Hawker shook his head in resignation. 'Very well. Go fetch the lad.'

They ventured down into the streets. A few sellers were late in fastening tight their shutters after the last customers had departed while nearby a group of boys ran yelling through the alleyways. Then quiet descended upon the neighbourhood. They began threading their way, cutting down cobbled alleys and making progress towards the white stones of Saint Rumbold's stunted tower, which lay just beyond. Jack grabbed Jacob by the elbow and pointed to a cart man selling pies on the far side of the tiny square they found themselves in. Jacob looked over to Hawker and inclined his head towards Jack. Hawker gave a nod and Jack sprinted to the vendor, the Fleming jogging to keep up.

Hawker again started thinking of Venice, and remembering the last time he had seen the woman. How she had sworn at him, berated him, hit him. He continued walking, slowly, across the square as the painful scene played out in his mind. A child ran by, bumping him, but he was oblivious, thinking how he might have changed her mind when he had had the chance. Convinced her to leave all and follow him to England. His feet carried him further down the street on the far side of the square.

He was less than a hundred yards down it when he crossed a second alley, deeply gullied and stinking of offal and piss. No sooner had he stepped out into the crossway than he caught movement out of his left eye. Two men had nearly collided with him. They both took a step back and gave a polite bow of the head. Hawker inclined his own in acknowledgement. They were dressed neither wealthy nor low and could have been merchants or artisans. He noticed that their eyes lingered on him, almost as if they knew him.

'Your pardon, sir,' said one in Flemish. His brown curls descended low around his woollen bonnet, dark eyes intently staring even as he spoke. His comrade, a bullish-faced man of middle age, said nothing. But neither seemed to be in any hurry to resume their way.

Hawker glowered. 'God give you good day.' He heard more steps on the cobbles, this time behind him. His hand instinctively moved to the dagger on his hip, but he was too slow. A few years earlier he would have beaten them to the attack. But not now.

He was propelled forward, down into the cross alley, his arms pinioned from behind. The bull-faced man sunk a punch into his belly that buckled his legs and pitched him forward in pain. He was hauled up again and this time he tried to shake off the man who held him from behind, seeking to ram his elbow into the man's ribs. But a fist caught him on his right cheek, staggering him. Hawker, head swimming, saw the curly-headed man reach forward for his belt pouch. He leaned back with all his strength and pushed with his legs in an attempt to off-balance the man who held him. Now all three assailants enveloped him.

The blow from some sort of cudgel knocked him to his knees, lights dancing in front of his eyes. Sickening pain enveloped him, skull throbbing. He felt himself falling deep, as if the alleyway was opening up to swallow him whole. He lingered, caught between oblivion and awareness – maybe the rotting stink of the place keeping him conscious – and then he felt himself being dragged along and rolled over. The voices echoed in his ears like someone speaking from the bottom of a well. They were guttural and urgent. Hawker heard them arguing as they rifled his doublet lining and yanked at the thong of his purse. He began writhing like a serpent to shake his attackers but a second thump on the back of his head finished the protest and Hawker knew no more.

13

In the crypt-like vaulted arches of the cellar tavern, lamplight
pooled across the glistening red bricks and the burble of fifty
or sixty men of Mechelen – soldier, merchant and tradesman –
echoed from one end to the other. Sir Roger Beconsall sat at one
of the long trestle tables that were awash in beer and greedily sank
his teeth into the whole roast capon that he had ordered from
the landlord. Opposite him, Sir Giles and Gaston Dieudonné
watched in shared amusement as the oafish knight tore the bird
apart like some palace-kitchen dog. They were both deep into
their second jug of Mechelen beer – strong and bitter but a taste
ever-encouraging of another swig.

Dieudonné's ears picked up on the voices around him: Flemish
mostly, but also a few French ones and a group of soldiers of the
Holy Roman Emperor speaking Swabisch German. Even as he
laughed, rubbing elbows with the young Englishman, his eyes
took in the others that had wandered in from the east end of the
market square. He had learned a long time before that one must
always know who is inside one spear-length, at all times in all
places. This, for now, was one docile gaggle, and so far he and his
companions had drawn little attention. It was still early though.

He turned back to his new comrade, this handsome royal
bastard. He thought the youth's week-old reddish-blond stubble
better outlined the fine cheekbones and chin, giving him a new
air of command. Dieudonné's conscience was rarely ever weighed
down with the rightness of a thing. For him, choice was a matter
of outcome, better or worse. And at that moment he was thinking
about what to do next. About this prize stallion that sat next to

him. About the wondrous jewel that Hawker had secreted away; the old knight's true reason for a journey to Venice.

At the same time, Dieudonné was painfully aware that he was being drawn deeper into this sad little company of defeated Yorkists. And aware also that he might soon need a better excuse to wear on his lips if he was going with them all the way south. Eventually Hawker would smell a rat and he needed to devise a motive that was more convincing to his companions of the road. And perhaps, just perhaps, the young man next to him might supply it.

He spoke in French closely into Ellingham's ear to cut above the noise of conversation around them. 'A damnable collection of rogues, wouldn't you say? How do you fancy signing on with the Habsburgers over there? Good pay, I'll warrant.'

Ellingham smiled thinly. 'My current adventure is enough to satisfy me, dear Gaston. And we've a long road ahead of us. Are you already bored of our little company?'

'Not in the least. On the contrary, my admiration grows stronger by the day. As does my affection for you all. We who fought loyally and survived treachery on the field.'

'I wouldn't have thought a Burgundian for hire would consider loyalty any great aspiration – or something worth his concern. That must make you a rare creature indeed.'

Dieudonné laughed. 'Rare, yes, perhaps, Sir Giles. We are not all driven by gold, not when the cause is right and just. So, you do not intend to stay here in Flanders?'

Ellingham peered into his cup, careful now not to speak of Venice. 'We journey onwards. You should ask Sir John if you desire to come along. For myself, I still cannot believe any of it, even now. Can't believe I'm outlawed. Or that I'm even here, in this place. You, on the other hand, have no tie to us. Surely your prospects are better here in Flanders.' He gestured towards the Imperial soldiery who were raucously drinking and singing. 'Perhaps that lot over there. Is not the German emperor's son the Duke of Burgundy? He'll exchange his ducal crown for his father's someday.'

'I have an interest in another crown. And in helping it return to the White Rose.'

Ellingham looked at the Frenchman, trying not to look surprised. 'How much longer do you intend to accompany us? And what reason could you possibly have to aid the House of York?'

'Because, Sir Giles, I've made a friend of a man whose blood is royal. One of the last of the White Rose. You.'

Ellingham went still. There was a long silence and then he ventured to speak. 'What do you mean?' His voice was quiet and dripping with apprehension.

'I know who your father was. I know who you are.' Dieudonné could see the young man blanch. 'And I would gladly serve to deliver the crown back to your house. It is God's will.'

Ellingham pulled back slightly where he sat. 'Who told you?'

Dieudonné's eyes flicked across the table to Beconsall, who was still concentrating on devouring his bird. 'I overhead Hawker and him on the ship. It was not Hawker's fault, close quarters and all. But I consider it a sign from God that our paths have crossed.'

'Your faith is misplaced. I am a bastard. The crown would never be my birthright.' He gripped Dieudonné's arm tightly. 'Nor would I ever wish it! I beg you, Gaston, say nothing of this to anyone. Not even among us.'

Dieudonné nodded and placed his palm over the youth's hand. 'You may be called upon to save your house one day. I would stand with you.' He would not mention the jewel. Not yet.

Ellingham's voice dropped even lower as he leaned in close. 'Madness. That is a struggle for my cousins, if they still live. Not mine. *Never* mine.' And he believed it. He wanted nothing to do with the backstabbing nobles who had plagued the kingdom for so long. Bad enough he was now a target. Hunted. Even if he was in line for the throne, he would have failed miserably in wearing the crown. He knew nothing about the world of kings. But he could see the dangers involved. Better to stay in the shadows.

Dieudonné pressed his hand tighter and whispered. '*You* do not know God's will. And a priest's oath can be bought, witnesses produced. Sworn statements to say that Richard married your mother in secret: youthful lovers whose union was blessed.'

Ellingham pulled his hand away. 'No more of this talk, or you shall risk our friendship. And I do hold you as my friend.'

Beconsall's bad French was beginning to frustrate him. 'What are you two conspiring at?' he called across the table. 'Are you going to drink or just talk all evening?'

Dieudonné hefted his cup and raised it towards Beconsall. 'Sir Roger,' he said in his halting English, 'we drink, of course!'

Ellingham smiled weakly and raised his as well. He glanced at Dieudonné and drained his cup dry. He then leaned in close to him. 'For pity's sake, tell no one of what you know. Understood?' The Frenchman laid a hand gently on Ellingham's forearm, only for a moment.

'So, my lord Gaston,' said Beconsall with a grin, 'you fancy joining us south? The wonders of Venice await. Cupid himself lives there, from what I have heard, so beautiful are the women.'

Ellingham's eyes narrowed, and he gave an almost imperceptible shake of his head as Beconsall's careless words left his lips.

Dieudonné's eyes widened in false surprise. 'Venezia you say? Sir John seeks business with the doge, then?' He ran a hand along his chin. 'Well… perhaps I might join you – if I am permitted, of course. I would hear from Sir John what the prospects are for a hired sword in that land.'

Beconsall now caught view of Ellingham's scowl and knew he had been indiscreet with the Burgundian. But he made light of the slip and scowled back at the young knight. 'What of it, Sir *Robin*?' He chuckled as he said the name. 'The Burgundian will guess where we're going soon enough, or else hear it from Sir John's own lips come morning. No harm among comrades!'

Dieudonné crossed himself and then set a forefinger to his lips. 'I say nothing! Sir John will say if he want me – needs my blade.'

'Then let us drink up and talk of other things,' said Beconsall. 'Such as love. Preferably where to find it!' He waved a drumstick at Ellingham. 'Have you a beloved you've left behind? Have you pledged your troth to some noble's daughter? We would hear your tale, Sir… Robin.'

'I have no lady,' said Ellingham flatly. 'Something my father was to arrange before the start of winter. Not likely now, I should think.'

'Ah, surely you have known love, my lad. Ladies of the camp, perhaps? You're not *that* young, are you?'

Ellingham said nothing but reached over for the pitcher to refill his cup.

Beconsall broke into a grin. 'Come now, not even a servant girl in your household?'

'You talk like a pig, not a knight of the realm.'

Beconsall drew back with a look of mock insult. 'Are we not comrades all?'

Dieudonné put an arm around Ellingham's shoulders and spoke quietly in French. 'Do not listen to him. Your *amours* are not his concern. Together we shall find Fortune and Love. I have some experience of both, you know. What do you say?'

Ellingham managed a smile, shaking his head. 'Gaston, you are the gentleman among us. And it was good fortune that you crossed our path. Very well, let us see what tomorrow brings. If you want to come with us to the south, I will stand for you.'

Dieudonné gave the youth another rough shake and leaned in, practically brushing his cheek with his own. 'We shall continue to be companions of the road, my lord!' He then gave the youth a knowing look. 'And my blade is your blade. Come what may.'

14

As he became aware that he was not dead, at least not yet, Hawker next saw a blurred face hover over him, a boy. His eyes were unable to focus on who he knew to be Jack and as he tried to raise himself on his elbows, the sudden pain in his head made him cry out. He sank back into oblivion, at first blackness and a ringing in his ears, and then, sinking further, a confusing sea of images pouring into his mind's eye.

Rippling black water, black as pitch. River water. He can smell the stink of it and hear it lapping hungrily against the stones. Then the crying comes to his ears. The crying of two children. Boys. Their words are indistinct but these two are pleading, sobbing and frightened. He hears the thump of a boat as it bumps into the slick, weed-strewn jetty, oars grinding on the gunwales. One of the boys is coughing, spasms coming more quickly, born of terror. And Hawker is as a spectator. There, but not there. Seeing through the prism of his disordered mind. And he is afraid too. There is urgency and dread in equal measure in the damp darkness. An echoing voice cries out, strident, in a hoarse whisper: 'Who goes there! Give me the word!'

His own cry brought him to consciousness. And it brought Jack rushing into the bedchamber. Hawker swallowed and let out a groan of pain, the ache cascading down the back of his skull.

'Rest easy, Sir John.' It was Jack, standing over him and grasping his hand. 'You're safe, my lord. You're back with us.'

'Some wine,' Hawker croaked. 'Give me some wine.'

Ellingham rushed into the garret room, stopping short at the foot of the bed. 'Sweet Jesus, he has come to his senses. De Grood!'

Hawker reached up and gently felt his head with a trembling hand. It was wrapped in bandages like a Moor's turban. 'What is that smell?' he asked, licking his dry lips.

'Vinegar, Sir John,' said Jack, moving to place a draught under the knight's nose as Ellingham helped to push him upright, jamming the pillows under his back. 'The apothecary told us what to do. Soaked the bandages we did and then wrapped you up. It's a mighty big goose egg, my lord. We feared your brains might be addled.'

Hawker sipped the liquid that was offered. Watered wine and something besides, but it was sweet and soothing nonetheless. 'Addled? Not yet, my boy. But the rogues made a good effort.'

Jacob burst in, his face lighting up at the sight of Hawker's open eyes and he fell to bended knee at the side of the bed. 'I prayed to the Virgin, my lord! And she has answered. I cannot forgive myself for letting you out of my sight as I did.'

Hawker waved an arm towards him unsteadily. 'Nonsense. I was the damned fool who wandered off. Get up off the floor.' He motioned to Jack for another sip of the posset. 'Did they catch who set upon me out there? How did you even find me?'

'I saw three men running fast down the alley when I caught up to you, lying there,' said Jacob. 'I thought they had slain you.'

Ellingham stood back and crossed his arms. 'And there's not a trace of them now, Sir John. But they did not even take your purse. It was left next to you where Jacob found you a few streets away from here. They tore open your robe and shirt.'

Hawker shook his head and let out another groan. 'There were three of the bastards.'

'So,' said Ellingham, 'if they were brigands they were particularly fussy ones. Or... they were not brigands at all. What do you think?'

'You know damned well what I think,' Hawker mumbled.

Ellingham nodded. 'The Tear. But what does it say about a company such as ours when we keep getting beaten up in the streets? First Beconsall at the tavern, now this.'

'That is not fair, Sir Giles,' said de Grood, mildly hurt, his cheek scar drooping, 'when a man is cornered on his own. My lord didn't have the benefit of the rest of us there to fight with him.'

Ellingham laughed. 'The rest of us? We're still a score short of even a wedding party, never mind a company of mercenaries. Sir John, your enemies know we're here.'

Hawker, annoyed, seized the pewter cup from Jack and took a swig himself. 'Where are Beconsall and the Burgundian?'

'They keep watch downstairs, my lord,' said de Grood. 'Monsieur Dieudonné thought it wise to do so. Until you are whole again.'

'Aye, well at least he's thinking like a soldier. I was a calf-headed sot for daydreaming. The town is probably full of Lancastrian spies. Probably was even before Henry Tudor stepped ashore back in Wales.'

De Grood put Hawker's purse on the bed. 'Here, my lord. It is still full. Even that straw trinket you took from the little girl in Leicester is there. I'm afraid it has not brought you much luck after all.'

It was peeking out from the purse and Hawker took it before reaching in to withdraw a coin. 'Here, Jacob, the penny I owed you for buying it in the first place.' Seeing the twisted straw led him to think about what had made him keep the thing: the remembrance of pureness of heart. Something he had lost a long time ago.

Ellingham put a hand on his dagger hilt and moved towards the doorway. 'We shall keep watch until you are mended. Then we can decide what to do.' He made to leave but stopped again and turned. 'Sir Roger is a bit free with his tongue. He let slip the word Venezia to Dieudonné at the tavern. I thought you should know.' He nodded and left, boots echoing down the staircase.

Hawker fingered his cup and looked down across the coverlet. Beconsall had his uses, though they were but chaff if his tongue waggled too much. And, to crown it all, someone in Mechelen already knew about the jewel – and had found out quickly indeed. 'How long have I been sleeping?'

'Why, more than a day, my lord,' said Jack.

Jack moved closer to the bedside. His voice was quiet but carried an intensity that was mature beyond his years. 'I would have fought for you, Sir John. If I'd been there with you. I'm not afraid. Not any more, leastways.' He nodded as if to reinforce his own words. 'I've killed two men now. I know how it is done. I would have stabbed them.'

Hawker looked at Jack, uneasy with the boy's newfound grimness, a coldness that maybe he had helped to birth by giving him salve for his conscience. 'I know you would have. Yet I'm glad that you weren't called on to do so. You are still too young to be eager to shed blood in my service.' His voice sank lower. 'The stone... you still have it on your person? Tell me so.'

'Aye, my lord, it has not left my pocket. I've even pinned it up inside so it does not fall out.'

Hawker let out a sigh. 'Good lad. That stone once adorned the brow of your king.' He watched the change come over the boy's face as his words sank in. A sense of great responsibility becoming just that bit weightier. But also, along with it, acceptance of what was asked.

'It lies cold in my pocket,' said Jack quietly and firmly. He paused a second. 'I remember when you gave it over to me... and Will. In the tavern. Is it a dangerous thing?'

Hawker closed his eyes again. 'My boy,' he whispered. 'It's brought ill to many I suspect, but I hope that it will do us some good.'

–

Hawker was back on his feet the next day, the blows of a dozen battles having inured him to broken bones and bruises. But the ageing knight had sunk into a foul mood since being set upon. Dieudonné's quips and whispered jokes were kept for Ellingham, who had found the wandering Burgundian a kindred spirit and, like him, a man without a home. About midday, the sound of the clacking loom spindles suddenly stopped. De Grood was first to realise this and jumped to grab his sword and fetch Hawker up on the top floor. As he did so, de Grood's father came pounding up the stairs, talking loudly to himself and intermittently calling out for his son. He met him and Hawker, now both armed, in the gallery on the first floor.

There was an explosion of guttural Flemish from Bertrand de Grood, so fast that Hawker could decipher none of it. 'What is he on about?' he shouted over the voice of de Grood senior.

Jacob held out his palm to interrupt his father's cascade. 'He says, there are halberdiers – guardsmen – outside, from the ducal palace. You are requested to accompany them.'

Hawker's brow rose. 'Requested?'

The son fed the question back to the father. 'Aye, Sir John. They are *asking* you to return with them. The duchess dowager wishes an audience with you.'

That the duchess knew he had entered Mechelen was bad enough. That the invitation had come a day after he had been left for dead in the alley was of more concern. Well, he had met all the brothers Plantagenet over the years, fought and spied for them, too. But King Richard's sister, the princess Margaret, he had never met. Now he would have the pleasure, whether he wanted it or not.

She had left England nearly twenty years earlier to marry the widowed Duke of Burgundy, a match that had produced no children, partly thanks to his premature end on the battlefield. She had ruled what was left of Burgundy on her own, guardian to the future duke, her step-grandson, the boy Philip. By all accounts, Margaret of Burgundy had far more brains than her husband ever had. The knight noticed that old de Grood looked almost elated rather than alarmed. 'What is he so happy about?' demanded Hawker.

Jacob shrugged. 'I think, my lord, he is relieved. He thought they had come to take *him* away.'

'Go down and meet them. Tell them I must change my clothes and that I will accompany them presently. Meanwhile, see if your father has found a merchant caravan we can join with.' Then another thought struck him. 'I shall take Ellingham with me. You stay here. Look after Jack.'

Jacob's scar twitched slightly. 'Aye, my lord.'

Four halberdiers in distinctly German garb walked in front of them, two more behind. Ellingham was sweating heavily in his green velvet robe, beads running down his temples from underneath the band of his black wool cap. 'Sweet Christ above,' he whispered across to Hawker, 'she is my aunt. And you say we must keep silent? Maybe she already knows of me.'

'We bide our time. We don't know what she's after, but I've a good idea. You say nothing. Understood?'

Ellingham nodded, feeling that he was about to enter the lion's den – but without Daniel's faith. 'Will she know of the king's fate?'

'Undoubtedly. It might be that she just wants another account of what happened. Or something else.'

The palace, bright white sandstone, lay upon a wide street in the centre of Mechelen. Large leaded-glass windows in its great hall gave it the appearance of a church, and Hawker had heard stories of the wealth that Margaret had spent in widowhood embellishing the place.

The guards took them through a pair of great, iron-studded doors and into a passageway that opened to a second great hall, perpendicular to the other. This was bathed in both light and shadow from tall windows at the western side. The high vaulted ceiling of blackened oak beams bore many escutcheons, brightly painted. Hawker watched as a black-clad figure approached from the opposite end, his footfalls silent upon the chequered stone floor. He was old, older than Hawker, and possessed of a round face, short nose and eyes that were set far apart, all giving him the appearance of an aged ram. 'Sir John Hawker,' he said as he stopped before them. He turned to Ellingham. 'Who has *not* come alone, I see.'

Hawker bowed. 'I am he, sir. At your service. This is my comrade, Sir Giles Ellingham.' He had almost given Ellingham's travelling name but thought better of it.

The man bowed in return. 'I am Sir Olivier de la Marche, chatelaine of this place. We were informed of your party's entry into the town – English voices, you see – and so would hear more news of England. The tragedy there has grieved us. Were you upon the battlefield?'

'We were there,' said Hawker. The sadness of it still carried in his voice.

'The duchess would hear your tale, then. But first, you must disarm and leave your weapons here.'

Ellingham shot a glance to Hawker but, seeing the knight unbuckle his sword belt, began to do the same. The chatelaine led them the way he had come and continued until they exited the hall and entered a vast ornamental garden entirely surrounded by the sprawling palace. The halberdiers remained two paces behind them as they made their way across the lawn. Reaching a bower, they halted. From it emerged a woman, tall and slender and dressed in a gown of black with silver lace and pearls. Her head was covered in a wimple of purest white cambric, sharply folded and creased. The high midday sun glinted on the metallic lace and the golden girdle she wore. Hawker went down on one knee and Ellingham, momentarily frozen, awkwardly followed suit.

'You are the John Hawker who was knighted by my brother at Middleham?' She spoke in French, slowly and clearly.

'I am he, your Grace. At your service.'

'And who is this man?'

Ellingham noisily cleared his throat. 'Your Grace, I am Sir Giles Ellingham, late in the service of his majesty King Richard.'

This was met by a studied silence from the duchess. At length, she spoke to de la Marche. 'You may leave us to walk in the yard. I would speak with these men.'

'But your Grace, you *must* be accompanied.' Olivier's voice carried a hint that she had done this before with guests. Many times.

'Then the guards may follow at our backs if you insist. I would practise my English tongue with these gentlemen for I fear I am losing it after all these years.' She looked down at the two knights. 'Rise, both of you.'

They did so, exchanging a glance with one another at the strangeness of it all. 'Walk with me,' she commanded in lilting English. The place was laid with rich green lawn and low box hedges shaped at right angles. Along the brick wall, calendula, Michaelmas daisies and roses still bloomed even in September's increasing chill. They made their way, slowly, like priests in a procession, Hawker not sure whether he should walk behind or at her side. That was quickly decided for him.

'I cannot hear you back there. Move over here – next to me. You, Sir Giles, may stay one pace back.'

Hawker studied the face surrounded by the starched wimple. She had large grey eyes, birdlike and almost unnaturally round. Her chin was as sharp as a rose thorn. Not beautiful but handsome, he thought, and her skin still milky translucent for a woman the same age as he.

'You were with the king, upon the field.'

'I was, your Grace.'

'Did you see him fall?'

Hawker swallowed, his throat dry. 'I did, your Grace. He fought bravely and took down a great many of the enemy until his horse went out from under him. It pains me to say that he came a hair's breadth from Henry Tudor. Slew the standard bearer next to him, but the Welshman retreated into his thicket of spears.'

She stopped and turned to regard him. 'You saw this with your own eyes? But you live to tell the tale.'

Hawker swallowed again, caught out by her slight to his honour. 'God saw fit to preserve me. I cut my way out after the king fell.'

She nodded. 'I have hope that the Earl of Warwick will make it out of England and come here. He is the last of the White Rose. Unless we find my brother Edward's children. You would know nothing of that, I suppose?'

'My lady?' Hawker's heart almost rose into his throat.

'You were Richard's retainer, weren't you? I thought perhaps you might know what befell them. Some say they were spirited out. I know what the Woodvilles and the Tudors say. Would you also say that Richard had them murdered?'

'Your Grace, with my hand upon my heart I would not. Richard would not have done such a thing.' His mind stumbled, calculating just how much he should say. How much he *could* say without ending up under arrest.

Margaret pursed her lips. 'Perhaps. But my brother was a fool. A fool who has destroyed his entire house. It will take a miracle to restore it. So much promise... wasted. First George, then Edward. Richard's impetuousness has finally undone us.'

Hawker could feel Ellingham's toes nipping at his heels as the youth strained to hear them.

'I believe, your Grace...' said Hawker hesitantly, 'I believe that Richard was trying to get the princes away. Away from the Lady Beaufort and her creature, Lord Buckingham.'

Margaret gave him a piercing stare. 'We have heard the same. The question is, did he succeed?'

Hawker was willing to go no further down that road though part of him strained to tell her that a Plantagenet prince walked just behind her, bastard though he might be. 'I have heard nothing, your Grace. But we may pray they are hidden and safe.'

She nodded, but Hawker could not tell if it was in agreement. 'Tell me, Sir John. Did my brother meet with you before the battle, at Leicester?'

Hawker felt his blood chill in his veins. 'He did, your Grace. He met with more than a dozen knights on the eve of battle.'

'I see. Did he entrust you with anything? Wise words from a fool, perhaps? Gold for your service, or jewellery?'

He noticed that she rarely blinked when she spoke. Intent, like the eyes of a cat. 'Why, he gave me this signet for my good service.' Hawker raised up the gold and silver ring bearing the charging boar for her to see. She smiled thinly at him, hardly glancing at the token.

'A generous gift from your king, Sir John. Was he so generous with his other knights?'

'I know not, my lady. But he also bid me look after one he had newly given spurs to – Sir Giles here.'

She turned around to look at the youth. Hawker noticed that she made to turn back to him but then, paused, her eyes fixed upon Ellingham's face. The youth bowed his head, embarrassed and not knowing whether to speak. 'Sir Giles... Ellingham? A Middleham lord, I seem to remember. That was your father?'

Ellingham bowed again. 'He is, your Grace.'

'And you acquitted yourself well, I trust?'

'I did my best and God preserved me.'

The duchess smiled at him and Hawker caught the briefest sign of a furrowed brow as she did so. She slowly turned back to the older knight. 'There will be other supporters of the cause arriving here. York has been dealt a mighty blow but it is not yet a mortal one. A true heir will be found.'

Hawker nodded. 'We all pray that will be so, your Grace.'

'We will need good men such as yourself – your company – to stand ready to return when the time is right. But I gather you are not remaining here?'

'No, your Grace. I have interests in the south that I must attend to. In Mantua... and Venice.'

'And commitments?'

He began to squirm inwardly. 'I have debts to settle. Affairs of business to resume. But, my lady, I will return to aid the White Rose when needed. When the time is right.'

She gave no reaction to this and they resumed walking, so slowly that even a hedgehog would have overtaken them. 'You should know, Sir John, that Margaret Beaufort and the Tudors have agents here already. One must take care if one has a price on their head. One such as you. I merely give you warning.'

'I am grateful, my lady.'

'My lord de la Marche will give you a purse of ducats when you leave. For your inconvenience.'

Hawker bowed his head. 'I am most grateful for such kindness, your Grace.'

'Did my brother not make any... confession to you... on the eve of the battle? You had known him since he was young, trained him in the art of war.'

Hawker stopped and she half turned to him as he did so. 'He had regrets, my lady. Many regrets. And so many enemies.'

She returned him almost a wry smile. 'Too late for those now.' She did not resume the walk. 'Remember,' she said, turning to Ellingham, 'keep a watchful eye. These are dangerous times for us all.'

Ellingham bowed low and she spoke to the guards, in the German tongue. 'Take them back to the hall!'

—

Ellingham watched Hawker clutch tight the purse of money as they walked through the streets, this time with no escort of Hapsburg pole-arm men.

'She looked... right *through* me, Sir John,' he stuttered. 'Did you see?'

'She saw Richard in your face.'

'Then she suspects – she *knows*.'

Hawker shook his head. 'Perhaps. But I doubt it. If she does not detain you and bring you back before we leave Mechelen then your secret is safe.'

'You're a true comfort, Sir John, do you know that?' He was quiet for a moment as they rapidly made their way across the cobbles. 'Was it she who had you set upon? Searching for it?'

'Of that I have no doubt. Now she has recompensed me for my lump.'

Ellingham made a rumbling noise in his throat. 'I'm not convinced. It could have been Henry's spies – or Lady Beaufort's – that attacked you.' He was still thinking about the duchess – his aunt – the only blood relative other than Richard that he had ever met. As they had walked he had almost blurted out who he was, but had held back, afraid of the consequences. And now, it was too late. But there could never be a bond, he knew that in his heart, and he felt a strange sense of loss already.

'If that were the case, then they would have slit my throat there and then. No, they were Habsburger henchmen, in the duchess's service. A little over-zealous, perhaps,' he said, rubbing at his scalp. 'But there to find the jewel without the awkwardness of having to drag me to the palace. They did not find it and she had to summon me anyway.'

Ellingham still thought it could have been either party that attacked Hawker. The worry now was that Margaret's henchmen might follow and ambush them in the countryside, looking for the jewel. It was not a comforting thought.

When they returned to the weaver's house, Jacob was at the door to greet them, face beaming. 'Thank the Virgin you are returned safe, my lord! And there is more good news to tell. My father has found a convoy of merchants for us to join with. Said they are grateful for escort. They leave in two days.'

Ellingham shut the door behind them and threw the bolt across. 'Tell me, Sir John. Do you truly know what awaits you in Venice *this* time?'

Hawker turned to him and smiled. 'You expect me to tell you your fortune? Or mine even? I give you a chance to *find* fortune – where there was none before.'

'I'll tell you this, Sir John. I'm tired of running away from things. Now, I need to run *towards* something.'

15

Gaston Dieudonné squinted over his limp riding boot, needle and catgut thread poised to pierce the leather where the stitching had burst. He pushed the needle through the hole and deftly brought the catgut through with an over-and-under stitch followed by a lock stitch. He knew he was as good as any cordwainer. A soldier must have many skills other than knowing how to kill. Such as when to strike and when not to. When to play the fool and when to play the wise man.

The party would be up before dawn to join the merchants' convoy and as Dieudonné watched the activity around him – de Grood lashing up the satchels, Beconsall oiling his steel, the boy Jack, Hawker's pet, wrapping cheese and bread in muslin – all his thoughts were focused upon the choices that danced through his head. Decisions that still had to be made.

Time was now running out if he was to keep to his original course. Hawker had been beaten and robbed in an attempt to find the jewel. That was obvious. But it only proved that the old fox did not have the gemstone upon him when he went out. It was either hidden or secreted upon another's person. He could not be seen rummaging for it, which meant it would mean luring one of the others – even Hawker – and torturing them to find the location. Possible, but complicated in execution.

His money was on the boy. De Grood was too obvious a choice to be the keeper, but the Fleming watched Jack like a mother hen when Hawker was unable. There were other concerns, too. Their presence in Mechelen was known to the duchess dowager and if she knew, then Lancastrian spies probably did as well. What if Lancastrians burst in and captured them all? He would lose the jewel and his prize cockerel, Ellingham. If *that* came to pass, where would he be? No prospects for fortune or title, sitting high and dry, bored in a land of bores. Assuming, of course, he wasn't slain. And just what was the purpose of Hawker's visit to the ducal palace? Did the duchess know what he carried with him?

If he was going to take the young Plantagenet back to Henry Tudor, he would have to act now: convince Ellingham to take the jewel and join him in a return to England to raise an army in the north. Dieudonné mulled the means of doing that, but decided that he had not earned Ellingham's complete confidence yet. It would come, given time. And it was this that had begun to intrigue him the more. He was now in a contest with Hawker, a contest for the loyalty of King Richard's bastard. That was a far more interesting game to his mind than playing kidnapper, and he smiled as he pulled the needle through the leather, tugging it with an upraised arm.

He thought of further possibilities. Henry Tudor himself was a usurper, newly sat upon a wobbling throne. What if his army deserted him and a Yorkist contender was successful in a bid to reverse their misfortunes? As the trusted confidante of a scion of York, he, the presumed Sieur de Orchamps, would have the means to attain what he wanted despite the hollowness of his own title. Perhaps Ellingham would never be destined to wrest the English crown back for himself, but as the son of King Richard, he could draw others to him. Others such as John de la Pole, Earl of Lincoln, or Edward, Earl of Warwick. These others had a clear claim to the throne, and that he knew.

He looked up and over to young Ellingham, who was sharpening his sword on his lap, running a whetstone lightly along the steel. Dieudonné could see from the look on the youth's face that his mind was elsewhere, far away. He knew he could teach Ellingham so much. The lad was intelligent and quick-witted, if a little green. He was handsome. That made the task a pleasant one, he thought, imagining the possibilities in a place such as Venice. Dieudonné had never been there — that itself influencing his decision to bide his time – but everything he knew about it told him that it was a nest of spies from every kingdom, duchy and republic. If things didn't go to plan for him, he knew the Tudors would have theirs there too. That gave him choices. One always needed to have choices.

A voice called over to him in French. It was Ellingham. 'Gaston, I cannot take this burr from the edge. Not particularly good at this sort of thing and I'm no armourer. Do you know how to smooth it?'

Dieudonné lifted his head and gave Ellingham a broad grin. 'Let me finish this last stitch and I shall come and help you.'

16

Ellingham pulled his cloak tight up around his neck as the wind whipped through the caravan. He, along with Beconsall, was bringing up the rear on this leg of the journey through the Alps while Hawker and the others led the four-waggon procession of Flemish cloth merchants. They had made it through the great pass, and they would soon be descending towards Aosta and into Lombardy. After that, assuming they survived the journey, it would be Verona, which lay under the rule of the Venetians.

Though the snow-capped peaks were behind them now, steep pine-covered slopes and grassy patches rose up on either side, funnelling mud and gravel down into the rutted track with every downpour. A rivulet of water rippled down the centre of this track, passing beneath the axles of the carts. They might make it to Venice inside a week. Or so Hawker told them.

He watched as time to time Beconsall paused, turning his mount and raising his chin, sniffing the air like some beast of the field. He himself was cold and sullen. The hospice at San Bernard had already warned them about gangs waylaying travellers for the past two weeks. The huge number of caravans, all racing to beat the onset of winter, had emboldened robbers and deserters looking for what might be easy plunder.

'You worried, then?' he called across to the hulking knight who was sitting hunched in the saddle and trying to keep warm.

'Hawker's not taking the threat of bandits seriously enough to my liking, lad. He's more concerned with telling you and me tales of Venice than keeping his eyes peeled for trouble.'

Rains the previous night had made the road treacherous, low cloud had descended upon them, bringing a drifting fog along with it. Perfect conditions for an ambush on a sleepy gaggle of merchants led by a clapped-out old mercenary, his four swords, and a boy.

Beconsall muttered a curse and Ellingham watched it become alive as his breath condensed. 'If we do get attacked it might go hard on us. There's just five of us – not counting the little crossbow killer – and twenty-three useless, fat merchants huddling in the carts.'

Ellingham didn't reply. The long hours in the saddle had made him question many things. It had been nearly a month now since they had departed Mechelen, and his mind had roved backwards and forwards, mulling over how he came to be where he was. His fingers were numb inside his gauntlets, his arse a lump of ice, and there was only the faint wisp of a promise of good fortune when they reached Venice.

Beconsall continued grumbling to himself for a while, every so often looking back from where they had come. Then, he halted, pulling his reins around to turn his mount behind. 'Hey ho, what's this?'

Ellingham turned to follow his gaze, scanning the slopes either side. Beconsall pointed. That was when he saw two men high up on the left slope, scuttling between the pines. What he thought might be shepherd's crooks were now looking more like cut-down war spears. Beconsall jerked his reins, whirled amid the splashing mud, and trotted ahead to where Hawker rode. Ellingham swore loudly and kicked his spurs in.

'To arms! We're under attack!' Beconsall bellowed. Hawker and Jacob looked up in alarm and then they too saw the men on the slope, bounding down to intercept them. Hawker halted and ordered them all to dismount when he saw the brigands were brandishing pole weapons. Ellingham knew that their horses would be skewered otherwise, knocking them all to the ground. They would be better off taking a stand in the waggons, giving them the high ground. Some of the merchants leapt from the carts and began running back along the road. Jacob grabbed his own bill weapon from the leading waggon and threw a short spear over to Jack.

'Jump into the waggon! Fight from there!'

Jack nodded and clambered up, pulling the spear up after him.

Ellingham counted twelve brigands. All had the look of lean desperation and were dressed in tattered doublets. They were a disordered mob, probably starving, all making a mad rush down into them. Before he could follow Jacob up into the waggon, they were upon him. He drew his longsword and picked the first man to engage. He charged in, a cry on his lips, and watched the eyes of the man grow large once he barrelled forward. Ellingham batted a spear thrust aside, kept his blade swinging and brought it back around to cleave the man at the shoulder, dropping him instantly with agonised screeching.

He wheeled for the next brigand approaching from behind and felt jarred as a spearhead slid across his backplate. Whirling, his longsword caught the shaft and struck the man's hand and the spear went spinning away. The man ducked but this didn't save him from Ellingham's second arc, which split his naked skull with a dull crunch.

Around him, Hawker and Jacob defended the waggons, protecting the Flemings who cowered inside. A brigand thrust at Hawker with a long spear, Hawker twisted aside and the thrust continued between the spokes of a wheel, becoming stuck. Beconsall, who stood his ground in the rutted road like him, laughed as Hawker kicked the spear, snapped the shaft and then chopped the man down.

Beconsall cast about for his next opponent and saw two robbers trying to pull down a merchant from the back of the last waggon. He caught up and yanked the wool cloak of the first brigand, tripping him up. He swung, the fellow went down on one knee, and Beconsall knocked him with a pommel blow and then followed up with a cut. The man crumpled and didn't get up again. The second brigand had managed to yank the merchant off, both tumbling to the ground. The bandit grappled for the fellow's overstuffed purse at his waist. Beconsall took the man's head off, sending it flopping, nearly severed.

He bent down and rolled the robber's corpse over and off the howling Flemish merchant and proffered a gloved hand. 'Get up before you drown, you fool!' he said, boots squelching in the deep black freezing mud of the road. The fellow, grey-bearded with huge eyes, and now looking brown-slicked as a farmyard pig and splattered with the brigand's blood, cried with joy and began thanking Beconsall with a stream of blessings, pawing at him in gratitude.

Ellingham, covering Beconsall, turned to see who was still left. Hawker and de Grood appeared to have finished off the remaining attackers and the sound of ringing steel diminished. He'd even glimpsed the boy standing in the lead waggon and thrusting down on a man trying to climb up. The lad was growing balls very fast indeed. He scanned the slope beyond the waggons and saw Dieudonné, alone, pursuing three of the robbers back up towards the treeline.

'Sweet Christ!' he swore, choking his left hand halfway up the blade of his longsword before running after the Burgundian madman.

–

Hawker was wiping down his blade on a dead ruffian's cloak. 'Well, we earned our keep at least. We were lucky none of us caught an arrow.'

'Fools didn't even have one crossbowman among them,' added de Grood, snorting his derision.

The merchants helped each other out of the waggons, shaking out their woollen cloaks and jabbering like magpies at their salvation. They set about embracing one another and their good fortune. The last of them was calling from deep in the branches of the pine tree he was trying to extricate himself from.

Hawker looked towards the treeline again. 'Sir Giles and the Burgundian went after a few up there.'

'I'll go after them,' said de Grood, hefting his spiked bill, glistening reddish copper with thickening blood.

Hawker shook his head. 'Better to get the waggons across the mudslide and onto drier road up ahead. We don't want to sit here much longer, especially if there is another band hereabouts. If the merchants want to give us thanks they can do so by helping push.'

'And Sir Giles?' asked Beconsall, scowling.

Hawker gestured towards the corpses around them. 'He and the Burgundian are more than a match for the likes of these poor, starving devils. Gather the merchants and I will see to the horses.'

Jack bounded out of a waggon and joined them, bearing his short spear and beaming. The spearhead was bloodied. Hawker saw this and put a hand on the boy's shoulder. 'Well done, my lad. You served well.'

Still shivering a little, Jack nodded, his smile slowly dropping away. He said nothing.

Beconsall looked towards the roiling whitish-grey clouds that tumbled over the mountains looming beyond. More rain or snow would bring yet more misery for them. They had to make good time and get into the valley below and into the lands of Lombardy. 'Your eyes are letting you down, Sir John,' he said quietly, twirling his sword in his beefy hands. 'That murderous rabble fairly jumped into your lap. And they would have, too, if I hadn't spotted them... from the *rear*.'

Jacob made to move on him and Beconsall smiled thinly, almost relishing the opportunity. Hawker shot Beconsall an icy glance and placed a restraining hand on the Fleming's shoulder, calming the moment.

'We *all* saw them. And I won't argue the point while we stand here freezing.'

Beconsall grinned, winding his cloak back up around his neck. 'Then let's get our geese back into the waggons and continue to market, shall we?'

Ellingham marvelled at Dieudonné's tenacity. The Burgundian was in the lead, his sword gripped in both hands across his body while he chased down the quarry over rock and hummock like a bounding wolf. Ellingham redoubled his efforts to keep up, breastplate and harness jangling. The slowest brigand had stumbled and Dieudonné had chopped him down with two ferocious blows before running onwards. The remaining two were running for their lives, all stomach for a fight gone out of them. One had already flung his spear away as they tore up the grass-covered limestone slope, but it was to no avail. The lead man, his ripped green hose and doublet covered in mud, slipped and fell, one of his short leather boots flying off. His companion turned to help and only then noticed that Dieudonné was nearly upon them. He froze where he was, instinctively crouching, cornered. He dropped his blade and fell to his knees.

The other man, scrambling for his boot, snatched it up hastily but, on looking up, realised there was no hope of escape. Still on his hands and knees, he sat back and clutched the boot to his chest. Dieudonné slowed his pace and Ellingham was soon at his side, lungs heaving. The brigands both began pleading in German and then poor French, begging for quarter and their lives. Ellingham took a step back, unsure of what he should do next. He looked over to Dieudonné. 'They're begging for mercy. Do we bring them back down and hand them over?'

Dieudonné threw a quick glance over to the young knight. Ellingham saw no mercy in the Burgundian's eyes. But he didn't see anger either. It was exhilaration, enjoyment and cruelty. Dieudonné didn't answer but kept flicking his blade back and forth in front of his prisoners, each swish of the steel eliciting winces from them. The man in green, his dark blond hair plastered onto a face streaming with tears, quietly mumbled some prayer. The other, hair shorn to nubs and with a squashed nose, kept looking from Dieudonné to Ellingham while he begged, not knowing which man gave him a better chance of Christian treatment.

'Gaston!' said Ellingham, his tone urging mercy.

His sword in a two-handed grip, Dieudonné stepped rapidly forward on his right foot even as he aimed a downward blow at the kneeling man, taking him across neck and collarbone with a spray of crimson, the head flopping sideways. Ellingham watched transfixed as Dieudonné's sword followed through, the arc of the blade converting as the *sieur* flexed his wrists. Up again and then down, cleaving the skull of the other brigand with a dull cracking sound and lodging the blade below the man's nose. Dieudonné stepped forward gently with his left foot and gave a quick tug to loosen his sword. The brigand fell forward on the white pebble-strewn grass of the slope, blood pooling. His body twitched.

Ellingham looked at the Burgundian. Dieudonné turned to face him squarely. 'And *what*?' he spat out. 'An objection?'

Ellingham glanced down at the Burgundian's handiwork. 'We should go back to the others and see what has happened,' he said quietly.

When they made it to the road, they found Hawker and de Grood pulling two horses while Beconsall and the struggling brotherhood of Mechelen merchants pushed the one of the waggons from behind, slowly inching it forward through the muck.

'Shirkers!' called out Beconsall, laughing, and wagging a finger. 'Get back here and put your backs into it with us so we can get out of here!'

Hawker stood back from the horse he was coaxing to pull. 'They got away, did they?'

Dieudonné laughed. 'They very fast, Sir John! As quick as hares. Is so, Sir Giles, no?'

Ellingham fixed his friend with a look of bewildered disappointment, even hurt, then turned towards Hawker. 'Aye. As fast as hares, Sir John.'

'Well, all the better reason to be on our way,' said Beconsall. 'And I'll ride up front now – with you, Sir John.'

Hawker shrugged and untied his horse from the waggons' mule team. 'That is no skin off my nose. My lord Gaston, will you take up the rear?'

The Frenchman smiled and bowed smartly. Throwing a grin towards Ellingham, he jogged to where his horse was tethered, gathered up the reins and mounted. He trotted back past the other two waggons and took up his position.

–

As the waggons rolled slowly along the road, the Flemish merchants busily restacked their load of wrapped woollens, all the while muttering amongst themselves. One looked up at Dieudonné riding close behind and gave a bow of thanks. Dieudonné pursed his lips in derision then slowly turned his horse in place, facing the way they had come.

The grey of the sky and slopes seemed to meld into the road beyond. But as he looked up the road, a few hundred yards distant, two dark figures on horseback came out from a clump of pines and stopped in the middle of the road. Watching him. He could just make out that they wore clothing of colour, reds or blues, long cloaks covering them. Wide berets on their heads. Men of importance perhaps, and no starving deserters from the Germans or Swiss. They stood rooted for but a moment, then wheeled their horses and rode back along the road, at speed.

Dieudonné cracked a slow smile to himself. The hunt was getting interesting again. He was willing to bet his last *sous* that they were Tudor men. They had either hired the most inept gang of assassins in the known world, or they were merely shadowing and observing them. For now, at least, he was going to keep all his choices open. When the caravan stopped and made a halt that evening, he said nothing to the others.

Part III

THE FLOATING CITY

17

To Ellingham, Venice was a floating city. Shining bright white against a blue sky streaked with wispy cloud, it grew and grew as the boat neared, a sea of red-tiled roofs and bell towers. Coming after the sights of the pilgrim road through France, the Swiss cantons and the Alpine passes, it was to him the crowning vision of their voyage. It seemed in his own mind, unworldly as he was, the most perfect, the most majestic, journey's end. A destination that would give birth to something new.

There had been times in the last month when he had wondered if their little company would manage a safe arrival. Only a little over a week earlier they had nearly been washed away in a mudslide in the Alps, the road disappearing before them in a rush of water and churning debris. As it was, it took the better part of an hour to get the horses and waggons through the aftermath, their boots sodden and filthy up to the knees. And then a second mudslide and the ambush shortly afterwards. He had acquitted himself well, though. Hawker had told him so. At least he had managed not to get himself killed.

They had entered Venetian lands two days ago, staying overnight at Padua at a hostelry filled with merchants bound for the Most Serene Republic. Their animated conversations, wild gestures and pulled faces built his anticipation for what lay ahead for them all once they reached Venezia. He thought that Sir John had visibly changed since they had come down from the hills of Milan and into the lands of Brescia: his mood had lightened, his distrust of strangers seemed to have lessened. It seemed to Ellingham as if the Lincolnshire knight had come home again. Even Sir Roger had noticed this peculiar shift of temperament, the Tuscan tripping from Hawker's tongue, bantering with innkeeper and servants alike. Beconsall grumbled to Ellingham one evening that this behaviour unnerved him. Ellingham could understand why: Hawker clearly was now on ground that he knew, but they did not.

Ellingham stood in the prow of the boat, one hand gripping the gunwale to steady himself. While he scanned the vista, Hawker stepped forward and placed a hand on his shoulder. 'Nearly there, Sir Giles,' he said. 'And a good journey, despite Beconsall's company, eh?'

Ellingham swivelled and faced him. 'Are you certain you still have a house here? Four years is a long time to be an absent lord.'

Hawker laughed. 'Well, I expect I still own it though whether it's fit for more than rats and mice will remain to be seen.'

Ellingham smiled, just a little, sucking in a lungful of the salt-laden air. 'I shall pray to God your reception is a good one. And ours.'

'My *casa*, such as it is, is in the bosom of San Polo, a district filled to the gills with good, God-fearing folk. They will find you lot... amusing, I should think.'

As the squat, broad-beamed vessel entered the mouth of the Great Canal, its lateen sail was lowered and oars then shipped by the crew. Huge red-brick towers – *campaniles* as Hawker said they were called – welcomed them on either side and Ellingham saw others, too, rising up further into the city. The waterway was full of life, throngs of people on either side of the canal and all manner of craft plying the rippling waters, forever moving, swirled by oar and tide. Though he had seen London, he was astounded by the tightness of the houses, churches and exotic-looking palaces here, as if they all jostled to keep a hold on this insecure mound of land no higher than the blue-green sea that surrounded it. He could spy no roads, no streets, only a ribbon of increasingly brownish sea that carried them deeper into the maze of brick and mortar.

Ellingham saw Hawker pull his felt cap down securely on his brow and nimbly move to the stern, where he had a word with the tillerman. The boat glided closer to the stone quay where Ellingham saw other vessels, barges and galleys both, moored. At this place, a great rope-and-wood boom stretched out and up to offload cargo and a dozen labourers were already manoeuvring it into place.

Gaston Dieudonné had been lying on canvas sacks amidships, eating an apple. He now pushed himself up and surveyed the quayside, carefully taking in this first sampling of Venetian life. Four cormorants were squabbling over half a dead fish as they bobbed next to the boat. Dieudonné took a final bite of the fruit then hurled the core with a quick snap of his wrist, the birds scattering as it hit the water.

Hawker whistled up a push-cart man to take their bags and they were soon off into the maze, him leading the way over a footbridge and into an alleyway. Faces peered down on them from windows above and Ellingham had the same feeling he had had in Bruges and Mechelen: they were always under someone's eyes. Did the others feel this, or was it only him? How Hawker after several years could remember his way through the twisting alleys, little paved courtyards and hump-backed bridges he could not imagine.

'There are no horses,' said Jack. 'Not a single one since we got off the boat.'

Beconsall laughed. 'They have probably eaten them all, boy!'

'They were forbidden just before I left,' said Hawker, not checking his pace. 'Too much bother and too many for so cramped and watery a place.'

'And too much shit in the streets, I suppose,' added Beconsall, giving a wink to Jack.

At length, they entered a square courtyard paved with large heavy stones, an octagonal marble well at its centre. Ochre-coloured houses both narrow and wide surrounded the place, all with louvered shutters painted red and green.

Hawker gestured towards the widest. 'This is my house. Not the grandest you will find in this city, but grand enough.' There was an archway at its base, a rough-hewn stone staircase glimpsed through the gloom within. The edifice rose up four storeys, all the shutters closed except for two. Ellingham saw Hawker squint at the windows. They all waited, watching. The handcart man coughed and held out his palm. Hawker hurriedly paid him off. He seemed distracted. Had he expected to be greeted by his caretakers? The house had a strange feel to it, inhabited but not quite lived in. Linen hung out over the top wall where the roof terrace was, waving down at them in the faint breeze.

Something inside, a door or shutter, slammed with a bang and a few moments later a woman appeared, practically falling down the stairs and out into the courtyard.

'*Ser Giovanni! Beata Vergine!*' She was tanned dark bronze, her roundish face surrounded by a white linen headscarf, sleeves rolled up high to reveal the sinewy arms of a house servant. She held her brown skirt up as she scuttled in her slippers across the paving stones.

Hawker's unshaven face split into a wide smile. 'Amalia! God bless you.'

The housemaid, though, looked more alarmed than delighted. As soon as the woman reached Hawker she went down on both knees onto the paving stones, seizing the knight's hand.

Beconsall leaned close to Ellingham. 'Had my own lady but given me such a welcome.'

Agitated words began to spill out of the woman. Hawker grasped her about the shoulders and pulled her to her feet. The knight spoke as though trying to calm her, but the woman appeared to be wanting to prevent Hawker from entering his own house. Rapidly, Hawker's joy seemed to wither into annoyance and his tone became more demanding.

While she implored and hauled on his arm, Hawker turned to the others. 'Amalia has been a servant to me, but she is insisting we wait until the house is made proper for my arrival.' Hawker swore and turned, prying off her grip. 'She seems to have lost her wits. But we are going up, now.' The woman wailed and then shoved her apron into her mouth.

Hawker led the way up to the house with de Grood at his back. Beconsall shrugged at Ellingham and then followed. It all seemed a very odd way to welcome a returning master of the house. Reaching the first floor, they entered a wide door into the high-ceilinged hall. And all drew up short at the sight that greeted them. Four young women, half-naked, stood opposite, bowing and smiling. A man came into the room from an adjoining archway, lacing the points of his doublet, his boots tucked under one arm. When he saw the knights, his eyes widened. He clearly wasn't sure who the men were, but they were armed and he assumed the worst. He froze, weaponless and in his stockinged feet. His boots flopped to the floor, slipping off his arm.

Dieudonné whistled softly. 'This is hospitality most pleasing, Giles.'

Beconsall started to laugh, but Hawker's face blotched red. 'Luca!' he bellowed. Hawker then turned to de Grood and pointed to the frightened man quaking on the opposite side of the room. De Grood strode forward, grabbed the poor Venetian by the back of his neck and propelled him out and down to the courtyard, tossing the man's boots after him.

Beconsall turned to Hawker and pleaded teasingly. 'Sir John, at least let the lovely women stay for a bit!'

Amalia caught up to them, whimpering miserably and trying to explain herself. Hawker cursed, walked over to one of the women and took a wine goblet from her hand before sniffing and taking a drink. 'A brothel. Sweet Jesus, my steward has turned my house into a brothel.' The ladies clustered together, frightened and pulling close their gauzy chemises. 'Get them out of here!' Hawker bellowed.

Ellingham wondered whether Hawker realised he was speaking in English as he waved his arm about. Amalia herded the women into one of the other rooms, directing her embarrassment and frustration through shouts and curses at them. 'And find me Luca Contanto!' Hawker shouted after her. Ellingham thought he caught something in Hawker's look. Not just anger, but a hint of something more. Was it his own embarrassment, or, perhaps, even hurt?

Dieudonné had ducked into one of the other doorways off the large hall. He came back, a sly smile on his face. 'There is a large bathtub in this room – and it has several people in it.' Hawker let out a groan and pushed past the Frenchman. A mix of English cursing and barked Venetian floated back out into the hall.

'Good folk and God-fearing people,' said Beconsall, nodding.

–

They gathered at table on the first floor of Sir John's *casa* after Amalia and Jacob had managed to evict the unwanted guests. Ellingham had taken the opportunity to explore all the floors. His eye told him that the place had seen little life for a long while – except for its time as a bawdy house, that is. The smaller rooms at the top were sparse, and in two bedchambers there were only beds and no mattresses, just the ropes tied to the frame. The green and ochre walls peeled and bloomed like drooping cowslips. Neglect had set in deeply, he thought; such a waste of a fine house.

The lower rooms were not quite so bad, though water had run down between the walls, melting the frescoes in two of the chambers. And sadly, the great wooden bathtub, a leaky and half-rotten affair, had stained and cracked the tiled floors. These now bounced precariously when one walked over them. Far more uncomfortable, though, thought Ellingham, was having to watch the supplication now ongoing where they sat.

A man stood across from them just over the threshold into the dining chamber. Luca Contanto was apparently responsible for the safekeeping of the house. He kept wringing his red-velvet bonnet in his hands while studying the yellow and green clay tiles at his feet. He was well into his best years, as they say, hair still brown with flowing curls and not a hint of grey. Obviously well fed and equally well attired, thought Ellingham, the poor man sadly looked as if he were like to collapse in a quaking heap any moment as he withered under the glare of Hawker.

The knight had just delivered a tongue-lashing to the man who had taken it all in silence, barely even whispering a defence. Behind him and off to one side, a woman stood, watching. This was Luca Contanto's wife, watching Hawker as one might observe a lawyer making pronouncement upon a stranger. She was lean as a greyhound but possessed of fine delicate features, the lines of age beginning to advance into her forehead and beside her sweetly curved mouth, but leaving the porcelain cheekbones untouched. She was dressed as finely as her husband, her slight frame covered by an emerald velvet gown, her bosom pushed up by the high cinched waistline, revealing hints of a fine silk chemise. A cambric skullcap topped a beautifully braided and coifed head of dark blonde hair.

Hawker shook his head and made a grumbling noise in his throat while his thoughts coalesced. 'I've told this jackanapes that he has betrayed the trust I put in him,' he said to his companions.

For her part, Amalia was scurrying as fast as she could to bring dried meats, pies, bread, hard cheese, fat green olives soaked in vinegar, and wine for them all.

'I cannot blame his wife,' Hawker went on, reaching for the cheese. 'As a wife is duty-bound to obey a husband it is he who bears the fault. And he says it was *her* idea to make money since they had no belief I would ever return. Does he expect me to believe that? Coward. And why a brothel?' Hawker waved a finger at Contanto. 'I can only put it down to greed. And, perhaps, because he enjoys the personal benefits of having such an establishment. He's a silk weaver, a member of one of the wealthiest guilds in Venice. I left him supplied with ample funds and a contract to guard my house until I should return. *Guard it*, not turn it into a bawd's paradise.'

'Can't blame them for being enterprising,' said Beconsall, chewing on his gammon and leek pie. 'Brothel keepers are more honest than bankers, in my experience. Seems to me the fellow just saw an opportunity to make use of what was going to waste.'

'Ill-judged, Sir Roger,' growled Hawker. 'Very ill-judged. How would it look for me to appear before the doge's council with tales floating about that I am now a pimp?'

Beconsall reached for the wine jug and stuck out his lower lip. 'How would it look? That you decided maybe the house was too big for just one man, perhaps?'

Hawker glared back. 'As I am the only one among us who knows this city I would be more circumspect in my japes, if I were you.'

Beconsall smiled and saluted with his goblet.

At the other end of the table, Dieudonné whispered into Ellingham's ear. 'Fear not, Giles, I will find us a proper bathhouse in this city, even if this one is now closed to us.' Ellingham frowned at him. Hawker was about to sentence his caretakers and the consequences of this sad homecoming were yet to be known. He worried that Hawker's retribution might yield them more trouble in the long run than letting sleeping dogs lie.

Contanto bowed low and began addressing Hawker in a creaking voice so tight that if he was a rebec his strings would have snapped. He then beckoned to his wife who dutifully approached, bearing a large leather sack, which she plumped down on the table in front of Hawker. It jangled loudly as it hit the table top. She stood back, hands folded in front, and stared at the knight. Contanto gestured towards the sack and spoke again.

Hawker's eyes grew large. 'He tells me this is the proceeds, which by right are mine. Six months' worth of coin.'

'See,' said Beconsall, wagging a finger, 'looks like you *are* a man of business after all. Now you can afford to treat us like proper guests. Perhaps a few feather mattresses and pillows to start with. Boy Jack needs some new clothes. Replenish the cellar with more wine.'

Hawker pulled back the edges of the sack and poked in a finger. 'This does not right the wrong.' He looked up and addressed Contanto in English, then rapidly repeated his words in Venetian. 'You have brought shame upon me by appropriating my house without my permission. You were compensated well for being its caretaker. You have other houses you oversee, other interests. But you wanted more.' His eyes drifted to Chiara, the wife. 'And you have brought shame upon this lady by making her your accomplice in vice and then blaming her for the scheme to lessen the blow on you.'

'*Don Falco, per favore!*' Contanto bowed again, a bit lower this time. But it was no use. Hawker's reply was as hard and cold as ice. Contanto's eyes shut for a moment and then he bowed and backed away and out of the room, a quick jerking movement of his hand to signal his lady to follow.

'What did you tell him?' asked Ellingham.

'I dismissed him from my service and have demanded the keys. I told him I have yet to decide whether to bring the courts in for malfeasance and breach of duty. She, I said, may continue in my service. But if I ever see that coward of a husband of hers again I shall throw him down the well out front. She's a good woman and deserves better than that fool.' Hawker's eyes met Jacob's for but an instant. The Fleming arched a brow.

'You are just, my lord,' remarked Beconsall, his voice laced with sarcasm.

Ellingham set down his wine. 'Well, Sir John, you have brought us all here as you said you would,' he said. 'And many was the time I thought we would not live to see another sunrise. For that, I raise my cup to you.' He lifted the goblet again and gestured to the older knight. Beconsall grunted assent and raised his as well. Dieudonné said nothing but tipped his goblet slightly towards Hawker. Young Jack looked to de Grood and then they both too, awkwardly, joined in the toast. 'But... now that we have arrived, my lord,' continued Ellingham, 'I would hear your plans for our little company. Or, if it is to end here, that we are to go our separate ways.'

Hawker put down his goblet and nodded. 'You are well within your right to ask. Though, I must confess, there is little more to tell you until I meet with the doge. After that is done, then we will know whether Fortuna smiles upon us.'

'And that could mean a commission to raise men under your command in the service of the Republic?'

'It could.'

'And where do the rest of us fit into that?' asked Ellingham. 'Under *your* command? Sir Roger too?'

Beconsall held out an outstretched palm like a priest about to offer benediction. 'I have said neither yea nor nay to anything, my lad. I will listen to whatever offer Sir John may make upon the day. I am here now if only to preserve my head from an axe, but I withhold my decision on where my feet will take me next.'

Hawker nodded. 'Understandable, Sir Roger. I would ask no more of any of you. But my intention is to raise an army – not just a company. And an army needs more than one captain to command it.' Beconsall and Ellingham exchanged glances. 'With the blessing of the Council, what money of mine I can call upon here, and of course what the Republic will pay, I would put into the field a goodly force. Perhaps one thousand. All under the lion banner of Saint Mark. What say you to that?'

There was silence. Ellingham felt uncertain and Beconsall rubbed at his chin whiskers, eyebrows raised. 'And, my lord de Besancon...' said Hawker, 'would you not consider raising a company of crossbowmen to serve in such an army? That is, of course, if you owe no further commitment to your liege lord.'

The Frenchman did not bat an eyelid. 'Sir John, I was paid to fight Henry Tudor. In England. That is over. I was mercenary. The contract is finished.'

Hawker nodded at this. 'Yes, you have told me that.'

Dieudonné sat back, raised his chin, and switched to French. 'But... I could see throwing in my lot with you here, in Venice. If you can obtain the commission that you seek and if you would have me.'

Jack reached across him to pull the platter of roasted pigeon over and de Grood grabbed his wrist. 'Ask, boy. *Ask.*'

'And this council of the doge,' said Ellingham, leaning forward, 'what power do they wield?'

. Hawker smiled. 'You will not find a place ruled as this if you searched for a thousand years. Venice is the domain of a few wealthy families. They share rule of this place by ancient agreement and choose a doge from amongst themselves when one dies. There is a senate – but that is controlled by the Council of Ten. They control all. And they see all – day and night. There is no king, for commerce is king.'

Ellingham muttered an oath. 'And you would raise a force of one thousand men. Seems we are but poor seed corn for such a crop, Sir John.'

Hawker laughed. 'I have raised men before, and the Council of Ten remember this. We stand a better chance than you might think.'

'And who are we to fight?' asked Ellingham, still doubtful of the enterprise.

'Venice has many enemies, so no fear of lack of work,' replied Hawker. 'The Austrians, Florence, even the Pope. Maybe the French next. All on our doorstep!'

Ellingham looked to the others and watched as Beconsall's lower lip curled downwards in contemplation. 'Well, let us see what tomorrow brings.'

—

That evening, Hawker lay in his bed, the candle on the stand next to it guttering in the draught that ran through the high-ceilinged chamber. Already the night grew chill in October's advancing days. And as he stared at the canopy over his head, his mind was filled with the thought of the woman. The memories of her had driven him back to Venice every bit as much as the jewel and the promise of renewed fortunes. But he worried. Worried that any approach to her would be spurned should he dare to speak. Four years was an age. Who could know her heart now? And he was older, more ragged.

He pushed these thoughts away by forcing himself to think upon the meal with his comrades and the justice he had tried to dispense. And of his plans for them all. But he had not revealed everything to them. And what he had revealed he had exaggerated. They probably knew that.

In truth, nobody knew how the doge and his council would receive him. He had handed back his command to the Council in order to return to England and serve Richard. Venetians never cared much for divided loyalties. But, even so, he was returning with something. A Tear of Byzantium. That had to be worth a new command and more besides. There was one problem he had not yet solved, though. Convention dictated that the doge could never meet any foreigner alone, only within council. So the question was: who other than the doge knew about the Tears of Byzantium? It would have to be the Capi, the three leaders of the Council of Ten. He had known a few in the past but, as they changed so quickly, it was like second-guessing a ball-and-cup trickster in a village market. Who of the ten *signori* could he trust?

A shadow moved across the doorway of the bedchamber for a fleeting instant. He slowly reached for the stiletto tucked under his pillow. A figure had entered the room, and it slowly edged its way, cautiously, towards the bed. He pulled himself up on his elbows and saw that it was a woman, her long face golden in the glow of the candle she carried. Her hair, tawny blonde with just a few strands of grey, was down, spilling over her shoulders. She placed the candle on the little table next to his burning taper. Saying not a word, she shrugged off her sleeveless russet robe and stood in her chemise, her face betraying nothing. Hawker, almost believing a vision or a ghost had appeared, froze, half propped on an elbow as he stared. Then, he smiled. He slid the dagger back under the pillow. Slowly, he pulled away the coverlet, and Chiara Contanto climbed in beside him.

She wrapped herself around him as he sank back onto the pillows, her head upon his naked chest. They lay there for a moment, in silence. Chiara reached up and combed her hair away from her ear.

'You have grown a little rounder, Giovanni.'

Hawker cracked another smile in the gloom. 'And you have grown bony.'

'We have both changed… a little.'

Hawker wrapped his arms around her tighter. 'It was all I could do not to jump up as you entered the chamber this afternoon. To see you alive and well, Chiara, my heart nearly burst.'

'Did I not act the part well? I could have flown into your arms there and then, husband or no. And your Fleming did not give the game away either.'

Hawker gently turned until she was on her back, nestled into the crook of his arm. He stroked her cheek. 'I didn't know what to expect, what you would think of me after all these years. Whether you would forgive me for leaving… leaving as I did.'

Her eyes were large and glistening in the glow of the two candles. 'You returned to your king's call, as was right. I cried for you, yes. But I never hated you for leaving Venice. Or leaving me. It was God's will. Maybe it was God punishing me for our sin.'

He gently kissed her upon the lips and she returned this with a passion infused by long anticipation.

'And now,' she said, her voice a whisper, 'we sin again. But my heart is glad of it.'

He straightened a stray tress that had fallen across her face. 'I am back, Chiara. To start again.'

18

Ellingham stood on the rooftop loggia of Hawker's *casa* and gazed out upon his new world. The morning haze was lifting from the city, streaks of pinkish cloud sitting low in the sky and cutting across the unending horizon of brick chimneys. Venice had been awake since before dawn, its narrow alleys and canals filling with merchants, costers, beggars, artisans and foreign visitors lost in the maze of stone. Strange voices floated up to him, incomprehensible, the people invisible. Shouts, laughter, the repeated calls of some hawker or waterman. The smell of the canals was earthy, almost rank. Nevertheless, he was here.

Despite his survival in both battle and skirmish, his bravado was wearing thin, the mask ever threatening to drop from his face, showing his companions that he was not the cocksure knight they thought he was. He was no better than a mummer. And one day they would all find out. If his stepfather had not driven him – prodded him – into seeking advancement as a man-at-arms, he might have ended up with the Church. At least there he could have had security and good food and drink without the risk of a bloody death. And even now, after the disaster at Leicestershire and the death of his true father, the flight from the sheriffs' grasp and the journey south, he still was unsure of his destiny. Unsure because none of it had been his choice. And the thought that King Richard had been his father clawed at the back of his mind most of all. Half of him wanted to believe it, the other half did not.

Now, the expectation was for him to become a captain of mercenaries in the service of a man he hardly knew in a country about which he hardly cared. He had toyed with the thought of the Hospitallers on Rhodes, those knights of worth who foreswore wealth and privilege. Was that so reckless a plan? He *had* proved he could swing a sword. And he was halfway to Rhodes already by his reckoning, a ship notwithstanding. But that path was also the path of celibacy. He sank further into dark melancholy, disheartened by the swaying pendulum of choices.

Dieudonné wandered up, running his hand along the parapet. The Frenchman let out a deep sigh, joining him in drinking in the view of rooftops under a sky now as blue as a starling's egg.

'What shall today bring us then, Giles? Better fortune, perhaps?'

'It is known only to God,' Ellingham mumbled in French. Dieudonné nodded thoughtfully at the reply and there was silence between them. Ellingham then plucked up his courage a little. 'You don't much like taking prisoners, do you? I mean… those Swiss on the road. The two who pleaded with you on their knees.'

Dieudonné pulled back slightly, seeming somewhat surprised by the question. A confused, awkward sort of smile spread across his lips. 'My dear friend, what an odd thing to remark upon. What else were we to do?'

'They had surrendered to you, asking for Christian mercy.'

'They were of no use to me, to us. Let them live so that they could escape and come upon us again with more of their friends once it grew dark? Not in my interest. They had made their choice. I made mine.'

'I see,' said Ellingham quietly. 'Like the innkeeper at Lynn.'

Dieudonné gave an emphatic nod. 'Just so. Exactly so. A liability must be dealt with, no?'

There was again silence between them as they watched sparrows bickering over bread crusts, the birds darting back and forth between the loggia and the one visible tree.

'He bedded the silk weaver's wife last night.' Dieudonné let the remark out half a moment after commenting on the rapaciousness of sparrows. 'Nice to have a bed-warmer after days on the road. But did he let those whores stay for our benefit? He did not.'

Ellingham turned to the Frenchman. 'Madame Contanto? He did? Well, perhaps she bedded him... out of gratitude for keeping her situation.'

'You are generous when it comes to the old man, I think, dear Giles. But it remains that he looks after himself first.'

'You deny a man the joys of love merely because he is old?'

Dieudonné chuckled. 'His grey hairs have nothing to do with it. But a captain needs to be thinking about his men and his ambitions – not behaving like some mooncalf of a boy, besotted by a woman.'

Ellingham shook his head, unable to see the wrongness of it. 'No, he's a man with a man's needs. Hawker has treated me as a friend since we fled the field all those weeks ago. I see no selfishness in his actions. We've looked out for each other, now that we are outlaws. And he has shared his intentions for us all... if we choose to follow.'

A smile flickered on Dieudonné's lips but his voice dropped lower. 'It never occurred to you that he might be using you? Keeping you close until he decides to bargain you away for his precious contract with the Venetians? There is more to the man than you know.'

'I cannot believe that,' said Ellingham, stepping back away from the railing. 'He swore loyalty to my father and nothing he's done since has given cause for doubt. What makes you so sure?'

Dieudonné tilted his head and made as if he was surveying the horizon, searching. 'The jewel, for one thing.'

Ellingham said nothing.

'Yes,' continued the Frenchman, 'I know about it. He plans to bargain it away for his own gain. Who's to say he won't bargain you away, too? Any oath sworn to a king dies along with that king. Hawker has fought for anyone who would pay the price. He doesn't know you from Adam.'

'Hawker says the jewel is more trouble than it's worth. Bad luck. It must be returned.' Ellingham's voice betrayed his doubt.

Dieudonné grasped Ellingham's wrist, not too firmly, but enough to get his attention. 'The only thing that is cursed is

Hawker. His luck ran out long ago. Giles, the jewel is rightfully *yours*. It could buy you half an army if you bargain it wisely. Why are we here? We could have stayed in Flanders. You could have revealed yourself to your aunt at the palace.'

Ellingham shook his head. 'I am Giles Ellingham. Or Robin of Middleham. I have no right.'

'You are the son of Richard Plantagenet! Now is the time to raise an army while there is yet time, before Henry Tudor secures his crown. If not for you then, well, in the name of your cousins. But it may come down to you in the end. To save the throne for your line.'

'What would you have me do?'

Dieudonné stood toe to toe with the youth and gripped him by his shoulders. 'You and I. We take ship from here back to Flanders, with the jewel. It is your proof to Margaret of York that you are of the blood. I bet she asked Hawker about it, didn't she?'

Ellingham was lost for words, the mere suggestion over-whelmed him. But he did not move away.

'I can find us a ship, allies. Do not blindly throw away the chance that God has given you.'

'Steal the jewel away?' stuttered the youth. 'Leave the others?'

'It is not his to keep, or trade. It is *your* birthright. And this city is not our city. It is Hawker's past, not your future.' Dieudonné looked into Ellingham's sea-grey eyes and cupped his cheek like a chiding lover. 'Giles, we can do this thing. Together. And others will join us.'

Ellingham gently pulled away. 'You talk of betrayal. That is not me.'

'I talk of what is *yours*. And what is your duty to your house.' His voice grew contemplative. 'I have suffered loss and defeat, but I grew the stronger for it.'

'What of your duty to *your* house? Why do you not serve your father or his lord?'

Dieudonné's eyes went dead. 'That is a story that must wait for another day. Tell me, what do you know of this Tear of

Byzantium? Why would such a thing be given back? And where are the other stones?'

Ellingham looked out over the city, wondering himself about the strange jewel. 'Hawker says he doesn't know. It was an original condition of the gift: it cannot be sold or given away, it must return here. Tales of ill luck that had befallen those other rulers who disposed of theirs wrongly – or held on too long.'

Dieudonné snorted with derision. 'So it passes around like a child's game. No, there must be something more to it.'

'Talk no more of this now, Gaston.' He had never seriously thought about his place in the royal firmament, or about the jewel. He was merely a royal bastard, and in his gut he still felt that he wanted nothing to do with any crown, or those who danced around whoever happened to be wearing it. It was poison, like the damned jewel that dictated Hawker's every move.

Dieudonné nodded, the cloud passing. 'You are right, my friend. Let us see what today brings for Hawker at the palace.' He wagged his finger. 'But I am sure I will be proved the wiser.'

–

Two storeys below, in Hawker's bedchamber, the knight and his squire huddled together on hands and knees upon the tiled floor near the window, its shutters wide to the morning light. Hawker's gnarled fingers pulled up a square tile that was already loose. 'See here, boy,' he whispered. 'It is three tiles from the wall, dead centre in the window frame, a cross contained in a circle.' His finger traced along the design on the vermillion glazed tile he now held. 'And only you and I shall know. Give it to me.'

Jack held out the dark ruby stone, its golden armature glinting in the daylight. Hawker took it and placed it into the cavity revealed in the floor. He then gently replaced the tile, which dropped back into place. Not snugly, but just as loose – and anonymous – as the others that rattled all around it. The concealment was complete, and his eyes quickly shot to the door to make sure no one had seen. Although he had no reason to believe the

Council would not accede to his demands, once he mentioned the Tear of Byzantium to them, they could just as easily search him and the party. It had to be hidden. And he alone could not be the sole possessor of its location. It was just a precaution, a measure of prudence.

'You did well, Jack, keeping it safe all this way. Though it be a small thing it is still a heavy burden. I'm proud of you.'

Jack smiled. 'And now will you teach me how to fight? Sir Roger gave me a lesson but only made fun of me for my efforts. Said I looked like a country clod swatting at a wasp.'

'Pay him no heed, I will teach you now. It is time you learn how to defend yourself and your comrades. We begin later today. And I won't be a forgiving teacher, my lad.'

Jack nodded, confidence renewed. 'I am ready. And I won't fail you, Sir John.'

Hawker winked and leaned back on his haunches. 'You have not failed me yet. And remember, you have already defended us in combat. Now we go down and fetch the others. It's time to go to San Marco and I need eyes all around me. To watch the watchers.' Hawker grinned and put a finger aside of his nose.

They found Beconsall and Jacob in the main hall and were soon joined by Ellingham and Dieudonné, Ellingham doing his best to conceal his guilt over the conversation on the roof. There was an air of expectancy among them, for this would be their first visit to the doge's palace. 'Buckle on your daggers but leave your swords here,' said Hawker. 'They would be taken off you when you enter anyway.'

Beconsall groaned loudly. 'In truth? I don't fancy being armed less than the fellows are where we're going.'

'The palace guard won't bite unless you bite first,' said Hawker. 'Trust me.'

Amalia, shuffled into the chamber, tugging at her crisp white linen kerchief while balancing in the crook of her arm something wrapped in scarlet cloth. Her broad face bore a wide, teasing grin. When Hawker saw the bundle his face brightened, head shaking in disbelief. 'Ah, Amalia, you still have it!'

She pulled back a fold of the fabric, revealing an ornate dagger with an ivory handle. '*Ser Giovanni, vostro cinquedea.*'

Hawker took it from her, hefted it and drew it from its scabbard. 'I had nearly forgotten it,' he crooned, fingering the wide blade, nearly the width of his hand at the hilt and finely etched.

'An unusual weapon,' said Beconsall. 'Though it seems it can't decide whether it be sword or dagger.'

Hawker waved it towards him. 'You have seen what passes for a street in this city. Not enough room to swing a cat never mind wield a longsword. The *cinquedea* is the answer to that problem. You might even find it suits you.'

'I shall keep hold of my little beauty for the time being,' replied Beconsall, tapping the hilt of the roundel knife at his belt. Hawker smiled, knowing that even the *cinquedea* would never replace his own *stiletto*, his final means of self-defence.

'It's a fine blade, Sir John,' said Ellingham impatiently. 'But I pray it's only for show and that we won't have to see it drawn in anger. Are you sure they will receive you at the palace after so long an absence? I might have worried that I'd been long forgotten.'

Hawker sheathed the *cinquedea* with a flourish. 'They will not have forgotten *me*. This day – this *good* day, my lords – we begin our new venture.'

19

Hawker led the way across the streets of San Polo and towards the Rialto and the Grand Canal. The alleys and *campi* channelled the streaming populace, all seemingly destined for the market stalls that spread out from the arched wooden bridge that spanned the canal. Along one street, a row of sombre-clad gentles in skull caps sat at their benches with their tabulating beads, slates and ledger books: bankers. Over the bridge and further east they passed through streets where overhead they were observed by women high- and low-born. Hawker made eye contact with one for a moment too long. She smiled, beckoning with a gloved hand. A movement not missed by the giant.

Beconsall chuckled. 'You have been here before, my lord, haven't you? Looks like they *do* remember you.'

Hawker gave him a snort of annoyance and continued the march through the Rialto while Jack gawped, de Grood's guiding hand upon his shoulder.

At length, they came upon the great beating heart of Venice, the square of Saint Mark. The magnificence of it all took the breath from even jaded Dieudonné. An expanse of huge slate slabs lay before him, down to the sea, a wide *piazza*. A stone triumvirate of imposing scale watched over all: the great basilica, a massive bell tower opposite – surely taller than Notre Dame de Paris – and then the sprawling palace of the doge. Four giant bronze horses looked down upon him from the portico of the cathedral and, above the tympanum, the winged lion of Saint Mark stood triumphant, one paw upon the open book of the gospel, a celestial field of blue and gold at its back. When they reached the centre of the piazza, their footfalls grew slower until all, save Hawker and de Grood out in front, had halted in wonder.

'Though I have not been there,' said Beconsall to no one in particular, 'it has the air of the East from tales. A new Byzantium.'

Hawker, realising the others had stopped to stare, smiled to himself and retraced his steps to his comrades. 'Aye, it is a masterful sight, but we must not tarry. Jack, boy, close your mouth. You look like a halfwit.'

'Who is that man hanging in a cage over there?' asked the lad. 'There, on the bell tower.'

The others saw it too. A wrought-iron cage that held a man instead of a bird, suspended about twelve feet above the paving.

'That is a prisoner of the Republic,' said Hawker. 'God knows what he is guilty of, but he will not leave the cage alive.'

'You mean he is to die there?' said Jack, sounding both intrigued and appalled. He walked closer. Hawker followed, placing a hand on the boy's shoulder.

'He is to be given no sustenance by anyone, no water either. That is his fate.'

Jack studied the bundle of rags that moved every so often. An emaciated arm hung from between the bars. 'Cruel enough to starve a man to death deep in a dungeon. But I think this is worse.'

Hawker gave the lad an interested smile. 'How so?'

A group of Venetian apprentices were clustered near the cage, pointing and laughing. A brief stop on the way to the workshops of the Arsenale, the cage and its occupant was entertainment and they were each placing bets on the day of his demise.

Jack looked up at Hawker. 'It's not just an execution, Sir John. It is to make mock. To take his honour from him.'

Hawker nodded, surprised at the boy's insight. 'I suppose you're right about that. But it is the same result as rope or axe, just a little slower. They give much thought to punishments in this city. And there are worse, I can tell you.'

They turned and walked to the great double doors of the palace, which were open and guarded by two tall halberdiers in white and red striped hose, barbute-style helms obscuring their faces. Beconsall's eyes ran along the colonnade of the palace, its soaring windows and strange dog-toothed crenellations. He smiled. 'Looks like they couldn't decide what to build so they built it all... Moorish, Byzantine, bit of French... the lot. I suppose it does what it is intended to do: overawe.'

'I shall tell the doge you approve,' said Hawker. 'In the meantime, I would ask you all to stay here while I seek an audience. Jacob, you will come with me.'

Ellingham nodded but caught Dieudonné giving him a knowing look. Beconsall shrugged his shoulders and continued to study the pink and white marble behemoth that loomed over them.

The courtyard of the doge's palace was far from empty. On the contrary, it was seething with diplomats, petitioners, councillors and guardsmen. To Hawker, it was familiar ground that had hardly changed since his last visit. He strode to the bottom of the great marble staircase that led up to the loggia and rooms of state. There, at a bench and table, sat the gatekeepers who controlled who could rise and who would languish below. Putting down a quill as he approached, the scribe made no attempt to hide his study of the strangers before him. Their boots and bearing would announce them to be soldiers – foreign ones.

'Your business with the State?' the man demanded in his slurred Venetian. 'Your name?'

'I am Sir Giovanni Falco, a former captain of the republic. I seek an audience with the Council that I may be granted to speak to His Serene Highness, Giovanni Moncenigo.'

The scribe looked at his companion and then turned to Hawker, a condescending smile on his face. 'You have been away a long time, I think. Giovanni Moncenigo is dead. The new doge is his Serene Highness Marco Barbarigo.'

Hawker could not conceal his surprise but refused to be daunted. He did not know the Barbarigo family, nor did he know if they knew of the Tears of Byzantium. He stuttered a moment,

first to find the words and then the Venetian for them. 'Then...
I would have you inform the Council that I have returned from
England with an affair of state for the ears of the new doge.'

The scribes whispered briefly between them and then the
other turned back. 'Are you sure you are in the correct place, my
lord? *Allora*... perhaps you should seek out the English ambassador with your... news.'

A voice came down from the great stair. 'I will speak with the
gentleman!'

Hawker looked up to see a man in black velvet robes
descending. 'Ser Giovanni is known to us, if by deeds only. Don
Falco. *Il grande Falco!*'

Hawker wracked his mind as the man approached, trying to
place the face somewhere in his past, but he could not. They
exchanged bows.

'I am Paolo Federini, of the Council of Ten. Please, if you will,
follow me up.' Federini looked over to de Grood. 'Your man must
remain here.'

De Grood pulled himself up straight. 'My lord?'

Hawker nodded and spoke quietly in Flemish. 'Wait here.'

The two climbed the broad marble steps that led to the first
floor, a loggia of great ornate arches. They walked along this,
taking in the commanding view it gave of the courtyard and its
denizens below.

'Your arrival was relayed to us yesterday evening in council,'
said Federini. The man noted Hawker's sudden slowing of pace.
'Why are you so surprised, Ser Giovanni? Did you think we had
grown lazy since last you were in Venice?'

Perhaps he *had* forgotten about the eyes and ears of the
Council, the wide circle of informants that kept the Council
and the doge aware of every new face that entered the Serene
Republic. Not that his comrades were inconspicuous, even in
England. But Federini held all the advantage, as Hawker did
not know who he was, to what faction he owed his loyalties or
whether the man knew what he was bringing with him.

'I have never doubted the intelligence gathering of the Council, nor forgotten it. I assumed you would know I had returned – and why.'

Instead of turning into the red and gold rooms of the palace revealed to them as they walked, Federini stopped and put his hands on the thick marble railing while he glanced down at those below in the courtyard. 'Why you have returned? Well, of that I have no doubt you will tell me.'

Hawker joined him and they nearly rubbed shoulders, neither looking at the other. 'First, I come to offer my sword once again to the Republic. I would seek a *contratto* that I may raise a company for you. The others of my party are my captains.'

'I believe there are still some on the Council who remember your past service in Dalmatia. They might look favourably upon such a request. And what is your second reason?'

This, thought Hawker, is where he must tread warily. 'I bear a message from King Richard. A message given to me by the king himself and destined for the doge – in person.'

Only now did Federini turn and face him, a sly smile on his lips. He was a little older than Hawker, silver hair showing from underneath his black felt cap, a bag of loose skin under the chin barely concealed by the high-necked velvet robe and gathered white collar. 'Richard? I think you are too late to be his messenger. I have heard you now have a new king. Just as we have a new doge. And I am sure you have not forgotten that no foreigner may meet alone with the person of the doge. That is very clear.'

'The message I bear has import far beyond the death of my king. Or your doge, for that matter.'

Federini smiled broadly. 'Indeed? Ser Giovanni, one might think you have come back to Venice to flee the grasp of your new king. Or is it you are just yearning for your old life here?'

Hawker returned the smile. 'Such motives are not to be considered mutually exclusive, are they?'

'They are not. You are right, Ser Giovanni. It is just that I would not want to introduce you to a countryman of yours who might be of the wrong faction. That would be awkward. Or worse.'

'Awkward for some. But infinitely worse for others.'

'Would you be willing to deliver your message to the three Capi of the Council? That would be the best that could be arranged, I'm afraid.'

'If that is the closest I may get to his Serene Highness, then I gratefully accept.'

Federini grinned broadly. 'Excellent! Come here tomorrow. At midday. I will inform the secretaries to expect you. And you need not bring your retinue again. We already know you are a man of worth and importance. The Republic is glad to welcome back one who has been so loyal.'

As he descended the marble stair into the courtyard, Hawker caught sight of Jacob watching him, his face lit with anticipation. The grizzled man-at-arms looked like some hopeful suitor, thought Hawker, repressing a smile.

'Well?' said the Fleming as Hawker joined him.

'Tomorrow. An audience with the Three. Hopefully, from the little I told him, they will be more than curious by the morning.'

'Then there is hope yet, my lord. We can say our prayers tonight that you will have a contract tomorrow, *na*?'

Hawker nodded. 'God willing. But I must go up there alone.'

'Aye, well, you understand how this place works. There is nothing gained without risk. And you should know, you were being watched while you conversed. That lady… over there.'

De Grood's gaze directed Hawker a short distance across the courtyard to where merchants and senators milled. A raven-haired woman of some prominence stood amongst her bodyguards, dressed in dark-red brocade decorated with silver lace. She was staring at him intently.

'Those in the retinue are *stradiotti*, are they not?' remarked de Grood.

'They are.'

'Is she Dalmatian? Or further east, perhaps?'

To Hawker, it seemed that she had not even blinked once as she watched him. Her eyes, large and dark – almost too large for her face – were piercing. Though he thought her not unbeautiful, her intensity heightened her allure. Her neck was graceful and long, her dark tresses wound up tightly and bound by a silver caul. Whoever she was, she was protected. The Balkan *stradiot* mercenaries she employed were known and feared throughout the region just as much as they were sought after for their ferocity and skill at horse. And these here were as he had known them from previous times: brass-studded jacks, short tunics, baggy hose, tall wide-brimmed felt hats upon their heads, and at their belts curved swords like those of the Turk.

Hawker's first guess was she was the wife of an ambassador, perhaps a Dalmatian lord of Ragusa. But the elaborate necklace she wore, heavy as a bishop's collar, spoke more of the East than the Adriatic. 'She is not of Venice, at least that much I would swear to.'

The woman still stared as he spoke and, slightly annoyed, Hawker made a dramatic bow to her. She did not reciprocate the honour but instead turned away to address one of her guards. Hawker was intrigued by her forwardness but also slightly unsettled by it.

'You do seem to attract the interest of women, my lord,' said de Grood quietly. 'I'm not your confessor but I trust you enough to believe you know what you're doing. With the mistress Chiara, I mean. I hope I was discreet enough yesterday, Sir John. It's just that, well, to take up with her again so soon and all.' The Fleming moved his head from side to side, as if contemplating the outcomes. 'Throwing her husband out on his ear. I mean, we've barely settled back in.'

Hawker threw him a stern glance. 'You are not my confessor or my priest. You would do well to remember that you do me service. And that service does not include pricking my conscience like some prattling old woman.'

De Grood bowed his head, chastised. 'Aye, my lord. I did not intend to question your judgement.'

Outside the *porta della carta* and past the guard post, they spotted their rather modest Yorkist company, looking somewhat lost as Venetian life swirled around them. Dieudonné appeared slightly more light-hearted, apparently joking with a stony-faced Jack and pointing towards the poor unfortunate suspended in the cage.

Beconsall looked up and caught sight of them emerging. 'What ho! Tell me, Sir John, what cheer do you bring? A bag of gold from the doge?'

'It is what I had hoped… and expected,' said Hawker. 'A further audience on the morrow. It's enough that they remembered me.'

'Hope against hope,' mumbled Dieudonné, near enough in range of Ellingham's ear.

'Tomorrow?' said Beconsall, his eyes narrowing. 'And what then? What kind of fools turn down a gift like yours?'

'Things here have their own pace. You'll have to learn that. Meanwhile, I now have business in the Rialto and there you will find much to divert you,' said Hawker. 'Or else Jack can guide you back to San Polo and the house. The choice is yours.'

Jack lifted his head and gave a grin. 'I spotted waypoints on the way here,' he said, voice suddenly changing to a honk. He paused, embarrassed. 'I can find the house.'

'I'm sure you can, Jack Perry. But it's for my captains to decide what they want to do with their day. Later though, you and I will have a bit of practice in the yard.'

The streets leading north towards the Rialto and the Great Canal were one vast stream of humanity, from high-born to low. It was as if all were being drawn towards the heavy-beamed, arched wooden bridge like some giant lodestone. Beconsall looked up at the balconies above. Women with bared breasts beckoned, cajoling passers-by to enter their house. He grinned up at them and made note of the location. Jack was out in front, leading them all, Hawker and de Grood coming after. Behind them came the three new captains of Hawker's company, but

Dieudonné was lagging back, further and further, until he was alone bringing up the rear. He reached out as he passed a rack of golden glazed pastries and snatched one quickly.

Jack paused in his tracks and Hawker caught him up. 'Sir John, what's that man doing feeding the stone lion over there?' A short Venetian was standing up on his toes to reach a sculptured lion's mouth on the wall opposite. He was dropping a paper into it.

Hawker nodded. 'That is a *bocca di leone*. A mouth of the lion. It is so that any Venetian may inform the Council of the wrongdoing of a citizen.' He prodded at Jack, giving him a wicked smile. 'And that includes *you*, my boy!'

'Every man is watched?' asked Jack, somehow not quite believing that such things were done.

'By every other man,' replied the knight.

Jack's eyes widened. 'Then who does anyone trust with a secret?'

Hawker smiled and gave him a small nod. 'We trust no one, Jack Perry. No one but ourselves.' He turned to his man-at-arms at his other side. 'After I meet my banker I will return to the *casa*. We need to make some plans for what lies ahead.'

De Grood frowned, pushing a street pedlar out of his way, sending the man tripping over his wooden tray. 'So you are expecting trouble from the palace?'

'From the palace? No, I am certain that will go well. We must talk of raising men, which means finding them. We must get the word out once I have my *contratto* from the Council.'

Jack, feeling part of the new army already, added his own thought. 'How do you find men that you can *trust* to serve you well? We're starting with only us.'

De Grood gave a little laugh. 'I forget you have never been in Venice before, boy. In this place one can buy nearly anything: food, clothes, weapons, women. And credit. But nowhere can I find a merchant under an awning selling trust.' He cast a glance behind to see where the others were. 'And it seems we have lost the Burgundian to the wonders of the Rialto.'

Hawker turned to see only Beconsall and Ellingham in animated conversation. Beconsall looked put out, disappointed. But Dieudonné was nowhere to be seen. 'You're right. But I have given them all licence. Besides, they can't get far. This is Venice.'

20

The Florentine picked his way carefully along the impossibly narrow street, avoiding the piles of dog shit and discarded food that dotted the cobbles. He had been in Venice more than half a year now and still disliked it with an intensity that had not diminished with time. Too many people and too many people speaking a dialect that sounded like the speech of a drunken man.

While he walked, his eyes scanned the coloured awnings of the street, taking in the painted signs of the moneylenders. One wooden board had painted upon it six claret-red balls arranged in a circle. The sign of the Medici family. His employer. The Medicis claimed these *palle* were cannonballs, proud symbol of a warlike pedigree. Carlo di Nofri knew better. They clearly symbolised coins, or even pills, since the Medici family had been nothing more than apothecaries and usurers when they had started out in Florence. Now they ruled that city with an iron fist. And they had sent him to Venice against his will. But at least they paid well.

The two clerks he had expected to see working on the bench out front were not there and he cursed under his breath. The door to the interior of the bank, normally open, was shut. He angrily grasped the iron ring, gave the door a shove and strode inside. Candles and rush-lights burned at the two long desks in the chamber, but his clerks were gone. The stench of excrement filled his nose and as he looked down between the ledger tables he saw one of the clerks sitting, hands clasped about his knees and eyes wide like some frightened rabbit. It was then that the door shut behind di Nofri, the bolt slamming into place.

'Little Cosimo here tells me you speak French,' said a man, stepping from behind. 'Do you speak French?'

Slowly, di Nofri backed away, seeing that the man was armed with a long dagger. 'And do you know how thievery is punished in this city?' he shot back, his voice calm. The man's wide eyes didn't look *quite* right to him. Protruding a little with a glassiness that bespoke a little of insanity.

'Ah, you *do* speak my tongue,' said Gaston Dieudonné, 'and rather well, I might say. But I am not here to take something. I've come to offer something.'

The Florentine looked over to his clerk on the floor. 'Cosimo?'

'He is unhurt,' said Dieudonné. 'But he has embarrassed himself, I'm afraid.' The Frenchman tapped his dagger against his palm. 'I will not trouble you for long, my lord. There is a new king upon the throne of England, as you no doubt have recently learned. My question for you, sir, is this: does Henry Tudor have intelligencers here in Venice? Maybe those that might handle his matters of money?'

'I imagine he does. But what has that to do with the House of Medici? Or more to the point, with me?'

Dieudonné smiled at the Florentine. 'Such beautiful French. You would not believe how my ears have been tortured of late by my English companions. I am here, my lord, because little of importance would not be picked up by the eyes and ears of the Medici in this city – yours.'

Di Nofri's voice grew quieter. 'What is it you want from me?'

'I want you to deliver a message to those that serve the new masters. I have intelligence of their enemies, their enemies here in Venice. My tale involves treasure and something more. Something of royal blood. They will know of what I speak. But it is important that they know – and you understand – time is of the essence.'

Di Nofri feigned indifference, running his hand over an open ledger, and retrieving a quill pen that had been dropped upon the table. 'And what do I gain from being your messenger?'

Dieudonné's lips pursed for a second. 'Well, I would imagine that the Tudors would pay you handsomely for passing on this intelligence to them. But, in addition –' and he raised a forefinger

'– I would not have to visit your apartments in the night. Where your wife is. You see, little Cosimo also speaks some French. Not nearly as well as you, but he does have much to say. Such as where you live.'

The Florentine was silent for a moment. Then he spoke, the words almost laboured. 'The new English king sends a delegation to the doge. They arrive in a week, maybe a little longer. But the Tudors have agents here already. They are known to me.'

'Excellent, Carlo. We shall help each other, then. You will arrange the meeting and I will tell you how to do it.'

Di Nofri nodded and lowered his gaze, cursing to himself. He still sorely wished that Lorenzo de' Medici had sent him to Paris instead of Venice.

Chiara Contanto stood on the threshold of the chamber, body tensed as if she was standing on a precipice. Although it was in her own house, a bright and airy room on the top floor, it was one she never felt comfortable entering: it was where her husband conducted his affairs of business. He was seated at a long table at its centre, the Persian-carpeted pearwood strewn with ledger books and pieces of silken cloth and trims of gold and silver. The morning light streamed through the high and narrow leaded windows on the east side, illuminating her husband in a soft golden glow.

She watched him as he flipped the pages of a book, intent on finding some entry or another, the ledgers, letters, books and ink stand arrayed like a table-top battlefield. When he noticed her presence, he slowly sat back in his carved folding chair, the leather seat creaking when he eased backwards.

'You did not grace our bedchamber last night. What is one to think?'

Chiara folded her hands in front of her. 'I did not wish to disturb you any more than you already were yesterday,' she said, her unease obvious despite her attempt at a tone of indifference.

'Nor did you sleep anywhere else in this house, according to the kitchen girl.'

'I stayed at the Englishman's *casa*. Someone had to prepare the place for their carousing and direct the servants. You may ask Amalia for she will swear to it.'

He swore under his breath, quill flicking onto the table. She had suspected he knew of her infidelity four years ago, but for several reasons had not pursued the truth. The biggest of all, no doubt, was that he had no desire to know for certain that he was a cuckold. That he wore the horns.

Chiara knew her advantage lay with heaping upon him the embarrassment of his own situation. 'Someone had to take the initiative. Or would you lose all that money the Englishman pays us to look after his pile of mouldy bricks? You have no one but yourself to blame, husband. It was your idea to tell Hawker that the brothel was my scheme. See what that cleverness has brought you.'

A veil came down across Luca Contanto's face. 'What a waspish creature you have become,' he said quietly, almost contemplatively. 'What did my brother once tell me? Marriage comes from love as vinegar comes from wine?'

She didn't flinch. 'I think there was precious little love to begin with... except your love for my dowry.' Her marriage was nine years old now, a frayed, brittle arrangement that stood only upon ceremony and served as an emollient for the silk weaver in entertaining his merchant guests. Her secret trysts with Hawker had rejuvenated her and even after he had hurriedly departed Venice, the memory of him kept her warm, hope still kindling in her heart. Now, against all chance, Hawker had returned to Venice – and to her. She knew it was wrong and that it was mortal sin she was indulging, but she did not regret her choice.

'You have never seen fit to give me children,' said Contanto, pushing back his chair and standing. 'Do I have to tie you to our bed that you may serve your purpose?'

She might be barren, she did not know. But for the past few years she had avoided his touch and syringed herself with vinegar to prevent conception when she could not escape his rough lovemaking. 'Perhaps God has seen fit not to give us children that they should grow up in this poisoned household. You never understood certain things. That a woman can be an adornment to her husband but that she should never be only that – merely a jewel to be shown off.' Her anger was building; frustration at her lot never far below the surface now came forth as small darts aimed at the man she once thought she had loved. She took a step forward, crossing the threshold. 'And how can you cast blame upon me for your fumbling attempts to sire children. With a prick like yours it is a miracle you can even find it when you need to.'

He covered the distance between them in an instant and she stood her ground, body tensing. As he seized her wrist, jerking it upwards, she barely flinched. 'Why must you make me give you correction? Your tongue does you no favours, Chiara.'

She smiled, the taunt silent.

The flick of his wrist was rapid and forceful, his hand striking her ear so hard that her head rang. Chiara felt her knees go weak and he seized her now by her upper arm, holding her up where she stood. As the sting subsided, she nearly blurted out her infidelity, wishing to throw it upon him with all the force her tongue could muster. But just as quickly she realised that doing this would end the only thing that now gave her joy of life, cutting the thread she clung to. She managed to muster a muttered curse at him, chin dropping.

'I shall be watching you, wife!' Contanto hissed. 'I will tolerate you running the household of the foreigners. But I will be watching. Do not think that you can play me.'

Chiara retreated into submission, but defiance burned inside her still. She would go on playing him until the circumstances changed or God intervened. She gently covered his hand with hers. 'I understand you, husband. Forgive my insolence.'

Contanto nodded, studying her for what seemed more than a moment. His hand released her and she steadied herself. 'Send up Massimo from the workshop. I have need of him.'

Chiara bowed and withdrew.

—

'No, boy,' said Hawker, drawing back and lowering his sword. 'You must press home your advantage and try a different blow when you see me block your weapon. Don't stop and retreat. I can *see* you thinking about your next attack.'

'I'm trying,' said Jack. 'But I'm not doing it fast enough.'

Hawker smiled. 'It must come without thinking. Your arm will know what to do, not your head. Comes with practice! Let's try again.'

They were out in the courtyard near the stone well. Every parried blow made the little *campo* ring with the echoing of steel upon steel. A few neighbours in the tenements that encircled them leaned on their windowsills. Others had already closed their shutters to the racket. But no one would dare complain to the *condottiere* in their midst, a man most had thought had long departed this Earth but who had now returned like a ghost.

Jack retreated a few steps, resting the blade upon his shoulder. Hawker could tell that the boy's mind was drifting. 'How am I supposed to be like you, Sir John?' He lifted the sword and hefted it, the acrid smell of metal and oil filling his nostrils. 'Not just fighting.'

Hawker smiled again, more broadly this time, and dropped his guard. 'What do you mean, boy? You're supposed to be *you*, not me.'

Jack's brow furrowed. 'How should I act if I am to be a knight one day? I know that I must learn to fight well. But what else is expected of me?' He gestured with the point of his sword. 'What do they expect of *you*?'

Hawker made a low growl in his throat and lowered his blade. 'I have not been asked that before. I suppose, if you press me... it is to be Godfearing. It is to defend one's liege lord when needed. To help defend the helpless. Be virtuous.' He paused, flummoxed a bit. 'And women. Protect and defend them and their honour.' He rubbed a gauntleted hand across his brow. 'God's wounds, boy! You're getting ahead of yourself. I don't even have a king any more that could give you spurs or chain!'

Jack grinned. 'I know. But I have to learn to behave like a knight — not just fight like one.'

He didn't have the heart to tell the lad that such things existed only in books. The tales of balladeers. 'Indeed you shall. But first you must learn the lessons of the sword. If you cannot fight well, you won't live long enough to practise being virtuous.'

'Or to protect womenfolk.'

'Just so.'

'Do you love Chiara? Will you marry her?'

Hawker's eyebrow shot up as he dropped his blade even lower. 'Boy, you are far from where you should be and seeing things you should not. And behaving like an unmannered pup who needs a thrashing.'

Jack's face fell. 'I'm your squire. I would not say a word to any. Even if they put me to the rack. Or inside that cage in the square.'

Hawker nodded gravely. 'Speak nothing of this, do you understand? Madama Chiara is under my charge. You do what she asks of you... She likes you, boy. Don't change that.'

Jack shrugged. 'But I don't understand anything when she speaks to me.'

Hawker beckoned with his hand for Jack to raise his blade again. 'Then that is what you should be doing. Learning Venetian when you are not practising at arms. Come on!'

Jack moved into a stance, raising his blade. He paused. 'And... when is it right for a knight to kill?'

Hawker lowered his sword again, a bit taken aback. 'Aye, well, in the service of one's liege lord – in battle. Unless your opponent yields and begs for quarter. To kill without conscience makes one no better than a robber knight, a common murderer. You understand me?'

Jack knitted his brows a second. 'But when you killed the bowman – at the Bull in Leicester – he had already given up, hadn't he?'

The candour embarrassed Hawker. He rubbed at his earlobe a moment thinking how to square that circle. And the memory brought forth more from his past. Other times when he had given no quarter to those who begged. He exhaled slowly. 'I'm not your best teacher of some things. Like virtue.' He raised his blade again. 'Take your guard.'

Jacob and Beconsall approached from the *casa*, and they both stopped to watch the lesson under way. 'He needs a helm, Sir John,' said Jacob, 'that you may thwack him in earnest. That's how one learns the quicker!'

Hawker turned, scowling. 'All in good time, Jacob, all in good time. The boy will get his armour soon enough.'

Beconsall stepped forward and picked up one of the spare blades lying near the well. 'Here, I'll show you a trick, young Jack! How to master your opponent's blade.'

Hawker shook his head in frustration but gestured for Beconsall to proceed. Jack raised up his blade in both hands and planted his feet squarely apart. The burly knight took his stance and raised his blade a little above level with his waist.

'If you thrust at me – straight out – I just use my wrists to make contact with your blade and use mine to walk it round yours, moving it out of line. And my blade ends up at your chest. Like so.' He nodded at Jack. 'Right then. Begin your thrust!'

Jack licked his lips once and then thrust out the sword straight towards Beconsall. The knight rotated his wrists and the blades made contact, both twisting around each other. But Jack's didn't stop with one revolution and continued for a second. At the same time he took a half-step forward with his lead foot. Beconsall's blade was now pointing towards the base of the well and Jack's poked the knight's belly.

Jacob roared with laughter and Hawker too broke into a wide grin, slapping Jack on the back.

'I'm sorry, Sir Roger,' said the boy, sheepishly. 'Sir John taught me that an hour ago.'

Beconsall's flash of anger disappeared and he too broke into a grin. He lowered his sword and tousled Jack's hair. 'Well played, boy. Well played. Maybe you should be giving lessons to us all!'

'He's a quick learner,' said Hawker proudly.

Beconsall nodded. 'He's a good lad. I watched him deal with those brigands in the mountains. He handled that spear well enough then.'

Dieudonné and Ellingham came out of the *casa* to join them. Hawker laid his sword into the crook of his arm and stood, feet spread apart.

'Sir John!' boomed Dieudonné in French. 'It is well past the time for us to pay a visit to the bathhouse and my comrade here has agreed to come along for the sport. Will you not join us?'

'I have other matters to attend to,' Hawker replied. 'But you may do as you please.'

'What about you, Sir Roger? It is not far, just around the corner in the Rialto.'

Beconsall nodded. 'Aye, I spied it and a most welcoming place it did seem. Leastways, from the ladies who adorned it, I would say.'

Hawker grimaced slightly. 'You'd better hope they change their water from time to time. Sir Giles, you're also game for this sport, then?'

The young knight nodded and Beconsall threw one enormous arm over his shoulders, shaking him. 'The lad must cleanse all his humours, top to bottom.'

'Then choose wisely,' said Hawker. 'The burning sickness does not announce itself beforehand. You should have a care. And wash your cocks. Otherwise you'll be scratching your privates for weeks.'

'The voice of experience?' replied Beconsall with a half-bow and an arched eyebrow.

Hawker smiled thinly. 'Only the advice of a friend.'

Jack tapped at Hawker's arm. 'My lord, over there.'

Eleven men had entered the square.

Hawker weighed their intent and then waved a hand towards Jacob, signalling him to attention. For one, they were not soldiers of the doge. They were dressed in motley array: leather jerkins, hose of many hues, some azure-blue tunics, one man sandaled and bare-legged while others were booted or shod. There were a few grey-haired fellows among them, but most of a younger sort. Artisans and tradesmen, Hawker reckoned, but it was very clear that they had come to see him. The other knights silently crowded behind Hawker and Jacob. Beconsall slyly threw his short cloak up and over his right shoulder, the better to wield his blade. Ellingham drew the hilt of his sword out by a thumb length.

'Maybe they've come to welcome you, Sir John,' said Jack.

'Would appear so. But to what end?'

The group stopped a few feet from the mercenaries, just opposite the stone well. One of the number looked back awkwardly towards his comrades and then faced forward, swiping his small round felt cap from off his head. A few of the others followed suit. The reluctant leader took a step forward, crushing the cap between his hands.

'Ser Giovanni, Don Falco, may God keep you and give you His blessings of this day! We are come from the neighbourhood of San Polo. We are from the guilds and it falls to us to make arrangements for the festival.' He paused and again glanced behind for some support. 'San Polo is relieved you have come back to us after so long.' He waved his arm expansively towards the knights. 'And that you return with friends from afar to grace us. Welcome to you all.'

Beconsall leaned towards Hawker. 'What is he jabbering about?'

'He's happy you're here,' said Hawker quietly. He then took a step forward and gave a quick bow of his head. 'I thank you for your kind welcome. What is it you seek from me?'

'It is because of the festival. The little battles upon the bridge.' The man's eyes darted to Beconsall, head and shoulders taller than the others. 'It would honour us – the entire *sestiere* – if you would join us in the fight against the men of the Dorsoduro. We join with Santa Croce—' He broke off suddenly, clutching at his cap again. 'Your pardon, Ser Giovanni, I do not presume that you *don't* know of the event. But it would be such an honour if you would stand and fight with us. It is Sunday next.'

Another of the artisans had the courage now to speak. 'And we will give you the weapons – the sticks and the shields. We've worked hard this year. Tondo here has sharpened the canes up nicely. Boiled the tips in oil so they don't splinter so easy like they did last time.'

Hawker nodded politely during these pleas. They were in such earnest he could see no deceit in them and the wondrous glances towards the giant who stood behind him made their reasoning all the clearer.

Beconsall pushed forward. 'What is it these fellows want? And if they do want something are you seriously thinking of doing it?'

'They want us to fight in a tournament. On a bridge over one of the canals. Something Venetians do every year, neighbourhood against neighbourhood.'

Beconsall let out a guffaw and turned towards Ellingham and Dieudonné. 'Did you hear that? They want *champions*! Us!'

'I think it more likely they want you,' said Hawker. 'But they are well aware of protocol.'

'To the death? Or just first blood? Blunt swords?' Beconsall was already enthusiastic for the plan.

'They use swords – batons – made of heavy cane. Leather round shields. They fight for control of the bridge. No rules.'

Beconsall was nodding like an excited child at every word Hawker uttered. 'Now that is truly a tournament and – by Christ – none of the bollocks one usually has to put up with when fighting in the lists back home.'

Ellingham spoke up. 'I think it unwise, Sir John. Why would we wish to draw attention to ourselves? What does it benefit us to do this thing?'

Hawker looked over to Jacob, who was slowly shaking his head. He squinted for a second, scratching his cheek scar, weighing things over. 'Sir Giles is right. It benefits us nothing and we would be the centre of the fight – and all the attention. The whole city turns out for these.'

'Well, so bloody what?' Beconsall spat on the flagstones. 'Sounds better than sitting in this house on our arses every day until the doge feels like meeting you. Might even help *your* cause if we get noticed flinging a few folk off the bridge.'

Dieudonné held whatever view he had to himself and was content to smile, amused at the exchange among the English. At length, Hawker nodded slowly and turned back to the delegation of tradesmen.

'I will think upon your invitation and let you know tomorrow. God keep you all.' He gave them a wave of his hand. The leader bowed low and they turned to shuffle out of the square, looking if not crestfallen then somewhat confused by the less than emphatic reply of the English *condottiere*.

'It's dangerous, my lord,' said de Grood, not waiting to be asked. 'Foreigners such as us battling on the bridge for all to see. But if we refuse the offer – and it is an honour in their eyes – then you will have made enemies of every man in San Polo.'

'Bah!' said Beconsall, shifting his scabbard and returning his cloak to cover both shoulders. 'You Flemings are all the same. Boring and pedantic. I'm going where the company is more enlivened. Who's coming along?'

Beconsall set off and Ellingham touched Hawker lightly on his elbow. 'I will abide by what you think is best. You know this place. I do not.'

Dieudonné followed the young knight but not before giving Hawker a bow and wave with his hand. Hawker sheathed his sword and let out a sigh.

'Can we not *watch* the bridge battle, Sir John?' said Jack softly. 'Even if we do not fight?'

'Jacob, spar with the boy for a while. See that he learns to parry and strike in one move.'

Jacob nodded and gave Jack a good-natured shove. 'Let's go, *jongeman*, raise that blade!'

Hawker ascended the stone stairs into the *casa* and caught a glimpse of Chiara lurking in the shadow of the hall. He followed her and she pretended to look for something she had dropped, standing only as he approached her.

'You heard then. What the guilds have asked for.'

Chiara nodded. 'I did not know. I swear it. Luca said nothing to me. Otherwise I would have given you warning.'

Hawker reached for her wrist and gently pulled her into the darkness of a brick alcove. 'I know that. I was not reproaching you.' His arm encircled her waist and she moved her long-fingered hand up to his shoulder, her eyes searching his face with pleasure. 'What did Luca say to you then? After you returned home the other morning.'

Her right hand unconsciously stroked across her ear and she gently inclined her head. 'He was angry. Angry that I stayed. But he is also greedy and is relieved that I may still manage the *casa*. And serve you.' She smiled thinly. 'I know he suspects me. But, for the moment at least, his hunger for your gold keeps him at bay. I will stay here as long as I can.'

Hawker raised his other hand and brushed her cheek. 'He's your husband, Chiara. It is his right to compel you to his house. I worry that he might get the *sestiere* watchmen to drag you out of here while I'm away.'

She laid her good ear against his chest. 'I will not be forced by him. I would rather be the mistress of an English lord than the wife of a whoremonger the likes of him. I am not so foolish, or so young, to think you came back for me. You came back for yourself. But I am glad of it just the same.'

'I came back because I have no other place now. But it is you who have put Venice in my heart as much as England ever was. And now, I will make this place a home again... with you at my side.' He tilted her chin with his fingertips, studying her long face in the gloom of the alcove. 'Has he beaten you, Chiara?'

She gave him a weak shrug as an answer.

'Does he know he wears the horns?'

She looked up at him. 'Four years ago you and I were more careful. I cried when you left and he did not know why. But I do not have to tell him this time. Because I've remained under this roof after you sent him away. Now all the neighbourhood knows he is a cuckold.' Her voice dropped lower. 'I hope he wears his horns well!'

'You must have a care... should his anger get the better of him.'

'I know this. The dagger I carry is a lot longer than his.'

'No, Chiara, I will be the one to kill him if he hurts you.' He gently gripped her by her hands.

'Not if I stab him first. I am already damned by what we do.' The rage began to rise up in her anew.

'Do not goad him. When I leave to go to San Marco you must bolt the door. Do not open it for anyone until we return in the afternoon.'

'And the *battagliola* next Sunday? Will you fight as they ask, or will you refuse? It is a strange request, even if it is an honour from the guilds.'

'I'm praying that God will give me a third choice by Saturday.'

—

Just off the Rialto, Beconsall pushed open the door to a house and led the way inside. A few stone steps led to a high-vaulted chamber, lit by tall, leaded-glass windows. The floor was tiled dark red, its border edging filled with white, yellow and blue flowers, intermingled vines and tendrils spilling amongst them. It looked to Ellingham like it had been a chapel – or still was. What did not belong were the three vast wooden tubs, each with a green fabric canopy over metal hoops, and the laughter that emanated from one of them.

A dark-haired man splashed bathwater over his face while the two ladies who were in there with him sponging him cooed into his ears. The man reached out of the tub and retrieved a pewter goblet from a small round table. Raising it towards the new arrivals, he winked and took a sip.

There was the slap of slippers on the tiles and a woman approached from the next room with open arms. '*Signori*, come in and refresh yourselves!' she said in her languid Venetian dialect.

Ellingham understood next to nothing of this. 'We have travelled far, good lady. From a troubled England and over sea and mountain.'

The madam tilted her head and smiled. She did not know English but gambled on trying French.

'We have wine and sweetmeats and hot water to soothe your tired muscles.'

This Beconsall understood – for the most part, at least. 'What else can you soothe, good lady?' he chuckled.

'That would depend upon the size of your purse,' said Dieudonné as he strode to one of the tubs and ran his hand through the water, brimming with rose petals. He looked up towards the madam. '*C'est trop froid!*'

She clapped her hands twice and two young women entered wearing white muslin gowns and nothing more. She ordered them to fetch more hot water and to bring wine. Dieudonné nodded his approval and began to unbutton his doublet. 'You're too big to share a bath, Sir Roger, so take your own. You'll still be lucky if there's any water left once you get in. Sir Giles and I shall take this one.'

'Your prodding is tiresome, Burgundian,' said Beconsall, spying yet another courtesan approaching. 'I shall take my pleasure first and bathe later.' She took his hand as she approached and, twirling around him, began to lead him away. The madam quickly followed, demanding in broken French that someone pay for the visit first and not afterwards. The two courtesans reappeared bearing buckets of steaming water and proceeded to pour it into the tub.

'What are you waiting for, Giles? Undress and climb in before it begins to cool!'

Ellingham smiled awkwardly and obeyed, pulling off his boots and piling his clothes on a chair that was nearby. He tucked his belt and dagger under his doublet and peeled down his hose as Dieudonné did the same. As he pulled off his cambric shirt and stood in his braes, he felt the chill of the large chamber on his naked skin. The bath, smelling strongly of rosemary and roses, was now beckoning him. He undid the ties of his braes and pulled them off, flinging them on the pile.

Dieudonné seemed to watch him approvingly as he continued to disrobe.

'Now, where have our ladies got to?' he said as he climbed into the tub. 'Come, Giles.'

Ellingham threw a leg up over the rim and balanced precariously on his arms as he brought his other leg over. Dieudonné's hand reached for his hip to steady him as he climbed in. The sound of the lapping water echoed in the vaulted chamber and they settled in, Ellingham submerged to his chin in the boat-sized tub. He watched as the two courtesans disrobed, supporting each other while their slender alabaster legs stretched over the top and into the bath.

As soon as the women entered, the one closest to him practically landed in his lap, laughing and muttering in a language that did not sound Venetian, to his ears at least. He didn't have much choice in the matter. Her companion already had her arms wrapped around Dieudonné's neck as she spoke softly in what seemed to Ellingham a mock warning to the Burgundian to be good. There was little room to move now with the four of them bobbing among the rose petals. One of the women reached over to a nearby round table for a sponge and gently began scrubbing his back. Gradually, he felt the anxieties of the trip melt from him, the scent of the water and the perfume of the girl filling his head, the warmth of the bath relaxing his body even while her caresses to his back invigorated his manhood below the surface.

Dieudonné's courtesan reached across him and retrieved two wine goblets, handing them to the men. She spoke what Ellingham thought was Venetian, smiling when she quipped something and then drawing a forefinger gently down Dieudonné's long nose. The Frenchman smiled in return then drained his goblet in one go, tossing it to roll about on the table. Ellingham took a long sip, the liquid warming him on the inside as it slid down his throat. It was a situation he had never previously found himself in and his uncertainty must have shown on his face.

'Ah, Giles, one can always atone for sin later. Forgiveness is but one short confession away.'

'Do you think I'm worried?'

'Well, you do look a bit torn about it. But the arts of Venus are as important as the arts of Mars, wouldn't you say?' Dieudonné hefted his woman across his thighs, her breasts bobbing, and shifted himself so that he was next to Ellingham. 'Did you leave a lover behind? Someone you miss even now?'

Ellingham finished off his wine and let the goblet sink to the bottom of the tub. His courtesan had now begun to kiss the nape of his neck, running her fingers through his hair. It was making conversation difficult. 'Left behind? A love? No. The cook's daughter took me to the buttery a few times. If you're asking if I have been made a man.'

Dieudonné shrugged and nuzzled his woman, his hands disappearing into the gently swirling bathwater. His woman squealed. 'No matter, dear Giles. No one is sitting in judgement here.'

'What of you? Who have you left behind?'

'Me? Alas, my friend, there is too little time left to a man to give it to one woman. One may find pleasure in many ways of the flesh.'

Already, Ellingham felt the wine going to his head. It had tasted a bit strange, he thought, probably doctored with wormwood or maybe *theriac*, that magical substance of the ancients. Ground poppy and viper flesh and God only knew what else. His woman had wrapped herself around him, mouthing him upon his neck and collarbone, hands exploring his belly and teasing his manhood. His head felt almost weightless. Conversation died away. He was vaguely aware that it was all a jumble of arms and legs. Slowly, it came to him that his loins were being attended to by more than one pair of hands and whose they were he was not altogether sure. He shook off the fumes from his head, managed to push off the woman and somehow arose, swaying in the tub.

Dieudonné leaned back, arms encircling the rim of the bathtub. 'Giles? What's wrong? Pinched by a crab?'

Ellingham ran his hand through his hair. He climbed out and then reached to pull out his woman as well. She looked a

208

bit confused, her lips mumbling in her unknown tongue, but nevertheless she let him extract her from the bath. 'I'm taking her to bed. I'm done swimming.'

Dieudonné frowned a moment then reached for the wine ewer.

'Ah, Sir Robin! The bedchamber is free.' It was Beconsall, emerging from the other room, dressed in a muslin gown and his arm around his woman. 'Something in this wine makes for a rather quick tilt at the ring! Suppose that is how they move their customers out to make room for more, the clever little things.'

Ellingham paid him little heed, his own courtesan now understanding his intentions and leading him by the hand into the bedchamber ahead. He caught a glimpse of the brothel's madam behind a wooden screen at a table, counting out coins from a pouch. He fell into a goose-down mattress, the woman falling down upon him and, head spinning, he let his Venus lead the way. She was alluring, but despite her best efforts, Ellingham found himself too distracted to accomplish anything. He was feeling rather drunk from the wine now – or drugged – and he began to grow anxious. Thoughts kept flooding his mind about Hawker's risky optimism, the strangeness of everything around him, and the overwhelming feeling that a calamity was about to strike. The woman pushed herself up and laid a hand on his chest. She asked him something but all he could do was cover her hand with his, lie back, and close his eyes. She seemed to understand, stroked his brow a moment, and then set her head down on his chest.

–

Beconsall had slid into the tub that had been vacated by the Venetian and his *amour*. He sighed loudly as his courtesan poured a jug of steaming water into the bath. The Frenchman pushed away his own attendant as she tried to mount him, twisted a bit, and raised himself up on his elbows over the rim. He spoke in his broken English, something that Beconsall already suspected was an affectation. 'Sir Roger, we share secrets, *non*? Secrets of the brothel that go no further.'

Beconsall splashed his face and hair and plucked a straying rose petal from out of his mouth. 'What are you prattling about, Burgundian?'

'A secret has been under your very nose for over a month and you are none the wiser about it.'

Beconsall grunted. 'Aye, I know a secret or two that you don't. About why we're here and not someplace else.'

'I not so sure. You speak of the gemstone. Am I right? Well, your face tells me I'm right. Such a secret cannot stay secret when one is on the road for so long.'

Beconsall sat up straight, annoyed. 'For such a little man you have very big ears. What else do you think you know?'

Dieudonné nodded and wiped dripping water from his eyes. 'Very well then. Why you think Hawker has taken this new knight – this young man – under his feathers?'

'Wing.'

'Bah, *le même chose*! I mean, why drag him along? Because he take pity on him? For good luck? Who is Sir Giles?'

'All right then, who is he? Tell me.'

'He is the bastard son of Richard, your dead king.'

A smile spread slowly across Beconsall's face like a cloud moving away from the face of the sun. 'You're a joker, Burgundian. Has the cheap wine got to you, too?'

'Hawker is entrusted with his safety. Sworn to it, by Richard, *before* the battle. Think, man. Why he take the lad with him to the palace at Mechelen? Because the duchess is his aunt. *De toute façon* – anyway – Giles admitted it all to me. *Tout*. Go ask him.'

Beconsall's smile melted away, replaced by a frown.

'*En fait, cher* Roger… we are all on a fool's errand in Venice. Do you really think that old soldier will get his contract with the doge? With what money? What army? *We* are his only army.'

Beconsall's reply came slowly, from a deep rumble in his massive chest. 'Hawker is sworn to return the jewel to the doge, by Richard himself. That is why he is here. That is why I am here. To see it done.'

'He will *trade* it,' hissed Dieudonné. 'For a worthless *contratto*. And we are but passengers on his ferry to nowhere. You want to end your days living in camp, fighting for the Venetians? That is, of course, if we don't end up dead before.'

'Your talk is beginning to worry me, Burgundian.'

'He might trade any of us to gain what he want. You really believe his promises? We should have stayed in Flanders. Revealed Sir Giles at the palace in Mechelen. I think Hawker changed his mind when he meet the duchess. He wants the jewel here. To bargain with. We should help restore the true royal house. *That* is where your fortune and my fortune awaits. Not here. We must convince this prince among us to return. He is of the blood. What do you think she give us if we restore her nephew to her? The last White Rose.'

'Not quite white, is he, though? More like grey. Bastards can't inherit the crown.'

Dieudonné smiled. 'No,' he whispered. 'But they can *take* it. Like Henry Tudor did.'

Beconsall tore the sponge from the courtesan's hand as she tried scrubbing him. 'What is it you are proposing exactly?'

'The Tear of Byzantium by right belong to King Richard's son. Not the man Hawker will deliver it to. Why not we convince Hawker to restore Giles to his rightful place? We find a ship here, return to Flanders in few weeks. In the end, this place will only be death for us. You know that… in your heart.'

Beconsall's great square chin rested on the rim of the tub. 'I am growing weary for England already despite all the dangers waiting there, if truth be told. But what if Hawker does not agree?'

Dieudonné raised his eyebrows. 'My friend, there are always choices. One just need to look in right place.' And then, like some water serpent, his long arm encircled his pouting courtesan and pulled her in to him again.

22

He wore hose of forest green, round-toe shoes of black leather, a cream linen shirt frilled at collar and cuffs, and over all a *cioppa* of black velvet, fluted from the chest down to his shins and secured with a red leather, brass-studded belt. Chiara had packed these away in a chest when he had left Venice, liberally sprinkled with lavender buds and shut fast. An act of hope in the expectation that he might one day return.

She had helped him dress upstairs to the sound of Jacob and Jack sparring in the courtyard, the ring of steel upon steel a special music to Hawker's ears. Chiara helped blouse his *cioppa* from behind, pulling and plucking at the fabric over his belt until the robe lay just right on shoulders and hips. She fastened the scabbard of his *cinquedea* dagger to the hanger on his belt and his hands moved to adjust its angle. Hers gently enfolded his for a moment, pausing.

Hawker smiled. 'These will be glorious times, I promise you. I will have my command again.' For the first time in an age he had felt young upon waking, the prospect of his *contratto* as close as it had ever been. He gathered Chiara into his chest and folded his arms about her delicate frame. 'I was a fool for ever leaving here, leaving you. You are the only one I have loved since the death of my wife. I thank the Lord you were still here for me.'

She squeezed him tightly and looked into his grey eyes. 'The thought of you is what has kept me alive these past years, what has saved me.'

Hawker slowly pushed her away and stroked her face with his palm. She grasped his wrist for a moment then gently broke away.

'You must be covered. Here.' Chiara handed him a felt cap, a tall baggy thing the colour of dark wine. He placed it on his brow and pulled it down, frowning, for he had never liked the style. But he needed to look like a man of worth and not a broken outlaw knight down on his luck and looking for one last chance at redemption.

Hawker placed a hand on her shoulder. 'Remember what I said. No one to enter until I return, lest it be my comrades.'

'Well, if you want to eat I must go to market at some point. I won't be a prisoner in here – not even for you, Giovanni.'

Hawker sighed. 'Then I shall leave Jacob here with you. You can take him with you to market. It is time he learned some Venetian.'

When he appeared on the steps leading down to the flagstones of the *campo*, Jacob came over, beads of sweat running down his sloping brow. 'I am ready, Sir John!' Jack was in his wake, grinning at Hawker's new attire.

'You're staying to guard the *casa*,' said Hawker. '*He's* coming with me.'

Jack's eyes started and his grin widened further, ears blushing red.

Jacob stuttered a reply. 'But... my lord... is that wise?'

'No, Jacob, it's not wise. And you're letting him borrow your dagger, too.'

—

When they entered the doge's palace from the piazza, Hawker bade Jack remain just inside the *porta della carta* and near to the guard post. To safeguard Jack's presence, he hastily introduced the boy as his retainer. The guard, no doubt a boat builder on loan from the Arsenale quarter and rather smug about his scarlet suit and extra pay, barely acknowledged Hawker and merely tossed his head, allowing the knight to pass inside. Hawker cast one more look behind, noting Jack's rather worried, pale face in the shadow of the vast ornate stone portal. Still, he thought, safer for the lad there than in the corrupt wilderness of St Mark's outside.

They were waiting for him at the top of the marble stairs. And it appeared he had chosen the appropriate colour. They were all in black from head to toe. Federini gave a sharp court bow. 'Ser Giovanni, it is good to see you again.'

'And you, sir.' Hawker noticed a guard standing in the shadows of the loggia, halberd at the ready. Federini failed to introduce the two other gentlemen with him but Hawker was in no doubt they were part of the Council of Ten.

'You may leave your *cinquedea* here with this man,' said Federini, gesturing to the guard in the shadows.

'I *may*?' said Hawker, a small smile on his lips.

Federini gave a light laugh in return. 'No, Ser Giovanni, you must, I'm afraid. Fear not, it will be looked after well. Guests may not bear steel in the council chamber.'

Hawker bowed, unclasped his scabbard and blade, and handed it to one of the Venetians to pass on. 'Shall we go, then?'

They entered the half-lit loggia and a great marble archway leading to a staircase that seemed to rise up forever, lit by wall sconces. Federini led the way and Hawker found himself flanked by the two councilmen and tailed by the halberdier. He knew this was the protocol but he also knew that prisons lay not just below the palace but above it, too. The cream-coloured walls appeared to glow in the light of the torches, red and black Byzantine-like border edging guiding his eye ever upwards.

They turned right at the top of the staircase and emerged onto the third floor of the palace, vaulted ceilings overhead. A narrow corridor of dark wood panelling beckoned. They did not walk very far before stopping at a simple, unadorned door that opened even as they approached. Federini turned and whispered to Hawker. 'The Chamber of the Council of Ten.'

The room was windowless, stuffy and barely lit. So dark was it that Hawker had trouble even seeing how large or small it was. The floorboards creaked loudly when they entered and he was guided forward to a great chair near what he took to be the centre. Federini gestured for him to take a seat, then disappeared off to the side with the others. Hawker saw the halberdier leave, closing the door behind him. His eyes began to adjust and he found himself facing three figures in shadow, all seated in towering, carved chairs. Candles burned on a stand at Hawker's right side. A clever way of obscuring his vision towards the men opposite. They had no illumination behind them while the proximity of his candles blinded him to anything more than a few feet distant.

The floor creaked around him. Someone had now taken up station behind where he sat.

'Ser Giovanni Falco. We are told you have urgent business with this council. Affairs of state.' It was the man in the middle. Old, thought Hawker, from the timbre of the voice, at least much older than himself.

'*Signori*, my message comes from my king, slain in battle this past month of August. It is a message for the ears of His Most Serene Highness, the doge.'

The figure to the left spoke up. 'My lord, you have served this city in the past and should be aware of the conventions of our state. There are no private audiences granted to foreigners, be they servants of Venice or not.'

'And I am grateful that the Capi have granted me this one. It is only my intention to deliver my burden and then to serve the Serene Republic as best I can.' He could hear a chuckle emanate from the man in the middle.

A third man, on the right, now spoke. A thin weedy voice also past its prime. 'There are those in the *signoria* who remember your past service, Ser Giovanni. The campaign in Bosnia and our victory alongside the Hungarians at Srebrenica, short-lived though it was. But that was near upon ten years ago.'

Hawker sat straight as a ship's mast, both feet firmly together, his hands folded on his lap. He had no idea if the Council knew what he had borne from England or indeed if even the present doge, Marco Barbarigo, knew. He decided to plunge straight in. It was his only stake in the game.

'Richard Plantagenet, upon the eve of the battle that took his life, bid me to return a gift of Doge Pietro Mocenigo. I carried that gift from this place to King Edward, his brother, when I departed Venice. I have now borne it back. It is a Tear of Byzantium.'

Hawker heard muffled voices off to the side as the name of the jewel left his mouth. The three in front of him said nothing for a few moments. Finally, the man in the middle spoke. 'The Tears of Byzantium are known to us. Most are now returned, except the Plantagenet jewel.'

Hawker's vision had slightly improved now, the glare not as bad as before. It seemed to him that the man in the middle wore a tall, bulbous hat where his companions did not. Moreover, his garb was lighter in colour, almost shimmering when his body shifted on the chair. Was this the doge himself? The man had paused. Was he waiting for Hawker to say more? Hawker raised his chin slightly, hanging on.

'Do you bring the jewel with you today?'

There it was, thought Hawker. Now the game would turn tricky. 'No, my lord. I have not.'

'But you say your mission is to return it to the palace. And you have not brought it with you?'

'Something of such worth requires care and some subterfuge, my lord. Surely you can appreciate the need. I have risked my life in this mission to Venice.'

Again, a pause from the man in the shadows. 'And will you bring it to us?'

Hawker shifted his feet, some sand rasping underneath them. 'I have sworn to my late king to do so. But such matters are delicate.'

'Forgive me, Ser Giovanni, but there is something in your tone that carries the whiff of ransom.'

Hawker knew about this place, this chamber, though he had never entered it before. There was another door that led upwards again, a narrow wooden staircase that brought one to an even darker place. He again heard the boards behind him creak as someone shifted their weight. Would he be hauled up, dragged to that secret wooden door and led up the steep stairs to the interrogation chamber above? Where next his feet and hands would be trussed behind and his body then raised by a rope, inverted, to hang until his joints popped. The thousand agonies of what the Venetians called the *strappado*. Probably not, he reasoned. At least, not yet.

'Good my lord,' he began, voice steady. 'Ransom? Surely not. I am arrived to deliver the Tear – and to seek a *contratto* that I may continue to give loyal service to the State. As a *condottiere* – as I did before.'

The man in the middle – Hawker was now certain it was the doge himself – let out a laugh as if he was genuinely amused by Hawker's cheek. 'A *contratto*. I see.' His companions were content to let this man speak alone, further convincing him that it was Barbarigo himself he was sparring with. 'And I trust that the jewel is safe? At your *casa*?'

'It is safe where I have placed it, my lord, and precautions taken. Precautions should a thief try and force me to divulge its location. It is quite safe from harm.'

'I am glad you are taking such care with what belongs to the ducal treasury. May I ask you what colour is the stone?'

Hawker nodded once. 'Indeed, my lord. It is a ruby, yes, but of a dark complexion, like a bloodstone. In the light of the sun it shines almost from the inside, as if it contains a glowing ember.'

Hawker could see the man on the left lean in and whisper something to the doge. The doge exhaled loud enough for Hawker to hear it across the chamber. He raised his hands. 'Then we shall welcome you back into our service. A six-month agreement plus pension to offset your expenses in raising your squadrons.'

'My lord, I have travelled very far to come here. Shall we say twelve months, plus generous pension for life, in the event I may be wounded?'

The doge laughed easily. 'And shall we say the *contratto* will be signed and paid at the same time you deliver over the Tear? Does that suit, Ser Giovanni?'

'Most generous, my lord. I am here to serve the Republic as I once did. Honourably and with all my heart.'

'One week for the Council to draw up the *contratto*. And you shall again come here.' The doge raised his left arm and made a sweeping gesture. Federini was again at Hawker's side.

'Ser Giovanni...'

Hawker stood and gave a deep bow. As he was ushered out and into one of the vast corridors of the upstairs palace, he felt a surge of pride in himself and not a small sense of relief.

Federini placed a hand on Hawker's forearm. 'That went well indeed. I am glad that you returned to enter service again. I've arranged an entertainment for you, Ser Giovanni, something I think you will like.'

They walked across an enclosed stone bridge that crossed the narrow canal behind the palace. This was a place that Hawker had not been before. Fortress-like, undecorated, this part of the palace had a far different purpose. They wound their way down a deep spiral stair and the air grew close and damp, stinking of canal water. They reached the bottom and Hawker saw iron gratings – cells – set into the dripping stone walls. Federini was silent while they walked, and Hawker felt his balls begin to pull up tightly, his stomach a knot. Sweat instantly prickled in his armpits, his *cioppa* suddenly feeling far too warm. This place smelled of rot and death. The 'wells', as they were called. He swallowed, his throat dry, and Federini gently guided him by the elbow as they turned in to a new corridor, the rough blocks of stone under their feet slippery and green.

Federini put an arm out and they halted. Before them was a large dungeon chamber, lit by a single tallow torch in the wall, a wall festooned with hanging chains and manacles. At its centre sat a naked prisoner, tied to a high-backed wooden chair. As Hawker peered between the bars, he saw the poor creature had a thick rope around his neck, hauling his head against the chair back. The man was barely recognisable as human: hair as matted as an old goat, body smeared with excrement, sores the size of ducats visible.

'He is a corsair,' said Federini, nodding slowly. 'A Ragusan working with the Turk.'

'Why show me this?' replied Hawker, in a tone he hoped would convey calm disinterest.

'We thought you might find a personal interest in this one, Ser Giovanni. You see, this fellow – and his crew – last attacked an English ship before we captured them. They murdered the merchants and the crew. All of them.'

Hawker sniffed loudly. 'English ship, you say?'

'I thought you might take some satisfaction in bearing witness. I had intended to execute him yesterday but as I knew you were coming back today...' Federini gave Hawker a wide grin. He then turned towards the guard within the chamber who was wiping his hands on his stained leather apron. 'Begin!'

The executioner nodded and stood behind the chair. Hawker watched as he began to turn a thick stick that was tied to the rope. He turned it slowly, as if he was winding a delicate clockwork. As it gripped the poor wretch's throat, the man's mouth opened, gasping, his body writhing where he sat. Hawker heard the rope groaning and pinging against the hardwood chair as it twisted tighter. Soon he could see the whites of the pirate's eyes, the man choking, face beginning to purple. Wrists tied to the chair arms, the man could only clench and unclench his fists as the agony progressed. The choking noises grew in intensity and finally, a tongue – now blue – stuck out in a horrible parody of insult towards the observers, the eyeballs protruding grotesquely from the shaking skull. Moments after, it was over.

'Satisfied?' asked Federini, turning to the knight.

Hawker nodded. 'An honour to see justice meted out, my lord.'

'Venice believes in justice, Ser Giovanni. Justice, reward and punishment.' His shoulders twitched and he pulled up his cloak.

'Ugh! This damp. We've stayed down here long enough, haven't we? Let us go back up!'

Out in the open air of the palace courtyard, Hawker took a deep breath, having risen from the Venetian version of hell. Federini handed him back his *cinquedea*. 'You are a bold one, Ser Giovanni, I give you that. A masterful performance in the audience chamber.' He threw Hawker a sly, comradely smile. 'And it is good to have you back. My own brother was at Srebrenica with the army. It was a great victory, wasn't it?'

'It was, my lord. Pity it was all lost in the end. But, God willing, I will help give the Republic other victories.' Hawker paused a moment. 'Was that His Highness, Barbarigo, I spoke with?'

Federini smiled. 'What does it matter? You have your agreement. Did you really expect to kiss the doge's hand?'

Hawker smiled too and shook his head. 'No, my lord. It matters not. We have our bargain and I can still believe what I wish to, can't I?' He almost admired Federini's calculated boldness in demonstrating what happens when the Republic is crossed. Whether it be a pirate or a *condotierre*.

Jack was sitting on his haunches between a portico column and the marble statue of a Grecian nymph, his head resting against her cold thigh. He sprang up at the sight of his lord, face coming to life. 'Sir John, Christ be thanked! Did they give you your army? What did they say to you? Did you see the doge?'

Hawker reached over and clapped Jack on the shoulder. 'All shall be told, but not here or now. It is enough to say we are one step nearer. Come, we're going back to San Polo.'

Saint Mark's was teeming as they entered the piazza. It seemed the centre of the world, a vast conurbation drawn from the corners of the Earth: liveried ebony slaves from afar, priests and nuns, traders and their squeaking pushcarts, young gallants of the nobility bedecked like peacocks and the ubiquitous black-draped senators of the Serene Republic like so many crows ambling among the pigeons. Hawker felt relieved that he had come this far in his scheme. He had not pushed too hard, he thought, and it was little cost to them to give him what he wanted. And it was clear what they wanted. It was only for him now to wait until the Council had drawn up his contract and placed a seal upon it. He would give them the Tear and good riddance to it, if it would buy him a new life. Beconsall and the Burgundian could do as they pleased – stay or go – but Sir Giles he would try and protect for as long as he could, at least until the youth had matured in the ways of the world and had gained a foothold on the ladder of life.

When they reached the corner of the great basilica, a man stepped out in front of them, blocking their way. Jack tensed and reached for the hilt of his dagger, but Hawker instinctively pulled him back and to the side, close to the stone columns of a portal recess. The man was no Venetian. His dagged tunic, mantle and conical felt hat marked him as a man of the eastern mountains, and his bronze skin, drooping moustaches and chin whiskers completed the exotic appearance. He smiled and dipped his head towards Hawker, holding out a small square of paper. 'For you, Ser Giovanni,' he said, almost reverently, in stilted Venetian.

It was a note, a small dark purple smudge of signet wax holding it shut. The messenger did not linger but bowed again and left, going back towards the Great Canal. Hawker hissed to Jack to join him, stepping backwards into the shadow of the pillars underneath the portico of the basilica. He opened the letter and squinted, angling the paper so that it picked up some daylight. The hand was delicate, spidery and most definitely a woman's. The language Florentine. Before Hawker even began reading the short note, he knew it was from the woman he had seen the previous day in the courtyard of the palace.

> *If you value your life and liberty you must meet me at the very moment you read this. Do not wait upon it, for time is not something you possess. Unlike the jewel, which for the moment remains with you. Meet me in the basilica, in the chapel of San Isadore. I will be at prayer. — MH*

How she knew of the Tear he could not conceive. That alone meant he had no choice but to meet her. And if this woman knew of the treasure, who else did?

His nose was hit by a swirl of smells the moment he entered the basilica. Heavy incense mixed with a certain dampness and salt tang, colder than the air outside. Above them, the domed heavens were filled with phantasmagorical wonders dancing on a canopy of shining gold. Hawker could hear Jack mumbling as he walked. He was praying. '*Ave Maria, gratia plena, Dominus tecum…*' The tessellated mosaics at their feet, like the domed ceilings above, told the magnificent stories of the Faith, of the Word. It had been years since Hawker had entered the basilica and, for him, it was almost as if it were the first time. Hawker's hand lightly guided Jack to stop him from walking into a table. He did not know which of the several chapels at either side of the church was Saint Isadore's, and he stopped a black-robed priest who was carrying an armload of tall beeswax candles like so much firewood.

The man indicated with a toss of his head. 'Over there. In the north transept.'

Hawker saw that Jack could not take his gaze away from the marvels overhead. He placed an arm about the boy.

'I told you I would take you to a cathedral, didn't I? Would you like to stay here and pray while I meet with someone?'

Jack smiled and nodded. 'Aye, Sir John. That would please me much.'

'Good. I will return here for you.' He handed the lad a small silver coin. 'Here, so that you may light a candle – over there – for whomever you wish.'

Jack took it and nodded again, smiling. Hawker watched him as he made his way across the aisle to a small chapel illuminated with the glow of a hundred red votive candles.

Hawker then made his way through the forest of stone columns, the massive rosette window of the south wall failing to shed its light for them. He was not sure it was the right chapel until the *stradiot* standing near the entry gave it away. The mercenary gave him a stare that would curdle milk, but let him pass.

Inside was a figure, seated on a bench that stretched the width of the white marble altar. The chapel glowed warmly in the mixed light of dozens of candles and lamps. Over the tall altar a mosaic depicted Christ standing with two saints. Hawker took a few steps towards the altar, made the sign of the cross before the golden crucifix and then walked around the bench. The figure, dressed in a dark-red cloak and hood, gestured for him to be seated. Awkwardly, he grasped his *cioppa*, gave a little cough to clear his throat, and sat down. Not too close, but enough to listen.

'Ser Giovanni Falco, I thank you for coming.'

The woman drew back a voluminous, wired hood and turned her head towards him. She was compellingly beautiful. An almost olive complexion, high cheekbones and eyes so large, irises tinged so verdant, they seemed otherworldly. The raven hair he had noted from a distance the day before was coiled and plaited under a short, flat-topped felt hat decorated with silver braid. A gossamer veil formed a halo around her head and face. Her high-bodiced gown, dark saffron, was set off by a string of grey pearls and pendant. Hawker inclined his head towards her in greeting.

'You have the advantage of me, my lady,' he said his voice low. 'I know neither who you are nor what you require of me. But I have come, as you asked.'

'I am Maria Hunyadi, kin to Matthias Corvinus. He who is king in Hungary and of the lands of the east.' Despite her youthfulness, her voice was deep, he thought, deep like a woman far older, a Byzantine lilt eclipsing the fluency of her Florentine. 'I know your errand, sir, and I would make you a proposal of mutual benefit.'

Hawker twisted his torso on the bench more squarely to face her. 'I don't like that you assume to know my purpose. Why should I entertain any offer from you?'

'I said, Ser Giovanni, my proposal is of mutual benefit. I do not talk of mere recompense for the jewel you guard. I know things that you would know as well. Things that could save your life. Also, the life of the man of royal blood who travels with you.'

Hawker felt his throat muscles tense. 'Speak what you will.'

'The doge knows you bring back the Tear, yes. He and the Council also know of the Plantagenet bastard. I am sure they did not reveal that to you.'

'I have made my bargain with the doge. The jewel was always supposed to return here. I will fulfil that and gain my commission again. For me and my comrades.'

'You will not.' She pulled her veil closer. 'The jewel does not belong to Venice. None of them do. It is a lie. They belong to my family.'

Hawker couldn't stop himself from grinning despite the fact that his concealment and secrets were dissolving before his eyes. 'The doge is custodian of the Tears, lost when Constantinople fell.'

'A custodian is not an owner. He is an overseer. And this overseer has claimed more than is his right. I swear that they are of my family. Indeed, it was my family that gifted them to the other crowns of Europe. It was the doge that added the condition that they must be returned here. Our condition was that the jewels revert to *my* family. The doge has not honoured that. What you hold is mine, whether you choose to believe or not.'

This was indeed a new wrinkle, thought Hawker. He had been told when he was tasked by the Council ten years before that the Tear was a gift from the doge. And he had no proof of what this woman claimed other than her own word. 'My bargain is made. The jewel is not for sale. I am fulfilling the task I was sworn to undertake.'

She turned towards him, those huge eyes almost pulling him towards her. 'The jewel will bring you nothing but misery. The Council has no intention of giving you what you wish. You are already sold.' She looked down and her long thin hands opened the velvet purse that hung from her girdle. She pulled out a small, clear glass phial and handed it to Hawker. He took it, brows beetling, and held it to his eye. It contained white crystals, tinged brown and coarsely ground.

'Salt? What is this? You're saying I've been betrayed for salt?'

'It is not salt. It is alum. Did you really think the doge would give you a commission and money? Let you keep the Plantagenet in your company? Another bargain has already been struck, my lord. And you, your friends and the jewel are the prizes.'

Hawker shook his head. 'What? Why alum?'

'I would not expect you to know these things. The Council would keep English wool cloth coming here. England needs alum to dye its wool. The doge would have your king buy it from him and not the pope. It is near monopoly between the two. Henry Tudor will have a gift of the jewel and of the Plantagenet bastard to seal the arrangement between the Serene Republic and England. What they will do with you is very doubtful.'

'How do you know of the Plantagenet? I have guarded that carefully.'

'Do you really think that? I have my spies about just as the doge. And Henry Tudor's have already been here for days. You have been careless.'

Hawker felt a bitter taste flood his mouth. It could be a well-spun tale, a fantasy. But deceit was all around him. Venice had been built upon it. 'My lady. What you tell me is hard news indeed... if I am to believe it.'

'I would urge you to believe it, to accept my word. They will arrest you the minute you hand over the jewel.'

'What would you have me do, then?'

'Give me the jewel. I will get you away from Venice. You and all your comrades. If you like, I will give you commission in my service. And wealth. Even a cause worth fighting for.'

Hawker gave a desperate chuckle as his alarm grew. 'In *your* service?'

He watched her lips move as she replied, almost as if he was an observer standing away from himself. 'I will take you to Buda. You will be paid handsomely. You will be rewarded and find good service with the court.'

'So, either I believe you... or I believe them.'

'That is the choice for you, Ser Giovanni. But I am the one who is rightful in this. I will not fail.'

'You've given me much to ponder. How will I find you?'

She smiled at him. 'You are never far from my view. I will find you. But you do not have long. Deliver me the jewel and my galley awaits you.'

'If I did do what you ask – and without proof I must be sceptical – you would only have the one Tear. What good would that be to you? The Council has told me the doge holds the others.'

She smiled to herself, looking down into her lap. 'You are like the scribe who can see nothing more than the page his nose touches. What makes you think I do not already hold the other Tears of Byzantium?'

Part IV

THE CONDOTTIERE

23

Striding through the *calle*, intent on making it back to San Polo, the sights, sounds, stinks and spices of the Rialto barely penetrated his consciousness. His head was spinning, full of likely enemies and betrayals, working out of those which were the greater threat. As if he had the power to sort them into most likely, least likely and most lethal piles. For now, he was less inclined to believe this Maria Hunyadi. She believed the Tears were hers – fair enough – but she had no doubt concocted a story of treachery to scare him into handing the jewel over. But her threat was clear: she would take the jewel by force if he did not cooperate.

Jack Perry's slightly shorter legs did their best to keep up with Hawker's, even when the old knight fairly leapt up the steep wooden stairs of the bridge over the Great Canal, elbowing merchants both on the way up and down the other side.

'She knows about the jewel, doesn't she? This fine lady.' Jack kept pace now that they were on level ground again. 'So she's either wanting it for herself or trying to get money from you to keep it secret.'

Hawker was reminded how sharp Jack was. 'She knows, aye. Now I have to do some thinking.' He stuck out a forefinger towards Jack. 'Keep your mouth shut when we get back, understood?'

Jack's eager expression crumbled. 'Sir John... do you think I would? I am sworn to you!'

Hawker relented. 'No, I do not doubt your trust. It's that this could... trouble the others. Come!'

'You think so?' mumbled Jack, his sarcasm out of earshot as Hawker set off.

They arrived at the *casa* to find that the others had already returned. Chiara scolded a serving girl fixing their meal while Beconsall sat with his head on the great table and Ellingham and Dieudonné conversed in low tones, both sprawling in their chairs across from the giant. They sat up when Hawker entered, tossing his felt hat onto the oak cupboard opposite them.

'I see you have all returned from your little campaign,' Hawker said, reaching for the pewter wine ewer and then swiping a goblet from the cupboard shelf. 'I hope you have not brought back any tiny pets with you into my house.'

Beconsall lifted his head, annoyed at Hawker's airs. He had sworn no loyalty to him and owed him nothing. 'It was a bath-house. We bathed.'

Ellingham stood up. 'Well? Tell us, Sir John. Did you get the *contratto*? Do you have a bargain? Do *we* have a bargain?'

Jack dared a quick glance towards Hawker then hurriedly pulled his brown woollen cloak off over his head. Chiara emerged from the other room to tousle his hair and coo. She handed him a stick of marzipan, having had it ready for his return.

Hawker took a long swig of wine and then sat in an oak armchair next to the massive ornate cupboard, stretching out his legs and slumping back. 'I have agreement for the contratto. I do not have the contratto yet. The Council says in a few days: paperwork.'

Ellingham's brow furrowed. 'So we wait, then. And hope they don't reconsider in the meantime?'

Beconsall sat bolt upright. 'So what are they playing at, Hawker? Perhaps they are scheming something themselves. We must be on guard. I wouldn't trust these Venetians to pay up for a pie from a market stall let alone a commission and a bag of gold too. You should have just given them—' He stopped, catching himself, and buried his nose in his goblet.

Dieudonné rose and refilled Hawker's goblet. 'Did they tell you exactly, Sir John? I mean, *exactly* which day to return for the contratto?' The French rolled off his tongue, honey-sweet.

'And who the hell are you all? The Council of Three?' Hawker rose, his chair scraping, and glowered. He then swore and drank again. 'Very well. One week, they said. From this day. The full Council must agree and the clerks put to preparing it. And...' He waved the goblet towards them all. 'And to draw the pension from the treasury, which ought to please you lot.'

Dieudonné turned to the others and shrugged. 'Seems reasonable, does it not? Why doubt them?'

Ellingham gave Dieudonné a look of stone. No one said a word. Amalia came in, shot Hawker a smile, and placed a bowl of apples upon the table. Dieudonné plucked one out straight away and polished it on his doublet.

Hawker changed the conversation. 'I was earwigged by the master of the weaver's guild on the way back here. Wants an answer if we will fight alongside the San Polo men on Sunday. I told him I would leave it to my comrades.'

Beconsall's voice sounded as flat as a tombstone in a church nave. 'Better than sitting in here watching the walls peel. Do as you will.'

'Discuss it among yourselves,' said Hawker, trying to salvage their spirits. 'You can tell me your decision when we eat at table later.' He heard voices downstairs in the main hall. Chiara's, and a man's. Then Chiara appeared in the room, beaming with pleasure, two liveried servants in her wake. One carried a wooden chest that tinkled as he walked while the other carried a muslin-wrapped bundle, the delicious scent of which wafted to them the moment he entered.

'Ser Giovanni!' said Chiara. 'Gifts for you! From the palace. They bring wine and prosciutto – the biggest leg of boar I have ever laid my eyes upon.'

Hawker relaxed, his thin lips spreading in a wide smile. 'You see, my friends! Our welcome has begun. The Republic does not forget those who have done it service. Jacob, relieve that man of his burden of wine and set it here upon the table!'

The others exchanged looks of surprise, Beconsall mumbling oaths when the smoked leg of boar was revealed and placed on the table in all its glory. 'A prodigious beast it must have been,' he said, stroking the haunch. 'May we do it service, Sir John?' He was drawing his dagger even as the words left his lips.

'It is the first of many feasts, Sir Roger,' replied Hawker, feeling vindicated. 'Cut away and open a bottle to wash it down.'

Dieudonné stuck out his lower lip, genuinely impressed by the bounty, and reached into the casket for one of the terracotta flasks that rattled within.

Ellingham stared at the feast that had been laid out. For some time he had been thinking – agonising – about who he was and where he might be destined. There were no easy choices for him, he knew that. But over the last few days a feeling had been building within him, something that told him to stop drifting with the current. To stop running away. To stop denying what was.

Hawker refilled his goblet, nodding with enthusiasm as his comrades began to attack the meat and wine. 'Fill yourselves! I will join you presently but have some things to attend to in my chamber.'

–

After Hawker had left the great hall, Ellingham waited a few minutes until the others were tearing into the doge's gifts. He then slowly got up and left the room just as Jacob was beginning to regale them with a tale of the bridge battle he had witnessed years earlier. Rather than retiring to the chamber that had been granted him, he made his way to Hawker's instead. He found the knight seated on a three-legged stool at the foot of his bed, sipping his wine. Hawker looked up as he knocked on the doorframe and then beckoned him to enter.

Ellingham took just a few steps inside. 'So now you're open to the idea of us parading into this tournament on Sunday when you were against it before?'

Hawker leaned his elbows on his thighs. 'It does not signify to anger the neighbourhood. Not if I'm staying on now. And I am. I hope you will stay with me and lead a squadron or three.'

Ellingham shook his head slowly, his anger welling up inside him. 'You can lead the others around by the nose if you like but I'll need more convincing than that. You expect me to believe anything you've told me? *Anything* since we met?'

Hawker's brow creased. 'Do you mean that? After we have journeyed together all these days?'

'They *know* who I am... Dieudonné and Beconsall both. Gaston said he overheard you on ship.'

Hawker sat up. Ellingham could see he was playing with the corn dolly in his left hand, turning it over and over. 'That is the damnedest thing. I took great care. Beconsall too, you say?' It struck him hard, following so close on what the Hungarian noblewoman had revealed to him.

'They are both professing loyalty now. To *me*. And Beconsall has told me more about *you*. That you served the Duke of Buckingham at the Tower. Before his rebellion two years ago against King Richard.'

Hawker reached down and placed his goblet on the tiles. 'I did not follow him into the rebellion. I stayed loyal to Richard.'

Ellingham's anger and frustration darkened his face. He took a few steps closer to Hawker, fists clenched at his sides. 'What else did you do, goddamn you! Did you kill my cousins at the Tower? Did you do Buckingham's bidding? Murder children?'

Hawker's mouth opened, but words did not come.

'Where are they, Sir John? Where is Edward, the rightful king?'

'I did not kill them.' Hawker's face was haggard but his sea-grey eyes pierced Ellingham. 'Shut the door,' he hissed.

Ellingham turned, keeping one eye on Hawker, crossed the chamber and quietly closed the studded oak door. He returned and stood over the knight – now looking even older – the man's bowl-shaped haircut marking him as practically a living relic. 'I want to know what happened there. And you're going to tell me.'

Suddenly, Hawker's demeanour changed. His head sank between his hands, eyes to the floor. The corn dolly rubbed against his temple, as if he expected it to remove his pain like some talisman. 'I did not... kill the boys.'

Ellingham squatted down next to him, his voice low. 'Then tell me. Who did?'

Hawker raised himself, sat back until his head touched the bed curtains, and exhaled a long breath. 'Lord Buckingham announced his treachery. Many at the Tower obeyed him. Henry Tudor's mother, Margaret Beaufort – that great bitch – probably put him up to it. He had the crown in mind for himself but she would use his ambition to gain what *she* wanted: the crown for Henry. The princes were in the way.'

Ellingham's mouth gaped in sheer amazement at what he was being told. 'Who gave the order?'

Hawker's eyes then focused on Ellingham, as if his mind had been far away for a few moments. 'The order? The order to dispose of them was given to Sir James Tyrell. And to me. A few days after the rebellion started. But we did not obey.' He swiped his thumb and forefinger down his nose. 'We did not... we did not. Tyrell told me a man in London loyal to Richard – a Jew trader who had converted and who Richard had knighted a year earlier – was arranging a rescue, a scheme to free the boys. A wherry would come at night, to the walls. Tyrell would distract the guards by ordering them elsewhere while I led the princes out of their chamber and down to the Cradle Tower gate on the river.' His gaze moved towards the window, but his mind was back in the bowels of the Tower in the dark of night.

Ellingham took half a step backwards, his fists unclenching. He pulled himself up, head reeling. 'Did you save them? Get them out?' he whispered urgently.

Hawker's voice seemed to catch thickly in his throat. 'I had them wrapped in cloaks. They were so frightened... so frightened. I got them out of the royal apartments and down to the alley. A soldier stopped me outside. He was suspicious – alarmed – once he saw the princes. I started making my excuses, then... I cut his throat. Richard started crying when he saw that and all the blood that covered me. God will judge me for making them witness it. Edward was ill, always coughing. Had been for weeks. He was so weak I thought I would have to carry him. His brother helped pull him along. My heart was in my mouth that we would be discovered. Thank God it was not far to the Cradle postern. I had the keys.'

He stopped for a moment, swallowing hard. 'So dark. There was no moon at all. And cold. My God, it was cold.'

'Jesus, what then? What did you do? You opened the gate?'

'Aye. Through the door of the gatehouse. There is a footbridge over the canal. I got them over that. We were on the wharf. It was slick with slime and the river was high and wild with wind. Churning. I saw a bobbing lantern out near the edge. It was a small boat. They must have seen us because someone hailed me. They asked for the word. I gave it. Richard slipped and fell on the planks and I lifted him up and somehow managed to get him into the boat. Grinding and creaking, up and down. I practically tossed him into the bottom. Then I turned back for Edward.' Hawker stopped there, his eyes scrunched up tight.

'Sir John, tell me what happened?' Ellingham's voice was strained with tension, yearning to drag the truth from the old knight.

'He fell.' Hawker opened his eyes and looked hard at the young Plantagenet. 'He fell. Slipped down... through my hands.' Tears welled up in Hawker's eyes and Ellingham's heart went into his mouth. 'The boat pitched up and out. He went down underneath. Jesus, I reached for his cloak but he... he wasn't in it any more. He was gone... gone.' Hawker nodded and wiped his cheek with the back of his hand. 'The boatman told me to jump in with him and Prince Richard but I didn't. I waved him off from the wharf and staggered near the edge, peering into the lapping, mad water. Praying the boy would break the surface. The tide was strong. That boatman cursed me and shifted his oars, and he was away.'

'What did you do?'

Hawker shook his head. 'I should have jumped into the river myself.' His voice had grown tired and thin. 'But I went back inside. I didn't even look for Tyrell. I just left the Tower before the alarm was raised. Took horse and went north, to find your father's camp.'

Ellingham walked to the leaded window, his head still spinning. 'Where was the prince taken?'

Hawker was silent for a moment. 'I don't know. To this day I don't know. I pray to the Almighty that the boy yet lives.'

And for the first time, Ellingham understood the knight's mawkishness. Holding a child's simple gift as if it were gold. His devotion to the boy Jack. Even perhaps his protectiveness towards him, honouring the promise to a dead man. It was remorse, eating away at Sir John Hawker's soul. The knight stood up, knees cracking, and shuffled over to face him.

'Giles, there is more to tell. News this day. Others know of your presence here. And the jewel.'

Ellingham's back stiffened.

'A noblewoman has made contact. A Hungarian princess. She says that the Tears of Byzantium are the property of her family, that the doges have hoarded them, and that she means to have them back.'

'What?'

'And she says that the doge and his council know who you are and will bargain you and the jewel for trading rights with Henry Tudor, the damned wool trade. When I hand over the jewel they will arrest me and take you away.'

Ellingham felt his face flushing as he drank in the import. 'Christ save us. Do you believe this woman?'

'I don't believe her. But she has her own little army. The Tears came from those lands, that fact I do know. They might well belong to her family. She is offering safe passage out of Venice

– and service in her kingdom. Wealth, she said. If I give her the jewel first. She could just as easily set her men on us as soon as I hand it over.'

It was indeed ill news just when he had hoped there was a way out. 'Then what will you do?'

'Do? For the moment, nothing. She has given me no proof of her claims. The Republic has welcomed me back and given me my command. They will honour the bargain.'

'This noblewoman. You say she has promised safe passage and money?'

Hawker sniffed derisively. 'She has. But after she has the stone what need does she have of us? Is she even who she says she is? Perhaps she is just part of a clever ruse set into motion by the Council to test my loyalty to the Republic.'

Ellingham wasn't sure which was worse. A new pursuer or Hawker's weakening control over their circumstances. 'Then you've overestimated your bargaining position. We are in grave jeopardy.'

'No. Do not think that. But I have underestimated the duplicity of this place; that fact I should never have forgotten.'

'Will she send her men to take the jewel?'

Hawker shook his head. 'That would be a foolish gambit. We would hold off her *stradiots*, kill a few, and then she would have nothing but the Council of Ten hounding her back to her ship for breaking the peace of the Republic.'

'Perhaps there's another way.' Ellingham's voice seemed to have suddenly gathered years, laced with a gravelly rasp.

'Speak your mind.'

'We go back, back to Flanders. Whatever favour you once enjoyed here is gone. You have made new enemies but you have no old friends.'

Hawker bristled. 'What do you know of Venice? What do you know of *my* time in Venice?'

Ellingham drew himself up and gestured to the room. 'I see all that is around me. Time has moved on, but you have not. I've abandoned everything, such as it was. I don't want the crown. I don't deserve it and I'm a bastard. But all who believe as I do will now be gathering at the dowager's court to save what *was* ours. To find the rightful heir to King Edward, to fight for our faction. And yet we are here. Chasing the glories of *your* past.'

Hawker's head turned again to stare out the window and down into the courtyard below. When he spoke his voice was quiet, almost contemplative. 'Your faction? A family I remember you saying you wanted to forget. Someone has been pouring advice into your ear.'

Ellingham grew angry again. 'I will not deny my bloodline any more. Not to anyone. And yes, the company talks of these things. It does not make it bad counsel. Their lives hang by the same thread as yours and mine.' He saw Hawker's face fall for a moment, and he gave Ellingham a look that bespoke of shame and chastisement.

'I only want to give you a chance at a life of fortune, free from your past.'

'Sir John, I cannot run any more from my past, who I am. Nor can you outrun yours, the decisions that still haunt you.'

'So, then. Return to Flanders. With the jewel.'

'Yes. And fight for something we believe. Something you were sworn to. We find the true White Rose – and crush the usurper. And, God willing, you may find absolution for what you failed to do. Something you will never find in this place.'

Hawker rubbed his hand over the whiskers of his sharp chin. 'You're proposing a path that is even more dangerous than staying and taking service here. You realise it would be difficult to evade the doge and get off this island with that jewel in our hands?'

Ellingham nodded again. 'That is why we follow you. Our captain and *condottiere*. You will get us back. And you have our four swords along with yours to make it happen.'

Hawker stood up straight and took a breath. 'Giles, I will open my heart to you. This place is my home now. Where I can be happy, find pride in myself, serve in an army that will reward handsomely.'

'With your mistress, Chiara,' added Ellingham sharply.

'Yes, with Chiara. And with myself… content in myself.'

Ellingham's head sank and he slowly backed away. 'So, you will not lead us if we decide to return?'

'I did not say that. I'm saying that now is not the time. And if it were, the jewel would not guarantee you a place at the Dowager Margaret's palace. It is better gotten rid of… for everyone's sake. Maybe it is cursed.'

'*You* are what's cursed. One you placed upon yourself.' Ellingham shook his head, frustrated. 'If not leave this place now, then when? When the Tudors have entrenched themselves in England and enriched themselves? Turned all to their side with bribes?'

Hawker looked at him, his expression almost pleading. 'I'm telling you to return with an army of your own, with money of your own, not as a pauper looking to his blood claim to rescue him from misery. What could you offer the cause of the White Rose in Flanders now? Just your sword arm.'

Ellingham swallowed and clenched his teeth. Part of him knew that Hawker spoke sense. But another part chafed, not believing that the bounty of Venice would fall into their laps. 'So you expect me to wait. Until I am some great captain with an army of spearmen behind me and sacks of golden ducats. How old will I be by then, Sir John? How old will you be?'

Hawker put a hand on the youth's shoulder. 'I have not been wrong yet. My counsel is to give it time. If I can't raise an army in a year, then I will just raise a company of stalwarts and go back north with you. But to leave now is madness.'

Ellingham looked up to the ceiling for a moment as if he was expecting God to tell him what to do next. 'I have followed your counsel this far. I'll think upon what you have said. But I can make you no promise to join your little army.'

Hawker nodded. 'I respect that, Sir Giles. You are your own man and must follow your conscience. But trust me, a man driving a wagon of gold with an army behind him is listened to.

A man without money or power is just a minstrel singing pretty songs. And minstrels are but a short-time fancy.'

Ellingham still felt a gnawing doubt. Doubt that the old knight was keeping his best interests at heart. He was new to the ways of the world but old enough to know that John Hawker had been blinded by the love of a woman who was still another man's wife. Blinded to lurking dangers and swayed by empty promises.

24

Ellingham leaned against the stone well in the paved courtyard, contemplating the residents of the *campo*, while the sun dipped below the red rooftops. As soon as he had emerged from the house, the few women who had been drawing water hastily made for their own houses like scurrying mice.

He could see a shadowed face, half-hidden by the green wooden shutters. A face that was watching him from the far end of the square. And all was strangely silent. It was clear the people feared foreigners in their midst. Perhaps they had believed Hawker long dead, never to return. Now he was back and this time with others. He thought this ironic. It was he and his companions who were the ones in danger from Venetians, not the other way around.

More than this was eating at his conscience, though. Since he had confronted Hawker with the past that afternoon, he was worried. He knew Hawker felt shame for his failure to safeguard the princes. Ellingham desperately wanted to believe that he had given Hawker new purpose as he had given such purpose to himself by embracing his bloodline, by resolving to carry on the fight against the usurping Tudors. But something told him that Hawker was perhaps losing his own way, losing his confidence to lead, and that the others might then look to him instead.

Ellingham knew very well how his father had taken command during the battles at Barnet and Tewkesbury when he was only eighteen. Dealing death, meting out justice to the vanquished, relishing the yells of fealty from his victorious soldiers. But he was not his father's son, despite the blood that ran in his veins, and he felt he had neither the skill nor the charm to lead even this little band of mercenaries if Hawker faltered now. He had delivered brave words to the old man. But he had not yet delivered deeds.

Self-belief was the most difficult of all beliefs to sustain. Far easier, he thought, to believe in the risen Christ and the paradise of Heaven to come. He glanced up again. The figure peeping through the shutters across the square had gone. He dragged a sleeve across his sweating forehead as more ill thoughts flooded his mind. If by the grace of God they made it back to Flanders, would he even be recognised as the bastard son of Richard? Or would his aunt and her court throw him out into the street, or worse, brand him a pretender and have him executed?

He wished that he possessed just a cupful of the Burgundian's boldness. Dieudonné seemed to think that Fortune only favoured those who leapt into her arms and perhaps he was right. But Ellingham knew in his heart that he would need Hawker's wisdom of age and experience to temper the blind boldness of Gaston Dieudonné. In truth, he believed he would need both men to guide him. As for Sir Roger Beconsall, the man was still a cipher. A sometime buffoon who also, underneath, he suspected, was calculating and without scruple.

There was a crunch of boots on the grit of the paving stones behind him. It was Dieudonné.

'Giles, we were wondering what you had done with yourself. Lost your appetite? Beconsall is already devouring your portion, I fear.' He settled in next to Ellingham, matching his posture against the stones, thigh to thigh.

'I wanted some solitude,' replied Ellingham quietly.

Dieudonné put a hand on the youth's arm. 'Understandable. Are you worrying that the doge is playing us for fools, maybe? Who is the spider and who is the fly?'

Ellingham didn't answer.

'You know, when I was your age – not so long ago – I was nearly penniless. My father's estate run down, the wars taking their toll. I had only my title, a *sieur* with land so worthless that even a peasant might turn his nose up at it. So, I decided to seek my fortune elsewhere in the duchy. I became the hammer and not the anvil.'

Ellingham smiled a little. 'Gaston, I thought that is why we're both here. To seek our fortune.'

'That is true. But one has to have the vision to look ahead. To change course when it's necessary. Have you not thought upon what we spoke of these last days? You know I was in earnest.'

'I have, dear Gaston. Gaston, I must—' He checked himself. It was too early to confide what he and Hawker had spoken of, the choice of a return to Flanders now or later. Too many details that had to be thought through. No, they needed to lay out one plan, a plan that would convince the others to keep the company together.

Dieudonné leaned closer, his voice almost a whisper. 'Giles, I beg you. Come with me. We'll take ship back. We *two*. Seize sweet Fortuna by her tits and lead the cause of your bloodline.' His hand moved downwards, palm gently laid upon Ellingham's thigh.

Ellingham caught the scent of desperation on him and gently brushed his hand away. 'Gaston, we're under eyes here. Always.'

Dieudonné clucked his tongue and gave a toss of his head. 'And what should we care for these peasants, hiding behind their walls?'

'I cannot take my pleasures as you do, my friend. On that we must agree, as friends and comrades.'

Dieudonné twisted around at that, again leaning in close, his face contorting. 'You *judge* me?'

'I do not, Gaston. I know only my own conscience. But I ask you to believe in *me*, if not Hawker. We will succeed. Maybe, I say *maybe*, we even take the path you urge.'

Dieudonné drew back slightly. 'There is something afoot, my friend? Secrets?'

Ellingham looked down. 'No… there is not. I am asking you to be patient. Give the old man a chance. For my sake.'

The Frenchman sighed. 'You sound, dear Giles, as if we have all the time in the world. Even when you know very well that we do not. I beg you. Come away... while we still can.'

'Gaston, it is time enough. If we hang together a bit longer.'

Dieudonné pushed himself off the lip of the well and brushed his hands. Ellingham felt the man's look of coldness go right through him. He thought it carried a hint of something more than rebuff.

Dieudonné cleared his throat and the look just as suddenly melted away. 'Patience is for old women who have no choices left. A soldier *always* has choices. You will have to make yours sooner than you think.' He pulled his cloak about his shoulders. 'I am going for a walk. Maybe find trouble on the Rialto. You coming?'

Ellingham shook his head. 'No, I will go back inside, eat Beconsall's table scraps, I suppose. You should go back, too. It will be dark soon.'

'Are you judging me again, dear Giles?' replied Dieudonné, an impish grin forming.

'Keep yourself safe.' Ellingham stood, gave him a nod, and walked slowly back towards the *casa*. Dieudonné's words rang in his head. *A soldier always has choices.* And he knew then that it was time to make a bargain with Sir John Hawker. One he hoped they could both honour. He still needed the ageing knight. He was simply far too innocent of the world and its ways. But he swore to himself that he would learn quickly enough.

–

Dieudonné had walked briskly through the *calli* and across the main *campo* of San Polo, past rows of tilting, ochre-washed tenements that looked like crooked, yellowed teeth. At the Great Canal, in near gloom, he climbed the steep covered stairs of the wooden humpbacked bridge, passing over and entering the Rialto. The oarsmen of a few gondolas plied their trade with sing-song calls but, for the most part, street traders had left with the failing sun. Under an awning, two young women in the tight multi-coloured hose and unbuttoned doublets of male fashion beckoned him with kisses, but he moved on. He continued until he reached the *merceria*, the main thoroughfare that led all the way to Saint Mark's Square and upon which the best shops and inns were situated. He had an assignation for the hour past Compline and this was fast approaching. He had made the mistake of not scouting it earlier when the banker had informed him of the meeting place, but he had not wanted to draw attention to himself. Now he hoped he would not be late.

At last he found the inn, set back down an alley, its pigeon-stained sign illuminated by a brazier set underneath near the doorway. There was no keeper there to meet him and he instantly suspected a trap had been set. Why not? He had threatened the Medici banker and his clerk into arranging the meeting. He could only hope that the desire for reward was more firmly entrenched in their hearts than that of revenge. He climbed the stairs to find two doors shut and one ajar. Body tensed, he slowly pushed this door further open. It creaked loudly on its wrought hinges.

'*Entrez!*' The voice said.

Dieudonné peered cautiously around the corner and entered. It was a large apartment with a great fireplace and heavy dark wood table at its centre. Two men stood opposite: finely dressed and puffed with self-importance, he thought. They were neither old nor young. One of them spoke again in French, the same voice that had beckoned him inside. 'You are the Frenchman who desired to meet us?'

Dieudonné nodded.

'Then shut the door and be seated.'

Dieudonné hurriedly scanned the rest of the chamber. There was no one else. One doorway led to another room. Two leaded windows faced north. A large Turkish carpet covered the table upon which sat two things: a large candelabra and a small leather pouch. Dieudonné moved to the table, hesitating to sit. 'I speak English,' he said.

The same man who had spoken before, sallow-faced with large dark eyes, addressed him again. 'Very well then. Tell us your name.'

'That not important. But for sake of friendship I tell you. I am Dieudonné.'

The other man, dressed in black satin, his bald head glowing in the candlelight, exchanged a glance with his companion. He answered Dieudonné's halting English with French. 'Perhaps French would be better… and quicker. Will you not be seated, friend?'

Dieudonné began to bristle but he replied in his native tongue. 'I find it better to negotiate standing, thank you.'

'You have sought us out because you have intelligence that may concern us. Here we are.'

'And are you agents of the king? I have told you who I am.'

The dark-eyed man smiled. 'We represent the interests of Jasper Tudor, Earl of Pembroke, now that we are arrived in Venice. And also those of Henry, his nephew and king. Does that satisfy?'

Dieudonné nodded. 'Then you now know I have gained the confidence of your enemies. Yorkists who have something you might want. I can deliver them up to you without much trouble. Indeed, I can bring them to your door. Their leader, Sir John Hawker, is outlawed. He might be brought to you by kidnapping his young squire for whom he has great affection.'

Now, the bald man spoke. 'And tell us what these Yorkists possess that might be of such interest to us?'

Unnecessarily derisive, thought Dieudonné, and not in the spirit of things.

'I have no doubt you already know what. I communicated this to our intermediary. There are two items. One, the great jewel that Richard gave away before he was killed. A gemstone that ought to be Henry's now along with the rest of the royal treasury. Second, Richard's bastard son, who goes by the name of Sir Giles Ellingham. I am prepared to deliver both for a modest price.'

The two Lancastrians exchanged amused glances. The bald man spoke. 'What is your price?'

'I am a modest man. So, a modest estate confiscated from a Yorkist noble. And five hundred florins to keep it up... and get me there from here. That, to me, gentlemen, seems a fair price for the value on the ledger. I would also be willing to serve you on future enterprises – of a secretive nature – when required.'

'Dieudonné, Dieu... don... nay.' The dark-eyed man rolled the name on his lips. 'This is a name we already know. A preening man-at-arms to my lord Pembroke who claimed to have come from a noble French family but who went missing after our glorious victory at Bosworth field. And also, a desperate sodomite who looks to have murdered a young servant of the earl's before he fled. Something of a madman, I hear. *Untrustworthy* was the word that was used, I think.'

Dieudonné's brow beetled. 'My lords, you blacken my reputation by believing the lies of others. I gained intelligence of the outlaws while in England. *I* insinuated myself into their company, their trust, a cuckoo in their nest. And now *I* have sought out my lord's agents to deliver the enemy into their hands. I was doing the earl's work all along, serving the new king. Surely you can see that.'

The dark-eyed man shook his head in mock disappointment. 'What I can surely see is that you offer us what is not necessary. The intelligence you bring we already know by way of the doge's council. But I was curious – intrigued actually – to know who was peddling the same news.'

Dieudonné suddenly felt as if the ground was opening at his feet. '*I* am the one who holds the enemy in my grasp. And I am prepared to deliver them at your command.'

'In your grasp?' said the bald man, breaking into a grin. 'When the doge says Hawker will walk into the palace with the jewel in a few days' time? When Richard's bastard can be taken by the doge's army of constables the instant the word is given? The Yorkist knights are of no interest, except perhaps to the shires where they did murder. The bastard, well, the king has yet to decide upon that score. But the doge will keep him on a short lead in the meantime. He will dispose of the problem when we request it.'

The dark-eyed man shook his head in disdain. 'The bargain you offer, *monsieur*, is no bargain at all. We have our bargain sealed. You should feel lucky that we do not have you sent back in chains. We know now the lords of Liancourt died out thirty years ago. You are a murderer *and* an imposter.'

Listening to the torrent of insult, a cold calm came over the Frenchman. He felt ashamed that he had let his own confidence get the better of him, leading him to a weak strategy, half-formed. But, like a revelation delivered by angels, he suddenly realised that Lancaster or York did not really matter for him. It never had.

The dark-eyed man leaned across the table and pushed the leather purse towards Dieudonné. 'But I will at the very least reward your initiative, *monsieur*. However, that is the total of our largesse in this matter. You should think yourself fortunate it ends thus.'

Dieudonné gave a most sincere expression of obeisance, a slight incline of his head, and reached forward to take the purse with his left hand. As he did so, his right reached into his waistband and pulled a blackened steel stiletto. His left clamped down on the wrist of the dark-eyed man and his right drove the thin blade through the agent's hand, impaling it to the wood.

So rapid was the strike that the man did not even scream as the stiletto went in between the knuckle joints with the skill of a barber surgeon. In one motion, Dieudonné was over the table top and scrabbling for the bald man, who began to windmill his arms in a futile effort to beat off Dieudonné. But the Frenchman, coiled and precise, had him gripped by the collar and, throwing him against the wall, drew a second dagger, wide at the hilt. He rammed it deep into the man's throat, ending his cries.

Even as the bald man dropped, the other had managed, groaning, to pull out the stiletto that had impaled his hand and turned to grapple with the Frenchman. Dieudonné elbowed him in the ribs and the man bent double, winded. Dieudonné twisted at the waist, seized the man by his hair, and propelled him into the dark-stained panelling. He then hauled him up, raised the dagger, and took aim. The blade sank into the man's eye socket until hilt scraped against bone. He collapsed in a lifeless heap. Dieudonné then wiped his sweating face on his sleeve. Quickly retrieving his stiletto, he began to think about how to get out.

He looked down at the bodies under the table. He'd been rash, true enough. Something he could chastise himself for later. But now the concern was that the dead agents would be found and that he might have been seen entering. That the little spies of the *sestieri* of Venice were everywhere was a given. Something would have to be done to lessen the chance of discovery.

He was still for a moment, listening for the sound of an alarm being raised. There was only silence. He went into the adjoining chamber. There was a large bedstead and curtains, an ornate walnut cupboard bereft of any silver. In one corner there was a garderobe closet, set off by a suspended curtain. A varnished wooden plank lay across the trough, a circular hole cut through the middle. He lifted this off to reveal a stone chute that led straight down. The smell made him wince but, peering down in the failing light, he saw that a man could just fit down it – upright or head first. A tight fit would be best. He did not want the bodies to fall all the way and into the canal at the bottom where they would be spotted.

He worked quickly. He pulled the heavy coverlet from the bed and rolled the bodies into it, using the ends to mop up the pooled blood on the floorboards. He then dragged the grisly pile into the bedchamber and to the garderobe. He cursed at the weight as he hefted the first man, remembering – if not quite understanding – how a man seemed to weigh more dead than alive. He shoved him in head first, guiding the corpse by its ankles until it was down the chute. The second corpse proved an effort to ram down by dint of the first proving to be a tighter fit than expected. At last, he managed to wedge them both down, leaving more than enough space to replace the plank. He balled up the coverlet and pushed that down as well before he put the wooden lid in place.

When he turned from his labours, a movement at the foot of the bed caught his eye. It was a man, climbing out from where he had been hiding. Dieudonné swore. Dagger in hand, he extricated him – pulling him out by the scruff of his collar – for the poor man had become wedged trying to crawl out from beneath the bedframe. He curled himself up, pleading in Venetian. He wore a *cinquedea* blade at his back and must have been a guide or servant to the Englishmen. But, obviously, he was no bold swordsman. The man babbled fluently but Dieudonné understood not a word of it.

Dieudonné put a gentle hand to his lips, hushing him. He spoke like a mother comforting a son. 'You had two courses of action, *monsieur*. You could have charged me while I dealt with the other two. Probably could have stabbed me before I even saw you. Or, my friend, you could have made for the window and jumped to the other roof. Cowardly, yes, but a valid choice. Sadly, you chose a third way. Something, I fear, that has not worked in your favour.' The Frenchman sighed, genuinely aggrieved. 'But, thankfully, there is still room for you with the others.'

A few minutes later, he left the rooms by the window to the adjoining roof. He left the purse of Florentines where it sat upon the table. He was no thief.

25

Dieudonné retraced his steps back to San Polo, his climb up the bridge of the Rialto far more circumspect than last time, his eyes piercing the darkness for any signs he was being followed. His mind raced to weave a plan to salvage what he could from the ruins of his rampage and he caught himself mumbling aloud.

A bargain with the Tudors was now beyond hope and he would have to revert to what had always been the other alternative: the conquest of young Ellingham and the cause of the White Rose.

His furious pounding on the *casa*'s door brought Jacob de Grood down the rickety staircase, cursing as he made his way into the hall and to the heavy oak door, fashioned from old ship planks. Jacob frowned at the sight of the sweating, slightly wide-eyed Burgundian who, if anything, looked more drunk than sober. His eyes looked down and drank in the ruin of Dieudonné's doublet, dark crimson smears on the grey velvet. 'Sir Giles said you went out for some adventure. Looks like you found some.'

'Some brigands tried to rob me. They failed.'

Jacob smiled as Dieudonné walked past him, and shut and bolted the door again. 'Knowing you these past days, that does not surprise me.'

Beconsall gave a loud whistle when Dieudonné entered the main chamber, the prominent bloodstain on his chest unconcealed. 'Trust none of that belongs to you, my friend,' he said.

Ellingham put down his goblet and stood up. 'I did not take you at your word when you said you were looking for trouble.'

Dieudonné waved a hand dismissively. 'Ruffians. Thieves. They did not profit, I assure you.'

'You are not wounded, then?' said Hawker.

Dieudonné shook his head.

Hawker pointed to the wine ewer on the table and then indicated an empty chair. 'My lord, Dieudonné, we of this company have much to discuss.'

Dieudonné had begun to compose himself. He nodded, reached for a goblet, and filled it before taking a seat.

Hawker wrapped both hands around his own goblet, sitting forward at the head of the long table. 'I confess I've been less than open with you all. Sir Giles has rightly reminded me that we are in this venture together – a company of free men – and that you all deserve to know what I know.' He cleared his throat and took a swig. 'And so, I will confide to you things I have learned of late. For one, I know that you, Sir Roger, and you, my lord Dieudonné, have discovered Sir Giles's truth. Something I obviously did not conceal with any great skill or success.'

Dieudonné, his goblet halfway to his lips, froze for a moment. His body tensed, waiting on the knight's next words. He set down his goblet slowly, his earlobes beginning to heat. He imagined the rest of his face was flushing the same.

'And you all know what it is I bring with me,' said Hawker. 'What I was sworn to return. Well, others have learned of it too. To speak plainly, they mean to take it for themselves. We may have been betrayed.'

Beconsall's voice was a low growl. '*May* have been betrayed? Who has betrayed us? What have you learned?'

'I have been told that the doge and his council have no intention of honouring the bargain. Apparently, they intend to seize me and Sir Giles as soon as I deliver up the jewel.'

Dieudonné exhaled, long and slow. He lifted up the cup again, his worry about having to cut and hack his way out of the *casa* subsiding. At least for the moment.

Beconsall slammed down his goblet, splashing the table. 'Christ's nails! Where did you find this out? Do you believe it?'

Hawker tilted his head. 'I'll tell you first that I do not believe it. The woman who has told me this desires the jewel for herself. That is her motivation for spinning this tale of betrayal.'

Beconsall's tone became even more incredulous. '*What* woman?'

'A noblewoman from the court of Hungary, of the royal blood. Or that is what she claims. She says the doge has sold us to Henry Tudor. A sugar loaf, if you will – an offering – to sweeten the future trade in wool and wine.'

Beconsall seemed to sink into his chair. 'Hungarian?' he muttered. 'How did she come by this morsel?'

'That, Sir Roger, seems a less important question than what we should do now that we know it. None of you, save for Jacob and Jack here, are sworn to my service. You are all free men – knights and gentlemen. You may take what path you think best.'

Beconsall drew himself up in his chair, anger bubbling. 'So that is that. We are at an end. Is that what you're telling us? We who have risked our bollocks to get this far.'

Hawker shook his head slowly. 'No, I do not believe this woman. It's a lie to force my hand to give up the jewel.'

Dieudonné chewed his lip. This was more confirmation of the Council's treachery, but Hawker was unlikely to have gained this news from the same place he just had. Whoever had whispered to Hawker must have made a bargain of their own. Of that, he was most certain.

'But, Sir John, what if she is telling the truth?' he said.

Hawker looked at Dieudonné. 'Then we have three choices. We do nothing and I go to the palace in a few days to sign my *contratto* and take my gold. Or, we believe the noblewoman, deliver up the jewel and trust she will get us out of Venice. Or...' He paused again as if searching for the words and the courage to utter them. 'Or, we devise a way out on our own if the worst befalls us. We take a ship and head west, back to Flanders.'

Beconsall pursed his lips and said nothing.

Ellingham's voice rang out, steady and confident. 'I am King Richard's son. But the jewel was given to Sir John to dispose of. It is his task and therefore his decision. I don't want it. And it should have been given back a long time ago. The jewel will return to the doge. Sir John has asked for my trust that he may build a company of men-at-arms and bowmen. One that, in time, we may take northwards. To Flanders. Sir John and I will seek out the duchess dowager in Mechelen. We will gather the followers. And we will find the rightful heir and help put him on the throne.'

Jacob de Grood's eyes started out of his head. Jack backed away carefully from where he had been standing, leaning nonchalantly on the back of Ellingham's chair.

Beconsall looked straight at Dieudonné for an instant as his eyebrows moved skywards. He then turned in his chair towards Ellingham. 'You, Sir Giles, would lead this rebellion?'

Ellingham nodded. 'By the grace of God and the help of my aunt.'

Beconsall tripped over his tongue. 'Sir John, you agree to this... this scheme? Bold, I give you that, but what chance do you have? Begging you pardon, Sir Giles, but there are only you two, the Fleming and this boy.'

Hawker's rough voice was firm. 'I have always served the White Rose. First and last. If Sir Giles gives me his time now, I will give him my time later. And an army and treasure to go with it.'

Ellingham stood up and extended his hand. 'Sir John has made his bond with me. Will you do the same, Sir Roger?'

Beconsall rubbed at his face vigorously, shaking his head with disbelief. 'It is madness. Sir John, you've had nothing from the doge but a leg of pork and some wine. Now we're told there is a new enemy pursuing us even while Tudor men are probably searching the city for you... and Sir Giles.'

Before Beconsall could say anything else, Dieudonné stood, raised his chin, eyes giving away nothing of his true thoughts. 'I am honoured to serve, my lord.' He extended his hand, his bloody doublet unbuttoned to his stomach.

Ellingham grasped it and shook firmly, sealing the promise.

Beconsall swore under his breath, pushed his chair back and rose, slowly extending his hand to Ellingham. 'My lord, I will fight with you, and for you. Even if we are pissing into the wind.'

'Gentlemen,' said Hawker, 'we stand firm. I trust in the Council, unless we learn otherwise – with proof. In the meantime, we keep on our guard here in this place. And we scout for a ship. Just in case.'

'Scout for a ship?' said Beconsall, his great head jutting forward. 'So we are to become pirates now?'

Hawker folded his arms over his barrel chest. 'I see no other way. We must go to the wharf at Dorsoduro. Find a ship that we could take by force, given our numbers.'

There was silence. Dieudonné began calculating how much time they had before the Council would close their trap upon Hawker. He reckoned they would hold to their bargain and welcome him back to the palace – where they would seize him. The only question – the trump card in the deck – was whether the Council had discovered his own handiwork of that night. And again, he thought about the loose ends: the Florentine banker and his craven clerk. Somehow, he would have to convince Ellingham to flee the city before the trap closed upon them all.

'If I do not return from the palace on Monday,' continued Hawker, 'then you will know it has gone ill for me. You will leave here and head to the docks. Your belongings will be at a warehouse nearby. Just in case, mind you.'

'But are we to fight upon the bridges on the Sunday?' said Dieudonné. 'We have been asked and the guilds await their answer. Or do we stay here, hiding behind closed shutters?'

'No,' said Hawker. 'We will take part. It is expected of me. Not to join in the tournament would raise suspicions. It is a great honour.'

'And our belongings?' asked Beconsall. 'Not that I have much more than two sticks to rub together any more,' he added.

'Jack will take a handcart with the bundles,' said Hawker. 'We take a chamber at a storehouse I know and drop them off under lock and key.'

'I will?' said Jack softly, looking like he'd been hit over the head.

'Tomorrow I will scout the wharf,' said Hawker. 'See what ships are in.'

'I will come with you, Sir John,' said Dieudonné.

'If you like.'

Beconsall shook his head. 'You realise, Hawker, every one of your choices is nothing more than a dice throw. And they are terrible odds.'

Hawker smiled. 'We will get what we want. I have a bargain with men who know me – and I them. But one always must have an unlocked door at one's back, eh?'

They all drank deeply and brought the pewter down with a clang onto the scarred oaken trestle. Dieudonné looked at Ellingham and, when he had caught the youth's eye, gave him a sly smile of knowing. Of shared concerns. Hawker was not infallible and needed watching. As for himself, his ship of purpose was spinning still, quite rudderless, in the maelstrom of his heart. But he alone knew that they would be having to turn pirate sooner than the rest expected.

'Sir John,' said Dieudonné, 'if we fail in that moment of seizing a vessel, then we are trapped. As good as dead when the Council catches us.'

Hawker turned to him, a challenge in his eye. 'It is a gamble, my lord Dieudonné. But I see no other way of getting off this island without being arrested or killed. And, of course, you are free to remain if you wish. The Serene Republic has no complaint against you, does it? Tonight's little street affray notwithstanding.'

Dieudonné smiled back. 'They do not, my lord. But I have thrown my lot in with you and Sir Giles. I suppose you are saying that the price of our failure is the incentive not to fail.'

'That is exactly what I'm saying. Tomorrow we'll have much work to do. I will grant you all the liberty of the morning as you see fit, but Jacob will fetch the wooden weapons from the guilds and give you some instruction later. I will make my way to the wharf to scout. My Burgundian friend may join me, as is his wish.' He slowly stood up and drained the last of the wine from his goblet. 'I am off to my bed. I suggest you all do the same.'

The moon, enveloped in a halo of gossamer, had not yet begun its descent. It had just gone midnight, the bells of a distant clock tower, somewhere near San Marco, striking the hour. Hawker's arms enveloped Chiara in his voluminous black *cioppa*, holding her tight against him as they stood at the stone balcony of the *casa*'s roof terrace. They had hastily dressed after their lovemaking; Chiara was fearful of the lateness of the evening and more questions from Contanto, but Hawker had soothed her worries and begged her to take the air with him.

This night he had been even more passionate, as if he might never get the chance to lie with her again. It was almost desperate, and it troubled her. He was reluctant to let her go from him after they were spent, and he had poured out his plans to her as they lay together. Recruitment of men on the Terra Ferma would be his first endeavour – as he had done years earlier. Building his mercenary company, finding camp and training through the approaching months of winter. She had listened, content in his embrace, drinking in his scent. But worry clung to her nonetheless. She worried that Hawker had forgotten just how devious the Council could be. And the doge was the fat spider sitting in their midst, spinning his web near and far.

Now as they stood silent overlooking the shadowed rooftops, she felt before she left for the night that she must seek more assurance from him. That he was certain of his prospects and wise to those that might wish him ill.

She grasped his hand as he stroked her cheek, pausing him. 'Do they believe you? Will they follow?'

He tilted her chin up to look at him. His face was stark in the lamplight. 'I have soothed their distrust and fears. I am certain of that. What they needed to hear was that they can escape if all goes against us. But it won't come to pass.'

'I believe you believe that. If you give them what they want you will have proved yourself. But you must be careful.'

He smiled. 'I will. Far more in it for them that I serve the Republic. I am not important enough to the Tudors that the doge would hand me over. And he wants the jewel for himself, not to hand it back to Henry.'

'What of Sir Giles?'

Hawker's brow crinkled. 'I won't let anything happen to the youth. He is safe with me.'

She was silent for a few moments. Then she placed a hand high up on his chest. 'I do not wish to lose you a second time. Luca seethes with jealousy. Suspects everything. Everyone. But, if you were ever betrayed... by this Hungarian creature... it would kill me. My husband we can fight. But this woman, she has a ship full of men. And you... you have...' Her small voice trailed off.

His reply was low and soothing. 'Chiara, all will be well. I feel it in my bones.'

'Then I must believe as you do, my love. It is time for me to return lest I stir more trouble for myself.' She smiled at him, not wishing to show her doubts.

Hawker squeezed her close to him again. 'I long for the time that we may spend the whole of a night together. Not like the past week. We've been like two children stealing away from our elders.' He loosened his embrace of her. 'Come. Jacob still stands guard downstairs. I will have him escort you back.'

—

Below, in the cool of the buttery, lit by flickering lamps, Amalia pretended to rearrange the stacked cheeses, each carefully wrapped in muslin. She felt a hand rubbing her ample backside but ignored the caress, even though she was enjoying it.

'Why do you linger here, Massimo?' Her tone was purposely bored and haughty. 'You've been pestering me for an hour.'

'I would spend every hour I own, here with you… if the master would let me,' said the manservant, moving his hand along her back to trace the laced points of her tunic.

'You're a besotted fool,' she chided, wiggling under his roving hand. 'Go away.'

They heard Hawker's voice upstairs followed by the Fleming's. 'She's leaving now,' said Amalia, pausing to listen.

'Does the *donna* always linger this late? What does she get up to?'

Amalia twisted around to face Massimo. She gently swiped a forefinger down his sharp nose. 'That is none of your concern as this is not your household. Nor that of your master. Not any more.'

He grinned at her. 'I was only asking, *cara*. But she has caught Don Falco's eye, hasn't she?'

She gave the most imperceptible of smiles whilst plucking a stray piece of straw from Massimo's doublet. 'It is not for the likes of us to gossip about those who give us work.'

Massimo laughed. 'If not them then who else? Come now, they are lovers, no? He must have bedded her.'

Amalia raised a finger in warning, gave him a stern look, and then delivered a dramatic wink of her eye and a sly smile.

26

The next day, late morning, the company again gathered in Hawker's great hall. Amalia had put out a few trenchers of bread, cheese and apples to tide them over before a larger meal later. When they had finished, Beconsall interrupted the quiet reverie with a loud resounding belch.

'So,' he said, 'who told the guilds we have accepted their invitation for the tournament? I'm already beginning to lose my enthusiasm given the sword that's hanging over all of us.'

Jacob spoke up from where he stood behind Hawker. 'I informed them earlier – while you were still snoring upstairs or else out for your walk.'

'And this is not a tournament like the ones we know back in England,' added Hawker. 'More a melee than anything else. No rules. Whoever holds the bridge by driving the other side off is declared the winner.'

'Tell me about these wooden weapons,' demanded Beconsall.

'Wooden canes – solid marsh reed – dried and sharpened. One may strike or thrust. Most also carry wicker round shields. And you may wear a breastplate or mail. Or a helm.' Hawker grinned. 'Seems to me what you've been waiting for, Sir Roger, in your boredom of the last days.'

'Aye, well, I suppose you're right,' said Beconsall, his voice coming from deep within his chest. 'We'll prove the champions against street rabble and tradesmen. Any prizes?'

'Honour,' said Jacob, without irony. Ellingham smiled and looked over towards Dieudonné, who raised an eyebrow in reply.

'You should not be thinking about prizes until you have trained a little,' said Hawker. 'Go outside and Jacob will show you and the others.'

A few minutes later the little company, without Hawker, had assembled near the well in the square outside the *casa*.

'It's a basket lid, isn't it?' Beconsall handled the wicker *rotella* shield with obvious disdain. 'But this,' he said, hefting the sharpened cane the thickness of a man's wrist, 'this could knock someone's brains out.'

Jacob de Grood brought up his own round shield to his chest and raised his wooden sword up over his head. 'My lord, if you will but spar with me I believe you will get the feel for the form.'

Beconsall grumbled and went into a guard while Ellingham stood back to await the clash.

Dieudonné sat and watched from the edge of the stone well.

De Grood rushed the knight, aiming an overhead blow, which Beconsall blocked with a punch of the light wicker shield. He instantly threw a side-shot of his own, shoulder height, aimed at removing the Fleming's head. But de Grood rolled his arm up from the elbow and intercepted the blow even as he thrust his cane straight out – and into the rolled flesh of Beconsall's paunch.

The *oomph* from Beconsall was audible across the courtyard and he staggered back, swearing, before breaking into a chuckle of embarrassment. 'Well struck! But I'll not be as easy a mark next time.' They engaged again, trading blows, and this time Beconsall landed one of his own.

De Grood called out the hit and stood back. 'But remember, Sir Roger, you will have blows raining down from front and side. Not a duel like this.'

Beconsall smiled. 'Even so, it will be a light sport compared to steel.'

De Grood gestured with his cane. 'My lord Ellingham? Do you wish to try your hand?'

Ellingham shook his head. 'I would save my strength for the morning, Master de Grood. But the lesson isn't lost on me, I assure you. It is quick sport that requires a keen eye and fast arm.'

De Grood bowed. 'As you wish, my lord. How about the Frenchman?'

Dieudonné's eyes narrowed. 'Burgundian.' He then picked up his own *rotella* and stick, twirling the latter with a snap of his wrist. He feigned a relaxed pose and suddenly lunged for de Grood in an explosive leap. Blows rained down so fast that it was all de Grood could do to keep from being struck, his cane held out point downwards, locked onto his shield to better defend against the onslaught. But one blow blew past the lip of the shield, striking the Fleming square on the ear and sending him to the ground. Dieudonné raised the cane again, preparing to strike, but Ellingham had seized it from behind.

'Gaston! Hold!'

Dieudonné stepped back and tossed the stick and shield to the pavement. 'The lesson is ended, no?'

'Have a care, my lord,' growled Beconsall. 'That was most uncivil among comrades.' Ellingham said nothing, alarmed by the sudden, unprovoked ferocity of it all and the wild look in Dieudonné's eyes.

Dieudonné turned to de Grood, now back on his feet and rubbing his ear. 'Your pardon. That was unfair exchange among comrades.' It came out, at least to Ellingham's ears, as insincere – just so many words.

De Grood shook his head. 'You are fast, my lord, I give you that. You'll need that tomorrow, you can be sure of it.'

A short time later, Hawker came out of the *casa*, still buckling on his *cinquedea* with Jack trailing behind. 'My lord Dieudonné! If you wish to accompany me, I suggest you strap on a blade. A sword made of wood will get you only so far in the neighbourhood we're visiting.'

Dieudonné bowed and went inside.

'I'm coming as well.' Ellingham handed his wicker shield to Jack, who eagerly snatched it and then retrieved a cane from the ground. 'I'd like to see where we might be making our last stand… *before* we have to make it.'

Hawker nodded. 'Very well. Get your blade.'

-

Though it was not far to the wharfside of Dorsoduro as a San Marco pigeon flies, for one on foot it was a journey of detours, slow cart men, narrow sewage-strewn alleys and tiny footbridges with no railings. The brick maze that was Venice challenged any stranger to the city, particularly a stranger in a hurry. Hawker led the way, single file, trying his best to remember the route he used to frequent four years earlier. Luckily, the landmarks he had known remained: a collapsed balcony here, a red and white awning on a leather shop further along, even the little black dog on the stone stoop, still sleeping but with a muzzle of grey now. People along the *calli* half watched the progress of these three men of obvious money, but with that clever Venetian way of avoiding staring while taking in every detail.

Slowly but steadily, Hawker made his way towards the wide canal that opened on the south of Venice, towards the island of San Biagio. They crossed the last of the several small canals, a simple set of wooden planks forming a bridge, passed between two tall tenements and found themselves on a wide promenade looking out onto the water. San Biagio, green with trees and orchards, lay a quarter of a mile distant. Tied up before them were ships and boats of every description, from sleek double-prowed fishing vessels to the tubby cogs of Adriatic traders.

'Enough of a choice,' remarked Dieudonné as he walked alongside Hawker. Ellingham came up on the other side, placing Hawker in the middle as they walked parallel to the docks. 'Maybe too much choice. And maybe they won't all even be here when we need them.'

'But some *will* be, my lord,' said Hawker, annoyed. 'And we keep an eye on the stretch where the most are moored up.' A stiff chill breeze out of the north-west hit them – the *bora* – stirring up dust into whorls along the cobbled street and announcing the imminent arrival of the winter. 'Up ahead at the next corner.

That is the tavern where we can meet if all goes ill. Large and boisterous, which is what we want.'

Dieudonné smiled. 'So that we will look like traders from abroad, and not fugitives.'

'You have a tongue that is sharp, my lord,' said Hawker. 'Take care you do not cut yourself on it.' He resumed his way then suddenly turned back towards Dieudonné. 'And we're not fugitives yet.'

The tavern was weather-beaten, shutters falling off and rising up three storeys. As they stood out front, the low steady burble of many men in conversation floated out to them, occasionally interrupted by laughter or cries. Ellingham turned to Hawker. 'Do we go in now?'

Hawker shook his head. 'On the way back. I want to carry on further down the wharf. We are in the market for a ship after all.'

They kept walking. Sailors gamed on upturned tubs and fishermen spread out nets for repair. Hawker hoped they looked like foreign traders, captains from afar. But part of him was nearly certain that some informant of the Council was dogging their heels even now. They would never be able to approach a ship's master for a friendly conversation. After a few minutes, he spied what he was hoping to find. A large galley, its single great lateen sail furled up tight along its spar and oars stowed on the open deck. It was not of the Venetian fleet; those would be anchored at the Arsenale on the far side of the island. This ship was foreign, and Hawker was willing to gamble that it belonged to the Hungarian noblewoman so keen for his Tear.

As they drew closer, passing it on their right, Hawker could see its sailors: from their dress clearly Dalmatians, while the turban of another spoke of Bosnia, Serbia or Ragusa. He stopped and turned to see the distance from the tavern. Certainly close enough. He tapped Ellingham lightly on the arm. 'The salvation that has been offered to us,' he whispered, and his eyes indicated the galley.

Ellingham's eyes scanned the deck. 'Would not trust that lot as far as I could throw them.'

'Thinking of pirating this one, then?' Dieudonné had managed to come up alongside on Hawker's left. 'Looks like we would have our hands full taking on that crew. They look to be pirates themselves.'

Hawker shook his head. 'No, my lord, not our prey, this one. Time we headed back to the tavern to take a cup of wine. Then back home.' He gave one last, heavy look towards Ellingham and then turned away, not waiting for the other two.

'*C'est tout?*' muttered Dieudonné.

Ellingham called after Hawker. 'Have you seen enough? Which ships are laden and which are empty?'

'I have seen enough,' replied Hawker, without slowing his pace.

–

'This is all madness, you know,' said Dieudonné in hissed and rapid French. 'You could have relied upon me to buy the two of us onto a merchant ship. Hawker will get you killed before this is all done. And me as well.' He and Ellingham were following Hawker back to the *casa* but lingering a dozen paces behind.

Dieudonné moved closer to Ellingham and spoke, his voice low. 'It is clear Hawker does this as a sop to our fears… fears that are well justified. And yesterday you told me to have patience. Now, you seem to agree with his fantasy that we are the seeds of some great army. And you're not telling me something, my friend. Like… who passed on the intelligence that you have been sold out by the doge.'

'Our circumstances shift like so much sand,' Ellingham rasped. 'Maybe… I have finally seen what must be done. You don't need to know more. For now, at least.'

'Very well, my friend,' said Dieudonné. 'I give you my hand in trust. But we are still in grave danger. I feel it.'

Two can play at keeping secrets, he thought.

As soon as they had returned to the *casa*, Jack bounded into the great hall and began excitedly hounding his knight, regaling him with how he had mastered *rondello* and sword under Jacob's tutelage.

'I beat his low guard, Sir John! I did! Ask him, if you doubt me. He said I have a quickness for it, he did.'

Hawker clapped a hand on the lad's shoulder. 'Why would I doubt you, Jack Perry? You will be a formidable opponent before the month is out – *if* you keep at practice.' He took a seat at the long oak table where Beconsall was already ensconced and looking jaded while he swirled the wine in his goblet.

'Might there still be some boar's flesh about down in the kitchen?' he asked, half to himself. Hawker was about to tell him to use his own legs to find the answer but then Chiara entered from the back stair, smiled at Hawker and curtsied. She made her way to stand behind his chair where Jack already had taken up station, leaned in, and placed her hand upon his shoulder. She passed Hawker a small, folded note, sealed with a few careless blobs of purple wax. 'After you left, a street child came knocking. Handed me this with one word… *Falco*.' Her few words did little to conceal the anxiety in her voice. Hawker wasn't surprised to hear of the boy messenger. It would have been fatal for one of Maria's *stradiotti* to knock upon his door with Jacob on watch and the eyes of the *campo* upon him as well.

Ellingham and Dieudonné came up the main stone stairs, their animated French echoing in the archway. Jacob followed close behind them, his face expressionless. Beconsall sat up straight, interest renewed. 'Well, now I might have some *appreciative* drinking company,' he said, grasping his goblet and hefting it again. He turned back towards Hawker, his eyes settling on the small square scrap in his hand. 'Some message from the palace?'

'No doubt,' lied Hawker. 'Probably to arrange my next audience to gain the *contratto*.' He looked over to Ellingham, who had just taken up his chair. 'Sir Giles, join me, if you please, in my chamber.'

'So now you take counsel without me?' Beconsall was like a dog being deprived of his bone, his voice a growl of annoyance.

Hawker levelled his gaze on the knight again. 'I take counsel with whom I choose. On other matters it might be you and not him.'

'Having court favourites isn't for soldiers, Sir John. It stinks of secrets to me.'

'Nothing holds you here. If your honour is sullied, you may depart.'

Beconsall chuckled lightly. 'You will not rid yourself of me that easily, Sir John. Go and have your counsel. I will stay and drink your wine.'

Chiara moved over to Jack, put her hands on his shoulders, and spoke to him softly in Venetian.

'She wants you to help her and Amalia in the buttery. Wine flasks to be filled,' translated Hawker without taking his eyes from Beconsall. 'Says there will be payment in marzipan for you.' Hawker's thumb and forefinger worried the letter he held, as if it were burning him. He turned towards the boy. 'Go on, then!'

Jack gave a frown, looking just as put out as Beconsall, but he nodded and let Chiara lead him away. Hawker rose and strode out of the room, and Ellingham, puzzled, followed. But the Frenchman merely gave a smile as light as an empty wasp's nest and just as paper-thin.

–

By the time Ellingham had crossed the threshold to Hawker's bedchamber, the greying knight had already cracked open the letter. He read it quickly then proffered it to Ellingham. 'Here. Read it.' His leaden voice set Ellingham's stomach to tumble.

'If it be in Venetian I cannot read it, Sir John.'

'It is from her.'

Ellingham looked at the parchment again, the thin spidery script a cipher to him. 'The Hungarian?'

'She is asking me to meet her again. At vespers in San Silvestro. She says things have changed. More urgent.'

Ellingham held out the letter, anxious to be rid of it. 'Will you meet her?'

Hawker sighed. 'I must. But I want you to come with me. That you might judge her for yourself.'

'Judge her? Are you weighing her so-called offer to get us out of this place? You told me she was scheming some lie to gain the jewel. You said she would never risk attacking us.'

Hawker walked to the window and looked out over the forest of painted chimney stacks, smoke wafting up into the afternoon sky, streaked with dull red. 'I have been thinking of your words yesterday. Your counsel. We must consider our situation carefully, with open eyes. Keep her believing we are considering her offer even if we are not.'

Ellingham swore under his breath.

'You've seen battle now, Giles. I swear to God it's easier to fight upon the field than it is to fight these phantoms and spies in the dark of night.'

'What do we tell the others?'

Hawker shrugged. 'Tell them we are going to Mass.'

Ellingham frowned. 'Gaston is suspicious of everyone anyway. And do you think you can trust Sir Roger any better? They'll both be curious.'

Hawker laughed lightly, sounding tired. 'We truly are a miserable band, aren't we?'

'Aye, miserable,' said Ellingham. 'But so is blood and family. You can't change those and at this point, we can't change either.'

27

The bell sounding vespers had ceased. Ellingham's eyes scanned the cavernous church, which was aglow with candlelight. The air was filled with the lifted voices of choristers, singing the prayers, while the golden-brocade-clad priest did his office. '*Deus, in adiutorium meum intende. Domine, ad adiuvandum me festina.*' The sound reverberated across the domed ceiling, an ethereal chorus of angels on earth.

Hawker stood by a great fluted pillar near where they had entered by a side door, his arm laid lightly across Ellingham's chest while his eyes tried to pierce the darker recesses of the church. 'There! She's sitting over there. Two men stand in the shadows behind.'

Ellingham's eyes were adjusting quickly. He could see a veiled woman where Hawker had pointed. Hawker touched his elbow and guided him forward. They made their way to the back of the church where no one sat, the few Venetians attending all near the altar, and they took up station near the heavy studded oak doors. Ellingham realised that they had been seen for one of the men standing guard leaned over and spoke to the woman. 'Do we approach?' he whispered.

'Nay, we hold here. It is her move.'

After a few moments they saw her make the sign of the cross and rise. She seemed to float towards them, a wide, dark form, both of her men-at-arms following closely behind. She stopped just a pace from the two Englishmen and reached up to lift her gossamer veil. Hawker gave a quick bow of his head and Ellingham did the same. But Ellingham soon found himself staring at the lady's striking beauty, the dark skin, the glistening hair of jet, the sharp cheekbones of her oval face, and the large eyes that had shifted quickly from Hawker to him. She was unlike any woman he had ever seen, emanating an otherworldliness – for he could not describe it otherwise – that held him as fast as if enchanted. Those eyes, glistening like polished green marble, were studying him even as he stared back at her. She then blinked slowly and returned her gaze to Hawker.

'My lord, I am glad that you heeded my call.' Her voice was commanding but not haughty, just enough to be audible to them but still barely above a whisper. Ellingham did not understand what she said but the sound of her voice, an exotic lilt of eastern lands, gave her a quiet nobility. She paused, realising that Ellingham did not speak Florentine. 'I speak some French too,' she said, smiling faintly.

Ellingham bowed his head again. 'My lady.'

Hawker followed, in his soldier's French. 'We have come as you asked. What has changed since we last met? I have yet to make up my mind as to your offer.'

Ellingham saw her make a subtle sweeping gesture with her right hand, held low. Her two guards, goat-bearded *stradiotti*, moved back, fading into the shadows.

'What has changed is that your time is running out. Two of Henry Tudor's agents here were found murdered this afternoon.'

Hawker's voice was cold. 'It was not my work, my lady.'

Ellingham realised it did not matter whose work it was. It was bad for them all.

'The remainder of the English delegation has arrived. You can imagine their fury. Particularly at the ignoble end their comrades met. Much blood, I understand. And the assassin sought to cover the crime as best he could. The finger of suspicion will fall fast upon you.' Maria looked at Ellingham. 'And you as well, sir… by the blood you carry in your veins.'

Ellingham tried not to look overawed by her and her news. 'Yet you offer no proof that the doge intends to betray us. Or that these men have been murdered.'

She smiled and gave him a look like a tolerant elder. 'My lord, did you expect me to bring their heads to show you? Or a letter from the doge to Henry Tudor telling of his wonderful promises? What I can give you is my word and bond as kinswoman to the King of Hungary. A promise that I will get you away from this place. Give you service in a great task. Wealth, if you wish it. All I ask for is something Ser Giovanni already knows.'

'Aye,' said Ellingham softly. 'That which belonged to my family.'

She wagged her finger mischievously. 'That which your father willed be given back to the giver, which is why Ser Giovanni is here in Venice. The Tears belong to *my* family. The doge was ever only an intermediary for these transactions. And your Tear, Sir Giles, is the last to come home.'

'You ask much of us today for a promise of bread tomorrow,' said Hawker. 'And still you haven't told me your kinship to the throne in Hungary.'

'Did I not?' she replied. 'My uncle is Matthias, the king. Does that reassure you?'

'I have just the word of a woman I don't even know. I'll decide my course when I am ready.'

'Your prospects are dimming with the light of this day, Ser Giovanni. If, by some miracle, the doge's heart is changed, even then you would have nothing but a handful of mercenaries in a city that cares little for your skill or service, past or future. I am offering you much more. Much more than escape from this place.'

'And what is that?' asked Ellingham.

Maria turned again to the young knight. 'A purpose fit for the son of a king. The defence of Christendom...' She trailed off for a moment, almost wistful. 'The rescue of a saint,' she continued, her voice barely above a whisper. A cloaked figure approached them, another *stradiot*, who bowed curtly and spoke rapidly and softly to the noblewoman. She looked at Hawker and raised her chin. 'You desired proof? Then come with me.'

Hawker and Ellingham exchanged a worried glance but followed as she gathered her skirts and made for the west entrance, one *stradiot* leading the way and the other two behind. Outside, the sun had nearly set, the Venetian sky now as purple as spilled ink. Across the small square not a soul could be seen, almost as if the neighbourhood had been deserted and left to the rats, cats and dogs. The smell of a nearby canal floated to them, richly noisome. The *stradiot* led them to a buttress arch nearby, a corner shielded from easy view and now lying in shadow. Ellingham could just spy a crumpled heap of rags at the base of the church. As they closed in, the *stradiot* reached down and grasped something. Ellingham swallowed as he saw that the *stradiot* held a man by his hair, the throat open wide and glistening faintly.

'A spy of the Council,' said Maria. 'Here to find out what I was doing. Or maybe you. My man caught him by one of the pillars inside. When he was seen he ran out here.'

Ellingham could see, even in the last of twilight, the look that overcame Hawker. A look that almost said he had met his match.

'If you doubt, then look at this.' She handed over a small black enamel medallion on a crimson ribbon. 'It is the badge of a *sbirri* – the Council's enforcers. You see, the noose tightens. For me as well.'

'What will you do with him?' said Ellingham, transfixed by the dripping gore of the unfortunate eavesdropper.

'He will go swimming over there,' Maria replied, gesturing towards the canal. 'A deep swim.'

Hawker pulled his cloak about himself and seemed to regain his composure. 'We cannot stay here any longer. My lady, send your messenger for us on the morrow.'

She bowed her head and then issued orders to her men. 'Do not take much longer with your decision, Sir John. You probably have a day at best – before the Council comes calling.'

Hawker grasped Ellingham lightly by his elbow and nudged him back. Even as the two briskly made their way, Ellingham found it difficult not to look back, driven to take another glimpse of her while her cloaked form was still visible, a dark angel standing before the church's stones.

They entered the maze of alleys.

'A strange creature,' said Ellingham, working hard to keep up with Hawker's strong pace. 'Her uncle a king – but where is her father, her brothers? *Who* is her father? A noblewoman on her own in a foreign land with her own retainers under arms? I mean… it is not *seemly*. For a young woman with no master to her?'

'She is not of your world,' came Hawker's curt reply. 'And she is her own master.'

'But was that dead man a spy for the palace? Does she speak the truth?'

'It's likely. But since her *stradiot* gave him a second mouth the poor bastard won't be telling us who he was from either of them.' Hunched over at a plodding, determined pace, Hawker bulled past the few Venetians still walking the *calli*, his cloak flailing about him as he moved.

Ellingham found himself walking behind, hand on his dagger, the fear of pursuit taking on monstrous proportions in his mind. His heart was in his mouth at every corner and Hawker seemed to pay no heed to stealth or caution as he plodded forward. When they had reached the little square outside the *casa*, Hawker stopped by the stone well and stared up at his house.

'It was Dieudonné.'

Ellingham felt his stomach tighten. 'The dead man?'

'No,' said Hawker, his voice quiet but tight with anger. 'The murdered Tudor agents. Dieudonné's work.'

Ellingham knew, reluctantly, it was more than a possibility. His blood-spattered arrival the night before was no distant memory. His difficult, impulsive friend had now become more than difficult. He had become dangerous. 'Sweet merciful Lord,' he whispered. 'He will bring the dogs down upon us.'

Hawker did not reply. He tore off his cloak and made his way up the stairs into the house.

'Sir John! Wait!'

Dieudonné and Beconsall were seated at the table, a jug of wine between them. Even as Beconsall broke into a smile at his arrival, and Dieudonné began to swivel round on the bench where he sat, Hawker was on the Frenchman without even a word. He shoved him with both hands, sending Dieudonné flying off, and as he rolled onto his back Hawker had him by the doublet, hauling him up again, laces popping. Dieudonné tried to prise away Hawker's hands, but such was his surprise at the attack that he froze while Hawker pulled him in close.

'Bastard! It was you, wasn't it? You sliced up those Tudor men last night. Confess it!' It felt as if his entire world was closing in on him, everything he had planned for – and hoped for – now about to collapse.

Dieudonné flexed to push away the old knight but Hawker was a mass of coiled muscle, stocky where Dieudonné was leaner and faster. The Englishman held him firm. 'I want to know how you met them.' He shook Dieudonné, hard, jolting him again. 'Confess it!'

The Frenchman stopped struggling and his cold eye met Hawker's. 'Release me.' The two words were uttered quietly, the menace implied. Beconsall was on his feet by now, his jaw slack. He was about to step in when Ellingham shook his head and waved him off. Hawker's breaths were coming on hard, a bubbly rasp underneath. His face was mottled, deep red.

'Sir John… let him speak,' said Ellingham softly.

Hawker slowly relaxed his fists, releasing Dieudonné's doublet. He took half a step back, raising palms outwards. 'Speak then.'

Ellingham moved closer to Dieudonné, worried that he might draw his blade then and there. But the Frenchman slowly pulled his doublet down, back into place, and stood his ground. 'Very well, I will tell you.'

'Goddamn you all!' said Beconsall. 'What madness is this? Who has killed who?'

Hawker did not take his eyes from the Frenchman. 'Two of Henry Tudor's men were killed last night. Here, in the city. And I will wager every ducat I own that it was this fool who did the deed.'

Beconsall swore again. 'They will surely come for us now. What possessed you, Dieudonné?'

Dieudonné did not answer but Hawker did. 'Our comrade here either tried to betray us and it went wrong… or his keenness for the cause got the better of him and he decided to turn assassin. So, which is it?'

Dieudonné stood motionless. When he spoke, in French, it was slow and measured. 'It was reckless, my lord, and I confess to it, now and before God.'

Beconsall moved away from the table and drew his dagger. 'And by God, I will deliver the justice if need be, Burgundian. So speak plainly.'

'I was in the Rialto. Looking for… women.' Dieudonné kept his eyes on Hawker. 'As I walked, I heard English voices near a stall. I grew curious. They were loud… incautious. Talking about what money they would gain from King Henry for making arrangements. I followed them, back to their hostelry. That is when I sought to eavesdrop upon them, learn if they knew about our venture.'

Hawker spoke quietly and took a step back. 'You stink of lies.'

'Judge me as you will, Sir John.'

'Let him finish,' said Ellingham. 'If we are damned either way I would still learn the why of it all.'

'I will tell you,' said Dieudonné as he glanced to Ellingham. 'I moved as close as I dared, making my way into their chambers, one room removed. But they had been drinking and were loud, confident that no one speaks English here. They began to speak of the jewel, that the doge would offer it back to them – a gift of sorts. And you, Sir Giles, another gift for Henry. They said that you would enter the palace – willingly – but that you would never leave it alive.'

'Then what?' said Hawker, his voice tight with anger.

Dieudonné nodded and swallowed visibly. 'I grew so intent on trying to hear them – my English being so poor – that I did not hear another man enter behind me. As soon as I was discovered I lunged for him. Stabbed him. The others heard and rushed in and we fought. I killed them both. Did my best to hide the bodies.'

'Where?' asked Beconsall.

'Down the garderobe. The privy.' The latter word in English.

Beconsall's eyes grew wider and he lowered his dagger. 'You shoved them down the privy?'

'I only wanted to learn of the plotting against us. I grew… reckless.'

Hawker's stare had not grown any less hard. What the Burgundian said was plausible, but equally, it could have been treachery. 'You do not give me any reason to believe you.'

'I believe him.' It was Ellingham. 'Let him swear upon the crucifix as a man of God and as our comrade these last weeks.'

Hawker glanced to Beconsall, who merely raised his eyebrows in reply. He then looked at Ellingham. 'You would trust him? With our lives?'

Ellingham looked at Dieudonné and nodded slowly. 'I will take his word. To believe otherwise would break my heart that all honour is dead.'

The Frenchman reached over and touched Ellingham upon the shoulder. 'I will swear any oath asked by my comrades.'

Hawker exhaled and looked at his boots. 'So that's it then, is it?' He moved to the table, took Beconsall's goblet and downed it. 'I give up my *contratto*, give up the gold. Give up my *house*! My…' His words trailed off. 'All on the word of this liar?' He shook his head ominously. 'That is much to ask.'

'But what of the Hungarian's revelations, my lord?' Ellingham pleaded. 'She has told you the same dread news.'

'There is *no* proof of treachery by the palace. Only by *this* man!' Hawker's finger jabbed towards the Frenchman.

Ellingham swore and closed the distance between them. 'You will not get proof, my lord! It will never come. They will close the trap and you will be in it. It is *my* life they are offering to my enemies, not yours. Would you give me up so easily?'

Beconsall's sonorous voice echoed across the chamber. 'It is done, Sir John. We are betrayed. Believe it.'

Hawker seized the wine jug upon the table and hurled it towards the stone archway. It shattered with a dull crash, followed by a tinkling of terracotta shards upon the tiled floor. Its contents spattered the walls, dripping red. He cursed. He cursed his God, the doge and his own foolhardiness that he thought he could recapture what he had lost. He could feel himself begin to sag in his *cioppa*, shoulders rounding, as if he was melting away.

Ellingham stood still, uncertain whether to offer comfort. 'Sir John, what are we to do now?'

Hawker's reply was barely above a whisper. 'What do we do now? By Lord Dieudonné's little misadventure we are on borrowed time. Some of you wanted escape, I know that.' He turned towards the others. 'Well, that is all that is left to us now. We take a ship. Tomorrow night, after the bridge fight... when the whole city will be stinking drunk.'

Ellingham looked at Dieudonné, searching his face. Hawker knew the youth was wondering why Dieudonné, his comrade and friend, had done what he had.

From his vantage in the darkened chamber adjacent, Jacob de Grood — with Jack peering over his shoulder — lowered the spanned crossbow he had held aimed at Dieudonné's chest and gave a low grunt of dissatisfaction.

—

The house was nearly still, its occupants each keeping to themselves, turned inwards upon their thoughts of what might lie ahead. In the atrium, Jacob de Grood stood first watch, naked blade across his knees and crossbow upon the trestle table. Jack Perry slumbered fitfully in a pile of woollen blankets on the floor nearby, curled up like an exhausted hound. Ellingham, in darkness where he lay on his bed, stared into his own mind. Beconsall, exhausted himself, stared at the ceiling. Gaston Dieudonné paced the rooftop balcony, weighing the alternatives as rigorously as a banker with his scales.

And John Hawker sat upon his bed, his mistress beside him. A single candle struggled valiantly to illuminate the high-ceilinged bedchamber; it guttered frantically in the draught that swirled through the room. Melancholy hung over them like a smothering pall.

'You want me to flee with you? Leave everything? Venezia?' Chiara's face was flushed, her dark almond eyes moist with tears, and Hawker could feel her shaking as he held her by both hands. The sibilant Venetian tongue came to him with difficulty and he stumbled over his words.

'I beg you, Chiara. Come with me. I can leave this place... this house. But not you.'

'You have just come back after four years. You drive my miserable husband away, you take me into your bed again, and now... now you leave again? And ask me once again to leave with you. A day ago you said all would be well.' The anger turned plaintive. 'What did I do to you to make you treat me this way?'

Hawker winced under her assault. 'Chiara, the Council *will* come for me. If not tomorrow, then the next day. If I go to them, they imprison me... or kill me. And they will most certainly kill Sir Giles. There is no other choice but to flee the city.'

She pushed him away. 'And what is your great plan? You do not even know how to get off the island. Or where to go. You might even die trying. And you want to take me with you?'

'I tried to find favour here again, but I've failed. I've failed my comrades with my wilful blindness to things. I've failed you.' Hawker put his hands to his temples and closed his eyes. 'But I *will* protect you, I promise. I can get us out and away. Away from the Council. Away from your husband.' But how could he? He did not know if they could even find a ship moored up, defenceless, ready for them to steal. Nor if they would all die, Chiara too, even attempting it. He pulled her back into his arms. She pushed back for a moment then sagged, her head falling on his chest. 'I think that you have killed me, Giovanni Falconi,' she murmured. 'Who can give me protection when you are gone?'

And that he could not answer.

After what seemed an eternity, she spoke again. Her small voice was flat. 'I am married, Giovanni. Under the laws of the Holy Church and in the eyes of the Lord. Fleeing with you will not change that. We have both sinned. And I cannot run away from all that I know. Even for you.'

He tightened his grip on her wrist, his frustration flaring. 'I can drag you out of here if I need to.'

She did not resist him. 'No, you would never do that, my love.'

He loosened his grip, and felt the sudden sting of welling tears. 'Do not do this to us, Chiara, I beg you. Think upon it!'

Her body kept very still even as Hawker soothed her face. When she spoke, her voice was like one resolved to death, quietly calm and certain. '*Giovanni*. It is God's will. Something even you cannot challenge.'

Part V

THE BYZANTINE CHOICE

28

It was midday, holy Mass just ended, and the sounds of music reverberated from the walls of the towering houses: the high-pitched drone of shawms and the pounding bass of tabor and kettle drum. Band after band was parading San Polo, dressed in dizzying colours, ribbons streaming from arms and legs. The day of the fight. The day the tradesmen of San Polo, allied with Santa Croce, would battle the fishermen and wharf men of Dorsoduro.

Under the stone arches of the open-air ground floor of Hawker's *casa*, Jack watched Jacob hurriedly lash a piece of sail-cloth over the wheeled pushcart that Sir John had hidden at the back of the dripping stone walls. Underneath the sailcloth, satchels of clothes, a sack of gold and, at the bottom, sheathed longswords wrapped in their belts. Jacob pulled at the rope to test the load was safe, and stood up. He shot Hawker a look of deep misgiving, shaking his head for good measure.

'My lord, are you sure of this? The boy and me to stand guard over all this until you catch us up at the tavern? I would rather we stash it and that I join you on the bridge.'

Hawker's eyes followed the steady stream of revellers laughing and prancing as they made their way through the little square, passing southwards out the other end. 'All our choices are poor ones. This one is the least bad. Get the cart into the tavern storehouse and stay close. Jack will afford you an extra set of eyes and ears.'

Jacob nodded but didn't object. Jack had seen Hawker visibly change in the last day – wearier than he had seen him in months, weaker in spirit. No one needed to tell him how thin a thread their fates all hung from now.

He spoke up quietly. 'And the other thing, Sir John? What of that? Should I...'

Hawker put a hand on the boy's shoulder. 'You have borne it long enough. And this lot here is enough to look after on its own. No, it is for me now. Me alone.'

Jacob grumbled. 'Well, that does not sit well either, Sir John. If you should be stopped, or struck down...' He trailed off, shaking his head again.

'It is safe. Safe for now. Have you your weapon, lad?' asked Hawker.

Jack's right hand gripped the thin handle of Hawker's stiletto that he now wore on his belt. 'Aye, and I will keep that safe for you, too.'

Jacob smiled at the boy's bravado. 'If you lose it, it should only be in the chest of an enemy.' He patted his own dagger, the twelve-inch battle blade he had worn at Bosworth field, wire-wrapped hilt and silvered pommel protruding above his wide leather belt. 'I'd be a happier man with my sword, but this will do for a tavern brawl, if needs must.' He placed a large floppy brown felt *beretto* on his head.

Hawker stepped forward and embraced him. Jacob returned it awkwardly, making Jack grin. 'Be off with you now. And God go with you!' Hawker then pulled Jack roughly into his chest, hand around the back of the boy's neck. Jack felt suddenly overwhelmed and strange, as if he was being hugged by a kindly uncle even though he had none. His chest ached, heart full. Hawker slowly pushed the boy back, gripping him by the shoulders. 'And you, you keep your wits about you this day.'

Jacob, grunting, manhandled the cart around and out from under the arches. It was then that Amalia and Chiara came down the steps. Chiara held a gathered napkin, tied, in her hands. She avoided Hawker's eye and went to Jack. She handed him the bundle and cupped his chin. 'For you,' she said in halting English, 'apples and marzipan. From Amalia.' She teared as she spoke, lapsing into Venetian. 'Have a care and may blessed Maria watch over you and keep you in her hands.'

Jack blushed and gave a bow and Chiara nodded towards Jacob before quickly walking back up into the house above.

'She stays then?' asked Jacob quietly.

'She does,' said Hawker, and Jack could clearly see the pain in the knight's unshaven, ragged face.

Jacob nodded. 'I am sorry for you. For all of this. God be with you upon the bridge, my lord!'

Hawker watched the two make their way, rattling, across the undulating paving stones of the square. He then returned to the house where his other comrades were making final preparations before the escort of San Polo arrived to usher them to the place of battle. Beconsall, nervous, had been gone for two hours early in the morning, telling Hawker he needed to walk and to prepare himself for the street fight. He was back now, an uneasy peace declared with Dieudonné. Each wore simple garb: hose, tall boots, thigh-length tunics of coarse wool, and breastplates over these. Four sallet helms without visors sat in a row upon the long table of the hall. On the floor lay their weapons: stout, heavy canes sharpened at one end and round shields of woven rattan.

'I'm going to feel naked as Adam out there,' mumbled Beconsall, picking up his shield. His eyes were wide, giving him the look of one confused – or scared.

Hawker opened the double doors of the great oak cupboard and brought out an oilcloth bundle, which he carried in both hands to the table. He untied it and threw it open. 'This might provide a fig leaf for Adam.' There were three short war hammers, black iron glistening with oil, about the length of a man's forearm. Not the heavy war hammers of the field, these were shorter and lighter, but the faster for it. 'I could only find three – we will have to draw broom straws.'

'I will keep to my dagger,' said Dieudonné. 'It will serve well enough if things go awry. You take them, gentlemen.'

Beconsall shrugged and hefted one. Ellingham followed suit.

'Now,' said Hawker, 'you know why I told you to wear a second belt over your hose and under your tunic. These are to be concealed. Here are some leather laces to fashion a hanger.' He tossed some rawhide pieces onto the table.

'You will still carry your cow-tongue of a dagger, Sir John?' asked Ellingham as he picked up a delicate war hammer and examined it.

'My *cinquedea* is just a deterrent to the adventurous. The war hammer is there to settle things in my favour – if it comes to steel against steel.'

Tunic hiked up, Ellingham began tying the raw hide on his belt to fashion a loop. 'Do these people not have any marshals to keep order during this thing? I mean, as we do in England?'

Hawker finished hanging his hammer and adjusted his tunic over it, the end of the iron haft just concealed by the hem. 'Marshals? This is a very different kind of tournament, Sir Giles. One of the few where you can kill your neighbour and never have to worry about meeting justice for it.'

The noise in the square had increased noticeably. Three heavy knocks sounded on the door outside the hall. 'Pray that is our escort to the bridge and not to the palace,' said Hawker as he made for the door. Beconsall and the others were right behind, sticks and shields in belt and under arm, helms settled upon heads. Hawker opened the door – cautiously – and a great cry went up beyond. Fully three score and more men filled the *campo*, marsh canes raised to the sky. 'Giovanni *l'inglese*!'

An army of tradesmen and apprentices cheered them as they emerged. It was a ragtag force, one of leather breastplates, chainmail shirts, tight-fitting helms of hard-boiled leather, gloves, and one fellow with two feather pillows strapped to his belly. Their sign: wide satin armbands of azure blue, tied in a double bow and worn as a badge of San Polo honour. They pulled the knights along, laughing and shouting, a babble of Venetian that never paused once. Like a torrent narrowing to exit a dam gate, the mob thinned when it approached the alley at the south of the square, folding back on itself in the press of men. Chiara Contanto watched from a shuttered window, above it all.

I will come back to bid you farewell… before I leave the city…

Let us say our goodbyes now, Giovanni. My heart cannot do this thing twice.

I promise you, Chiara…

Have we not sinned enough?

—

Surging through the *calli*, the army made its way south, towards the little bridge that crossed the San Barnaba canal, deep into Dorsoduro territory. Other tradesmen, these wearing green armbands, blended in with them from other *calli*, the men of Santa Croce. Wine in huge leather vessels passed over heads, more spilled than drunk.

Somehow, Dieudonné managed to link an arm with Ellingham as they were propelled along by the crowd. He pushed his head close to the young knight and shouted in French to be heard above the din. 'What has this noblewoman offered? Why have you not shared this with me?'

'It is not for me to share this intelligence. It is for Hawker.'

'Why, Giles? Hawker is spurning her help, isn't he?'

Ellingham snapped. 'Leave it where it lies! The die is cast!' He shook off Dieudonné's grasp. 'We have other things to worry about first!'

They reached a large *campo* with a great stone church at its centre and the *capi* of the armies, wearing tabards in their colours, began pulling men into rough ranks. Pointing and gesturing, they herded the foreign guests together near the front ranks. The mob began to coalesce. From another side, a great many prancing musicians joined them, a cacophony of horns and drums.

And then, the combatants – some hundred strong – made their way down a wide street, swung to the right and then followed another, straight to a little humpbacked bridge at its end. Beyond, the ancient pale walls of the church of San Barnaba rose up. The sky was cloudless and bright in the warm October sun. The pale red of the tiles met the sky in a rippling wave of colour, azure and gules. Yet it was the sheer noise of humanity converging on the spot that stirred hearts and set blood pulsing.

–

Hawker could see their Dorsoduro opponents on the far side and on the bridge, sticks waving. On every balcony, on roofs and in doorways, people yelled and cheered. The canal itself was covered in boats – enough to walk clear across – and they too were filled to the gunwales with onlookers. The bridge was no wider than fifteen feet and the span was no more than thirty. There were no walls on either side. One mighty push and you were in the water. He could see that sawdust had been liberally spread on the paving stones to aid footing – and soak up spilt blood. Hawker had once fought on a drawbridge and knew full well the danger. The press of bodies could become so thick that one could not wield a blade or raise a shield: hemmed in tight and helpless only to see an enemy's halberd arcing downwards towards your head...

They walked forward, leading the San Polo and Santa Croce men, Hawker in the centre, Ellingham and Beconsall on either side and Dieudonné to the left, next to Ellingham. Hawker found himself leaning backwards to try and slow the press. There were two ranks in front of them, big Venetians – most likely butchers or bricklayers and stonemasons. The *capi* were yelling and urging them all forward, some hurling insults over to the opposite side.

'At least we need not worry about drowning if we fall off,' Beconsall said laconically. He pulled his sallet down a bit lower on his bull-like head, tamping it a few times with the butt of his stick. Hawker leaned in towards Ellingham and shouted to be heard above the roaring. 'Keep your weapon high in your hand. Point down – like this! And shield covering your chest!'

Ellingham nodded nervously. 'And then what?' he yelled back.

'Hold fast! They will push as one to drive us back!'

A townsman with a great spear stood at the apex of the bridge, his tall red-felt hat a head higher than those around him. The spear he held at chest height, parallel to the bridge and blocking any overeager combatants. A series of trumpet blasts broke out from a balcony on the far side. Hawker tensed and shifted his stance: lead foot forward, the rear turned out to brace himself. A brief hush ensued, interrupted only by a few catcalls, and then Hawker saw the red-hatted man move towards the edge of one side of the bridge. In an instant, the spear was raised high and he jumped over the side into a gondola below. Immediately, a great cry went up and the two sides collided in a dull crash of steel and wood.

Within seconds, men were falling and being trampled, scrambling out on hands and knees. The fools who wore no helms were the first to go down, some knocked senseless. One was rolled over the side while another was dragged out feet first by those behind. As one went down and didn't rise again, the man behind stepped forward. It was all muffled grunting and cries of pain, cane sticks rising and falling. Hawker heard a high-pitched scream of pain and caught sight of a man clutching his face, stabbed through the eye.

The knights moved inexorably forward, a step at a time. At the centre, it was Hawker and Ellingham who engaged first. Hawker felt a flaring pain in his thigh. Some bastard, crouching one place behind the front man, had stabbed at him, aiming for his bollocks. Hawker shifted his stance and punch blocked with his shield. A snap of his wrist brought the heavy cane arcing up and then down onto the head of man directly in front of him, a stunning blow that staggered the Venetian back. There was a concerted roar from the Dorsoduro side and a new push. Suddenly, half a dozen San Polo men fell over the side. Hawker heard his *capo* screaming for others to push up and fill the gap, but the Dorsodurans had already gained ground, a third of the bridge already yielded.

Beconsall, a towering mountain of muscle, was flailing away rather than thrusting. He had already taken out half a dozen men, none of whom rose again. Hawker managed a quick glance towards Ellingham at his left shoulder. The youth was holding his own, but Hawker could hear the ping of wood on his helm and Ellingham's eyes were wide and darting about watching for the next incoming blow. It was relentless.

Pressure from those behind was now pushing all the lines forward. Hawker was shoved from behind and faltered. A sideswiping blow across the side of his head dazed him, bright lights swimming before his eyes. He felt his shield dropping but Beconsall gave out a cry and thrust diagonally against Hawker's attacker. It gave a pause just long enough for Hawker to recover. He shouted and punched his shield outwards, pushing back the man.

And so it went on, time disappearing for them all. How Dieudonné was faring on the end of their little line he did not know. Suddenly, Hawker realised they were near the end of their side of the bridge. One more enemy push and they would be driven off. Another great cry from the fishermen of Dorsoduro and a sudden rush of bodies. San Polo and Santa Croce broke, collapsing inwards from the centre and sending men on either side tumbling out into the canal, landing in and slipping between boats.

Trumpets blared again and there was cursing all around as the Dorsoduro side raised their clubs in victory, their compatriots on the far side cheering and waving handkerchiefs and banners. Hawker hauled Ellingham backwards and out of the fray. Despite their loss, Beconsall was being slapped on the back and mobbed by all around him, a hero for his prowess. He had taken out more of the other side than anyone else. For these Venetians, it was not about winning the bridge, it was about winning the fight. And winning it well with honour. Hawker wiped the sweat from his chin with his forearm. That much was over and he hoped their luck would hold out until sunset. The crowds alone meant it would be difficult for either the Council's *sbirri* or Maria Hunyadi's men to take them on now.

'Sir Giles, are you whole?'

Ellingham nodded, catching his breath still. They both turned to see Dieudonné at the far end, looking grim and with blood pouring from his punched mouth. Some fellow combatant proffered the Frenchman a large tankard, which Dieudonné readily snatched and drank from. Soon other tankards were being passed around, filled from a large nearby cask. The first battle was over.

Dieudonné moved unsteadily to Ellingham and Hawker. 'This is supposed to be an enjoyment?' He managed a sly smile, teeth bloodied and bottom lip split wide.

Hawker slipped off his helm. He gestured towards Beconsall, who was drinking in the adoration of the mob. 'It was for some. But we have done what we needed to: shown people we're not running away. At least, not yet.' The San Polo *capo* came up and gripped Hawker by the shoulders, jabbering and smiling. Hawker bowed and smiled back as the man drifted to Ellingham and did the same again.

Beconsall came up, dragging another *capo* with him. 'Hawker! What does this fellow want with me? I cannot understand him!'

Hawker rapidly understood that they wanted Beconsall for the next entertainment. A champion's fight on the bridge. One against one.

Beconsall, beaming, was led back out onto the bridge.

The bridge was cleared by all the *capi*, the red-hatted official insisting on showing his prominence, and after some chaotic milling about, the trumpets sounded again and Sir Roger Beconsall plodded up to be met by his opponent. It was some equally ursine fellow, a wharf man and cask hauler by the look of him, thought Hawker. They squared off for a few moments, the man wearing a chainmail shirt and leather helm while Beconsall's steel breastplate and sallet shone in the sunlight. But Beconsall was a knight and a swordsman. The Venetian was not. Beconsall put him down with half a dozen well-delivered blows to head and body. The poor man collapsed in a heap and was dragged off by his comrades. Beconsall raised his stick in triumph. Some cheered, others jeered.

Dieudonné sidled up to Hawker. His face was now a puffy and bruised mess and there was worry in his eyes. 'We should leave now, my lord. With all speed.'

And Hawker knew he was probably right. He told Ellingham and shouted for Beconsall to join them. A large gang of combatants swarmed them without warning, all smiles and claps of camaraderie. They were both of San Croce and San Polo. One was imploring them to take some drink at a tavern nearby, on the north side, and despite Hawker's best attempts at placating them, all four found themselves being propelled along, enveloped in camaraderie and laughter and divested of shields and sticks.

'Well,' said Ellingham, as a dark, lean, wall-eyed Venetian grasped his neck good-naturedly and gave him a shake, 'we're alive, but should we not be on the other side of the bridge and heading towards the docks?'

'We still have some time,' said Hawker. 'But we must stay together.'

They were travelling eastwards now, parallel to the canal along a *calle* that was narrowing as they progressed. Several Venetians – Hawker recognised them as San Polo men – led the way, but after a few moments those behind them were falling off, leaving for other routes or turning back. The high houses cast shadows along the alley and the sunlight now blocked made the path feel cold and damp. The group ahead turned left into a new *calle*; as the knights followed, they saw it opened onto a tiny square with but one exit at the far end. After they had rounded the corner, a large cart scraped along the paving stones and blocked the alley behind them. Opposite, a new gang poured into the square blocking the only way out.

Hawker and the others warily moved off to one side. Those that had joked with them now hung back, smiles evaporating. Where once they had extended hands eager to clasp in friendship, these now drew blades. Looking across the square, Hawker saw that the new arrivals were armed with knives, clubs and boat hooks. Hawker counted eleven. Whether the five San Croce men who had led them into the ambush would join in – or stand off to enjoy the fray – remained to be seen.

One of the Venetians stepped forward a little and gave a richly flourished mockery of a court bow. 'We come with greetings. From Signor Luca Contanto.'

Dieudonné stepped next to Hawker and slowly drew his long dagger from out of his tunic. '*Merde*,' he mumbled. He shot Hawker a look of disgusted disappointment, his lower lip swollen and cracked. 'I did not expect to have to pay for *your* adultery. Why could you not just go to the brothel like the rest of us?'

29

Slim iron war hammer in one hand, *cinquedea* in the other, Sir John Hawker, an ageing English adventurer in a city he thought he knew well, took a few steps towards the ringleader and halted. 'We can settle this if you like. You and I… alone. Let these others pass.'

Massimo was sweating, face blotched red like a cooked crab. Excitement and fear mixed, contorting his face. He had fought and killed before for his master, yet that had been against street thieves or tradesmen swallowed by debt, not against the sort who faced him across the little square. '*Bastardo!*' he bellowed, wagging his dagger towards Hawker. 'You think I'm a fool? You are *condottiere*. Not odds in my favour. *We–*' and he gestured to all his comrades '–we fight together. And when we kill you I go find your whore and slit her throat, too.'

'Pig! I'll gut you here on these stones!' Hawker started to rush forward, his war hammer arcing higher, but Beconsall jumped in and wrestled him back to where they had stood.

'God's nails!' swore Beconsall. He could not understand the exchange but knew well enough it was just loud bravado. 'Not like that, you old fool! We're outnumbered. We must stand together.'

Ellingham stepped forward to join them. 'He is right, Sir John. We have some armour at least. We can beat them back and reach the alley.'

Hawker, nodding, took a deep breath, filling his lungs and stretching the straps of his breast- and backplates. His grip tightened on his weapons. There was indeed only one course to take if Chiara's life was at stake. 'Giles, keep to my left. Sir Roger, I need you to anchor my right, over here. Remember, *that* bastard is mine.'

Dieudonné joined at Ellingham's left side. He inverted his grip on the dagger, blade pointing down, the better to block and punch with. He spoke quietly in French to the youth. 'I stand with you, my friend. We hit them hard and pass through, yes?'

Ellingham nodded.

'My lords!' said Hawker. 'Stay close. Don't let them split us. If they get behind us we fight back to back. Understood?'

But Massimo was already making a dash forward. Half an instant later his comrades rushed in at the knights. Massimo bulled his way into Hawker while another San Polo man took a swipe with a four-foot boat hook. Hawker's war hammer blocked the blow while his wide-bladed dagger intercepted the Venetian's with a dull ring. He roared curses at the Venetian, blocking and thrusting by instinct alone.

Beconsall was facing fully three opponents, all lunging or chopping at him with club and blade. He roared like a beast, his bellowed curses echoing through the square. A club landed on his breastplate and he fell back, staggered. Beconsall roared defiance, even more infuriated than before. His hand lashed out, seizing the club from the amazed tradesman with one deft motion while his war hammer came down to brain him. The first opponent downed.

Like two packs of fighting dogs, the battle swirled in on itself, the combatants circling even as the knights held together, moving as one. Hawker, intent on keeping Massimo engaged, was in danger of getting separated from the ragged line the company had formed. Ellingham deflected a thrust from a boat hook even as another struck, smashing into his helm. He felt an explosion of pain, lights dancing, and he felt himself go to his knees. Dieudonné stepped in over him, punched the attacker with a balled left fist and then brought his dagger down squarely, past the man's collarbone and deep into his lung to the hilt. The man crumpled, joining Ellingham on the pavement, blood gushing from his mouth. 'Get up! *Vas -y!*' Dieudonně screamed. The young knight hauled himself up just in time to raise his hammer and stop a club blow aimed at crushing his head.

Hawker had dropped two men flanking Massimo: one stabbed in the face and the other having his skull shattered, and Massimo now back-pedalled to get out of range. These men were tavern brawlers, but seeing friends begin to fall – and not get up again – was taking the edge from their attack. Their courage began to wane. Sensing that their rush was faltering, Massimo yelled at his comrades to spur them and they obeyed, making another sally. Massimo picked up a nail-studded club and came on again – bulling his way straight into Hawker. A flurry of blows rained down on Hawker from three San Polo men, one glancing off Hawker's helm, while a pole-arm thrust dented his breastplate and winded him. Hawker's knees gave way and the knight sank down, fighting to regain his breath.

Massimo stepped in quickly and snapped a blow to Hawker's head, sending him collapsing, sprawled out and dazed. Hawker rolled onto his back, struggling to raise his war hammer in order to ward off the coming blow to his face. But it felt heavier than it had ever before.

Suddenly, Dieudonné was there, stepping forward to Hawker's aid. He wrapped an arm around Massimo's neck from behind just as the Venetian was about to rain down the killing blow. In one smooth motion, Dieudonné had pulled Massimo backwards and arched against his chest. The Frenchman's dagger flew up to the man's neck and was driven in, twisting as it went. Massimo gave a high-pitched cry and Dieudonné punched and pushed the dagger forward twice, ripping out the man's throat. A torrent of bright blood covered the Frenchman's arm and splashed into his face. Dieudonné spat and pushed the Venetian away, sending him tumbling into one of the other attackers.

Hawker saw the San Croce men – all of whom had been holding off – begin to crawl underneath the wagon to make their escape. When the remaining San Polo gang saw Massimo fall, they pulled back, almost as one. They exchanged worried glances one to another, all saying the same thing. *Stay? Or run?*

Beconsall hastened their decision. He let out a battle cry that echoed off the surrounding houses, and raised up his war hammer, shaking it in his fist. First one and then the others of the surviving four turned and ran for the alley. Ellingham wobbled towards Hawker, head throbbing from the blow of the club. Dieudonné reached Hawker first and looped his forearm under Hawker's armpit, helping him to stand again.

Hawker's head had begun to clear and he pulled himself up straight. He saw that Dieudonné had received a deep slash on his left arm during the fight and this was rapidly blossoming across his entire sleeve, dripping down into his hand. Ellingham, too, saw that Dieudonné was wounded. He grabbed the Frenchman's wrist and ripped the sleeve up to the elbow.

'Not too deep, I think, Gaston.'

Dieudonné stood wordlessly while Ellingham tore and cut off the bottom half of the Frenchman's sleeve and fashioned a bandage. 'That will hold until we get to the tavern. *If* we make it to the tavern.'

Dieudonné grunted in reply.

'I owe you thanks,' said Hawker, sounding almost surprised by the words. 'If you had not jumped in they might… *would*… have finished me.' He nodded at Dieudonné. 'You are a wolf in a fight, my lord.'

Dieudonné swallowed hard and wiped the blood and sweat from his face with his other arm. 'Then have I redeemed myself?'

Hawker's face gave away nothing. 'Let's just say the ledger is improving.'

Above them, they heard shutters opening and with the fight ended, the awareness of other sounds returned: raised voices and cries, music, laughter. They were still in mortal danger and far from a safe haven. 'We need to get off these streets,' Hawker said. 'Before the Watch comes. Or the doge's guard.'

Ellingham's eyes ran over the bodies before them, some spread-eagled and others curled up from their agonies. Massimo, whom he had only glimpsed once delivering food to the *casa*, lay face down, dark blood pooling around his head. 'At least his master will be proud. He fought with honour. But, by God, they will hang us for certain now. We have to find a ship. We may not even have until nightfall.'

Blood was running into rust-coloured puddles. Hawker hurriedly cleaned his *cinquedea* on a dead man's cloak. 'His honour be damned! He was going to kill Chiara.' He stood up and sheathed his weapons. 'We've avoided the Republic's dogs this long… we can make it until dark. Only a few hours more.'

Ellingham gave Hawker a look of incredulity. 'Only a few hours? You remember what *she* said? Time has run out. Only the grace of God has got us this far. For all we know, the doge's men could be heading this way as we speak.'

'You've asked much of us,' said Dieudonné. 'I've seen little in return and the prospects are looking even slimmer.'

Beconsall's silence and fixed eye said he was of the same mind.

Hawker cursed under his breath. 'The Council knows of the murder of the Tudor agents. And they think it was me. And now, another one of their spies is dead at the hands of the Hungarian woman. We're between two rocks now.'

'Then if we make it to your tavern on the quay alive,' said Dieudonné, 'perhaps you can tell us the whole story. Right now, I suggest we move this waggon out of the way and take to our heels.'

—

They pulled the waggon further into the square such that they could squeeze past.

Avoiding the way they had come, Hawker found a narrow footbridge further on that took them over the canal behind the Church of San Barnaba. It was now only a matter of threading their way single file through the maze of *calli*, south by west, until they reached the wharf. Hawker prayed passers-by would think it only the bridge battle that had left them so bloodied. When

Venetians came near them, many drunk and without as much as a raised eyebrow, he got his answer.

It took a quarter of an hour for them to cover the distance. At last, he could just spy clear space ahead at the end of the alley. A glimpse of green far beyond, the isle of San Biagio.

At the corner, Hawker scanned the wharfside. He saw the usual commotion – carts and cargoes, sailors and fisher folk – but no visible sign an alarm had been raised. Yet they were too far up the docks and the tavern lay further down. 'We go around behind and work our way towards it,' he said.

Hawker glanced at his men. Beconsall was breathing heavily, eyes bulging, still fired up from the brawl. Ellingham's face had a lost look to it; he appeared overwhelmed. Only Dieudonné was calm. The four moved quickly, Hawker leading, through the narrow passages and along the open sewer of a small canal that ran parallel to the wharfside. They then turned left onto another *calle* and out onto the wide quay.

Hawker lifted his head sharply. 'There is the tavern. Find a dark corner and stay there. I will join you shortly.'

Ellingham grabbed him by the arm. 'Where are *you* going?'

'I must retrieve something.'

'Sweet Jesus!' said Ellingham, pulling back. 'You forgot the jewel?' He checked himself, suddenly thinking of another possibility. 'Or is it her? You are bringing her!'

Hawker pinned his shoulders against the bricks and held him fast. 'Now listen to me, Giles. I did not forget the Tear. But I was not about to carry it into a fight. I go back now – alone – to get it.' He released the pressure on Ellingham and looked over to Beconsall and Dieudonné. 'My lords, leave your armour and helms here. Try and look like you... *belong*.' Even as the last words left his mouth, he saw that they all looked like brigands, faces bruised and dirty, stinking of sweat and spattered with their own blood and that of others. If they lasted without discovery until dark it would be a miracle of faith.

Dieudonné pulled his sallet off his head, kicked it away, and began unbuckling his breastplate. 'This is madness. As I have said before – many times. But there is no turning back now.'

Beconsall said nothing and did the same.

Hawker pressed his palm flat on Ellingham's chest. 'Giles, do not lose hope. Not now. You must trust. If not me, then trust yourself and your own wiles.' He gave him a fatherly pat and stood back. 'Go inside the tavern. Find de Grood and the boy. And by all that is holy don't get into a fight.' He backed away and then loped down the alley. Stopping at the little canal, he tossed his helm and breastplate in before carrying on. He knew full well that it was madness for him to go back to the *casa* after what had just happened. But he was depending on others believing that too.

30

The tavern, its ceiling thick-beamed and low-hung, reminded Jack Perry of nothing more than the innards of a ship. He did not like ships. But, much to his relief, it was largely empty of patrons. If this was as big a day as Sir John had said, then the Venetian sailors and wharfmen would never miss the grand fights that were raging on the bridges. He wondered how Sir John and the others were faring in the midst of it. Even from inside the place he could hear the distant cheers and low elephantine rumble of the thousands that watched the spectacle of the bridge battle only a short distance away from the docks.

'Well, boy,' sighed Jacob, focusing his attention on the lad, 'Christ alone knows how long we will be waiting here and praying that Sir John isn't knocked on the head. Or worse. But here I am... with you.'

Jack crossed his arms, giving de Grood a basilisk's glare. 'I am no boy. I am squire to Sir John. And *I* should be with him now, not sitting on my arse here. Even Sir Roger treats me better now. He told me my guards were good. And my swing.'

De Grood snickered. 'You're an ill-mannered nosepicker, is what you are. Since we look like father and son maybe I should box your ears so we look more the part.'

'You're too ugly to be my father.'

De Grood's cheek scar rose when he cracked a smile, showing the shattered stumps of his teeth. He waggled a forefinger at the boy. 'I shall remember that when I give you your next lesson.' He snatched up his wooden wine cup and took a drink, all the while staring the lad down. 'We shall be here a while, so we can trade barbs or we can treat each other like comrades. What say you to that, eh?'

Jack merely hugged himself tighter and looked around the tavern. De Grood gave a slow nod. 'Very well, as you like.' He took another swig of the stale wine and set the cup down again. His head swivelled and he studied a group of three men that had entered wearing Eastern-looking felt hats. 'I hope Sir John knows what he is doing.' He turned to focus on Jacob again. 'But he should not have left her alone to fare for herself. Mistress Chiara.'

De Grood looked at Jack again and gave a small shake of his head. 'You worry about things you should not. Why are you in such a hurry to be a man? You think you are a soldier already just because you killed someone? And how shall you help the mistress? You going to drag her down here?'

Jack looked at the table and began picking at a crack in the boards. 'I think we should be defending the company. Not sitting here… drinking.'

De Grood raised his mug. 'I'm the one drinking. Not you.' Not getting a smile in return, the Fleming scowled. 'Bah! I am going for a piss.' He pushed a coin towards the middle of the trestle. 'If you see the landlord, get us another. One for you, too – if you're such a man now maybe you should start drinking like one.'

–

There was a privy out back in the small courtyard that de Grood's nose guided him to with no difficulty. As he relieved himself, watching his dark urine splash into the granite sluice, he reluctantly accepted that the boy was right. It was stupid for them to be sitting on their arses, as well as dangerous.

Sir John did seem to have lost his way, even his cunning, and he himself didn't have the balls to tell the knight when he'd had the chance. Chiara Contanto had changed everything, he reasoned. To be sure she was a virtuous and good woman – though of course not to her husband – but she was a distraction. A distraction, he knew, that a returning *condottiere* did not need and could not afford. And Sir John had blinded himself to all else. Blinded himself to the Burgundian, a man de Grood would never have even diced with, never mind trust. It was plain that Dieudonné would sell his own mother if it was to his gain. He finished his business, hawked and spat, and retied the points of his hose. When he returned to the tavern room he saw that Jack Perry was gone.

—

Jack Perry had a rat's sense for finding direction. That is what his father had always told him. He had only to make just a single run somewhere, and he would then be able to find his way again without a second thought. This was not unusual if food were the object, which was more often than not the case. The stealing of which normally led to being beaten black and blue by his sire. But this had never changed how fast he could travel, no matter the twists and turns of the alleyways of Stamford. Thus, he made it back to the *casa* quickly, finding the square deserted of life.

He knew his disobedience would likely be punished by Sir John but, he believed, his oath as a squire to a knight demanded more of him. The mistress was unguarded. The house was unguarded. The jewel – a treasure he had secreted on his person for weeks, fearful of its loss – was unguarded. And Sir John, in his worry and his haste to plan their escape, had neglected their rear. At the great battle near Leicester had he not stayed behind to guard the camp? This was no different, and the knight would surely see that.

Jack entered the crumbling archway, the stone staircase an open mouth inviting him to the rooms above. As he reached the great chamber he heard sobbing, the sobbing of a woman, suppressed and muffled. At the top of the interior stairs off to the side stood Amalia, her apron shoved into her mouth, her body shaking like some quivering great brown dumpling and her eyes wide with fear. She saw Jack and started – a stifled cry making its way past the crumpled linen in her mouth. But she recognised him and the apron fell from her lips. '*Vada Via!*' It was half whispered but vehement and she repeated it, shooing him with her hands. Jack did not understand but took her meaning well enough. That was when he heard the voices up in Hawker's bedchamber, those of a man and woman fighting. Fighting like he had often heard his mother and father do. Ignoring Amalia's pleas, he carried on up.

Before he reached the chamber, he heard the woman cry out in pain. He knew it was Chiara. A chair or table smashed and she cried out again. But quickly thereafter came her own fire. Her Venetian poured out at her attacker in a scornful flood. When Jack reached the doorway, he could hear the scuffle of feet on the floor and the strained but furious voice of the man. Looking in, he saw Chiara fall to the floor under the full force of a blow from the man. It was Luca Contanto. The man exploded into what sounded like cursing and then hauled her up by her bodice only to strike her down again. Jack had seen such sights before but had been too young and too scared to ever intervene. But now he was older. And now he knew what was expected of him.

He hurled himself straight into the back of Contanto just as the man hunched, fist raised, over the figure of Chiara on the floor. Jack's arms wrapped around the Venetian but at that point he was at a loss as to what to do next. Contanto recovered from the attack and tried to shake off the intruder that clung to him like a limpet, twisting and yelling. He quickly had Jack pulled around to face him even as Jack tried to push him off. Contanto struck him across the side of the head and lights flashed before his eyes. A second blow sent him off his feet and sliding across the tiles.

Even as his head swam, he could see Contanto pointing at him and screaming at Chiara. And then, Contanto went for Chiara again. His hands were about her throat and Jack watched for what seemed an age while her husband throttled her. She did not raise her hands to pull him off but instead kept still as if she was already dead. Jack could see her face go from red to a mottled purple and all the while Luca Contanto spoke through his gritted teeth, cursing her.

Jack rubbed his temple, his face burning, and pulled himself to his feet.

Defend the helpless. Be virtuous.

Hawker's blackened steel stiletto was in his hand and he half stumbled, half fell, towards Contanto who was then on his knees, energies fixed on extinguishing his faithless wife. Jack Perry had neither skill nor craft, but he drove the needle-like blade through Contanto's back – to the hilt. The Venetian cried out, but this stopped as soon as his left lung collapsed. Contanto tumbled over sideways and Jack fell over him, his hand still firmly gripping the hilt. His falling weight shifted the blade sideways and Contanto's body jerked sharply once – when the tip bit into his heart.

Jack pulled the blade out and pushed himself away, his breaths coming fast. Chiara seemed not to move upon the floor and Jack knew not if life remained in her. Luca Contanto was dead though. He was in no doubt of that, watching the dark blood creep from the man's mouth and begin to slowly pool on the russet-red tiles.

He was a squire and he had defended a woman. He saw the colour of Chiara's face return to pink, her body curling up where she lay.

And behind him came laughter.

Jack, still upon the floor, moved like a frightened crab and then righted himself, jumping to his feet and brandishing the dripping stiletto. In the doorway stood two men, both armed with curved swords. Strangely dressed, great brimmed felt hats on their heads and pointy, waxed beards. He remembered that he had seen them before, at the palace with the foreign noblewoman. One of them said something, which Jack could not understand, and his comrade let out a hearty laugh again. Jack felt his hose begin to soak through as he stood there, the piss tickling as it trickled down to his shins. He dropped his dagger. It clattered to the tiles.

31

Hawker reached up quickly and plucked a long, forest-green cloak and hood from a washing line and hurriedly pulled it on. He had staggered back to San Polo through the winding alleyways, his breaths laboured and wheezy. Even as he feared a hundred eyes were following his every step, he had kept up a steady stream of cursing the whole of the journey back. Cursing his own hubris. For the promise of fortune, fame and a rekindled love, he had ignored the signs and the warnings all around him. Ignored instincts that had kept him alive through countless battles and the palace intrigues of Plantagenets and Venetians alike. Now he was trying to claw back a small remaining chance of salvation and escape from his enemies.

He slowed his pace the closer he got to his square, peering from each corner before rounding it and pushing forward. The sun was low and the revellers were fast disappearing back to their homes after a day of pandemonium. Cautious until the very end, he at last made it to the square.

A woman was filling her bucket from the well. It was not Amalia or Chiara. He paused, hanging back to scan every way into the place. The only sound was the scraping of the wooden bucket on the stones as the woman hauled it up. A flock of starlings squawked overhead, darting and diving as they began their evening feed. Keeping to the edges, Hawker walked around two sides and came to his house. There, sitting on the stone steps, was a young boy, no more than eight or nine, dark with grime and eyes like two small lumps of coal. When he saw Hawker, he got up. His voice was cautious.

'Are you the one who lives here, sir?'

Hawker nodded. The boy extended his hand and held out a small square letter, sealed with a wax the deepest hue of purple. Hawker gently took it from him and the boy darted away without a backward look. Hawker went up a few of the stone steps, turned to make sure no one had entered the square, then carried on up into the house. The studded door was ajar. It was deathly quiet, the house filled with shadows and not a single lamp burning. In the gloom Hawker could see the doors of the heavy cupboard in the great hall had been left open. Plates and goblets lay strewn across the floor. Chiara was nowhere to be seen. He listened carefully, proceeding to his bedchamber. The mattresses had been flipped off the bedframe, his table smashed, an oak chest emptied of clothes and trinkets lay upended in a corner. It was then that he spotted a crumpled body on the far side of the bedstead and a copper-red smear of gore that led to it. Heart pounding, he walked around the bed and saw the upturned grey and lifeless face of Luca Contanto staring back at him.

'Sweet Christ above,' he muttered, falling back a pace. His mind filled with a dozen ways it could have unfolded and Chiara was in all of them. But had she slain him? Hawker threw back his hood and went to the window. Carefully counting the lozenge floor tiles, he quickly knelt and with his fingers prised out the heavy red clay square. And then he hurled it against the wall with all his strength. The jewel was gone.

He slid down and backed himself up against the wall under the leaded window, clutching at the letter in his hand. His gut churning, he opened it and read, eyes squinting.

> *You have waited too long. Regretfully, to safeguard my own life, I have had to take action. I offered you something you have been too blind or too proud to see. So, I tell you this: bring the Tear or you shall not see your boy again, nor your gold. My terms remain unchanged and generous. You know where my ship lies.*

Hawker's fist scrunched the paper into a ball, the wax seal pricking his hand as it crumbled. His stomach felt sick. She had taken Jack as hostage.

Sitting on the cold tiles, legs splayed, he fumbled into his belt purse. A few coins rolled out and then his rosary spilled, black beads coiling onto the floor. His fingers found the corn dolly, which he pulled out and held to his eyes. It had not brought him much luck, other than that he was still alive. But perhaps, just perhaps, that was its only purpose. He shoved it back into his pouch, crushing it. The child that he had bought it from was no doubt that day in Leicester selling a hundred of the little charms to the sentimental and the gullible – like him.

He was awash in anger, frustration and regret. For a moment, the desire to just lie there until the Council's men came for him – and come they would – overwhelmed him. But then the despair subsided, an ebbing tide, replaced by a rising resolve to fight on. As he always did. He swept up his rosary and picked himself up off the floor. He plied the beads in his right hand, rolling each as he worked his way up towards the silver centrepiece. Yet he wasn't praying, he was thinking.

Clearly, Maria Hunyadi didn't have the jewel. Jack Perry, ever loyal, had asked him if he should carry it, and had accepted the decision that he would not. And the *casa* had been ransacked. Had the doge's men already been there, looking for the jewel? Or had Luca Contanto come here first, planning on finding him in Dorsoduro afterwards? Hawker decided it was more likely the palace that had paid the call. If the doge's men had found the Tear, then it was finished, over, his scheme in tatters. He might beg for Jack's return from the Hungarian but he would have nothing to offer up, nothing except his own life. Had they killed Jacob? He could not see how the Fleming would have let Jack be taken without a fight.

Chiara…

The only other who might have discovered – or guessed – the hiding place. She may well have watched as he and Jack squatted on the floor and placed the jewel pouch under the tile. Hawker wound up his rosary, briefly kissing the crucifix, and hurriedly placed it back in his belt pouch. All her anger, her sense of betrayal and her abandonment, leading her to take that which was of most value to him. He had to find her. And he had to hope it was not she who had slain Contanto.

We have sinned enough.

He could see her saying that again, her heart broken, looking up at him. The memory of it felt like a dagger thrust. Remorse. Yet her guilt might direct her to seek out forgiveness – absolution. But where? He walked out into the hall again, his mind travelling outwards from the little square. Remembering the chapels nearby, the churches that lay closest. Which did she favour? He remembered one. A tall but narrow whitewashed church, a tiny bell tower above its heavy iron doors. It was nestled between two houses a few hundred yards away. And if she was not there? He had no choice but to search out each and every holy place. Search until he found her, or until he was taken.

He returned to the oak cupboard and retrieved paper and quill pen. The ink had been splattered across the cupboard and floor when it had been ransacked, but enough remained in the pewter well for him to write what was needed. He wrote rapidly in a shaky hand, tearing the brown paper as he scrawled out his poor Venetian.

Folding his paper and tucking it into his pouch, Hawker put the hood of his stolen cloak up over his head and descended the stone stairs to the doorway, hand on his dagger hilt and ears alert to any new arrival. The square was as quiet as when he had entered and he slowly made his way around the perimeter to the north, slipping into the alley. The sky was changing its hue as it did in Venice during the hours of fading light: azure blue to ultramarine, to amethyst. He thought about his men and whether they had been discovered or indeed what they might have done when they did not find de Grood and Jack where they were supposed to be. He reasoned that Beconsall would follow Giles's lead, but Dieudonné had a mind and will of his own. That made him the more dangerous.

He reached the narrow, tall double doors of the church that sat, squat and low, in a wide alley. Three cats on the granite stoop hissed at his arrival and fled. Two old women passed by, deep in conversation, and barely glanced at him. The door was partly open. He pushed it and entered. A hundred votive candles burned near the altar and rising above it was a painting of the risen Christ.

His eyes fell upon the church's only occupant: a veiled woman kneeling at the front. Pushing his hood back, he approached her. She turned as she heard his footfalls, the edge of her veil pulled back to see who it was. He heard her gasp echo as she sought to rise. Hawker rushed ahead, and his arms enveloped her, forcing her back down to her knees and he with her. Her veil fell off and he saw the mass of bruises upon her face, the red finger marks upon her long neck.

'Chiara, Chiara,' he whispered. 'What happened? What happened at the *casa*?'

She had already broken into quiet sobs, her frame heaving as he held her. He tried to lift her. 'Tell me, did you kill him?'

She shook her head, swallowing hard, more sobs wracking her as the memory flooded back.

'My love, who came? Who was it?'

She turned her eyes upwards to him and found her voice. 'It was your boy. He saved me. He had returned to the *casa* and found... Luca. He killed him.'

Hawker pushed her head onto his chest, nuzzling her, as the truth of what Jack had done – and what he now was – swept over him. He remembered the boy's words weeks earlier.

I'm not afraid... I know how it is done.

She continued, her voice small and detached of emotion. 'And then... the other men came upon us. Took your boy and tore up the rooms. They wanted the jewel. I lay upon the floor unable to move. I heard them speak with a woman in the hall. A foreign tongue. They left me alone and I fainted away again.'

She shook her head, wordlessly imploring him. Her eyes began to fill and Hawker felt her body go almost limp. She spoke again, barely audible. 'My fault. *Our* fault, Giovanni. Our sins.'

Hawker swallowed hard. 'Contanto would have killed you.'

She looked up, her voice empty. 'I deserved no less.'

Hawker winced at her words. 'You deserve to live. And you will live. It is not too late. We can get away. Come with me now.' He gently touched her chin and guided her face towards him. 'Chiara, I beg you. The Hungarian has Jack. I need the jewel… to free him. It is what she wants.'

Her eyes shut tight at his words, more tears welling past the crow's feet above her cheeks. A small, anguished noise came from her.

Hawker swallowed the lump in his throat, feeling as if his heart, long ago dried to a husk, suddenly had filled near to bursting. 'They will kill my boy. They *will* kill him. I need the stone. I beg you.'

Her head lowered and lolled a bit, her mind seeing something terrible. Hawker felt her arm move down and into her tunic. She twisted slightly, and her hand withdrew. She held up something between them. It was a folded piece of cream-coloured muslin. She pushed it into his chest and kept pushing. Hawker folded his hand around hers and then took it from her grasp. He could feel the jewel inside, cold and hard.

'I watched you hide it. With the boy.' Her voice was small.

Hawker swallowed. 'I was wrong to abandon you before. Selfish… prideful. For the love of God, I beg you… come with me.'

She looked at him again, a great sadness flooding over her long, thin face, handsome despite her bruises. She slowly shook her head.

'Chiara, please. I will take you away from here. From all that has happened. I won't let you escape me twice. I never should have left you the first time.'

She shook her head slowly. 'You don't understand, Giovanni. Running away cannot undo what was done. What I have done before you came. And after. My pride at being the mistress of a lord.' She looked down again. 'I must prepare to bury my husband. Then… then I shall prepare to receive my punishment, if that is what is to come.'

Hawker slowly released his hold on her and she fell away, collapsing onto the stone steps, her eyes, in her bruised face, seeking out the altar and a lit candle. She seemed broken, the fight gone out of her. He needed her to rekindle the fire he knew still burned inside her for life, and for him.

He gripped Chiara by her shoulders and shook her. 'Punishment? Woman, if they don't hang you they will slash your face into ribbons!'

She shoved him away. 'I do not fear Venice. I fear the wrath of the Lord. My fate is in God's hands! Not yours.'

He instantly regretted his brutality and felt the sting of tears in his eyes. His shoulders sagged and he leaned back against a stone pillar. 'Chiara, the *sbirri* will say you killed him. There were no witnesses.' The words came out in a dry rasp.

'No. Amalia was there too. Before she fled. She will swear to it.'

He could feel Chiara slipping away from him again, though she was still right there. He swallowed, trying to wet his throat. 'I could carry you out of here. What I should have done years ago.'

She looked at him, her face full of sorrow. 'You could. But you won't. It is not my will to go with you, to leave my home, to end up God knows where, even if you succeed in escaping. To go into battle with you? No, Giovanni. I will stay.'

His chest hurt as if he'd been punched. He reached into his doublet and pulled out a folded piece of paper from his purse. 'You will need more than the word of Amalia. This is my confession. It says that it was I who killed your husband.'

She tried to push it away, but he placed it in her palm and folded her fingers. 'No. You will need this. I suspect they will have little trouble believing it. My time here is at an end. The *casa* is yours to do with as you will. The deed is in the sideboard. I have signed it over to you. It was witnessed by the parish two days ago.'

312

She blinked a few times, her head shaking. Hawker opened his mouth but the words would not come. He helped lift her up, his own knees cracking. She touched the side of his face, gently pressing her palm to his cheek. 'I will pray for you, Giovanni. Always. May God protect you.'

'Chiara…'

'Find your boy. And then find your way.'

32

Beconsall wrapped his hands around the clay wine pot and hunched lower on an old table marred by a thousand knife gouges. 'The deepest and dampest corner of this damnable hole of a tavern would not save us from looking like murderous bloody Saracens,' he hissed. 'See how they over there are watching? Then they look away. And where the hell is the Fleming? He should have been here long ago. Hours. And, for Christ's sake, *where* is Hawker?'

Ellingham leaned in. 'Have a care, my lord,' he growled. 'Pretend you are in church. Pray and keep silent.' But he was getting worried, too, as they seemed to have been waiting an age.

Beconsall was so nervous that his leg was twitching and shaking the table. Ellingham cast his own eyes about the place. It was a sprawling den of traders and seamen, thick wooden pillars fashioned from old masts holding up the undulating ceiling of the floor above. The brick-laid floor stank of stale wine, and stray dogs wandered between the trestles and benches, searching for discarded scraps.

They had taken seats towards the side of the tavern floor, halfway back towards where the wine casks lay propped in their cradles. They had a clear view towards a doorway at the rear and line of sight to the main entry at the wharf. For his part, Beconsall had already spotted and pointed out a bench that he could use as a ram to clear a way through if it came to a hasty exit and a fight. The denizens were boisterous but, for the moment at least, all good-natured.

Dieudonné, too, was twitchier than usual, thought Ellingham. He could just see the glint of the dagger in the Burgundian's hand at the table's edge. He had ceased running the tip of the blade under his fingernails and was now absently rubbing his thumb over its edge. His lip was swollen where he had been struck, the cut dried a dark reddish brown. His hair, sweat-soaked and stringy, was pasted down over his forehead. Every few moments he would slowly turn and survey the room behind him.

Ellingham could not fault him for his caution. They were deeply exposed now, fully expecting either the doge's men or else a party of Dorsoduro artisans bent on *vendetta*. As the hour went by and the serving boy brought more wine, they each were thinking the same thoughts: that Hawker had fallen or that Hawker had recovered the jewel and escaped on his own with his caretaker mistress. Even Ellingham had now begun to imagine the worst had occurred. It was time to think of another way to escape. And in his usual, uncanny way, Gaston Dieudonné seemed to sniff this out on him.

When he caught Ellingham's eye he spoke in quiet French. 'Eh, my friend? Your little mill wheels are spinning, I can see. Tell me about this woman then. This *Hungarian*. I know you are scheming something. You and Hawker both.'

Beconsall's French was hole-shot and patchy, but he hunched over further when he heard Dieudonné pose the question. 'Tell us, Sir Giles.'

Ellingham cast his eyes down towards the sodden table for a moment. 'She is a noblewoman. She says… she says that the jewel belongs to her. It is of her family. And she is determined to get it back.'

'More determined than the doge?' asked Beconsall.

Ellingham pinched the bridge of his nose. 'Don't you see? We can trust *neither*. Hawker has been doing his best to keep them both guessing, but now we have run out of time.'

Dieudonné's voice was calm. 'What is she offering?'

'She offers us wealth and an escape. She has her own ship. Just further along the docks. She told us something about service in her household… or her uncle's.'

Dieudonné rolled his hand outwards, urging Ellingham. 'Her uncle? Who is…?'

'The King of Hungary, Corvinus.'

Dieudonné stuck out his lower lip and then nodded. 'I know what you're thinking. The jewel is your proof of who you are to the duchess dowager. But in truth, Giles, it is not. There are other ways to prove yourself. If it is the price of safe passage – and the path to riches – why not?'

'You're forgetting,' said Ellingham. '*We* don't have the jewel. And if Hawker doesn't any more, then who does?'

Dieudonné fixed him with a look of steel. 'If we do not take a ship this night then we are dead men. If we steal one, we are pirates – and penniless pirates at that. If we bargain with the Hungarian we stand a chance of gaining far more.'

Beconsall sat back and pushed his mug away. 'De Grood is missing. Hawker is missing. We are nearly as naked as the day we were born, with neither swords nor money. The Burgundian speaks sense. I will wait here for Hawker. You two should go now. Move down the wharf and find this noblewoman and her ship. We will join you.'

Ellingham inhaled deeply of the tavern fug. It was time to decide. He thought of both his fathers – the one he had never known who had sired him, and the one who had raised him and ignored him. He thought about the precious little he had accomplished in his short life, nothing of which had prepared him for such decisions – or to lead men. The few retainers he once had now lay dead in the marshes below Bosworth, a thousand miles away. But his blood was the blood of kings. God and fate had brought him across kingdoms, duchies and seas. All the way to where he now found himself. He suddenly remembered what he had told Hawker all those days ago in Flanders. It was time to start running towards something. Towards his destiny.

'The lady knows my blood, who I am. I will take us to her. If it is in my power to deliver up the jewel to her then I will do so. We must get off this cursed island. If we can do that, then we live to bargain another day.'

Dieudonné slowly sheathed his dagger and sat up straight. 'Well then, I suppose it is time we met your noblewoman. While we all still draw breath.' He looked from one to the other. 'Are we ready?'

'We should all go,' said Ellingham, looking over to Beconsall. 'We stand a better chance that way. Sir John will figure things out soon enough.'

Beconsall shook his head, looking doubtful. 'The arrangement was for here. He'll come here first. You two must go. I'll stay.'

Ellingham looked to Dieudonné. The Frenchman shrugged. 'Let him. Better two of us get out of this cesspit than none.'

'Sir Roger,' said Ellingham quietly, 'this is rash.'

But Dieudonné was already pulling at his elbow.

'It's all rash, my boy,' said Beconsall, giving him a wistful look.

The two made their way out, weaving around gangs of porters. As they emerged onto the wide wharf, a strong, sea-tanged breeze wafted past and Ellingham, for one, could smell freedom was close. The sun was nearly set and the drinking holes were lighting their lamps and braziers. Cart men still laboured even on this the Lord's Day, for the cargoes came and went without stop in Venice, ship masters eager to finish their ladings in order to set sail at dawn's light. Ellingham led the way, Dieudonné in his wake.

'What vessel is it?' asked Dieudonné.

'It is a good-sized galley, further on,' replied Ellingham, not slowing. They walked for a few minutes, Ellingham desperate to lay his eyes on the familiar lateen mast, picking it out of the dozens that reached up to the sky in the fading light.

Dieudonné smiled. 'I see it,' he said. He then swivelled his head back to check the way they had come. Two men were watching and keeping pace a few yards back. They were dressed in long dark mantles, short felt caps upon their heads. Dieudonné faced forward and kept walking. He turned back again and saw they still followed. As they passed a chandler's, two more men joined them, similarly dressed in dark cloaks, the tips of sword scabbards just visible below their hems.

'There it is!' said Ellingham, pointing. 'The long vessel with the single great mast.'

Dieudonné drew up alongside Ellingham. His voice was icily calm. 'Ready yourself. We are not alone.'

33

Hawker knew it was going to be the longest journey through the *calli* that he had ever taken. The Tear of Byzantium now joined the corn dolly, rosary and three gold Florentines in his purse. With his stolen green cloak drawn close, hood covering his face, he set off south once again.

His muscles ached and his head was light. Too much fighting for one day and nothing to eat had taken its toll. He was pushing himself now, he could feel it. Nearly too old to lead the life of a mercenary but too stubborn to accept the fact. He purposely took a different way through the winding alleys and prayed he would not run into a survivor of the afternoon's butchery in the Dorsoduro square.

As he neared the seafront, it seemed the streets were quieter and he assumed word of the murderous fight must have spread. People returning to their homes out of fear of both the combatants and the dreaded *sbirri*. He lost his way, redoubled his steps – twice – and eventually made it down to the docks. But he had wandered too far to the west, still a distance from the appointed tavern. Thus far, it had taken him almost an hour by count of the quarter chimes.

Hawker scanned the wharf and then began walking again. Those that still worked loading vessels were too busy to bother even giving him a glance. He passed unnoticed, head down, looking up every so often to see the path ahead. At length, the tavern hove into view. He entered and weaved his way into its depths. He quickly spotted Beconsall, hunched over a trestle. Alone.

'Where are the others?' Hawker couldn't mask the note of desperation in his voice.

Beconsall turned and looked up. 'Sir John. Your Fleming and the lad were not here. I have stayed behind for you. Ellingham and the Burgundian have gone out down the wharf looking for the ship.'

Hawker cursed under his breath. 'Get up. We have to find them now.' He remembered that Ellingham knew exactly where Maria Hunyadi's galley lay – if the Hungarian had not moved it. Pushing Beconsall in front of him, they hurriedly departed and turned left along the wide cobbled wharf. Beconsall kept abreast while Hawker looked ahead, scanning for signs of the others, his left hand clasping the hilt of his jangling *cinquedea*.

'I'm sorry,' said Beconsall, quietly. 'Sorry about all of this.'

Hawker didn't slow his pace. 'What have you to be sorry for?' he said. 'We still have a chance.' Everything depended on the jewel now. And getting it to Maria.

Beconsall slowed and came to a stop. 'Forgive me, Sir John.'

Hawker stopped too and looked at the big knight. His eyes were wide open, almost frightened. Conflicted. Hawker's brow furrowed then instantly relaxed. He understood now, and it was too late.

A man sidled up next to him. It was Paolo Federini. 'Don Falco, stay your hand. Do not be a fool. There is a crossbow at your back.' Hawker felt the gentle prod of something in his ribs. Hawker craned his neck to see three or four long-cloaked *sbirri* arrayed about him. Beconsall moved back, slowly. He was wincing.

'I had no choice, Sir John,' he said, head shaking. 'You were going to get us all killed, for nothing. I gave you every chance to prove you could lead us out. You failed.'

Hawker swallowed hard, letting the betrayal wash over him. He remembered Beconsall's absence for a few hours the previous afternoon. A trip to the brothel, he had assumed. He snorted at the irony of it. His own blindness. 'Honour is dead.'

'Our *king* is dead,' said Beconsall. 'You should have accepted that, given them the jewel. I had no wish to do this to you.'

'Move forward, Don Falco. My men are keeping an eye on your companions up ahead. It seems your ship has forgotten you. There is no one aboard her. I'm afraid you have lost that gambit, too.' His English was perfect.

Hawker felt a prod again. He began walking. People ahead stared and receded, setting down their loads, moving away. 'What will you do with the others? They merely serve me. They have no guilt in all this.'

'That depends on you. Where is the jewel?'

Hawker threw Federini a thin smile. 'It is somewhere.'

A *sbirri* closed tight on Hawker's left, grasped his shoulder harshly, and steered him forward. 'Then the others of your company we will sell,' said Federini, 'to the Turks. The boy will no doubt fetch a good price. As for the young man of a certain family, well, the Council has plans for him. In the interests of the Republic.'

Hawker could see the galley now. It was dark without a lantern in sight. He could also see Ellingham and Dieudonné standing next to its mooring, conversing. Across the wharf, a gaggle of long-cloaked men milled about, trying to look uninterested. Hawker knew that Dieudonné would not be ignorant of them. He was waiting for the moment to unleash.

Beconsall was still following alongside, slightly distant from Hawker and his captors. 'You never told me you would enslave the boy!' he blustered. 'You told me you wanted the jewel and the youth.'

'And you will have your gold and your passage back to England. Subject, of course, to the desires of King Henry's commissioners.'

Beconsall shut up, blinking furiously. Hawker looked over at the knight. Beads of sweat poured down his wide, sloping forehead. In the torchlight of the wharf he could see the man's face mottling darker. Beconsall began mumbling. 'Not what you told me. Not what I wanted.' Hawker could see that he was bubbling like a steaming cauldron.

A moment later, Beconsall's cape flew back and the knight drew his dagger in one movement, shoving it into the man behind Hawker. Hawker moved to seize Federini, twisting him around as a shield. Beconsall began slashing his way through the shaken *sbirri*, who had now drawn steel themselves. He then yanked his war hammer from his belt and began swinging. Another crossbowman dropped back and fired, hitting Beconsall in the back, but the bear of a man kept raining blows on the Venetians. He bellowed at them, cursing them for all they were worth.

'Hawker! Run, you fool!'

Hawker saw the other Council ruffians opposite the galley begin to trot towards them. He pushed the spitting Federini into the dogfight, drew his *cinquedea*, and launched himself straight for the men heading his way.

–

Heads bowed in false conversation, Ellingham's heart pounded while Dieudonné whispered words of encouragement. He could see the commotion further down the wharf from where they had come. Then he heard the ring of steel on steel. When he saw the cloaked men make a dash to intervene, he heard the rasp of Dieudonné's blade a second later.

'Now!' shouted Dieudonné. The Frenchman whirled about and ploughed into the closest of the men, knocking him forward and down to the cobblestones. The Frenchman raised his dagger and stabbed down. Seeing they were under attack, the others turned to defend themselves.

Ellingham held out his dagger at full arm's length while reaching with his left for the war hammer lodged at his waist. He blocked the arc of a Venetian's sword, but his dagger went spinning out of his hand. Instinctively, he threw up both hands in expectation of the next blow. He was briefly aware of a rushing figure behind his attacker and in the next instant, just as the

Venetian was about to unleash a crossing blow to take off his head, his attacker suddenly arched up, head thrown back, mouth wide open. The Venetian slumped to the stones and Ellingham saw it was Hawker standing before him, wheezing for breath, his bizarre dagger dripping. Ellingham dove down to retrieve the dead man's sword.

'Sir John! Where are the others? Where is Sir Roger?'

Hawker didn't have time to reply, whirling again to block a sword cut. Ellingham looked ahead to see Beconsall, an enraged giant, roaring oaths and grappling with the other Venetians. Ellingham raised the longsword over his head and brought it down, cleaving the skull of the man running at him. He caught another glimpse of Beconsall beyond. The giant staggered and shook, his war hammer flying out of his hand. Ellingham could see three fletched bolts protruding from him. And then he toppled over.

Hawker stumbled to Ellingham and grabbed his arm. His words tumbled out as he fought for breath.

'We must get onto the galley!'

Ellingham could now see more soldiers or *sbirri* heading towards them, some officer waving a blade and urging them forward. They surged around the body of Beconsall, numbering at least a dozen men.

'The galley is abandoned!'

'Then we shall take it!' spat Hawker, stumbling back towards the mooring and gangplank.

Dieudonné appeared half mad, ranting at the assembling crowd in French, waving his bloody dagger. Hawker grabbed him and pulled him back. 'Onto the ship!'

Something whistled past Ellingham's head. And then another whizzing blur, which hit the galley's side and bounced, clattering to the cobbles. Crossbow bolts. They were but three against a dozen, and now Ellingham could spy other Venetians pouring in from a side alley, all studded leather armour and shining helms. A high-pitched sound – trumpet or ram horn – sounded behind

323

him. It came from the galley. To his amazement, Ellingham saw a dozen archers rise up from concealment along the gunwales between the raised and locked oars of the vessel.

The Hungarian's *stradiotti* were drawing back their bows, taking aim at the Venetians. Lights appeared fore and aft as lanterns were uncovered. His eyes searched out the deck. Aft of the mast he saw Jack. He was standing, a *stradiot* holding him by the shoulder. At his side was Maria. She was dressed as a warrior: Ottoman pantaloons and boots, a short thigh-length tunic and belt. In her hand was a naked sword.

The way up the gangplank was blocked by her men, wicked curved swords glinting in the lamplight. Maria moved across the deck and approached the rail.

Hawker seemed to have frozen in his tracks once he had seen her with Jack.

Ellingham saw more Venetians fanning out on the opposite side of the wharf, some taking cover behind barrels and crates when they saw the *stradiotti* on the galley. They began to close ranks, unsure of what to do. A voice called out from deep inside the group of hesitating *sbirri*.

'Giovanni Falco!' It appeared that Federini had escaped Beconsall's wrath. His *sbirri* fanned out in front. Ellingham could see that two had levelled crossbows at them.

Dieudonné moved closer to him, his reddened dagger tapping against his palm in anticipation. 'Too many this time, my friend. Can you swim?'

Ellingham was frozen, too stunned to reply.

Dieudonné grinned, his wild eyes darting from man to man across the wharf. 'One always must have choices.'

—

Federini shouted again. 'My lord! Did we not have a bargain? I will still honour it, I swear to you! Why are you running? Give me the jewel! We will not pursue.'

Porters and cart men scattered like startled deer at the impending skirmish.

Hawker looked up again to the Hungarian. Over her head a red banner rippled, lantern light dancing on the silk. It was emblazoned with something he had seen before, a memory that evaded him.

Her voice was calm but commanding, carrying across the deck and wharf. 'Do you have it, Ser Giovanni?'

'I do!' Hawker replied, hoarsely.

'And do you accept my terms?'

Venetian blood had now been spilled. There was no way back. Hawker glanced over to Ellingham. The youth must have understood her. He gave a slow, deliberate nod to Hawker. Whether it was right or wrong, whether it was cursed or not, whether it belonged truly to the Hungarian or the doge, the jewel was going to buy their escape. Hawker shouted up to Maria.

'I accept your terms!'

She nodded and gestured towards the gangplank.

Hawker swallowed, his eyes on the crossbows that stood ready a dozen yards away. 'My lords,' he said quietly, 'get on the ship.'

Ellingham began to move towards the gangplank. Federini's voice, more strident this time, echoed across the wharf. 'I won't ask you again!'

'Dieudonné,' said Hawker, 'you go next.'

'You do realise that the crossbows are aimed at *you*. Not me.'

Hawker managed a thin smile and laid his *cinquedea* across his chest. 'I am old, my lord. But not yet blind. Move, sir, while you have the chance.'

Maria shouted in her tongue to her men-at-arms. They moved away from the top of the gangplank. Ellingham, at a crouch, scrambled up the slick wooden plank and Dieudonné followed him, nimbly darting up and onto the deck.

Hawker, his eyes still on the crossbowmen, took a step towards the gangplank. An instant later, a loud metallic ping and a slap on his chest sent him stumbling to the side. He went onto one knee, caught his balance, and rose again, pushing himself off and dashing up the gangplank. As he did so, he heard the twang of bowstrings. Maria's *stradiotti* standing at the stern rail. One crossbowman sprawled back, shot through, and the *sbirri* scattered in all directions as the arrows continued to fly from the short horn bows on the galley's deck.

Hawker clutched at his chest. Stunned, he wobbled forward and into Jack's arms.

'Sir John! Thank the Virgin!'

Hawker was roughly hauled back under the poop deck's heavy canvas awning. Maria's shipmaster shouted to his crew, the last *stradiotti* now straining to pull in the gangplank from the dock. Her crew were casting off lines, bow and stern, and readying the oars to be lowered. Hawker watched as two of her men carelessly aimed their arrows towards the Council's men, seeking merely to keep them from charging the vessel before it could pull away.

Hawker searched for Federini but in the weird, gloaming light and the glare of torches on the wharf, he could not find him. He would be returning to the doge empty-handed and Hawker had a suspicion that the waterlogged dungeons of the palace would be that man's next abode. The galley creaked and groaned, its crew shouting and pushing a pole against the granite stones of the canal wall until the ship came away. Slowly it drifted out. Hawker heard a few crossbow bolts hiss past, holing the awning above his head. The galley entered a wide turn to send it eastwards past San Marco, and the yelling and shouting from the wharf began to recede.

Ellingham went to Hawker and put a splayed palm on his chest. 'You are unhurt!'

Hawker looked at his wide dagger. Its ornate etching had been gouged, a long scratch drawn at an angle across the width of the blade. 'Deflected,' he muttered.

'Sweet Jesus!' said Ellingham, catching himself as the vessel heaved. 'Perhaps the jewel is good luck after all.'

Hawker stood with some effort, wobbling on his feet. He turned to Jack and put a hand on his shoulder. 'I know what you did. Chiara... she is safe now.'

Jack nodded, features haggard for one so young. 'I told you I could fight – and kill – to defend us.' There was resignation in his voice as well as fatigue.

Hawker wrapped his arm firmly around the boy. 'I know you did. I never doubted you.' He scanned the deck around him. 'What happened to Jacob?'

'He's below, Sir John. They surprised him, outside the tavern. They must have thumped him something wicked. Then they dragged him back here. But they wrapped up his broken head for him. He still knows me... he can talk... so that's a good sign, isn't it?' His grime-streaked face brightened suddenly. 'And they took back our cart. With our things. And your gold. All stowed below, Sir John.'

'Well, *that's* something at least,' said Dieudonné flatly, while he watched the continuing chaos on the wharf, men running to and fro, others dragging away the injured.

Ellingham steadied himself on the railing. 'I saw Sir Roger fall. He bought us a chance. It was brave. Very brave.'

'Yes,' said Hawker. 'He fell.' And he said no more.

A wayward gust snapped the banners that hung from the stern, unfurling them. This time, his memory did not fail him. One was the banner of Hungary, the family arms of the Hunyadis: a raven holding a jewelled golden ring in its beak. But the other, a long red banneret, held far more significance for him. Upon it was a crouching dragon, its tail encircling its neck, the cross of Saint George cut into its spine and across its folded wings. And this time, he remembered where he had seen it before.

34

The oarsmen pulled hard, the galley completing its turn close to the shore of San Biagio and making its way east past the piazza of San Marco and the ducal palace that had so very nearly been Ellingham's last destination on Earth. The noise of the straining oars, rising and splashing, the chants of the rowers, was reassurance that they were finally seaborne, if not entirely safe from danger.

Maria stood at the rail and watched while they passed the great marble palace, darkness descending around them. 'They will no doubt pursue us,' she said, little trace of concern in her voice.

'But it is nearly pitch,' said Ellingham. 'We continue through the night? We might run aground.'

The woman turned to him and smiled. Ellingham saw a wild creature of the East before him, dressed in rich raw silks, her white-turbaned head adorned with a golden chain. 'You would prefer we go back, son of Richard?' She gestured with her thin curved sword towards her ship's master standing near the main-mast. 'He knows these waters by both day and night. I trust him with my life.'

Hawker found it difficult to look away from the piazza. He thought of Chiara, now alone. He thought of his dream of new command, of becoming once again a *condottiere* of the Serene Republic. A dream now in tatters. And the pain in his heart was far deeper than the aches and wounds of his body. He tore himself away from the rail, unable to look any more upon the city. He turned to Maria. 'So, my lady. Where are you taking us?'

'We journey to Senj. Less than two days' sail. It is a friendly port in Croatia.' She gave him a broad grin. 'Out of the doge's grasp.'

A horn sounded on the long, narrow deck that ran along the middle of the vessel. The crew scurried to raise the great sail. The rowers lifted the gigantic oars in unison on both sides and lodged them in holding pegs. The galley now resembled some monstrous water spider, legs reaching skywards. The screeching of the pulleys stopped. Once set home, the triangular sail billowed and they gathered speed, white foam churning along the galley's sleek sides.

'And now,' said Maria, 'it is time to go below. We have yet to seal our bargain, Sir John Hawker. And you owe me something of importance.'

The galley rolled and the bow cabin creaked and groaned in reply. Oak benches stretched along the sides of the hull, piled with colourful velvet cushions, upon which sat four rather grubby, bloodied men and one boy who had become a man before his time. Two ornate, punched-metal lanterns swayed overhead, bathing the cabin in warm, if somewhat sparse, light. And Maria Hunyadi stood at its centre just in front of the ship's stem, legs braced, lithe frame gently rocking in motion with the galley.

Ellingham studied the *stradiot* standing in front of the cabin door, arms folded. The man possessed a full jet beard that drooped onto his chest – something never to be seen in England – and a flat-brimmed, red felt hat that would have made a cardinal jealous. At his hip was a long, wide-bladed dagger that reached to his knee. The man's eyes, dead as two black pebbles, looked straight through him, and Ellingham, discomfited, turned away towards his comrades again.

Jacob de Grood sat glumly, his head wound up in brown linen bandages, right eye blackened. De Grood had said little since being reunited with the band. Ellingham thought that the poor Fleming must have felt shame for being captured along with Jack, having failed both him and Hawker. This even though Sir John had greeted him with a bear hug and warm words.

Gaston Dieudonné, on the contrary, sat looking relaxed, with outstretched arms, watching Maria like a curious cat. He had been doing so since he had first laid eyes upon her. Next to him sat Sir John. Ellingham saw that the knight looked older than he had done since he had known him. In his heart he knew it was more than the bloodletting of the day. Hawker had lost much. This day, it seemed, he had lost control of his destiny as well.

Their rescuer looked at each of the men in turn, but she appeared to rest her eyes longest upon Ellingham. 'Good my lords,' she said in her strangely accented French, 'I have done my part and plucked you away from your enemies. As I did promise Sir John and you, son of Richard. It is time for us to speak plainly, hearts open. Now, I trust, as friends and allies.'

'Friend and allies?' said Hawker, his voice hoarse. 'You force my hand by capturing and beating my man-at-arms and threatening this boy. What choice did I have?'

'Sometimes a stubborn bull must be forced to enter a greener pasture it does not know,' she replied, 'for its own good. Besides, your comrades had made up their own minds to ask for my help – before you showed up. Waiting in front of my ship.'

Hawker looked over to Ellingham. The young knight cast his eyes downwards.

Maria brought forth a large black velvet pouch and placed it on the little square table that stood in the middle of the cabin. 'This is what I have laboured for these past months. That which Sir John holds is the last piece of the puzzle.' She reached in and pulled out an armature of gold wire, set with enormous rubies. It formed the shape of a cross, and Ellingham found himself leaning forward along with Dieudonné to drink in its beauty. She turned to Hawker. 'Sir John, it is time to bring forth your Tear and deliver upon your promise.'

Hawker reached into his purse and drew out the muslin scrap that Chiara had given up to him. He opened it, flat on his palm, and another ruby wrapped in gold sparkled for all to see. He extended his arm towards Maria. 'Take it.'

Her eyes fastened on to the jewel like a magpie's, her lips parting slightly. She plucked it from Hawker's palm, leaned over the table and fixed it to the foot of the crucifix, the final piece. She stood back, eyes still fixed on it. 'Behold, the Tears of Byzantium. Faith renewed.'

Ellingham sat staring at the crucifix. It was as if an old wives' tale, first told to him by Hawker on a Flanders evening, had now come to be true and real; all the stones now come together again after many different journeys.

'How?' said Hawker. 'How did you regain all of them? Stolen, more like. From under the nose of the doge.'

She tilted her head, brow creasing. 'Stolen? Is it a crime to take from a thief what he had himself stolen?'

'How did you do it? He would never have given them willingly to you.'

'I gave the doge a gift a few months ago. A sort of gift that I knew he had a liking for. I sent him a beautiful youth I found on the market in Ragusa. A Greek. The old man took him and kept him in the inner apartments of the palace. It was a small matter for the youth to find the Tears and take them. The doge mourns the loss of his young favourite but is none the wiser that the jewels in his keep are really just the finest Murano glass, set in gilded lead.'

Dieudonné smiled and leaned back, his amusement undisguised. 'And how did you pay back the lad for his... service?'

Maria turned to Dieudonné. 'You walked past him on the way to this cabin. He remains in my service.'

Hawker slowly got up, swaying slightly. The *stradiot* behind nervously shifted his stance, hand moving to his hilt. 'I have delivered the jewel to you,' said Hawker, his expression written with distrust. 'But you spoke of other reward, not just getting us out of Venice. What is it that you propose, my lady?'

'I will bring you money. Gold... if that is what you want. That is not important to me. What I propose is that you and your men join mine... in a great quest.'

Hawker smiled grimly. 'Then tell me why you fly the badge of the Order of the Dragon from your stern.'

Maria raised her chin slightly. 'I believe you have guessed why. You should know it. You served under that banner ten years ago.'

Hawker nodded. 'Aye. I did. The campaign that ended when we took Bosnia from the Turks. Now tell me by what right *you* fly that banner.'

'I am the niece of King Matthias, as I have told you. And I choose to bear my mother's name. But I am the first-born daughter of Vlad Dracula, the true prince of Wallachia. The warlord of Christ.'

Dieudonné sat up again at the name. 'The great crusader? He fell fighting the Turk. The pope himself ordered Mass sung for his soul.'

Maria shook her head slowly. 'He still lives.'

'His head was sent to Constantinople by the sultan,' said Hawker flatly. 'He is long gone.'

'After a battle it is easy to find a rotting head and set it upon a pole. My father escaped that battle but was captured. He is a prisoner still.'

'No, my lady. That is fantasy. The world knows he fell.'

Maria's eyes bored into him, glinting with a fierce confidence. '*You* once fought under his command, Sir John Hawker. You know his skill, his wiles. He has survived.'

'I saw him impale a hundred Turks on stakes outside the gates of Srebrenica. If that is what you mean by skill and wiles.'

Her eyes narrowed. 'Another lesson for the sultan who invaded our lands. My father has always done what was needed to preserve Christendom – when all the other crowns of Europe looked the other way and did *nothing*, nothing to help us.'

Hawker pointed down to the Tears of Byzantium, still glistening as if alive. He gave a sniff of derision. 'So what then is the story of these? How did they end up in Venice and then across the crowns of Christendom?'

She ran her hand along the assembled crucifix. 'Vlad had the Byzantine cross cut up. As a gift to his fellow Christian princes – along with a plea for assistance against the Turks. Each to receive a relic of Constantinople. He did not trust the pope to act as his messenger but he trusted the doge. But the doge and the Council betrayed this trust, taking these gems for Venice and sending them out as *profane* gifts, gifts for their own base advantage at trade.' She practically spat out the words. 'But I have forged this sacred piece anew. And it will lead us to him.'

Ellingham looked over to Dieudonné, who returned a raised eyebrow.

Maria pointed to Ellingham. 'The son of Richard understands these things. He has come.'

'Do not call me that,' said the youth quietly. 'I am the bastard son of Richard.'

She laughed, a full throaty laugh from deep inside her. 'You are of the blood! Bastardy is no bar to the throne in the kingdoms of my lands. You seek to regain the crown of England for your house, I know you do. I am willing to aid you in your quest if you aid me in mine.'

Hawker shook his head, giving her a weary, doubting look. 'So, where is Dracula then, my lady? Who holds him prisoner all these years?'

She wagged a finger at Hawker, her dark eyes going wide. 'The crown of Wallachia slips easily from the heads of those who gain it. Vlad's half-brother, Calugarul, wears it now while he licks the arse of the sultan. They call him the Monk. Has never hefted a sword in his life.'

Ellingham watched her as the venomous words flowed past her beautiful, full lips. In her eyes he recognised that she was seeing those she spoke of, her gaze distant but glaring. She flashed Hawker a nervous smile, which barely lasted a second.

'I tell you... if the son of the Dragon were free, then all would flock to his banner. That is why Calugarul keeps his brother locked away from the light of day in the fortress at Targoviste. And I will be the one to free him.'

Hawker leaned back, looking at her down his proud nose. 'So why did Calugarul not kill your father and be done with it? Because he is a monk?'

'Because he is kin!' she shot back. 'He would not want that sin upon his immortal soul. Would you?'

'And you want *us* to help you,' said Hawker, his voice cold.

'There is a reason, John Hawker, why you were the one to bear the jewel back to me. It is God's will.'

Hawker's expression remained unchanged. 'We here are a free company, my lady. My loyalty is sworn to the White Rose–' he inclined his head towards Ellingham '–and with this knight of royal blood. The decision of where we go next lies with him.'

She looked at Ellingham and the youth felt the full power of her gaze and her pale beauty. At length he found his voice, still unsure as to what to say. 'We will consider your offer, my lady. If you will afford us the privacy to take counsel one with another.'

She bowed, smiling at him, and he felt again something rising in his breast, fascination and infatuation intermixed.

'Then I will await your decision.' She motioned to her body-guard to open the cabin door. 'And remember this, Sir Giles Ellingham. My uncle, the king, is of more use to your cause than the Tear would ever have been. Free my father and the crown will aid you.'

–

They had been blessed by a large moon, not full but yet pouring its milky white light upon the sea, showing the way out into the Adriatic. Hawker stood with his back to the stern rail of the galley as it rolled and pitched, the canopy awning flapping wildly in the wind. He had his arm around Jack's shoulders, holding the exhausted lad close. Beconsall's treachery still ran unceasingly through his mind. He had not foreseen it, but he should have. Blinded by his own arrogance. It was so bitter a taste. To tell the others the truth now would serve no purpose. And it would make them doubt his wisdom even more.

Around him were gathered his remaining comrades, silent, waiting for him to speak. Ellingham looked towards the bow where Maria Hunyadi stood, the daughter of the Dragon of

Wallachia, her silks rippling in the wind, hand grasping a shroud line. His head told him she was a madwoman, believing only what she chose to, driven by a blind faith her father yet lived. But his heart was speaking to him too, in a much quieter voice. She was powerful, and, in truth, he was drawn to her like a moth to the flame.

Hawker reached out and placed a hand on his shoulder. 'I believe I've failed you. Failed you all – and myself – through my pride. But a choice is upon us. Upon you. Do we take a new *contratto* with this woman or do we make our way back north once we reach Croatia?'

Ellingham turned to Dieudonné.

The Frenchman grinned through his cracked lower lip. 'You would look to *me* for counsel?'

'I consider you my friend, if not my countryman. What say you?'

Dieudonné's eyes then took on a look of intense determination, playfulness evaporating. 'I have heard the tales of this great prince, this Dracula, his power over men. It would indeed be a noble quest, as the lady says. Make no mistake though, it is full of risk.'

'Speak plainly, Gaston. We dance on the edge of a knife. We must make our choice now.'

Dieudonné fixed him squarely. 'Very well then, I will tell you what I think. If we were to go back now to Flanders – on our own – what could we possibly accomplish? Would your aunt in the palace at Mechelen believe you? Penniless, with no gemstone? Those are poor odds, my friend. But go back a wealthy lord, armed with letters from the King of Hungary and from the scourge of the Turk, the warlord of Christ, this Dracula… that is the more convincing.'

'And what of Henry Tudor?' said Ellingham.

Dieudonné shrugged. 'The rebellion will wait. What is a year? I say, return later and be heeded rather than return now and be ignored. Return as Sir Giles Plantagenet, son of King Richard – a warlord of Hungary and Wallachia, friend and ally of princes and kings.'

Ellingham turned to Jacob, who was leaning on Jack's shoulder. 'Jacob de Grood. What say you?'

Jacob smiled awkwardly, looking over to Hawker. 'I have no say in this matter. I serve Sir John.'

Ellingham gripped his shoulder. 'Jacob de Grood, I value your counsel.'

'Then I will give it. Follow your heart.'

Ellingham turned to Hawker. 'Sir John, what say you?'

Hawker looked up and Ellingham saw the pain of loss in his face. Loss of love and loss of fortune. Maybe even loss of purpose. The grey knight reached out quickly to grab a shroud line to steady himself as the galley rolled again. He tried to crack a smile but it fell short, an expression of regret more than anything else.

Ellingham nodded, comprehending what was left unsaid. 'What course do we take then, Sir John?'

'That burden must fall to you now.' Hawker moved closer to Ellingham and held out something between thumb and forefinger. Ellingham's brow furrowed. He plucked it from Hawker's gnarled fingers. It was a ring. The gold and silver boar that King Richard had given the old knight.

'This is yours by right,' said Hawker. 'You are the son of the White Boar. I failed in keeping my first promise to your father, delivering the jewel. But I will honour the second vow I made to him: to stand by you.' Hawker pulled his aching shoulders back and stood a little higher than before. 'So... do you take the offer of the Dragon's daughter or do we journey back to Flanders?'

Ellingham slipped on the ring of his father and for the first time he felt a fire was now kindled in his heart. Perhaps the long road to Venice had not been for nothing, for he had found himself. His father, a man he had never known, was lost to him for ever. But Maria, mad or sane, still sought hers. It was any daughter's duty. And any son's.

'We are going east, my lords.'

Sir John Hawker gave Ellingham a curt, solemn nod and squeezed Jack's shoulder. 'So be it,' he said.

Suddenly, the wind snapped the dragon banner at the stern to its full glory. Ellingham watched the grey knight stare at it, almost transfixed by the undulating serpent embroidered upon it. And he saw that Hawker's face was a mask of cold, hard stone.

Historical Note

The Battle of Bosworth

The Wars of the Roses, an inter-dynastic struggle that lasted for more than thirty years (forty by some counts) resulted in the largest battles ever fought on English soil and the deaths of thousands. What we know today as the Battle of Bosworth Field, fought on 22 August 1485, was for many years originally called the Battle of Redemoor. The town of Market Bosworth is actually three kilometres from where we now know the battle was fought. In fact, we have probably learned more about this, one of the most famous battles in English history, in the last twenty years than we have learned in the previous four hundred.

Surprisingly, most of the accounts of Bosworth were written many years (or decades) after the fact and in most cases by men who were not even there. And as with most primary or secondary sources, some are more useful than others. The difficulty for historians has been in sorting the wheat from the chaff in these contemporary accounts. Even so, we will probably only ever be able to conjecture what happened that day in August. There are dozens of books about Richard III and his last battle. A plausible and thorough analysis is provided in *Bosworth 1485* by Mike Ingram (2012) and his more recent *Richard III and the Battle of Bosworth* (2019). Also of note is Chris Skidmore's *Bosworth: The Birth of the Tudors* (2013).

The advent of modern battlefield archaeology, using ground-penetrating radar and other tools, finally pinpointed the actual location of the battle in 2010. It lies just a stone's throw south of Fenn Lane and six hundred metres due west of the village of Dadlington. Many artefacts have been found. Lead cannon shot of the period, armour, arrowheads and, most poignantly, a small silver-gilt badge in the shape of a boar – Richard's personal badge.

As I have tried to portray in the preceding pages, the battle could have gone either way. Richard's army of around ten thousand probably outnumbered Henry's, and both armies had competent field commanders, veterans of conflicts on the Continent as well as previous battles on English soil. Young Henry Tudor, unlike Richard III, was not a warrior and had little if any experience of open battle. But his commanders took advantage of the terrain when they deployed for the fight and secured both flanks from attack. For whatever reason, overconfidence or impetuous fury over the rebellion, King Richard marched down from the heights of nearby Sutton Cheney, thus ceding the high ground. He may have been better off instead by forcing Henry to climb to attack him.

Once battle was joined, Richard was confronted with marshy ground on his left flank and 'hedgehogs' of mercenary French longspears on his right. This constrained the charge of his cavalry and the initial stages of the battle, after an exchange of bowshot and cannon fire, devolved into a brutal push of spear and pole weapon among the men-at-arms and militias of both sides, with archers joining in, armed with sword and buckler. After some two hours of fighting, Richard's vanguard began to break on the right flank due to the press of the spear formations. He and his commanders must have realised that the line would be 'rolled up' unless some action was taken. Around the same time, by several accounts, the Earl of Northumberland's forces to Richard's rear, mainly conscripted townsmen and farm labourers, began to slowly dissolve, fleeing north.

The king must have known that his situation was fast becoming desperate. But Henry's forces, under the command of the Earl of Oxford, had now formed into wedges, leaving large gaps along their line. Several accounts agree that Richard and his mounted knights charged in, deep into Henry's line, looking to find and kill him, thus ending the battle and the rebellion. King Richard himself was said to have lanced Henry Tudor's standard bearer, unhorsing him, before cutting his way through with sword, hammer or axe to get towards Henry's bodyguard. It is also believed that Henry may have sought refuge among the spearman rather than face Richard directly in combat.

But the final act that ended the Plantagenet dynasty was the intervention of Thomas, Lord Stanley, Earl of Derby, whose army had been waiting and watching on a rise of ground just to the rear of Henry's position. Richard had probably been counting on his neutrality (he had Stanley's son, Lord Strange, as a hostage), but if this was the case it would have been a dangerous gamble – and foolhardy. When these mounted knights and infantry rushed down and engaged Richard's men and not Henry Tudor's, the die was cast. King Richard was at some point unhorsed – quite possibly in marshy ground – and it is likely he was eventually cut down by a flurry of pole weapons such as halberds and bills. From the sources (and most recently the autopsy on Richard's bones found in 2012) it is likely his body was stripped naked on the field and ritually humiliated, with wounds being delivered long after he was dead. Richard's death ushered in the Tudor dynasty but the new king, Henry VII, would spend the next ten years fighting to secure his throne against Yorkist supporters at home and abroad and never felt truly safe the rest of his reign.

The 'Princes in the Tower'

It is one of the enduring mysteries of English history: the fate of the two young children of Edward IV who went missing in the Tower of London sometime after 1483 when Richard ascended the throne. The eldest of the pair, Edward, was twelve, the rightful heir, and already acknowledged as Edward V days after the death of his father. The younger brother, Richard of Shrewsbury, was only nine years old. Immediately upon the death of his brother the king, Richard of Gloucester was declared

Lord Protector and took the boys into custody. Soon afterwards, however, he seized the throne for himself by having the boys declared illegitimate due to the fact that Edward IV had had a marriage contract signed (and a mock ceremony performed) with a woman before he later married Elizabeth Woodville. Gloucester ascended the throne as Richard III and after a few sightings of the young princes playing in the Tower grounds, they were never seen after 1484 and disappeared from history.

There were several people with strong motives to do away with the boys. Not least of whom was Richard. Thomas More's damning history of the reign of Richard III clearly implicates him in the death of the princes. But More, a Tudor supporter, offered no evidence of Richard's guilt and in the centuries since many researchers have outlined theories that implicate others in the Lancastrian orbit who could have instigated the murders. That is, if indeed murder actually happened. In this novel, I have portrayed Richard as not directly responsible for what befell the young princes. That was mainly for purposes of plot, but there are historians who point out that Parliament had already declared the boys illegitimate, meaning Richard's claim was relatively safe and also that no one in the family – including their mother, Elizabeth Woodville – ever blamed Richard for their disappearance, even after Richard's death.

The 2nd Duke of Buckingham, Henry Stafford, from the Lancastrian side, had come over to Richard upon the death of Edward IV and quickly became a major ally, well rewarded for his support. But by October 1483 he was leading a rebellion at the behest of the formidable Margaret Beaufort, his aunt, in support of her son, Henry Tudor. Buckingham could have actually been lining up the throne for himself, being of royal blood, and may have been in a position as constable of the Tower to do away with the princes ensconced there. He may have sought to later blame the disappearance on Richard, either to bolster his own position or that of Henry Tudor by getting rid of the legitimate heirs. His rebellion petered out within days though, leading to his capture and execution by Richard in November. He sought a meeting

341

with Richard a few days before his execution, but Richard refused him. It is interesting to think what he might have confessed or revealed given the chance.

Margaret Beaufort herself had motive. The two princes were clearly in the way of her son's path to the throne and doubly so if their illegitimacy was overturned once King Richard was dead. Henry Tudor had come from a line long-declared illegitimate for inheriting the throne so he was already on shaky ground. Getting rid of Edward IV's young sons prior to Henry's subsequent rebellion made sense. As with Richard III, there is no credible evidence that she gave the order for the murders, but her spies or supporters may well have had access to the Tower. Whether Henry himself was a party to such a conspiracy is not known but he would have been a beneficiary regardless.

More recently, a few researchers including M. J. Trow have put forward a theory that it was a court physician, Doctor John Argentine, who could have poisoned the princes during their incarceration because he had been appointed to look after their health. It's also been claimed that he may have gone on to murder Henry Tudor's eldest son and heir, Prince Arthur, who as a teenager grew sickly and died at fifteen. If so, this would not be a political motive but the work of a psychopathic personality. Argentine, according to some accounts, was one of the last people to see the princes before their disappearance. It does appear that he garnered royal patronage immediately after Henry VII assumed the throne. Was he responsible for the deaths of the young sons of York (either intentionally or through bad medicine) but not the young Tudor heir? Once again, there is nothing beyond speculation to pin any murder on him.

Lastly, there is the theory that no murders took place at all. This is perhaps the oldest of all as it goes to the heart of Yorkist claims at the time that at least one of the princes had escaped confinement and was whisked to safety on the Continent. No evidence was ever discovered or produced that the princes were murdered. It is believed that young Edward, the uncrowned Edward V, had possibly been ill with tuberculosis even before his incarceration.

Did Edward die of his disease shortly after escaping, while his younger brother survived?

A Yorkist pretender, Perkin Warbeck, later claimed to be Richard of Shrewsbury and led a rebellion over six years culminating with an invasion attempt via Cornwall in 1497. He had been recognised officially as the lost heir by the Holy Roman Emperor and more importantly by Richard's aunt, Margaret, the Duchess Dowager of Burgundy. Was this mere political expediency or had they truly been convinced of his parentage? His rebellion failed, however, and he was imprisoned by Henry Tudor, though later released and placed under house arrest. This fact alone is cited by some as proof that Henry didn't believe he was of royal blood but just a clever imposter put up to the job by Henry's Yorkist enemies. It was only after Warbeck tried to flee that he was rearrested and confined. After a second escape attempt in 1499, he was recaptured, tried for treason and hanged at Tyburn like a common criminal. Interestingly, it appears that Henry's wife, Elizabeth of York, was never asked to identify Warbeck as her younger brother nor did she ever commit her thoughts on the matter to writing.

At the end of 2021, The Missing Princes Project, begun by Philippa Langley (who led the effort to find and recover Richard III's remains in a Leicester car park), gave new credence to an existing theory that postulates Edward V survived, was given sanctuary under a new identity in a village near Crediton in Devon, and lived into his early forties. The small chapel in St Matthew's Church, Coldridge, contains the tomb of one 'John Evans' and is filled with Yorkist imagery and symbolism for no obvious reason, including a stained-glass portrait of young Edward V. Moreover, it was built during young Henry VIII's reign. Could this be the last resting place of the missing boy king?

There are many books in print dealing with the mystery. In addition to Trow's *The Killer of the Princes in the Tower* (2021), other recent works worth looking at are John Ashdown-Hill's *The Mythology of the Princes in the Tower* (2018) and Matthew Lewis's *The Survival of the Princes in the Tower: Murder, Mystery and*

Myth (2018). For the Perkin Warbeck mystery, Ann Wroe's *The Perfect Prince* (2003) is a definitive work. For an older, pro-Tudor viewpoint readers might also try Alison Weir's *Richard III and the Princes in the Tower* (1992).

Early Renaissance Venice

Venice was arguably reaching its zenith at the end of the fifteenth century, one of the most powerful states in Europe and in control of a vast Mediterranean empire. The story of the rise of this powerful Italian city-state is fascinating and much has been written about its impact on European culture, society and development. A republic and not a monarchy, Venice in the Renaissance was essentially an all-powerful oligarchy of wealthy established families who maintained control through a highly effective spy network and an administrative machine that would be the envy of any modern police state. The head of state, the doge, was a nominally elected position for the life of the holder, which would be rotated among the most powerful Venetian families. A complex system of domestic informants kept the ruling Council of Ten and the doge apprised of all comings and goings on the island and its adjoining provinces on the mainland, while abroad, its spies and agents at the courts of Europe fed steady reports back to *la Serenissima*. All of this was supported by the profits of its trading empire and its treaties across the known world. Venice enjoyed continuing power and prestige well into the seventeenth century, but the Ottoman Empire on its doorstep had begun to chip away at its domain even in the 1480s, slowly sapping its wealth and security. Perhaps one of the most entertaining histories of the great city is Peter Ackroyd's *Venice: Pure City* (2010), which also contains an extensive bibliography.

Acknowledgements

I am grateful to my editor, Craig Lye, at Canelo for his unstinting support and keen eye and indeed to the entire team at Canelo for their hard work in making this novel a reality. I must also give thanks to those who volunteered to read early drafts of this work and took the time to provide some incredibly useful insights and suggestions. In particular, I must single out Maya Dafinova for her wisdom regarding the principal characters and plotting, and to Felix Rigg and Tom Charles for their views on the opening scenes and the overall feel and flow of the script. Lastly, I must thank my wife who has always been supportive of my writing but nonetheless became a 'keyboard widow' far too often.